DARK'S SAVIOR

DARK WORLD MATES

OLIVIA RILEY

BEFORE

The slate of cold metal stung in Aly's hands. The tablet —as best as she could call it— flashed on its screen a torrent of words, some big, some small, all readable in her language; comprehensible. But only sixteen words, one sentence, got Aly's full attention:

ASSIGNED LOCATION FOR REFUGEE ALY SMITH: LETHE MAWS: MINING CITY SECURED ON SYSTEM SARITIUS, ORBITAL UNDEREM.

Her hands didn't shake. She didn't feel the sting of tears. She was numb, in fact. Completely numb. Just as she had been since the beginning.

Three months since she had been abducted and she had no use for crying. For anger. The universe didn't answer her desperate prayers. At least not in this dimensional plane.

She sat quietly, thinking. Then, after a long pause, she set the tablet carefully down beside her. She looked up at the oracle that had been watching her patiently nearby.

"Do you understand the terms, Smith, Aly?" It spoke in an oddly realistic tone. Its expressionless eyes somehow regarded her, even under its white shroud.

Aly licked her dry lips. "How long?" Her voice cracked.

"The length of time is unknown. Tests and examinations are still being performed. Once they are complete and we have a better understanding of your kind, and of your unique situation, we can proceed forward to—"

"To take us...home?" Aly blurted.

The oracle paused, gazing at her. "Perhaps. We will try."

That's what they always said. She was beginning to theorize that one of the silions programmed them to say that and nothing more.

Somehow, Aly still managed to nod her head. "And the others?" she asked.

"Your group will be joining you. You will be given your own units as well as all necessary supplies."

Aly nodded again, only, this time, she frowned as well. "I don't suppose a nice, cushy office job was available, huh?"

The bot only looked at her, saying nothing. Aly couldn't help but smirk. For all their intelligence, they couldn't comprehend sarcasm. Then again, the silion scientists didn't understand it either. Maybe it was a trait they lacked.

Still, the frown returned, but Aly couldn't bring herself to open her mouth and argue. What good would it do? She was helpless. She had been helpless ever since she had been taken. They were going to send her where they liked, even if it was to the very pits of hell.

Because that's really what the Lethe Maws were. Like hell in the real world. Only not hot but cold. Just as dark, just as full of horrors. The silions didn't get it. Or, likely, they didn't care. Maybe they thought humans were pests that they had been forced to deal with. The enforcers had dropped the humans in their laps, forced the silions to complete experiments (which they didn't seem to mind as much), and then ordered them to house the humans where necessary.

The Xolis Emperiom had an obligation to keep order and balance on this side of the universe, or at least in this galaxy—this realm—that they ruled within. All outsiders had to be assessed and placed accordingly. Many went to prisons, and most were forced into slave labor. If you weren't a silion or a nillium, you weren't considered a citizen. You had to earn that right.

The Xolis—the so-called Galactic Council—had been "generous" enough the last three months, but that generosity only went so far. It was a miraculous wonder that Aly and the others were even being given their own housing units and supplies. They had tried to talk to them—to reason with them—and the Council had listened. But the humans were in their territory now, in their world. What hope they had of returning to human territory was slowly diminishing.

And now, with the final blow of being sent to the mines, Aly truly began to think it was time she let that hope die. She could ask the oracles (or even the silion scientists) a dozen times, but the answer would always be the same.

'Time you let it go, Aly,' she thought. 'This is your life now. Home is far away.'

An image of the night sky through a hole in a cave shot through Aly's brain. She closed her eyes and let out a deep breath that turned into a quiet, shaky laugh.

"Are you in distress?" asked the oracle.

Aly opened her eyes. "No."

"Then your examination is complete," the bot said in a lifeless tone. It took the tablet from beside Aly then walked over to the door. The door opened. "You may proceed down to the waiting dock for further instruction. All your necessary supplies will be transferred over and arrive in a timely manner. Safe travels, and may you be in Nihl's sight."

Aly rose. She passed the bot without a glance and left the room.

* * *

The blast was impressive, to say the least. Dust and bits of rock sprayed in all directions, hitting the sides of the cave wall then scattering over the floor. A light tremor shook the earth, and Ryziel was certain it would be felt all the way to the top, but, for that, he didn't worry. What he cared about now was what lay hidden on the other side of the wall they had just blown through.

As the dust settled, he looked to Nar, who still gripped the detonator tight. When Nar nodded his head, Ryziel stepped through the thick wall and came out the other side. He held up a metallic sphere in his hand and twisted it soundly then flung it into the darkness. The orb flew up and flared into a brilliant blue light, swallowing the dark as it hung effortlessly in the air.

Beyond lay a large cavern, about a hundred and fifty spans across, as large as the training field back home but not as large as the First House. Ryziel stepped forward cautiously as a wind picked up the dust and rock and blew it back into the chamber, picking up in a whirlwind at the very center. There, it flew upward into an opening in the ceiling, an opening that Ryziel was absolutely certain reached the very surface above.

He was certain because the ship that lay before him now couldn't have gotten there otherwise.

Ryziel stepped inside the chamber, with Nar following close behind. It was more of a shell than a working ship, actually. By the light that fell on it, Ryziel could see that some parts were indeed missing, some fallen away, and others possibly taken by scavengers for some unknown reason.

Carefully, he and Nar examined in and around its hull. The urk scurried up one side, and Ryziel could hear him squeezing himself through a tear at the top.

"Definitely a tradership, by the looks of it," Nar said. "The inside is surprisingly well intact, save for the holes in the walls. Some of the console is fried but probably fixable, definitely out of fuel." There was a light banging then. "Engine is intact, but some parts will need to be replaced in the engine bank, and the firing mechanism is shot."

The ship was indeed in bad shape, judging by the look of it from the outside, with one wing torn to shreds on one side and several panels missing under its belly. The traders must have snuck onto the planet looking for precious minerals, only for the ship to malfunction possibly. Or something grabbed ahold of it from below, only for it to come falling down and landing in the deep dark. Landing, not crashing, he noted because otherwise, it would have been in pieces. The traders, with their ship damaged, had flown it down in hopes of hiding it and fixing it. But clearly, something had gotten to them before they could. They were long gone, but their ship remained. Yes, it was in more disrepair than he had hoped, but one thing was certain: it could be fixed. It would fly.

Ryziel placed a gentle hand on its metal siding and closed his eyes. This discovery couldn't have come at a better time, and he breathed a sigh of relief, though he didn't smile.

Only a few days ago, he had come to find out of his father's death and of his uncle taking guardianship over First House. No one had come to tell him. He had found out through gossip from the Enforcers above. But that didn't matter to him. All that mattered was that his father was gone, and he could now return home. Return to challenge his uncle. And be by his brother's side.

Ryziel could see his brother now, a light in the darkness, smiling, with arms spread to welcome him. Ryziel opened his eyes slowly and dropped his hand. So long he had been waiting for this moment. For the chance to escape.

And his father was finally dead.

"I am coming, brother. And everything will be as it should." He backed away and tilted his head upward to look past the ship to the tunnel above and the light.

CHAPTER ONE

It had been raining for days. Only now did it begin to slow, the last remnants falling down into the earth, sliding over rock in waterfalls, and disappearing into the darkness below.

Aly pushed back the hood of her suit and wiped her brow, trying and failing to wipe away damp tendrils of hair from her face. She took up her mender once again and touched the tip of the tool gun to the bot, white sparks flying. The bot beeped and groaned to life, small blinking lights flashing sporadically.

"Come on," she whispered softly, placing her mender to another pinpoint on the bot's chest.

The bot jerked slightly then its lights beamed on, and it turned up its head. It clicked and beeped at her, and Aly gently placed it back on its feet. It wobbled on twig legs, looked at her with its bright eye, then went back to work as usual, as if it hadn't just fallen thirty feet off the side of the cave wall. Aly watched it go, still crouched on the metal grate platform, a chill taking hold of her as the bot climbed onward up the steep rocky incline. A soft light hit her from above, and she bent her head upward to see for the first time in days the moon peeking out from the angry clouds. Its light was dim but, being in the dark for so long, Aly could make out the beams of light just barely falling against metal and rock around her.

Aly stared at it for some time as if in a trance, her mouth falling open slightly, then closing and morphing into a little smile as bits of rainwater splashed her face.

Tonight, she'd go up to the cross bridge. Before the meeting.

She placed her mender back onto her belt and turned for the elevator car when her techband went off. Her smile faded and a small pang hit her chest as she let out a groan. She knew who it was before she even took the call.

"Smith, where are you?"

Aly raised up her techband so the hologram of a beastly face was eye level with her own. "Hello, Braxin. I was just leaving Level thirty-four, Section B—"

"I need to see you. Now." The hologram disappeared and the call ended.

Aly sighed. She didn't need to imagine why her so-called "boss" needed to see her. She had a damn good feeling she already knew. Returning to the elevator car, she waved her hand over the sensor and the door slid open. Water dribbled and sprayed down over the metal cage as she entered and pressed the button for level fifteen. The door closed, and the elevator started, moving upward with a whoosh.

Aly watched the landing she had just left fade away and looked around at the vast cavern before her. A big (really big) hole filled with twinkling orange, blue, and green lights scraping the edges of the surface and trickling down. Down into an unfathomably deep chasm.

There were other holes stretching for miles and caverns leading into deeper sections; a network of cave systems and tunnels leading into chambers and rooms, some as small as her unit back on her old ship, others as large as a small city. Vast, fathomless, dark.

Lethe Maws, her... troubling home away from home.

A wind picked up as she got closer to the surface, shaking the car slightly and pelting her with a mist of water and cold air. Her face felt the icy touch, but her body did not. If there was one thing that made working in the mines tolerable, it was the slipsuits; skin-tight and warm, like having an extra-thick layer of skin in the form of small, durable gray-blue scales. Her body stayed dry and warm but not uncomfortable.

She clicked on a light on the collar of her suit and checked her waistbelt, making sure everything was in place. The last thing she needed was to lose another tool given to her and have another reason for Braxin to scold her.

The belt was cinched tight and all tools accounted for. She checked her techband, and it, too, was secured tightly on her wrist. She definitely didn't want to lose one of those again.

The elevator came to a smooth stop, entering one of the many hubs. As the door opened, Aly stepped out and turned left, making her way down a narrow passage. She passed by a few grex. They eyed her with their reptilian gazes, their nostrils flaring, but Aly only nodded her head and gave a small smile, keeping her eyes down, to acknowledge she was no threat. She slipped by and quickly made her way to the central base of the hub.

There were more people as she got closer. She refused to call them aliens like some of her team. They *were* people. Just not human. According to the Xolis, in fact, some were silion. But not all.

Aly made her way down the passage until she came to a large opening where, inside, metal crates were being organized by various armbots.

"Smith, over here."

Aly glanced around and saw Braxin gesturing for her to come. She followed the burly, beast-like man into his work unit, where he sat down at his console and pointed to the chair beside him. "Sit."

Aly did as told. She sat quietly, with hands clasped on her thighs, waiting patiently. Braxin watched her with his yellow eyes. The "miserable lion," as Aly liked to call him, was looking more put out than usual.

"I received another report that you got in the way of an abbiot's work," he said with a slight growl in his throat.

Aly bit the inside of her cheek and pushed back the strawberry-blonde locks of hair that were getting in her eyes. "I wouldn't call it getting in the way exactly, sir," she said as quietly as possible.

Braxin tapped a dark, taloned finger on his tableboard. "What would you call it, then? And don't say you were trying to help."

Aly's face heated, water dripping down the side of her face to her neck, making her shiver. She had no response, and with that, Braxin let out a bellow of breath.

"Did they not teach you humans anything at the facility?" Braxin showed his teeth. "Or are you just looking to start something?"

Aly opened her mouth. "No—no, I just happened to be by and was trying to aid—"

"First mistake," Braxin said.

"—And I didn't realize that was seen as very rude to them," Aly finished softly.

"I'll say it again. No one here needs your help. The other humans have learned, why can't you, hm? You have one job. Stick to it. If I catch you trying to aid another group again, I'll send you to the warehouses. Learn your place. No one is looking to make friends. Just credits."

Aly nodded. "I understand." She got up to go when he stopped her once more.

"And stay in your designated area. I heard you were caught sneaking around past level fifty again. This is your final warning. It's your hide if you want to get eaten or killed. You know the rules." Braxin turned back to his console. "You're off-shift, so I expect you to go straight to your unit."

"Actually, we are having a meeting...my team. In the old station."

Braxin side-eyed her, his nose scrunching slightly. "Go to the meeting then go home. That's an order."

Aly nodded and gave a little smile, then left quietly. When Braxin's door closed behind her, she let out a breath and took her time leaving the hub. She would stick to his orders, but the meeting wasn't for another hour. She would take the long way over.

She thought of the cross bridge and of the moon overhead. A little detour, that was all. And likely, no one would be up there with the shift change.

She had only encountered the bridge a week ago, and only after noticing it while looking up from the platform of level twelve in section C, where the cavern was wider and had an opening above the platform where a long bridge could be seen. It was more like a set of bridges, actually, that intersected one another like a web. And it was set at one of the highest points, close to the surface. Close enough where light actually touched.

No one seemed to use it anymore as it had once been used to get across to other sections but now, with the elevator cars and other transports, the bridge (and many of the stairways) were seldom used. Only Aly cared to ever use them to sneak to various points outside her designated area.

As she exited the hub and made for an elevator once more, her pace quickened.

Just a little detour.

* * *

The sluth did not see him at first, but it certainly must have sensed him, for it shrieked loudly and shot away into a narrow hole as he passed by its hiding place. It must have caught his scent, but Ryziel didn't much care. It was funny how the sluth could be such nasty, vile creatures and cause even the toughest miner to go running for the surface, but they turned into simpering cowards the moment he made his presence known. They were at least smart enough to know what was prey and what was not.

It had been weeks since he had seen a sluth because it had been weeks since he had left his home. He had been so obsessed with fixing the ship and getting the necessary materials for the fix that he had lost track of time.

It wasn't until Nar told him the second mender had broken and that their drill was slowing that he had any thought to leaving and only because the tools were vital for the ship. Xilya could have gotten them, but she was on a personal mission already and wouldn't be back for another mooncycle. And Nar didn't leave the underground ever.

So, it was up to him alone and, surprisingly, he felt energized, not dread, at having to make his way to the surface. Though, he walked quickly, wanting the deed done so he could go back to his work. The ship still needed many repairs, but he was certain in only a season's time, it would be completed. Assuming they could get ionx.

As he made his way to the lift, he brought up his arm and sent a message on his band to Braxin, the head of Sector 1, warning him he was coming up and that he expected the lygin to have the tools ready for him. The lygin always complied, even when busy, and he didn't ask questions.

Not like most would. Certainly not to challenge him. He might be an outcast—a darkborn nillium—but he was still nillium. Royal nillium, at that. And though he never cared to take advantage of such a title before, here on Lethe Maws and with the vision of escape so close, he used his title to achieve his every whim. And no one challenged him.

Too bad such a title didn't give him the ability to demand the enforcers take him off this cursed planet. But soon, it wouldn't matter. He would get out one way or another. And then, back home to exact his revenge, reclaim his position, and be back beside his brother. Back where he belonged.

The plan had been set even before the ship had been found. And nothing was going to stand in his way.

Maybe after, he would finally stop being such a "rigid asshole" as Nar put it. But he doubted it.

Another sluth appeared, and this time, Ryziel hissed at it with such venom that the sluth seemed to jump out if its own pale, leathery skin and bolt into the dark. Ryziel might have chuckled but few things made him laugh these days. Honestly, not much ever did. He really was rigid. But he was also bitter.

He opened the lift door and stepped inside then hit a button to take him to level fifteen. As the lift door closed and started its long journey up, his techband went off. Ryziel checked it and growled. Braxin had just left his work unit for one of the stations close to the surface. Something about an incident with the cargo. He would be able to get tools, but Ryziel would have to meet him on level five. Being that close to the surface made Ryziel uneasy. He preferred to not be seen or near crowds as the higher one went, the more people there were.

He wasn't sure when he had become such a recluse but then, he had never been much of a socialite. He had spent his young life on Nihl being trained not to be seen or noticed or be close to anyone. Avoiding others came naturally.

'You're shaping up to become the perfect living wraith, Ryz,' his brother had joked. Korzien might poke fun at him but he also sympathized, even if he didn't always show it.

Ryziel thought for a moment as he ascended. He could wait or make Braxin come to him, but maybe he needed to see the sky. Maybe it would be better for him. To get him out of the darker place. He messaged Braxin back and waited until the elevator eventually slowed to fifteen and stopped. He got out without being seen and made his way to the stairs. He would climb the rest of the way. He could use the exercise and likely wouldn't run into anyone. Who the hell used the stairs anymore anyway?

CHAPTER TWO

ALY SPENT A GREAT DEAL OF TIME JUST STARING AT THE MOON as if it was some lifeline or anchor. The first natural light she had seen in many weeks. They said there was a sun, but she had never seen it; either it was always hidden by thick, black clouds or it didn't rise above the mines. Mark said it was because of the way the planet revolved, where its axis point tilted, and where the mine was stationed that the sun hardly made it near to pass, making it almost dark every day and the nights long.

And the stormy skies had made certain to keep even a sliver of light away. She hadn't seen this clear of a night in so long it almost felt like a dream. And who knew how long it would last? Aly made her way across another bridge to a wider central point that connected two separate bridges, like a crossroad. She slid down against the railing, her eyes never leaving the big orb in the sky.

And it was big. Huge, in fact. Much bigger than Earth's moon, with deeper craters and a tint of orange around the edges. She shifted her eyes away only for a moment so she could fish out the small sketchbook hidden in the side pouch of her toolbelt. She slid the pencil out of its pocket along the sketchbook's spine and opened it to a blank page. She could never do such a moon justice, really, without giving it some color, but all she had was the short, bite-marked pencil and so it would have to do. Her eyes flitted up and down as she attempted to recreate the orb in black and white, making sure to get every crater and mountain.

When she was finished, she quickly put the sketchbook away and stood. Rainwater from the surface still fell in small droplets, like a light mist from above. With both the light of the moon and the artificial lights beaming upward, it created a sort of strange, sparkling effect. Aly watched in wonder, smelled the freshness of water and earth in the air, and could hear the spattering of water all around her...and the soft beep of something nearby.

She looked around curiously and saw, not too far from her, a floater lying alongside the bridge. She walked over to it and crouched down, poking at its puffy head. The lantern was deflated somewhat, its blue light blinking softly. Though she was off the clock, she felt obliged to fix it. Those down below needed the light.

Taking up the strange, wiry lantern that reminded her of a jellyfish, she turned it on its side and took out her mender, switching it over to a patch setting. Focusing on the tear on its head, Aly began to mend, sealing up the hole with her tool. When it was done, the blue light stopped blinking and brightened considerably. Like a helium balloon, the floater began to rise out of her hand. She took it over to the side of the rail, stretched her arm out, and let it go, watching as it slowly made its way downward.

She wasn't sure how, but her body knew something was wrong before she did. As if on instinct, she went from relaxed, even—dare she say—content, to tense and frozen with fear. Something was watching her. She saw the shape at the corner of her eye. And, like a cornered rabbit, she jumped and inhaled a sharp hiss of breath.

Only a few feet away, a man stood on the same bridge as her. She knew he was a man because of his clearly masculine physique: broad shoulders, tall and lithe body, muscular build. His face also said male, with cold eyes and a hard-set mouth. But it was only these obvious features that gave him away. The rest of him was, of course, completely inhuman, with alien features she was unused to seeing, even though she had seen dozens. He was new. Different than the rest. Yet, oddly, he also seemed familiar. But she couldn't figure how. All she could do was stare at him in wonder.

His silver eyes met hers with the same sort of shocked wonder, and for a long moment, all they did was stare at each other.

When Aly finally started to come out of her wondering trance, she blinked and cleared her throat. "Hello," she said softly, then said it again a little louder, with more confidence.

The man didn't respond, even though he must be able to understand her as she spoke to him in Xolien (the Xolis so-called universal language). She thought to take a step toward him, and, when she did, he seemed to grow more still, as if he wasn't already standing there like some glorified statue in the moonlight.

"I'm sorry, were you trying to cross? I was just taking a walk and...I can get out of your way." He was a large male now that she got a good look at him and could see how he might not want to get too close to her as he passed by, since he would have to as the bridges were rather narrow.

Still, he said nothing. He just stared at her. For a moment even, he reminded her of a tiger or a panther standing completely still, watching her curiously. Maybe deciding whether she might be prey.

Aly shivered, wondering where he had come from. She could only guess someone like him came from below. Far below. She had been warned about those who worked deeper in the mines. Those who were so vicious and unafraid that the monsters of the deep didn't worry or bother them. Her heart began to race at the thought. Maybe he was one of them.

She went still again, and for another moment, they stood frozen, until the silver-eyed stranger broke the tension and moved, so slowly and silently that Aly wondered at first if he was even real or just a figment of her imagination, conjured up by the moonlight and the shadows. Really, he almost seemed to be made of the stuff, his skin a deep, dark blue, with tendrils of silver shimmering in the light.

She blinked again, and he was in front of her. She nearly jumped back but caught herself, gripping the side rail tight. He got so close she could see the specks of gold within the silver of his eyes. And it was then she realized why he seemed oddly familiar.

He was a nillium. He was...

She opened her mouth but, instead of words, a gasp escaped her throat as his hand shot out and almost touched her, stopping an inch from her face. His hand slipped down and lightly touched a lock of her hair instead. He grasped it gently in his fingers, his head tilting slightly, his eyes flickering from her face down to her body. His face gave little away, but it seemed he was torn by his curiosity of her, his bewilderment, and the dark shadow of something else, something more feral.

Aly wanted to say something but, for once, she was beyond words. She recalled someone saying that if you didn't move in the presence of certain apex predators, if you stared them down, then they might leave you alone. But she was pretty sure that was bullshit. Especially now. Still, she didn't dare look away, didn't dare move as this large nillium male assessed her. His body moved closer, close enough to feel his heat, and his head tilted downward, his face close to hers. He growled deep, a low purr in his chest, and his hand came around once more as if to touch her again. Aly closed her eyes and lifted her head slightly back. *He wouldn't hurt her* something told her. As surprised as she was, she put her fear aside and leaned into his touch.

As his fingers barely brushed against her neck, a hiss of breath escaped him, blowing against her ear. The air went from warm to cold, and when she opened her eyes, he was gone.

* * *

Aly stood there for a long moment, too shocked to move. Her hand still gripped the cold metal railing behind her, her eyes blinking away beads of moisture from the air. It took a moment for her brain to process what had just occurred. Slowly she loosened her hand from the rail and lowered it, staring into the darkness, her breath coming in short bursts, her heart thumping in her chest.

She didn't think she could be more tense if a bear had just come out and sized her up. She knew now who that had been. She had been warned...

Her techband beeped softly, letting her know the meeting was starting. She would be late.

Still, she stood there as if she couldn't move. Still unable to think clearly. She stared back at where he had come from, but something told her he was long gone now.

She turned away and carefully made her way off the bridge. Her limbs were actually shaking. Now that she knew who she had just encountered (and had somehow come out unscathed), the adrenaline in her blood was making her a little lightheaded.

So, this is what it felt like.

Using the rail for support, she made it over to a nearby elevator car and stumbled inside. The doors closed, but the elevator didn't move, and she realized it was because she had forgotten to press the button. She pressed for level eighteen, and the car began to move.

When she got to the old station in Section D, she opened the slide door and was met with several curious and annoyed pairs of eyes.

"Glad you could finally join us," Kate said at the head of the room.

"I'm sorry I'm late. I just—"

"Save it and have a seat," Kate said, waving to a chair by the wall next to Jamie and Mark. Aly did as told and silently made her way over. The room was a tight fit. The station was nothing more than an old observation room, hanging off the side of the cave face and supported by old, rusted metal. The lights were dim and flickered occasionally, and the machines inside were long dead. The station had been abandoned long ago, when the heads of Lethe Maws found it no longer useful, so here it was collecting dust, with a few large gashes along the outer walls from some unknown beast that had come up from below and clawed its way up the side.

And now it was their little meeting center.

"So, we were discussing," Kate said, with her husband Julian by her side, "about our continued efforts to persuade the Xolis Council to allow us to acquire a ship. But, as usual, they have given us no answers or decision. We are also still trying to persuade them to let us use one of their high transmitters to send a signal back to base, but we also have yet to gain any permissions. Julian believes he will be granted a small window of time to talk to one of the council members about it in a few nights' time."

"That's what they said before," Ethan, on the other side of the room, interjected. His eyes were sunken, and his skin looked ashen. He seemed to be taking the transition to the mine the worst; ever since he had encountered a nasty creature hiding in a crevice while he worked. Aly's eyes fell down to his leg, where still he wore the metal brace from when he had fallen. "They say it every time and then nothing," he snapped. "It's been weeks."

"We know," Julian said, bending forward in his seat. "But we don't have many options. They sent us here to work. It was either that or stay lab rats."

"Like they aren't still experimenting on us now," Mark mumbled beside her.

It was true. Ever since they had been saved by the Xolis enforcers and taken to the refuge facility to be treated, they knew they were being studied. It was funny being on the other side of the glass. As the silion medics cared for her and her team, they had taken their samples and recorded their data. Who knew what they were doing with the DNA they had extracted? And then there was Sarah.

"This is bullshit..." Ethan said, not so quietly.

"We all want to go home, not just you," said Cilia, her arms crossed tightly, her mouth set in a hard frown. "And Kate and Julian are doing all that they can."

"There has to be something more we can do," Ethan protested.

"Like what?" Davis said in the back. "We're stranded within a galactic system run by the equivalent of the Roman Empire. We're outsiders."

"We could get rights. I heard a miner talking about becoming a civilian...a silion," said Ethan.

Davis snorted. "It takes years to become a silion. Years of working for the Xolis Emporium on slave wages."

"But it is possible." Ethan's eyes got a little brighter. "And silions have access to ships."

"We will still be here a long time before it happens. Who knows if we will make it that long in this place," Davis countered.

Ethan had nothing to say to that. He scowled instead but remained silent.

"We will think about it," Julian said. "For now, I am going to continue trying to gain an audience."

The others stayed silent, though a few grumbled. Anger and anxiety were beginning to run high. A few weeks in Lethe Maws could do that to a person. Aly didn't want to think how bad it was going to get if they were here for months or even years.

The Xolis and their oracles had never stated how long they would be in the mines. They had only said that, in time, a permanent place would be decided. Where that was, no one could guess. But for all they knew, the Xolis could keep them on Lethe Maws forever.

The idea made Aly shudder. Forever. And with the endless possibilities of death always surrounding them.

For they had been warned about all the risks. And there were many. Monsters of all sorts lurked in the dark, ready to eat unsuspecting workers. If they didn't get you, maybe a long fall off a cave side would, or one of the many rocks that fell would crumble you into pieces. If you were lucky and one of those choices didn't befall you, you might just lose your way in the dark and get lost in the endless chambers and tunnelways, some still lying undiscovered. For some of the other races, they had little to worry about. Grex were agile and could see in the dark and had a venomous bite and spiked limbs for protection. Abbiots had tough skin like an elephant that not even a blade could pierce. Humans, however, had no such defenses. They might as well be made of glass or a sack of sand. Ethan was a terrifying example and the others remained wary.

Aly thought of the nillium and shuddered again. They had been warned about him too. But the heads of Lethe Maws never said they had to worry about encountering him above level fifty, certainly not so close to the surface.

"Whatever you do, stay out of the lower levels," Braxin had said to them on their first day. "Anything past fifty is off-limits, and if I even hear that one of you went to the bottom, you will be punished severely."

"What's at the bottom?" Cilia had asked curiously.

Braxin had looked on her squarely. "It is nillium territory."

Her team had glanced at each other.

"You mean an actual nillium lives down there?"

They had known what the nillium were even at the very beginning. It had been a nillium that had saved them from the trader ship. The captain of the Xolis enforcers, Marzin. They had thought him an honest to God angel at first. An angel without wings and with glowing yellow-bronze skin instead. It was only after that they learned the truth.

Braxin's eyes had narrowed. "Yes. He is...not like the others. He is housed here—the bottom is where he lives. And he doesn't like people in his territory. So, if you value your lives, don't incur his wrath. Don't go below."

And that had been that. The severity and finality in his voice was enough for them to obey.

Or at least most of them. Aly was, well, prone to "forgetting" the rules. Her curiosity, Mark had said, would probably get her killed. She couldn't disagree, but it didn't stop her.

Aly snapped out of her thoughts as Jamie piped up beside her. "Will you ask them about Sarah?" she asked in a soft voice.

The team went silent, some looking down at the ground. Or anywhere but at her.

"I will...consider it," Julian said.

"They said she would be joining us." Jamie's voice rose a little. She gripped her knees tightly. "Th-they said..."

Julian nodded. "I know. I will try to talk to them, I swear it."

Aly couldn't help looking away also. None would say it, but she knew they were thinking it. Sarah might never join them. Like with the ship and the high transmitter, they may never let them see her. They still had no knowledge of why the facility was keeping her and they feared to ask. Just like they had been afraid to ask why they had taken their DNA.

"That's all me and Julian have for you tonight," Kate said, looking at each of them. "Is there anything you guys would like to add? Anything you've heard or seen and would like us to know?"

This was the part, Aly guessed, when she should tell them she had run into the nillium from below. But she kept silent. Something told her the encounter she had was such a rare experience, it probably shouldn't even have happened. No one used the stairs and old bridges, especially not her team. And she had a feeling the nillium didn't care to be seen.

It occurred to her, in fact, that she should never have seen him herself. But she had. Because he had let her see him. That thought scared her some. Why did he let her see him? And what brought him to want to get near her? Everything she had ever heard about him made him sound more like a scary legend than a person. He was rarely seen— he didn't go near people. He stayed in the dark.

Aly's thoughts were cut yet again when everyone began to leave, and she felt a hand land on her shoulder.

"You okay?" Mark said beside her. "You seem more quiet than usual."

Aly smiled. "I'm okay. Just been a long day."

"As they all are now. Literally." Mark stood up and offered his hand. Aly took it, letting him lift her up beside him. "You want me to walk you back?"

Aly was seriously considering it. But then she remembered the chances of actually running into the nillium again were probably zero. Still, she shivered.

"I think I'll be okay, thanks," Aly said. "Are you working the lower tunnels again? Find anything?"

Mark shook his head. "Saw a few oriens dig out a good chunk of tython, and of course, there is always aulion, but that's always easy to find. Nothing rare, though they always say the hard to find stuff is deeper."

Aly nodded her head understanding. "I'd say I envy you but, really, I don't."

"I knew I should have been a mechanic instead." Mark laughed. "Fixing bots all day doesn't sound so bad."

Aly shrugged. "At least you get to interact with others."

Mark frowned. "Things here are different...I think our mission at this point is at a stand-still."

Aly had nothing to say to that, though she didn't necessarily agree. Once again, her mind brought up the image of the nillium standing before her on the bridge. It was the first time, she realized, anyone other than a human had interacted with her. How strange it was that it should be the one who seemed to avoid people the most.

"Well, see you around then," Mark said.

Aly smiled again and he left. She walked out of the old station and looked around the dark cavern. She couldn't see the sky, but she guessed, by now, the moon was gone, covered by clouds. Even so, she was thankful for the moment she had gotten.

Because tomorrow, she was sure, would be just another rainy day.

CHAPTER THREE

RYZIEL FELT LIKE HIS INSIDES WERE TURNING AND TWISTING, his heart thumping heavily against his chest. He crouched in the dark for some time, afraid he was slipping. That he was frenzying. That he was in his Drega's hold.

He hadn't had an episode in so long he had forgotten what it felt like. In fact, it didn't feel the same at all. When his Drega side came out, when his beast-like tendencies took hold, they were violent. Primal. There was no sense of self, just the need for blood and the thralls of rage. But, as he sat there taking deep long breaths, he didn't feel these things at all. He felt something else altogether. And it scared him.

That...female—whatever she was as he'd never seen the likes of her before but knew by her scent and her form that she was indeed female—had brought out his Drega side. No one had been able to do that by just sight or touch alone. No one.

Yet, she had. And, as he sat there in the dark and his mind and senses started returning to him, he could finally understand. It wasn't rage or a hunger for violence that had taken him. It was something more instinctual. Something he hadn't felt for many years and nothing as strong.

He didn't want to break her or kill her. He wanted to...

Ryziel growled, and his insides spasmed again. He bared his teeth and clenched his hands tight, his body shaking. He could feel his receptors vibrating.

That one little touch, that light brush of skin, and he had almost faded out completely. If he hadn't ripped himself away and blindly fled into the dark, who knows what he might have done?

His stomach turned at the thought, and he clutched his sides with a groan. Slowly, he stood back up and closed his eyes, taking another long breath.

The image of her standing there was still clear to him even now. The moon cast its light over her reddish-gold hair, blue eyes looking up in sheer wonder, pale face shining from the droplets of water, giving her almost a strange glow. Then her small delicate hands lifting the floater and letting it go and her breath of surprise at seeing him.

Even he was shocked that he had allowed himself to be seen by her, like he hadn't realized he had stepped so close. It was her scent he had caught first. A scent he didn't recognize but had drawn him away all the same. Then his receptors had begun to vibrate along his head, like a blasting signal trailing a strong beacon. Once he had come up the stairway and onto the bridge, he had halted and gone completely still. Once he saw her, his sixth sense had gone wild. The confusion and shock were understandable. Why was his body reacting to this person? This female who was *not* nillium.

Once the shock had faded somewhat, curiosity had taken its turn. He wanted to make sure she wasn't some strange hallucination. In the light of the moon and misty air, she had seemed otherworldly. Perhaps he would have even mistaken her in that moment for a lightbringer or one of Nihl's guardians. But that was clearly absurd. Because, again, his logic brought him sense. She was not nillium, so that was impossible.

Still, he felt a need to touch. A very strong need. And he never cared to touch anyone, so this was definitely another shock. Never would he have considered going up to some random person—one whose race he couldn't even identify—and demanding to touch them. It was unthinkable. But the feeling couldn't be helped. Not in that moment.

He had hesitated twice, fighting the urge. He had smelled her fear wafting alongside her scent, but her fear could barely hold him.

When she had closed her eyes and closed the distance between them, in that one second of contact, his Drega had torn its way to the surface, like a beast thrashing to get out.

And so, he had fled.

He didn't know how long he had been hiding now, but he had to go. He had to get back to the lair. But first, he needed the tools. And now, a quick, serious talk with Braxin.

As he pulled himself away from the rocky wall, his techband went off. Taking one last deep breath to compose himself, he took the call.

"Did you die?" was Nar's hello as his face was brought up before him.

"I'm not sure," was Ryziel's reply.

There was silence and Nar's little urk face—beady black eyes with sharp features— actually looked surprised. "What happened?" he asked.

"It was..." Ryziel didn't know if he even wanted to tell him. Not in detail. "I had a lapse in control."

"Nihl's hide," Nar muttered. "What set you off? Did someone get in your way?"

"Not...exactly." He really didn't want to talk about this now. "I'll tell you about it later. I still need to get the tools." He ended the call and stood straight. He began to climb the stairs again, the energy in him depleted.

* * *

Braxin was waiting for him on a wide balcony overlooking a large silion-made waterway, the pool descending into small waterfalls, turning through more pools, cascading all the way down the side of the cave face, and disappearing into the dark below.

He didn't see Ryziel at first, as most usually didn't. And when he did, he flinched, as most usually did.

"Nihl Ryziel," he said and bowed his head slightly, his eyes shifting around, making sure no one watched.

Even though he had been exiled by his father and uncle and sent to Lethe Maws, he was still treated with the same anxious civility and respect given to all nillium. Though Braxin's nostrils flared in irritation, even he understood a shunned nillium was still nillium.

"Forgive me for not being at my unit. The cargo..."

"Forget it. Do you have what I need?"

Braxin brought out the two menders and drill along with replacement parts. Ryziel took them and latched them to his own belt. "There is another thing I want," Ryziel said. Braxin's mouth twitched in a frown but he remained silent. "I want to know about the newcomers to Lethe."

Braxin's furry brows rose. "Newcomers?"

"The new race. One not seen in the Xolis system."

Braxin's eyes widened in surprise. "You mean the humans? They arrived many weeks ago."

"Where did they come from?"

Braxin blinked at him, likely curious as to why he wanted to know. Ryziel didn't care what he thought.

"They...they were rescued by Marzin, found near the border of the Xolis realm, near the blue worlds," Braxin began. "They had been taken by traders to be sold in the shadow market. Marzin brought them to the Xolis Council, and for many months, they were housed on Yilsand in one of their refugee facilities. They got the usual treatment, were taught what little they needed to know, learned to speak Xolien, and then were placed here...for the time being."

"Did anyone find out where the traders got them?" Ryziel could only guess some primitive world, as was the usual case but, still, he was curious.

Braxin shifted where he stood. "They say they caught them on some planet way out of the boundaries of the realm. But it was mentioned that they had a ship. Some of the parts, the traders collected and were confiscated by enforcers. That is all I really know."

Ryziel's eyes narrowed. "How many humans were taken?"

"Only nine. Eight now brought here."

"Were you given their records?"

Braxin seemed to hesitate then. "Yes, but only the most basic information."

"Send it to me. All of it," Ryziel ordered. "I want it before I make it back down."

Braxin stiffened, and he could tell the lygin wanted to protest. Only no one challenged a nillium's command.

"Very well," Braxin said, a soft growl catching in his throat.

Ryziel said no more and left him there. The clouds were rolling back, and the moon was gone before he made it back to the stairs and disappeared.

* * *

The great metal door rose. and Ryziel entered into a large chamber warmly lit by several floating lanterns hanging above. He stopped just past the door and waited as it slid closed. Ahead, in the very center, was the ship, black and silver metal shining dulling from the beams of dim white light casting down on it from above. The light reflected murky daylight, though it was artificial in itself, created by floodlights around the opening of the ceiling and a little way into the tunnel itself, which stretched several miles up to the surface.

A loud clang followed by a muttered curse sounded near the ship's side, and a tiny face peaked out over the metal wing.

"Great—you're back," said Nar. His head disappeared, and there were a few more clangs and shuffling noises before he reappeared on top of the ship. The little urk crouched and bent his head down to stare at Ryziel, his black, pupil-less eyes blinking at him curiously. "You look like you want to end a life," he said after observing him carefully.

Ryziel clenched his fists and unclenched them. His Drega was finally starting to settle away but he still felt on edge. 'Not exactly that,' he thought but said nothing to Nar. Instead, he turned toward the inner wall to the right where a large console station sat. He touched at the surface and the console lit up, displaying a holographic screen before him. He touched his techband to the console, connecting to the program. Braxin had sent the records right away like he asked. Ryziel transferred the records to the console, and a set of nine images were displayed before him.

"Soooo...you gonna tell me what happened?" Nar said behind him.

Ryziel swallowed hard. He didn't look at Nar as he said, "It's complicated."

"Complicated how?"

Ryziel searched the images before him until he found the girl from the bridge. He stared at her picture.

"Uh, hello? Ryz, are you hearing me or what?"

Ryziel's eyes didn't leave the image. His Drega didn't come back, thank Nihl, but he felt the stirrings of curiosity. His eyes finally shot over to the other faces, wondering.

"Who or what are those?" Nar asked beside him.

"Humans," Ryziel said.

Nar let out a little grunt. "They are an odd-looking sort. Always something new around here." Nar went silent for a moment when Ryziel didn't respond. "Why are you looking them up? They a threat or something?"

Ryziel let out a hiss of breath, a near laugh. "Honestly, I'm not sure."

He could almost feel Nar's wide eyes on him. "Seriously?" Nar said with unhidden surprise. "They look pretty unthreatening if you ask me," he muttered.

Ryziel's eyes narrowed back on the girl from the bridge. It was true. There was nothing about them that seemed threatening, nothing that should have set him off. Though, again, he reminded himself that the feeling hadn't been normal.

He tapped on the image of the girl, bringing her picture to the forefront. Beside her headshot, a short description and set of information was displayed.

Aly Smith
Human
Age: 24
Physical: gold-red hair along head, blue-green eyes, pale, soft-skinned, small
Home planet: Earth
Job Skill: Mechanic
Background: Found by Xolis enforcers, led by Captain Marzin, on tradeship, being transported to [undisclosed]. Brought to Yilsand for rehabilitation and integration into Xolis system.
Threat: low
All Vaccines given. No known illnesses.
Testing still underway

Nothing seemed unusual. It was known that all outsiders went through the integration program. Only that they were still testing might have seemed strange, given that the humans were off the program for the most part, but he knew nothing of the silion scientists' tests and what they entailed, so it could mean nothing. There was nothing that really gave anything away. All this information seemed to do was make Ryziel more curious. He wanted to know more.

Ryziel looked back at the ship and frowned. This wasn't the time to be curious about some other race just because one encounter had sparked the beast in him. He needed to focus on the ship. He needed to focus on getting home.

'Always so impatient to get the job done,' a ghost of his brother's voice laughed in his ear.

'You'll get it done, Ryziel. You have time,' he said to himself. 'One more visit up to the surface won't hurt. Just sate your curiosity now and be done with it. Xilya will be back soon with the information you need, and you can put this strange encounter behind you and focus on what matters.'

With that, Ryziel tapped the image of the girl away and swiped the group off the console.

A message came through and popped up before him. Xilya was on her way back.

"I'm going to the upper levels again tomorrow," Ryziel said.

"What for?" Nar asked.

"Just...personal reasons. I'll tell Xilya to meet me somewhere and get what I need from her. Then I'll be back. Be sure to have the tracer ready. Once I have what I need, we start searching and drilling again.

Nar made a little noise. "It is, don't worry. You just take care of yourself, heh? Don't lose yourself again."

Lose himself again. No, they couldn't have that. Ryziel closed his eyes and remembered moments on Nihl.

"Don't worry," he said and left the console. It wasn't the first time, and, as he thought of the girl again, he feared it wouldn't be the last.

CHAPTER FOUR

Aly sat within the crevice of a rock, crouching over her small sketchbook, carefully shading and outlining the beginnings of a face and upper body. There was very little light coming down, per usual—just a dull grayish-blue tint that barely pricked the darkness. She angled the light around her neck downward to see her creation more clearly. The face wasn't perfect, and she wasn't sure she had his horns right. She wasn't even sure if they were horns. Maybe antenna? The eyes were off also, but it wasn't like she could possibly remember every detail in the dark, though she tried.

She closed her eyes and tried to remember more clearly. His face was angular, with large eyes and a wide mouth. Like Marzin, the one who had found them, the nillium all seemed to have cat-like features. Though, she wouldn't necessarily say they resembled cats (not like the lygin, who looked exactly like cats, whiskers and all), just that they had a sort of animalistic appearance. Piercing cat-like eyes, sharp teeth, pointed ears, and straight, flat-ish noses. The strange horns that were straight as rods and grew from each side of their heads like a crown were indeed not cat-like, however. The horns reminded her of the kind she'd seen on a dragon in one of her childhood picture books.

They didn't have tails that she had seen, but their bodies were tall, long, and lanky, yet muscular and agile. Besides the color, she couldn't guess what their skin was like, whether it was soft, or smooth, or rough, though it certainly seemed tougher than a human's. And their hair seemed thicker, like a mane that went along the center of their head and down their neck.

Like a cat. Or a dragon.

Yes, that's it—cat-dragons. A new species.

Aly opened her eyes, shook her head, and snickered. She made a few more marks in her drawing, shading around the bright eyes. It was funny how she had been amazed by Marzin when she first saw him, as well, but, for whatever reason, she hadn't thought to draw him. With this new nillium (whom she secretly nicknamed Blue because she didn't know his actual name), she had a strong urge to do so. While Marzin came off cold, stiff, and as personable as a rock, Blue was a fresh mystery; alluring, dark, and different.

A low, distant howling started down in one of the far caverns below. Aly closed her sketchbook and pocketed it in the small pouch on her belt. Several more howls joined the first, and, when Aly looked over the edge, she saw a few bodies crawling along the side of the cave face opposite her. Ugly creatures with mangy fur on their backs and small beady red eyes, resembling something between a fox and a monkey, with flat pointed ears and curved tails. They shrieked and hissed at each other, clambering over rocks. They had extremely long, sharp claws that helped them climb. Aly called them howlers.

She had drawn a few of them in her sketchbook. She had portraits of each person and alien creature she had encountered. She and her team had lost all their devices when they had been raided by the tradeship, their ISpads lost or destroyed, so there was no way to take pictures or document like they were supposed to. The others hadn't bothered to continue with the mission once the ship had been destroyed and they were taken as prisoners. The only thing the team worried about now was getting home.

Aly couldn't blame them, of course, but she still felt the need to have something to show for all their troubles. And, honestly, she greatly enjoyed drawing the others.

The howlers disappeared back into a cave opening as a low fog began to seep its way down into the earth. Aly looked up and could see nothing above save for the faded blots of lights. She should get back to work. Surely there were a few bots needing fixing. But all she could do was sit there and think about Blue.

She really needed to see him again so she could get a more accurate portrait.

A few floaters began to descend, as if pushed by the thick fog. One hit a low moving fan vent and sparked, then fell to the ground before her. Aly sighed and forced herself to her feet. She picked it up and sat back down with this strange mechanical jellyfish now in her lap. A wire was hanging out, and she moved to push it back in place. Her slender fingers worked gingerly to unknot the few string lights that had gotten tangled, and, using her mender, she fixed yet another hole on its head, something that seemed to happen often.

From the corner of her eye, she noticed a few miners watching her, one grex and a couple of krull, their feathers puffed as they chittered quietly, their talons pointing toward her. There were only a few groups around, mostly keeping to themselves, drilling and scraping into the rock around them. The ones who watched her did so out of curiosity, but they never came near nor did they ever speak. She tried once to initiate a conversation, but they weren't interested. All they did was watch.

The floater tried to float away, but Aly caught it firmly and worked at another knot in its strings. It felt strange to be the one gawked at. To be the outsider. Funny how things could change so quickly. Now she understood how the other aliens must have felt being studied on the bases back home. The gyda were their first known contact, and they had taken it pretty well. But others...not so much. At least, if they somehow made it out of this dark underworld and back home, they could tell everyone how it felt being on the other side.

Of course, having to tell the foundation (and inevitably the government) that there was an advanced civilization whose domain reached several dozen known solar systems, unlike the handful humans oversaw, might open a very bad can of worms. WAR flashed pretty heavily in her head at the thought. It was something the team had barely discussed. Should they tell the others? Even if their whole mission was about finding advanced civilizations in the first place? Well, yes, except they hadn't actually been prepared for one of this magnitude. They had been looking in the realm of planet or planets, not...a portion of a galaxy.

Aly fixed the last knot then gently let the floater go. It went off to join the others, flashing its blue light.

She watched it go for a moment then turned her head and caught the eyes of one of the krull. Its hawk-eyes shifted to her hands and it gibbered something to its partner before turning away. Aly looked down at her hands also. They were dirty and full of calluses. She had gloves, but she used them sparingly. She always worked better without them, her slender fingers making it easier to work on tinier fixes that needed a more delicate touch.

She supposed it was why she had been assigned to be a mechanic for both the mission and now on Lethe Maws. She was good with her hands.

And really, she liked it. Though she preferred having a pencil or paintbrush in her hand instead of a screwdriver or mender.

The groups began to disperse, and Aly got a ping on her techband letting her know a fix was needed a few levels down in one of the lower, smaller sectors. She brought up her map and the holographic screen showed the location. She picked herself up and made for one of the narrow tunnels carved into the rock face. She passed through, making sure to not bump into others, then crossed a section bridge over to an elevator car. She took the elevator down, and it got noticeably darker.

When she exited the car, she found a large group of miners huddled in a circle, their heads bent as if looking down at something.

A few others crouched before them, and Aly saw the medic symbol on the backs of their suits. As the crowd parted, Aly got a good glimpse of a body. As she moved closer, she saw it was a tylian, its gray shell now looking noticeably whiter. Its eyes—usually brownish-black—were now filmed over. It looked mauled. One of its feelers was gone.

The medics were taking samples and touching around as the crowd spoke in whispers. Aly heard some of the words.

"He was found in a lift coming up from the lower levels...he shouldn't have gone down," a lygin spoke.

"What do you think got him?" asked another.

"Who knows. Something nasty down in the lower levels, for sure."

"Or maybe it was the Dark One. Maybe the tylian got too close to his territory," said a grex.

"Maybe the nillium is sending a warning."

"Hey, human!"

Aly looked around and saw a large lygin male waving her over. Aly did as told, and the lygin took hold of her arm and pulled her around to face a hole where a drill machine had drilled in the rock and was now inside, stuck. "Stop gawking and start fixing!" he said. He left her there to return to the crowd as the medics began bagging the tylian. Aly watched, wide-eyed, for a moment, getting one last glimpse of the torn body.

It wasn't the first body she had seen, but it still made her stomach twist. Many were found in caverns, and their deaths were usually not much of a mystery. Either they fell or something got them and, in that regard, there usually wasn't much to find save for bones. It was strange that the tylian, though shredded in parts, was still intact. Like something had toyed with it then just left it alone.

The unusualness of his death and where he had been found was likely why she heard them accusing the nillium this time; only now because the tylian had supposedly been where he shouldn't have been.

A shiver raked Aly's body. Maybe she shouldn't want to see the dark nillium again after all. If he supposedly did that to another. Then again, it might not have been him. He hadn't hurt her, after all.

But then, she hadn't trespassed into his territory.

"Why do you think he went down there?" she heard someone say. "He would have known better."

Aly stood there in deep thought, feeling sorry for the tylian, when she caught eyes with the large lygin, who gave her a nasty look. Heat rose in her face, and she quickly turned away.

Placing her hand on the cold, sharp rock, she crouched down and looked deeper into the hole. The drill was jammed in but not because it couldn't penetrate the rock. It had only malfunctioned, a red light blinking to tell her it just needed to be recalibrated. Aly crawled into the tight opening and stretched out her arm to open a small hatch on the drill's side showing the switches needed to turn on and off. The lygin could have easily done it himself but was obviously too large to get inside and reach. Aly was small enough to get through the tight spaces of the rock, making her at least useful in that regard.

She flipped the switches and closed the hatch, and the drill began to reload. She shuffled out of the hole just before it started again.

The lygin returned but didn't thank her. He didn't even acknowledge her. Aly watched him drill at the rock for a moment, wondering if he would find anything. She turned away before he noticed her staring and walked onward with a heavy breath.

* * *

She was working on fixing another crawler (the small bots that crawled up the cave walls and collected rock data) when she felt like she was being watched. And not in the usual way, like before with the Krull and their hawk-eyes or the grex with their lizard ones. It started with a chill running down her spine and the impulse to turn her head. When she looked around, no one could be seen, no matter how hard she tried to peer into the open cave entrances around her.

She finished fixing the bot and left the section where she was, but still, the feeling was there. She thought about the tylian again and felt a sudden great need to be around others. Mark was shown to be working on the twenty-second level according to her techband. She made her way up, thinking to just have a little chat.

When she got off the elevator, she found him in a small alcove against a cave side, taking apart rock and harvesting aulion, a silver-coated mineral, into the large buckets beside him. As she walked toward him, she admired the shine of his blue-black hair in the lamplight.

Mark turned his head and paused as he saw her. He placed the bits of aulion into the bucket and waved at her. She returned it with a wave of her own as she strode toward him. His face was dirtied by dust and rock fragments, but his smile was still bright, his dark eyes squinting slightly as the lights on his wrist blinded him.

"Hey, Aly, what's happening?"

Aly smiled, swinging her arms forward in a sort of shrug. "I was bored and came to say hello." She lied a little.

"Oh, yeah?" Mark straightened up and assessed her carefully. "You take your break pretty late, huh?"

"Not exactly," Aly replied sheepishly.

Mark made a silent 'oh' and smirked. "Braxin will get on your case again, you know."

"I know." Aly sat herself down on a flat-ish rock near the cave face. Mark watched her for a moment then looked around. No one seemed to be paying much attention to them, so he came over and sat down beside her. They sat for a moment just looking out over the wide chamber, and Aly began to feel more relaxed.

"It's crazy, huh...to think only a few months ago, we were on Grayhart 12 and just cruising along to that random-ass planet, all because Kate thought we homed in on some signal." Mark shook his head. He leaned forward, placing his elbows on his knees. "And we thought we were gonna be such big-shots. Like we were gonna discover the next civilization...or maybe even find the vrisha." Mark bent his head.

Aly eyed him and smiled sadly. "Well, technically, we did discover a new civilization. Just not in the manner in which we were trained."

Mark blew out a quiet laugh. "Yeah, for real. Though I didn't exactly sign up to get kidnapped and forced into slavery."

"We're not really slaves," Aly remarked.

"Might as well be for what they pay us," Mark grumbled. "And even if we could save enough together, they won't let us leave here. I know no one likes to talk about it but...we are prisoners, just without the name."

Aly didn't say anything because she couldn't argue. They knew it to be true when they found out the ships that brought them here didn't take people off. Not without strict permission from the Xolis council. The ships that were docked were for materials to be exported only. And they were heavily guarded by second-ranked enforcers. No one left Lethe Maws.

"Do you really believe Julian will be able talk with one of the council members?" Aly asked.

Mark shook his head. "Honestly? Not a chance. But he has to keep hope in the others somehow. Otherwise..."

Aly thought of Ethan and how awful he had looked at the last meeting. And how scared Jamie seemed. Once again, the image of the tylian flashed in her mind, and Aly wondered how much longer they would last before that hope died. And one of them with it.

Mark's hand fell on Aly's knee and squeezed gently. Aly didn't move away, though she tensed briefly. She smiled at him and placed her hand on top of his in a friendly manner. She locked eyes with him and noticed the dark circles forming underneath his gaze.

"You seem to be doing okay, though, huh?" he said. "You seem to be taking things better than the rest of us."

Aly wasn't so sure. If anything, she was just much better at hiding it. She was scared too, but she tried her best to focus on other thoughts, tried to see the better side of their predicament, if there even was one. It was the reason she drew the other people around her or the scenery or anything. And why she wanted to try to help the abbiots or strike up a conversation with a grex. She wanted to continue working at the mission and have something to show for it. And if she never did see home again, then she wanted to believe she was where she was now for a reason.

And maybe that reason was to integrate and start a new life.

Aly unlatched from his gaze in hope that he couldn't read her face and her thoughts. She would never voice this to him (or the others), but home didn't give her the same bright and fuzzy feelings that it might for them.

Because Earth hadn't exactly felt like home to her for a long time.

It was why she had joined the Grayhart mission after all. And though she might like to see the blue planet again, to see fellow humans, she didn't care to step back on Earth's soil. Not really. In fact, if they did ever get back to the foundation's base, she would probably hop right back on the next ship, ready to go on in search of the next planet holding its secrets of life and advancement.

Aly let her hand slide off Mark's and opened her palm upward as an invitation. Mark took it gladly, entwining his fingers in hers.

"You were always the optimistic one, Aly," he said.

Aly looked back at him but didn't smile. Instead, she leaned in and kissed him softly at the corner of his mouth. Mark tensed in surprise at first, then closed his eyes and returned the kiss.

She shouldn't have done it. But after the last couple days, after her encounter with the nillium and seeing the dead body of the tylian, she felt suddenly very alone and more afraid than before (though she was grateful in being able to hide her fears) and in need of comfort.

This wasn't the first time she had sought out comfort in Mark. And just like before, he was ready to comply.

They parted and looked at one another. Mark opened his mouth and Aly knew the words he was about to say. But before he could say them, both their techbands went off.

Breaking the moment, they drew apart from one another and looked down at their wrists.

The message was from Kate. There was to be another meeting tonight. Only this time, they were to meet at...

"She can't be serious," Mark breathed.

Aly's heart did a little jump of excitement. "I think she is pretty serious."

Mark snorted. "Great, just what we need. Another reason to be glared at."

Aly gave him a sly little smirk and elbowed his side. "Our shifts will be over soon. I should probably get back to work. I'll see you there." Aly got up from the rock and walked off, feeling just a tad better than before.

"Yeah, I guess you'll have to," Mark called after her. "But I won't drink, and I call the first seat facing the wall."

CHAPTER FIVE

Ryziel had perched high up on the rock, making sure not to be seen, watching the human woman carefully from his hiding place. Watching as she fixed the bot in her lap then paused to look around, her eyes passing over where he was hidden in shadow. She was alone like the others had been. Braxin hadn't cared to keep them together, maybe to ensure they didn't get to talking or be distracted from their work.

He had gone in search of the humans and had found each one of them. The first had been a man. He prepared himself, in case his Drega slithered its way to the surface at the mere sight of him. But, to his great relief, he had felt nothing. Only maybe a little guarded at first but nothing more.

When he found the next human and saw it was another female, it was as he had feared, only this time his Drega was not so quick to rise. But it was, indeed, there. It wasn't like the first time, when he thought he would lose himself. Not by far. But the instinctual urge was there, only more as an itch that he could at least ignore. For the most part.

When he found two more females, the itch was stronger, his receptors vibrating slightly, but he could still manage at least some, though it made him uncomfortable after a certain point and so he left. After that, it was men again and—again to his relief—he felt nothing.

When he finally found the area in which the lone woman from the bridge was located, he prepared himself first. Even her scent, now familiar to him, drew his Drega out even a little, unlike the others who, though making him stir somewhat, did not seem as appealing.

When he finally found the strength to look over the edge and see her, his Drega moved quickly and almost violently, making him shake. He stilled himself in time, enough to will himself to remain calm, though his receptors hummed, and his stomach clenched, hardening him between his thighs.

He should have left then. He had completed his little test, and he should just go, knowing now that these human females (and not the males) affected him in a way he still didn't understand but they affected him all the same. A mystery still with few answers.

Yes, he should have gone. But he found too soon that he couldn't bring himself to move, couldn't bring himself to look away from the woman down below. She wasn't nillium. She wasn't even a silion. Yet, he sat there all the same, staring down at her, wanting...

Wanting something he shouldn't. This was wrong. nillium didn't entangle with others.

Yet his body was telling him otherwise. He couldn't fathom the reason and it bothered him.

The woman fixed the bot and set it aside and looked around again with uneasiness. She hurried away, and, without even a logical thought in his head, Ryziel followed her.

He made his way up without being seen and found her again on the twenty-second level. He slipped into a shadowed corner just above the cave face where she had entered and peered down to see her walking toward another human man. His eyes narrowed on them as they talked, but he couldn't make out their words, not because he couldn't hear them clearly but because they spoke in a non-Xolien language that he couldn't understand. Likely their own common tongue. He watched them move together to sit on a rock almost directly above him. They sat close and Ryziel wondered if they were mates. They smiled at each other and talked without restraint, but they did not embrace in their meeting. But that could mean very little as he did not know human customs.

A breeze picked up, catching in the woman's hair, spilling it over her shoulders. Ryziel thought about the night on the bridge, and even now, he wanted to touch the silky strands once more, letting them fall through his sharp fingers. He shut his eyes tight and rubbed his temples.

This was foolish and ridiculous and what the hell was he even doing here, watching them, thinking these thoughts?

As he opened his eyes, he caught the pair taking hands. Entwining their fingers. Ryziel's brow tightened at the gesture. Yes, they must be mates.

A strange feeling welled up in him, but he couldn't quite identify it. His Drega moved, stirring slightly, and he forced it down. What did it matter? He shouldn't care. Didn't care. Yet, he found his body growing tense as if ready to strike.

Foolish.

He was about to turn away when he saw the woman lean forward and place her mouth on to the man's. The sudden show of affection made Ryziel stop and grow still.

The gesture was intimate to say the least, though not to a point where Ryziel thought the man would claim her there on the rock (thank Nihl). It was a tender thing, something Ryziel knew little about, but something he suddenly very much desired to understand and even experience himself. And with this human woman no less.

His body trembled again at the thought of her lips touching him as she touched this man, and once more, his Drega moved. He caught the growl in his throat but couldn't stop a low hiss. He shoved the forbidden thought aside.

No, forget it. He didn't need to know what it felt like to be touched by one of them. Why should he? He was just confused, that was all. And in shock by the sudden change of his Drega. That was it.

It didn't matter what it wanted. It was wrong because nillium didn't entangle with others.

Or weren't supposed to.

Ryziel let out a long, deep breath and couldn't help in that moment thinking of his brother. Korzien, who believed nillium were without any fault. That their desires and needs were always rational and acceptable. Unlike their father, who believed nillium had to be in control of themselves and their urges at all times. He could imagine what Korzien would think of him now, how he would laugh and say he was being dramatic.

A memory came to him then of a time in the First House. He remembered walking the halls, always so silent that people missed him, and turning a corner to see his brother just about to enter one of the spare bedrooms down the way. His brother had looked around and saw him and smiled. There had been someone behind him, a figure Ryziel had seen many times in the House before. Usually serving his family in silence. Ryziel saw their face, and he understood.

"It's okay, Ryziel. We are nillium and we do what we please. And take what we wish," his brother had said before closing the door.

They take what they wish.

He could hear his brother's reply even now. His voice still drumming in his brain.

It doesn't matter, Ryz. You are nillium, born of the First House. You can have whatever you want.

And, as if to reply to him in his very mind, Ryziel said, 'It is immoral to take someone else, mated or no. To take by force is to let your Drega have control.'

He could hear his brother's low laugh.

You are son of the First. You have the right to all. You could take her and make her yours.

'She is not nillium.'

So?

Ryziel frowned, thinking again about the times he had caught his brother taking a silion or a servant to bed. That first time had only been the beginning. Many in the House knew he indulged in more than nillium women and had kept silent. Perhaps even his father knew. But he would not condemn his prized son. Not for that.

The human pair had separated now and were checking their techbands as if nothing between them had just happened. A few words were spoken, and the woman left.

Ryziel didn't move to follow her this time. Instead, he drew away in silence, deep in thought.

He had never considered just taking someone, and he certainly couldn't imagine it going well for him. He took lives by his father's command, sure. That came easy, but to force one to please him and serve him alone was honestly unthinkable. Because he wasn't like other nillium, and, despite his brother's words, he was not his brother in that regard. Korzien was charming and talented at seduction. He took those he wished, certainly, but they never said no, never fought him because he knew how to talk, and he was handsome beyond measure, and he had the practice. His brother had many women, it was true. And Ryziel? Ryziel had never been allowed to be touched. He had been forbidden to be alone with any woman, and he'd only spoken to those of his House. He knew nothing of love (though lust, he certainly was familiar with), and he knew nothing of affection. Only the violence and death that was his training since he was young.

And when he had touched another, he had been severely punished. Because he wasn't like other nillium, regardless of his birthright. He was Nihl's master of death, his father's prized assassin, but he was not in-line with the others. And so, he was not allowed to be with one of them.

If he could have been born of the sun and the light and not of the dark, maybe things would have been different. He would have had many women. And he wouldn't have to ever consider taking one by force.

The thought appalled him now. And he hated that he was losing control again of his Drega over such an idea. It had taken years to master his darker self. To control his bestial instincts. And suddenly, it all seemed to be crumbling before him.

All because of a human woman.

Ryziel stalked the dark tunnels, roaming nowhere in particular, not knowing where to go, when his techband sounded. He checked the message and saw it was from Xilya. She was back. And wanted to know where he wished to meet her.

Ryziel stopped. He could meet her in any old, abandoned cave system and get the info he needed, but he was feeling frustrated now and could really use a moment to take the edge off. He'd garner more than a few shocked responses; he hadn't been seen in weeks, after all, and people were always bound to talk. But damn if he cared. He messaged Xilya back then continued onward, trying not to think about the past, his brother, or the human woman.

CHAPTER SIX

As soon as her shift ended, Aly rushed back up to her unit to take a quick shower and scarf down a meal before meeting the others. Her unit was small and needfully simple. A one-room apartment within a hub on the ninth level, fixed with a bathroom as tiny as a walk-in closet, a bed in one corner, and a "kitchen" in the other. It surprised her how similar it was to her unit on the ship. Until she discovered they had purposely redone the empty units to reflect human necessity, so that it felt familiar. The one thing Xolis seemed kind enough to do for them given the circumstances.

She had no other clothes to wear save for the slipsuits, so she threw the dirty one aside and put on a clean one. It wasn't like she was going out with the thought to impress, anyway.

Shadowpoint was a low dive place at best. A high dungeon dressed up like a bar. A drinking-hole shoved into an artificially carved room on the eleventh floor. One of the few places miners could go to drink their tasteless *Shvas* (the closest thing to beer) and their bitter *Nuri* (a strong, warm drink that Jamie said reminded her of sake from home). Neither of which the team had much taste for but downed, regardless. Only Mark refused to drink, and Aly hadn't tried, mainly because she was already a lightweight and didn't really feel like getting "white girl wasted" in front of the others. She had her share of those moments in her youth and hadn't been in the mood to recount them in a place like Lethe Maws.

They had only gone once and didn't stay long. Having felt too many pairs of eyes at their backs and hearing too many hissing whispers with the word "humans" thrown in, they didn't need to be told they were bringing too much attention to themselves that first time. It was why they had been holding their meetings at an undisclosed location for so long. Now, however, Kate and Julian had decided to give the place another try. Messages flew around, a couple not too happy, but the captain and his second were adamant about going. Perhaps they were finally coming around to the idea that they needed to mingle more with the aliens. Though Aly had a feeling it had something more to do with getting out of their units and not feel completely miserable talking in the old station.

To keep morale up in the others.

As Aly slipped into her clean slipsuit and reattached her techband, she looked in the bathroom mirror one last time. Her face was pale, her lips a light pink, eyes bright still but dull circles were beginning to form underneath. Before she forgot, she opened one of the cabinets below the mirror and took out a metal canister. She took out a honey-colored pill and stuck it in her mouth, then cupped her hands under the faucet and took a long drink of water.

Because Lethe Maws was always so dark, they had been given vitamins to keep their nutritional needs in check. Some of the other races had no trouble in the dark, but, even with the vitamins, some of the group still felt lethargic at times. Not a good thing to feel in this line of work, when a wrong step could mean death and one needed to always be alert.

Aly splashed her face also then dried it with a towel. She took a deep breath and turned away. As she exited her unit, she looked down the hall to a door opposite. She could go and knock on Mark's door and ask if he wanted to go together, but she quickly thought against it. She had already made her one mistake today. She thought about that kiss, and her stomach dropped. She shouldn't have done it. She had known too, as soon as he opened his mouth, what he was going to ask her. The same offer he had given her on the ship. Only, this time, she wasn't sure how she would have answered. She had been shamefully relieved in that moment for the message that had interrupted them and given her a chance to leave.

No, she would see him there. And they would talk again like nothing had happened.

Aly turned down the hall and left the hub in which they lived. She bounded over to one of the elevator cars, squeezing herself in with a few other miners, who gave her silent glares, and made her way down to floor eleven. When the doors opened, she stepped out onto a platform and went down one passage and then across a long bridge, over a deep chasm, and through a carved tunnelway lit across by deep red lanterns. She stopped just below the lanterns and waited by the wall until her party appeared.

"Oh, look, little miss sunshine made it before us. What a surprise," Ethan said, walking—or rather limping—past, barely looking at her. Aly rolled her eyes as Davis followed with a tight frown then Jamie behind him, her head low, eyes averted to the ground. She looked like she had been crying again. Cilia was beside her, patting her back. Kate and Julian walked up next, both speaking in a low whisper in their native French tongue before seeing her and nodding their heads. Mark came up last and gave her a quiet smile. Aly returned with one similar.

"Ready to get shamefully wasted?" Mark said sarcastically.

"I sure as fuck am," Ethan said before Aly could reply.

"Let's not get ahead of ourselves, now, Ethan," Julian said, stopping before the entrance. His steel-gray eyes looked over his crew, assessing them. Behind him, other miners strolled past, staring curiously. "Now, we will go in and be respectful as usual, yes? We will sit quietly. And—" he looked at each of them—" no staring and no talking about the others around us, we clear? Yes? Good. Ah and—" he pointed at Aly—"no trying to make conversation unless invited. Got it?"

Aly saluted. "Yes, sir."

Someone snorted behind her, but Julian only smirked. "All right." He clapped his hands and gestured down the tunnelway filled with the red lanterns to the large open doorway at the end. "Let's go."

Julian and Kate led the way, and the others followed. As they entered Shadowpoint, it took Aly all her mental strength not to stop in the middle of the doorway and stare just like Julian had warned them not to.

The place wasn't huge. Not by any means. But it was still a strange sight to see, like walking into another time or place. Even if this wasn't her first time inside, it still surprised Aly, like she was stepping into a great dungeon in some dark castle. Arched pillars rose up to a ceiling, where floaters of all sizes and colors hovered. The floor under her was paved in dark-blue stone similar to marble, leaving no shine. Tables were stationed by the walls and near each pillar, carved in the shape of a crescent moon and made of a heavy black metal, welded to the floor. A curved bench accompanied the outer rim of the table while stools were placed on the inner side.

Miners of all races sat and drank while oracles, programmed to take orders, zipped around in their white and gray uniforms, with trayboxes full of drinks to serve them. At the center of the chamber, down a small set of steps, large tanks were stationed in a circle behind a long crescent-shaped bar. There, Aly could see the drinks being produced and taken by the bots.

Aly followed the others as they made their way over to a seat by the wall, close to the door. Kate and Julian slid onto the long bench first, situating themselves at the center. Davis sat beside Kate on the left and Cilia took her spot by Julian on the right, leaving the stools for the rest. Ethan pulled his out next to Davis, and Jamie took hers next to Cilia. Mark gladly took the stool opposite Julian, where he could just stare at the wall, and Aly made do with the seat between him and Ethan.

They sat for a moment, saying nothing, looking not much better than they had at the old station.

"We doing this or what?" Ethan spoke.

Julian rubbed his mouth with the back of his hand then gently settled his palm on the table. The surface of the table lit up, and a screen displayed before them.

"I want two of each," Ethan blurted.

"You got the credits, my man?" Davis asked.

"We will pool our credits," Julian answered.

They each registered their accounts into the menu system and put in a choice amount of credits onto a single tab. Once drinks were picked, Julian sent the order. They waited but a few moments before an oracle appeared. They took their drinks, mumbling a thanks to the bot, though it was unnecessary, then looked down at their drinks, no one moving to bring the mugs and tiny cups to their lips.

Aly had ordered one small shot of Nuri, and even she feared what it might do. She hadn't had a drink in so long she couldn't say how she was going to react. But damn if she wasn't going to try something this time. As the others sat there uncertainly, Aly decided to take the first dive. She took the small metal cup between her fingers and held it up. She paused before touching it to her lips to look around at the others.

They stared at her then Davis took up his mug of Shvas, holding it up.

"Here's to...getting out of this hell-hole," he said.

Ethan put up his mug. "I'll drink to that."

The others in turn lifted their drinks.

"Here's to getting home," said Kate.

They each brought their mugs and cups to their mouths. Aly drank hers in one small gulp, as did Jamie, while Ethan and Davis took several swigs from their mugs.

They each grimaced. Aly coughed, the Nuri burning her throat and leaving a bitter aftertaste. Jamie's face turned beet red, and the rest coughed and gagged.

"Jesus, fuck me, that's rough," said Davis.

Only Mark hadn't responded in any way as he sipped on his water.

Despite their faces twisting with displeasure, the others forced their drinks down until there was nothing left.

"Another round?" wheezed Ethan.

"I'm in," said Davis.

"I'm not," said Cilia, pushing her mug away in disgust.

Julian nodded and went to order another round for those who wanted it.

"Another one, Aly?" Julian asked as he tapped on the screen.

Aly coughed some more and waved her hand, shaking her head. "No thanks." The Nuri seared her stomach, and the bitter aftertaste left her tongue dry. "Water," she croaked.

If it wasn't embarrassing enough that they felt completely fragile and weak in front of the others, this only cut even deeper. Aly caught a few eyes of those around them and saw more than a few snicker.

"You guys don't need to torture yourselves," Mark said beside her, taking another sip of his water.

"Yeah. We do," said Ethan.

"What's hell without a little torture?" said Davis.

Mark had nothing to say to that. He, instead, looked at Aly with concern. "You okay?"

"Fine," Aly croaked again. She cleared her throat a few times but shook her head when Mark offered her some of his water. No need to start sharing drinks.

Julian put in the second order, and several minutes later, the oracle showed. They took their drinks, and, without hesitation this time, drank their dark, bitter drinks down. Aly drank her water quickly, as well, cooling her throat some. As she set her mug down, she caught an odd look in Jamie's eyes. Her face went from beet red to pale, and before Aly could say a word, Jamie vomited all over the floor.

Aly shot up from her seat as some of the vomit hit her boot. She, in turn, felt her stomach begin to twist violently at the sight of the upchucked liquid. She put a hand tightly over her mouth and backed away as Cilia shouted and pulled Jamie from her seat. Jamie hurled once more, this time in the direction of the wall as Cilia held her and patted her back.

"Well, shit," said Davis. "So much for keeping attention off ourselves."

Cilia turned her head toward him, her face now as red as Jamie's had been. "Shut up."

A strange sound emerged from behind them, like that of a slow, rumbling hiss. Aly blinked and looked around to find the aliens around them watching. And laughing.

"Dammit," Cilia muttered. "I'm going to take her back," she said to Julian and Kate.

"I'll come and help," said Kate, rising. When Julian grabbed her arm, she merely said something in French to him, and he let her go.

Mark stood up as well. "I'll go too. Think I've had enough already. You coming?" he asked Aly.

Aly should probably just leave too, but she shook her head instead. "I think I'm gonna stay a bit longer."

Mark nodded and left with the three women. Once they were gone, Julian sighed, muttered something unintelligible, and forced down his drink.

So much for that.

Aly sat back and watched as the others drank in silence. She caught Ethan looking at her and raised her brows. "What?" she asked.

Ethan shrugged. "You gonna have another, or you just gonna sit there?"

Aly crossed her arms but said nothing. She didn't feel anything yet and wasn't sure if that was good or bad. Ethan bumped his mug against her shoulder.

"Here, just give it a taste."

Aly smelled the earthy odor in the mug and flinched. She looked at Ethan then back at the mug and took it.

What the hell? She already knew it was going to taste bad.

She took a quick, generous swig then plopped the mug back down on the table. The liquid went down thick, and the taste wasn't far off from that of grass and saltwater. Aly choked and coughed again, her eyes stinging, feeling someone patting her back.

"Dammit, we don't need another one getting sick!" Julian said.

"Sorry, Captain," Ethan said, patting her back harder. Aly sat straight and brushed his hand away.

"So, how does it taste, Smith?" Ethan chuckled.

Aly recovered herself, wiping her eyes. "Tastes just about as good as you look, Hathfeld."

Even Ethan smirked as Davis laughed, and Julian gave her a warning glare.

"What could possibly make this appetizing to anyone?" Aly said aloud, then felt her face heat as she looked around.

"Nothing. This is probably just the only piss-poor choice of beer they got, by my guessing." Davis took another swig and was able to do so without making a face. Ethan and Julian followed suit.

Aly had started to laugh a little when she turned her head to the side and caught sight of two figures by the entrance, and her laugh quickly turned into a sharp inhale of breath.

There he was, as if just appearing from nowhere. The nillium from the bridge. And beside him was—

"Think that's it for me," Ethan said, wiping his arm across his mouth. "It was a nice shot, Captain, but I think I'll pass next time."

He and Davis both rose. Aly opened her mouth to get their attention, but it was too late. The two figures had already gone to the back of the room, out of sight.

"I guess we'll be seeing you at the old station," said Davis.

Julian rubbed his forehead and sighed, too tired to try and get them to stay. "You got it." He took one last pull from his mug then set it aside. "Aly, you coming?"

Aly opened her mouth then closed it, unsure what to say. "I...you go on. I'm going to finish my drink."

Julian's brows rose, his tired eyes looking on her with slight uncertainty. "I can stay here with you."

Aly shook her head. "No need, Captain, I'll be fine. I'll probably be done before you even get to the elevator car. Really."

Julian frowned then nodded his head. "All right. Well, suit yourself, Smith. Just don't start any bar fights, hm?"

Aly smiled and nodded then watched them go. She took a few more sips of water then left the table, but she didn't make for the entrance. Instead, she snuck to the back. She could see it had grown quiet at tables; miners stared in awe at the back wall where the nillium and his companion sat in near darkness. Aly hid behind one of the pillars to stare at them herself. She looked to the nillium first, and her heart did a little jolt. Then her eyes peeled over to the one who sat beside him, and her heart dropped.

It was a vrisha. Plain as day. There was no mistaking it now, from this close. She had seen the footage. They all had. From the leak of information the Grayhart Foundation had given to them. This one's skin, however, was more a purplish hue then the telltale red of the pictures she had seen, and its horns were shorter and its body slimmer. Aly wondered if it was possibly female.

Then it opened its mouth and spoke and there was no wondering.

But what was she doing here? And did she know what had happened? Did she know how to get home to her planet, or was she stuck here just like them?

Endless questions wracked Aly's brain, but none of them gave her the courage to go up to the table and start asking. What did get her to eventually leave the pillar and approach the table was something much stranger and more troubling but much more wanting in her mind. And it didn't involve the vrisha.

CHAPTER SEVEN

Ryziel didn't wait long for Xilya to show up, though he did receive a few snide remarks about their meeting place.

"Your mythical status is waning, Nihl Ryziel," she said upon their meeting. "Since when did you feel the need to meet at Shadowpoint, of all places?"

Ryziel looked at the vrisha female with a sharp gaze. "Don't mistake my meeting you here as a need to interact with others."

"Hard to believe, when you want to meet in a place filled with workers," Xilya said bluntly. "Is it because you haven't left the bottom in weeks, and being alone down there with just the urk drove you mad?"

Ryziel gave a tiny, bitter smirk. "Not quite. And, for the record, I never cared if they saw me. It's not like these people don't know I exist."

"Yes, but as the monster who hides in the lower levels, not some silion simpleton that comes crawling up just to quench his thirst."

Ryziel would have laughed if that hadn't stung a little.

"Maybe I'm just not myself, all right?" And wasn't that the truth? Ryziel rubbed the base of one of his receptors.

Xilya looked at him curiously, her spiked tail flicking to the side. "I see. Very well. But you are buying."

They entered the place and went straight to the back, where it was darker and there were fewer wandering eyes. As they passed, Ryziel saw the faces of other miners drop, a few choking on their drinks; their eyes followed them and the whispers soon followed. Ryziel didn't care.

They sat at the very back table, under a small floating lantern that gave off the faintest orange light. They got two Nuri sent to them right away, and Ryziel ordered a smoking pipe filled with red bluym to relax him. Once in his possession, he filled the pipe and lit the bluym then took a deep drag. Red smoke curled out of his nose and mouth as he exhaled, and the effects were almost immediate. He hadn't taken bluym in some time. Not since he found the ship, really, and rarely even before. But he felt he needed its softening effects to loosen his nerves, even if the drug brought a bad taste in his mouth.

"So, let's get to it, as I assume we didn't come to chit chat and drink our senses away." Xilya carefully took up the cup in her clawed fingers and drank her Nuri in one swallow. She set her cup down then opened the bag at her side, taking out a small red sphere with black etchings and setting it firmly on the table. "The map is accurate, you will find. And I was told by the urk that there were loads of tython and byril in the area also. He gave us a good price for the trade, so I took it, but we can always get more if need be, since they hadn't harvested all the minerals; though he warned they are in largely more dangerous and rarely explored territory, mainly Yurza's Keep."

Ryziel grunted and took another drag. "So, the map can guide us to the low-level chambers too?"

"As the urk said, yes."

Ryziel's eyes narrowed on the red sphere before him, thinking. Yes, this was good. If the map could get them into those inner chambers, they could use a tracer to search farther in, and, just maybe, they would find a specific energy signature that would lead him to the one mineral he needed most. The one to power the ship.

Ryziel took the red sphere and placed it in his own bag at his waist. "I'll look it over with Nar. We will plan a route then get everything ready to go down. Likely, we'll be ready to go in two mooncycles. Maybe less."

Xilya huffed. "You aren't seriously considering taking that urk with you?"

Ryziel met her gaze. "Don't have much choice. Neither you nor I can get into some of those cave systems."

"Except one bad trip might cost Nar his legs again." Xilya pointed. "And that's assuming you don't run into anything foul."

"I'm aware," said Ryziel. "Are you coming?"

Xilya shook her head. "Not yet. I should lay low for a bit, as Vilson will wonder where I have been. But I will come down to the lair once it's safe, to see that everything is in working order. I tested the map myself earlier, but I'd like to see that it is properly transferred into the console system and—Nihl Ryziel, are you listening?"

He wasn't. Not fully. Because as soon as she had begun to speak, a familiar scent hit his nostrils and turned him hard as a rock. His eyes darted to the side by the edge of a pillar, and a low growl rose in his throat.

There, from the darkness of the pillar, the woman from the bridge stood, watching.

Ryziel went still, just like he had when first seeing her on the bridge. Xilya was trying to get his attention, but he couldn't bring himself to look away.

The woman approached cautiously, and it was in Ryziel to feel greatly impressed that she had the courage to face not only him but the vrisha also, who was equally terrifying in her appearance.

Brave or stupid, perhaps. It could also be true that she was just shamefully oblivious to the danger before her. Yet, still she came up to the table and even gave them a curt smile.

"Hello," she said softly, just like she had on the bridge. Her eyes darted to the vrisha then back to him. "We met on the bridge...remember?"

Obviously, he did, but he didn't answer. He took one last drag of his pipe in desperate hope that it would sedate him enough that his Drega wouldn't rise up and he wouldn't have the energy to leap over the table and pull her to him.

Out of the corner of his eye, he saw Xilya regarding him. Her eyes darted from the woman back to him. When he still said nothing, Xilya let out a soft growl, as if to clear her throat.

"And who are you, girl?" she asked, curious but guarded.

The woman looked at the vrisha female and blinked several times, as if coming out of a trance.

"My name is Aly," she said.

"Aly? Interesting." Xilya paused and looked at Ryziel, who was no more reactive than the cave wall behind them. He remained still and silent, watching the woman with acute intensity.

So, her name was Aly.

Ryziel's brow twitched. It didn't matter what her name was. He should just tell her to leave. To never approach or look at him again. Did she not know who he was? Did she not know to regard him as she did was a serious offense to any nillium? Even one such as himself? Yes, he should call her out now and tell her she had no business interrupting them—that she should learn respect. That her kind did not just approach his kind without proper respect.

"And from where do you hail, Aly?" Xilya asked.

"She's human," Ryziel blurted.

Aly's bright eyes turned back to him with shock. Ryziel had to keep himself from grimacing.

'Idiot. Why don't you just go on and confess you've also been following her and her kind around while you're at it?'

"Yes," she said carefully.

"I have never heard of human," Xilya said, ignoring the tension between them. "Which planetary system?"

"Um. Earth. It's not within the Xolis system."

"Ah, a 'refugee,' like me." Xilya looked at her more closely. "Far away, I take it?"

Aly nodded and seemed like she wanted to say more but wasn't sure how. Eventually, she said, "You really haven't heard of us?"

Xilya's tail swayed, and she crossed her hands. "Why would I have heard of you?" she asked.

Aly's face turned a little pink. "Sorry, I didn't mean..."

Xilya snorted and looked at Ryziel. "Another ego-driven species. You two would get along, I'm sure...or make great enemies."

For all her bluntness, he wished Xilya would stop talking. He needed to end this now. He took up his Nuri and drank it down then placed the now empty cup in front of him. He laid his tightly clenched fist on the table and slowly eased it open until his palm was flat. He looked up at Aly and prepared to say what he needed to say but maybe with a little more gentleness because she was new and didn't understand all the ways of Xolis. He would ask her to leave politely and not talk to him or his companion, and that would be that.

"I'm sorry," Aly said for no reason. Her face reddened and he could see a lick of sweat run down her neck. She blinked a few times more and shook her head as if trying not to fall asleep. " I just...I wanted to apologize for the moment on the bridge. I think I might have scared you."

There was a long pause as Ryziel stared at her in disbelief. She thought she might have scared *him*?

"You looked like you didn't expect to run into anyone, and you looked pretty shocked." She took a step closer, her hip brushing the tableside. "And, well, I was pretty shocked myself." She laughed. "Ah, sorry, I'm...not feeling myself. I saw you here, and I just wanted to say that, I guess." She started to turn, as if that was all, then she came back." And if I hurt you, I'm sorry also."

"Hurt me?" Ryziel couldn't help saying aloud.

She brushed a strand of hair back behind her ear, her soft lips curving ever so slightly, and the gesture almost made him shiver at its sweetness. He could feel himself growing harder, and he shifted uncomfortably.

"You seemed...in pain when you got close and..." She looked to Xilya then back at him and placed her hand against her throat, and he knew exactly what she was talking about. "Then you ran. I don't know. I thought maybe my skin was toxic or something. But maybe that's stupid..."

Stupid, yes. But not entirely illogical, he guessed, for someone to think who had no knowledge of other species besides their own.

Something welled in him, and a noise escaped his throat. Xilya nearly jumped beside him and stared at him in shock.

Because he was laughing.

This strange human woman was so innocent, so naive, about what she was saying. *Scared him? Hurt him?* If she knew his past and who he truly was, she'd see how funny—how ironic—such statements were.

He could hear his brother's laughter too.

The innocent ones are always the most fun to play with.

He stopped laughing and frowned at his brother's words. Oh, yes, how his brother liked to play. And suddenly, he had an image of him toying with Aly, and for some reason, it bothered him. Now, he was irritated.

"Your apology is a waste of breath," he said. "You didn't scare or hurt me. Perhaps you surprised me...barely. But it was because I thought for a moment you were one of the *ruk* that had somehow scurried its way up from the bottom."

Her brows knitted. "What is a ruk?"

"A giant sightless frog," Xilya answered. "Give or take."

Aly frowned, and the disappointment in her eyes almost stung him...almost. He shoved any guilt down.

"Oh." She smiled then laughed a little. "I guess I can see the mistake." A joke, he thought.

She nodded her head and went to take a step back when an abbiot walked past. Ryziel watched as she backed into him, and he, in turn, jutted his great arm out and pushed her back, letting out a deep growl. Ryziel watched as she stumbled forward, hit the table, and caught herself, smacking her hands on the tabletop. One hand landed on the cool metal, another landed on top of his own.

The touch was as electric as the last time. Ryziel's Drega tore its way up, ready to pounce, and in response, Ryziel shot his hand back and bared his teeth, a hiss escaping his lips. A violent surge of lust ripped his lower abdomen, pain throbbing between his thighs. He was ready to lunge over the table, grab her arm, swing her around, shove her against the table, bend her over, and take her right there for everyone to see, Nihl be damned.

Panic took him. He found himself leaping over the table, but he didn't touch her. She stumbled back in alarm then fell to the ground, and her fear was plain. He towered over her with a heaving breath.

"Stay away," he growled. "Stay away from me. If I find you anywhere close to my territory or near me again, you will regret it."

And that was that. And he could see in her that it was enough. He disliked himself in that moment, though being cruel had never garnered such shame in him before. But right now, it felt necessary.

Before he did something he might regret later, he turned away and left, leaving the girl on the floor and Xilya to sit there wondering what the hell his problem was. But it was a better scenario than the alternative. And so, he went without a word.

CHAPTER EIGHT

ALY SAT UP IN HER UNIT, STARING OUT THE ONE SMALL WINDOW next to her bed, her head pressed against the cool glass, watching the lights from outside. It had begun to rain again, and, based off the skymeter's readings beside the window, it would continue to do so for the remainder of the night and all into the next day. The temperature was to drop as well, and the wind would pick up after that. Another glorious day in Lethe Maws.

Aly sighed and lifted her head from the glass then begrudgingly made her way to the kitchen and made herself a cup of dark hyli tea. She wasn't going to get much sleep tonight, she knew, so she might as well make the most of it in some other fashion. She took her tea over to the bed and set it on the bedside table to let it cool then she picked up her sketchbook and opened it carefully. She flipped through it until she stopped and stared at the image before her and frowned.

The nillium's face stared back at her, only partially shaded from face to neck, his eyes glaring at her just like he had at Shadowpoint. Angry.

She was a fool. A real idiot. She didn't know what had come over her then at the bar, but she certainly wished more than once she could go back and just drag her intoxicated ass out of the situation, patting herself on the back and saying, "nice try." But no. The memory of only a few hours ago still lingered like an open wound in her mind: the nillium's face snarling above her, his more than serious threat, his eyes alight with a violent fire she cowered before. And what had she done? Well, she wasn't entirely sure where she set him off as he had seemed pretty put out by her even in the beginning; but, by her guess, it was when she had stumbled onto the table and accidentally dropped her hand onto his. He really didn't like being touched, if only by her. That thought hurt, though she told herself it shouldn't. There were plenty of people, humans included, who didn't like to be touched, so she shouldn't feel offended.

Except that she still couldn't help feeling the obvious hurt and disappointment of the...rejection. Yes, she had been rejected. It wasn't like it was the first time, but this one seemed to bother her a lot more than it should. Why, she couldn't say.

Maybe she was just confused. He had come up to her on the bridge, had wanted to touch her. She wasn't stupid enough to think he actually mistook her for some giant frog. She could take a hint at an insult when it was thrown in her face. But he *had* been interested. She could tell, even as he had cautiously approached her that night.

So why the sudden change?

Aly let out a frustrated breath and shut her sketchbook tight. Forget it. That's what she needed to do. Just forget it. Even the vrisha had told her as she lay there on the ground in shock. The vrisha had risen from the table as she had watched her companion go then slowly stepped over to peer down at Aly with little concern.

"Just let it go, girl. The nillium are an uptight race with a lot of pride. You're lucky he even let you speak to him, really. It is strange..."

And she left Aly alone on the ground, with a dozen or more pairs of eyes staring at her and the soft voices of laughter filling the room. When she had finally calmed down enough, she had gotten up and—like a dog with its tail between its legs—left the bar more embarrassed than she was sure she had ever felt in her short life.

Sometimes she wished she could just listen and obey. But maybe it was just in her nature to get into trouble. Her family back on Earth would certainly agree, but then, she had never liked playing by their rules.

Aly took a sip of the black tea, hot and soothing as it ran down her throat, and set it back when her techband dinged with a message. She looked down at it, and her frown deepened.

Braxin wanted to see her and the others first thing in the morning. Oh boy, they were in for it now.

Or at least she was. Once she had gotten back to her unit and settled down a bit, allowing the embarrassment of the moment to dissipate a little, her stomach had dropped, and she'd cursed silently, realizing that talk was going to spread quickly about what the others had seen. There was no stopping its spread to the top. Braxin would hear of it for sure, and he would send her to the warehouses, away from the others.

Panic welled up in her at the thought, and she tried to tell herself she could convince him to let her stay, though it was probably unlikely. She looked back out the window to the darkness beyond.

Maybe going to the warehouses would be safest, anyway. Now that she seemed to have made an enemy of the most dangerous person in Lethe Maws. She had never felt any inclination to go to the lower levels, mainly because she knew of the horrors that awaited down there. Now she knew if she did somehow escape the warehouses, she would never allow herself to go beyond even the fiftieth level. If she could obey no one else, she would at least take the nillium's threat to heart.

* * *

Ryziel stared down at the map before him with the intensity of a predator on the hunt. Yes, this was perfect. The tunnels led straight into the undocumented parts of Lethe Maws, out of Xolis' marked working grounds. They delved into Yurza's Keep as Xilya said, but that didn't worry him too much. He, instead, focused on the clusters of green and blue dots scattered within a holographic copy of a cave system in red.

"Can't believe it," Nar said beside him. He pointed to the cluster. "That's a lot of minerals. And they are closer than we thought. Xilya, you are amazing."

Ryziel nodded in agreement. He pointed to a tunnelway beyond which the minerals were said to be, to a network of caves. "And here is where I want the tracer to start looking. There's an entrance here"—he pointed to a narrow opening—"that goes down a little further."

Nar looked at it curiously, his beady little eyes blinking. "Looks like the urk party didn't go beyond that point...I wonder why."

"It is odd," said Ryziel. "What's more troubling is that they didn't harvest most of the minerals within the cluster. By the looks of it, they only maybe got two barrels' worth. Xilya had said they hadn't taken it all."

"Because they didn't want to be down there for long," Nar stated.

Ryziel rubbed at his nose and straightened. "Something keeps them from sticking around for too long."

Nar shrugged. "It is in Yurza's Keep. Who knows what nasty beast is lurking around...and stories of Yurza's corpse lumbering around have been told to my kind since I was a youngling. Though, they are just stories."

Ryziel crossed his arms and stared at the map, in deep thought. "We might have to use some of the brightburns, just in case."

"It's going to be a rough fit in some of these areas," Nar noted, pointing to where some of the minerals sat in tight tunnelways.

"You think you can handle it?" Ryziel said, forcing his eyes not to linger over Nar's two metal legs.

Nar snorted. "It's not about whether I can handle it. It's about whether I can be discreet enough. Metal clanging around on rock tends to echo. Whether we use drills or hammers, there's going to be a lot of noise. And someone is bound to hear it."

"We will use a different method to harvest them, then."

Nar glanced up at him and grunted. " I know what you're thinking, but that could take twice the time."

"It's that or we have to deal with whatever hears us. And it means having to constantly back off, like the urk party."

Nar grumbled. "Using liquid fire might damage some of the minerals."

"That's a risk we might have to take," Ryziel said. "Thankfully, there's a lot and, knowing anything, some of them won't even need harvesting. They could just be right on the surface of the rock."

"True," Nar said, though still not sounding entirely convinced. "Even if we decide on that method, me crawling around with metal legs isn't going to be totally quiet."

"Then you will just have to go slow."

Nar grumbled again but didn't argue this time. "So, how long?"

Ryziel took a deep breath and leaned forward, placing his hands on the edge of the console, where the map was projected before them.

"A couple mooncycles at most. Xilya will be down before then, and we will have everything ready to go, including supplies for the trip. Then we get to work."

Nar was silent longer than usual and Ryziel knew he must be thinking about something. He waited until the urk said, "So, I take it you figured things out above, right?"

"I don't know what you mean," Ryziel said, though he thought he knew.

"You know, with what set you off? Just making sure your head is clear now."

Ryziel closed his eyes and an image of the woman—Aly—lying on the ground, cowering before him, lit in his mind. His hands slowly formed into fists, and his jaw clenched, as if he were bracing himself for a hit.

"I'm clear. And ready to get this job done," he said, unwavering. And he felt it was the truth. He had made up his mind coming down that he wouldn't return above unless it was by ship. He would not go near the humans again, especially the one called Aly. Maybe when everything was said and done, when he had gotten home and took revenge on his uncle and reunited with his brother, maybe he would try to come back for her—

No. For them. And only to understand why.

Ryziel took another long breath then moved away from the console and the map. "Let's get to work."

CHAPTER NINE

ALY FELT AWFUL WAKING UP AND MORE AWFUL AS SHE GOT ready to meet the others at Braxin's work unit. With the Nuri from the night before mixing with the little sleep she had gotten, she had a recipe for the start of a very bad day. She took a quick, lukewarm shower and ate a small meal that was a near equivalent to sloppy oatmeal, then dressed in her usual slipsuit before inevitably slipping out the door.

Outside the hub, the rain made it down to the middle levels, pelting the ground in heavy splats. Aly drew on her hood and rushed for the elevator, quickly becoming soaked in the places her slipsuit could not protect. Great flashes of lightning lit the surface above, the light penetrating the dark even from where she stood, giving off a white, eerie glow against the backdrop of the cave. The elevator trembled as she took it down, and though the slipsuit was meant to keep her warm, she shivered regardless, hugging herself tight. Her heart leaped and her stomach rolled when she made it to the fifteenth level, where the rain still cascaded down in torrents. She feared what was coming, even if she told herself last night that she would be prepared for the reprimanding she was surely going to receive. She felt sick at the thought of being alone in those cold, metal-laid warehouses, working on the conveyor with bots to transport the minerals to a ship sent down to the mines.

Alone and no one to talk to. Nowhere to find a familiar face. It was an awful nightmare she couldn't escape.

She dragged her feet into the hub and forced her way over to the large entry of the storeroom, where Braxin's work unit was located. As she entered the space, she found her team already there, standing in a semi-circle around Braxin, whose snarling face looked annoyed, as usual.

Aly made her way over without meeting his gaze, knowing he was probably giving her the dagger treatment, and slipped beside Mark and Ethan.

"Now that you all are here," Braxin said as he sent a message onto his techband, "I have been contacted by several Xolis council members, discussing your placement on Lethe Maws. It is their decision that you remain here a while longer. Until a... better situation can be made."

No one moved or said a word. The news came as no surprise to any of them, and they knew arguing was pointless. At least where the lygin was concerned. Likely, there would be much to talk about (or argue over) at the next meeting.

"Is that all, then?" Ethan asked.

"No, that isn't all," Braxin nearly growled. "Marzin wishes to speak with you lot."

That got a few responses out of them.

"Why?" asked Davis

The lygin's eyes shifted over to him, his expression unreadable. "It is not my business to tell, only that it is the wish of the captain." With that, he disconnected one end of his techband, forming a slim silver ring, which he slid from his wrist then placed on the ground. He tapped on the remainder of his techband, and the silver ring lit up.

There was a brief shimmer of light. Then, as if appearing from nowhere, Marzin stood before them. He was not actually there, but the holographic ring certainly fooled the team into thinking he was. Every detail was exactly as Aly remembered, from his slick black hair down to the golden shine of his skin. His black, gold-flecked eyes stared at them with no hint of pleasure or amusement.

Aly noted that the horns (or antenna) on the sides of his head were smaller than Blue's and curved ever so slightly. He was more...stern and official; pride sitting plainly on his face. He looked over each of them with quiet regard before speaking.

"As you each know, it is the Xolis Council's will that you remain on Lethe Maws," he began. No curt greeting or 'how are you'—just down to business. No one dared protest or interrupt, as if to do so would end in a worse punishment than remaining in the mines. He studied each of their reactions and nodded, satisfied. "It is also the Council's will," he continued, "that you be further monitored upon request."

"Requested by who?" Aly blurted.

Marzin's eyes drifted over to her and lingered longer than she liked. She felt heat rise in her face and looked away.

"It is for your own safety, the Council finds, that you should be more closely looked after," he said after a pause. "As of today, you will be given new techbands to help keep you safer in the mines."

'Safer how?' Aly wondered. And she could see the others thought the same.

"Forgive me, Captain," Julian said, "But would it not be more beneficial and logical to house us in a more secure location?"

"These techbands are of a special design and will alert standing enforcers on Lethe of your location if you come into danger," Marzin said, disregarding him.

A few couldn't help glancing at each other with tight suspicion.

Why keep them in the mines in such a dangerous place but then suddenly care about their safety? It made no sense.

More disturbing was the indication, whether accidental or not, that the Council and enforcers who were going to know where they were at all times. Why did they suddenly care? What had changed?

"If you lose or destroy your techband, you will be judged under Xolis law and punished accordingly," Marzin stated, with little emotion on his face. "Already, your shifts have been confined to the upper levels."

They could see he was finished and there was no way to argue or question this odd new predicament.

Jamie, with her head low and face pale, tugged on Julian's arm and whispered in his ear, "Ask him about Sarah." Julian shook his head, but Aly felt it was a fair question.

"When is Sarah coming?" she asked aloud, ignoring Julian's warning hisses.

The nillium stared back at her again, and Aly barely met his gaze. The way he looked at her for that brief moment almost reminded her of how Blue had looked at her on the bridge, only there was something more dark and unpleasant about it. It wasn't the first time she had seen that look on him. She had caught it once on the ship taking them to the refugee facility, and even still, it made her stomach turn and chilled her to the bone.

"Sarah will not be coming," he replied. "Because she is ill and needs to be strictly monitored."

They all turned silent from shock.

She was ill? No, that couldn't be. She had been perfectly fine on the ship. How could this be?

"That is all I have for you. Let Nihl be in your sight." And with that, he disappeared and the holographic ring went dark. Braxin picked up the silver ring and reattached it to his techband then turned back to his office, leaving them standing there, stunned.

"Fucking bullshit," Ethan uttered quietly. "This is seriously fucked."

"There's no way he's telling the truth, right?" Davis asked. "Like, we saw Sarah, before we left. She wasn't sick."

"And why are they suddenly keen to look out for us? They certainly didn't care to throw us into this cold hell," Cilia said with a sneer. Jamie whimpered and came up close as Cilia put an arm around her.

Kate said something to Julian in hurried French, and he nodded. "Something is off. But there is little we can do right now."

"Seriously?" said Cilia. "They could be doing messed up experiments on Sarah as we speak. And now they wanna watch us every waking hour. We have to do something!"

"Julian's right," Mark said beside Aly. "What? Are you gonna try to call up Marzin again or get in touch with the Council and try to change their minds?"

Cilia opened her mouth to argue but cursed instead.

"You could talk to them again," Aly said to Julian. "Talk to the Council and ask why. Maybe we can't change their minds, but we have a right to know what's going on."

Davis snorted. "Like they are gonna tell us. You heard that golden stiff just now. He barely told us shit. Like the Council will be different. "

"If you are persistent enough, maybe..."

Julian rubbed his face, his tired eyes looking more defeated than before. "I don't know. Perhaps I can see. But for now, we should comply without issue. Let us just do as they like."

Braxin returned with their new shiny techbands. Their old ones were deactivated and shucked to the ground while their new ones were activated accordingly and clasped to their wrists.

"Remember, you lose these ones, and it's more than me who will come after you," Braxin warned. His eyes fell on Aly the longest as he said this ,and she had to turn her back so as not to give him a dirty gesture. "And from now on, you go no lower than level twenty. You disobey these rules, and you will be begging instead to stay on Lethe Maws."

* * *

The first few days of harvesting went about as slow and challenging as Ryziel should have expected. Getting all of their gear together had been no issue at, nor was figuring out their initial route to the Keep. The first day of actual harvesting, however, proved to be as tedious and time-consuming as Nar had warned.

Without the use of drills and hammers, getting to the necessary minerals took nearly an hour longer than usual. With the use of a dissolver or "liquid fire drill" as some called it, the process was at least much quieter, but even Ryziel's patience wore thin at the end of the day.

The chemical, once sprayed on the surface of a chosen area, would begin to slowly melt the rock away, but it wasn't instantaneous, and the deeper the minerals were buried the longer it took. And though it was meant to react only to rock—being completely harmless to skin or suit—it sometimes took a bad effect on metal if exposed too much and for too long. This being discovered on the fourth day of harvest when Nar's legs started to creak and grind, with one of the bolts coming loose, inevitably, not long after, forcing Ryziel to support the urk back to the lair, a not so pleasant journey.

"We barely scraped the surface of that blasted cave system, and I can barely walk," Nar complained after they counted the amount of minerals harvested in one of their converter tanks. "This is going to take ages."

Ryziel crossed his arms and glanced over to the ship. When they had first found it, it had been nearly a wreck. Only now could he finally start to see a fully functional ship. But it still needed a lot of work if it was ever going to fly. Which meant a lot more minerals.

And judging by the past few days, it would take several more weeks than planned to even get the ship off the ground, let alone travel quickly through space.

Ryziel rubbed his temples, his receptors humming ever so slightly. He hadn't spoken to his brother in nearly a year and a half now as any line of contact between them had been severed and strictly monitored by the Council and the enforcers. The more time that went by, the more he feared his uncle's influence within the First House and his brother's right to rule becoming compromised. Perhaps it was only a false paranoia on his part, but it was a fear like many others. And regardless of any political movement within the city of light, his brother needed support. He needed Ryziel just like Ryziel had needed him in his youth. And the longer he was gone, the more he feared for his brother. Their father had many enemies, regardless of status; and friends—even family—were quick to turn sides when it benefited them. Ryziel could be his brother's guard, a physical manifestation of terror itself, if he had to be to protect him. Even his Night Blade if he so wished it, an assassin and silent enforcer of his brother's vengeance. Just like he had been for their father.

He knew his brother would never ask him to do the things his father had. He had loathed what his father had made Ryziel do. But if he asked it—asked Ryziel to take out a threat to their family and house—he didn't think he would hesitate.

But he couldn't help his brother now, and each day their uncle remained with some semblance of power was one day closer to him overthrowing their house and taking what was rightfully Korzien's. If Ryziel didn't get this damn ship going soon, he could be hearing about his brother's death from some low-life miner. No, he needed to find a faster way to harvest, and, unfortunately that meant telling Nar he might have to stay behind and asking Xilya to come instead. The vrisha was way too big to fit into the areas that Nar could, but together, they could at least get to the minerals that were outside these tight spaces, even if there were less to be found. Meanwhile, they would have to find another way to get to the rest when the time came.

"You're sticking here for now, Nar," Ryziel said, turning back to him.

"Like hell I am!" the little urk protested.

"You don't have a choice. You will stay at the console instead and work the map, maybe get the tracer to search any of the areas for unknown dens and any threats lurking within. For now, I'm going on alone."

Nar shook his head as he sat on the edge of a worktable, his metal legs dangling, one more loose than the other. "You'll never get enough done on your own."

"I may ask Xilya for aid."

Nar snorted. "She's nearly as big as you. Neither of you can fit—"

"I know," Ryziel almost snapped, his receptors vibrating a little stronger now. "I know. But she could at least help me with the outer chambers."

"What are you going to do, then, when the inner ones are all that are left?" Nar asked. "And don't say ask one of my kind for help 'cause you know they won't. Or they will ask for an outrageous price."

Ryziel rubbed at his neck and smirked. "I could always wait for one to have its legs chewed off then save them before they get eaten entirely. Then perhaps they will repay me by helping."

Nar gave him a grimacing stare. "Very funny."

Ryziel let out a breath. "We will figure it out. Just have the tracer ready for tomorrow, and I will message Xilya. Until she can make it down again, I will go on alone."

CHAPTER TEN

THE RAIN DIDN'T LET UP THIS TIME. FEELING DRENCHED (EVEN if she wasn't thanks to her slipsuit) and weary, Aly worked tirelessly at one of the charging station generators meant to keep drills charged and ready for use. Only it had suddenly decided to stop working, and, by the looks of the bashed-in pieces of metal and ripped sides, she could guess why. She was able to repair one outlet easily, but the rest had her fixing and mending for at least half the day now, and the hours were slipping away fast.

Groaning and gritting her teeth as she pulled and wrenched at a piece of metal bent and stuck in between another outlet, Aly could see at the corner of her vision pairs of beady red eyes watching her. She tried to ignore the howlers as they climbed and jumped and ran nearby, some electing to perch up on a ledge above to observe her, but when they screamed, it was hard not to flinch.

Aly cursed them silently, both for wrecking the charging station and for making it more difficult for her to fix it. When she wasn't looking, they would come dangerously close, one even braving to tug at her bag, forcing Aly to keep a tight eye on them while trying to do her job.

Her shift was over soon anyway, and if she couldn't fix it by that point, then she would just forget it. Braxin could yell all he liked.

Finally, the metal broke off but not without a lot of effort, causing Aly to stumble backward, splashing into a puddle behind her. Muddy water scuffed her boots and dirtied her suit from ankle to shin. Though she couldn't feel it, she could imagine the feel of the cold mud on her legs, and it made her shiver. She shook each leg as if that would help then went back to the generator, wiping away the wet hair from her brow with her arm.

Lightning lit up a portion of the ground and the booming thunder followed, igniting a hoot and holler from the deformed monkeys around her as Aly attempted to dissect the generator one outlet at a time. Her techband went off, but she ignored it as she brought out her mender and stuck it into the set of wires before her, sparks flying at her face. She was alone on her current level, the other miners electing to take a break when the drill station went out then electing to move on somewhere else when she took too long in fixing it. Feeling worthless and annoyed, she stubbornly kept at it, even if it was unwise to be alone at that time within the mines.

It usually didn't bother her. But when her mind started slipping to images of the dead tylian from the day before, she suddenly felt a tad more anxious. She found herself looking to the shadows, jumping every time a howler passed her periphery or lightning lit the cavern. She also couldn't help thinking about seeing a pair of silvery eyes staring back at her in the darkness.

But no, he wouldn't be here. She wasn't even close to his territory so there was no way. She shouldn't have anything to fear.

Shouldn't.

Aly tried her best to concentrate on the work at hand. With the metal piece gone, all that was left was to reset the outlets, pulling back wires and twisting her mender around then shoving wires back in. Pull, twist, shove. Pull, twist, shove.

She was almost done. She just had one more outlet and the charger should be set. She pulled and mended the last outlet then shut the metal door soundly. She went to one side of the generator and turned on several switches.

Nothing happened.

Aly groaned and kicked the generator. She must have missed a wire or two. Feeling really put out, she hit the generator again with her fist.

"Damn thang!"

Great. Now her southern drawl was slipping out. This was not her day.

Aly stepped back for a moment and took a few deep breaths. She took off her hood and placed her hands on her hips, letting the rain fall on her bowed head. She probably should just give up. She would be reprimanded, but what did it matter? She felt miserable and wanted out of this damn rain.

Aly looked on the generator for a moment longer, thinking maybe she should give it one more go, when something tugged at her leg. She looked around just in time to see a howler run away, glancing back at her with curious eyes.

Aly turned to face them fully and watched as a few trotted closer to her then paused to sniff at her. All of them seemed to be studying her curiously, and Aly found herself staring back.

Maybe they weren't so bad. They were just animals, after all, and perhaps some were even friendly. She'd never seen one attack anyone, honestly. Usually they were too skittish.

"Hey, there little guy," she said softly, crouching down slightly to be more level with them. "You're just curious, aren't you?"

A pair of them circled her, and one got close enough that she could almost touch it, but she dared not to in case it did bite. Instead, she remained very still so as not to spook them. One tugged at her bag again and another pawed at her leg but nothing more. They did seem rather harmless.

When the others watching could see she wasn't much of a threat, they slowly padded closer. Carefully, Aly began to stand, feeling suddenly overwhelmed by the numbers.

Friendly but a little too curious as they tugged at her on either side, one even trying to climb up her leg.

"Yeah, I don't think so," Aly said, laughing nervously. She took a few cautious steps and they followed her.

Great, she should have just left them alone.

Aly went to turn her back and start for the elevator car when she nearly tripped over a howler cutting into her path. She stumbled forward and braced herself when another latched onto her arm and tugged. Aly pulled her arm away, and the howler came with it.

"Hey! Come on, enough!" she shouted as she swung the howler around, who was now latched to her wrist and, to her great horror, pulling off her techband.

Aly cursed not too politely and went to snatch her hand away, but the howler had a full grip on her band and was slipping it from her wrist. As the band began to loosen and fall from her hand, Aly flung her arm outward, causing the howler to let go and the techband to go flying. It went high then bounced on the edge of a rail before tumbling below.

Aly froze for a moment, in shock. Numb, yet, to any growing panic. When the panic did finally rear its ugly head, she rushed over to the railing and peered down.

She let out a little cry; both in relief and despair.

By some great miracle, her techband had been stopped in its endless fall to the bottom by a large bright-red floater, getting caught in its wiry tentacles. It was a relief to see that it hadn't fallen into darkness only to break somewhere unseen below; what was despairing, however, was that the floater was making its way to the very bottom, likely from the weight of the techband forcing it down.

She was really screwed this time. As she watched the floater drop farther and farther away, panic welled up higher and higher in her chest.

"Oh fuck, fuck, fuck!" Aly cursed.

Even if it had been her old techband, she would have still gotten into serious trouble. But this being the very band that had only been given to her a few days ago meant if she lost it, she wasn't just going to the warehouses, she was going somewhere much farther away. Alone.

Aly cursed some more and began to pace beside the rail. Then she looked down once more and saw the floater was almost out of sight.

Now, she had two options, and neither were good in any sort of way. She could either let it go and face the consequences—face being taken away to await a punishment she had yet to know. Or she could take the elevator down. Down past level twenty, where she wasn't allowed to go farther. Down past level fifty, where she had been warned never to go again. Then down into the nillium's territory, where awaiting her was nothing short of a swift death, if not by some monstrous creature then by the nillium himself, who had made it very plain he didn't want her there.

Aly stood there, unable to move, torn between her fear of being ripped away from the others to be placed somewhere somehow worse than Lethe Maws and her fear of the darkness and the nillium waiting in it below.

When her brain finally started working past the senseless panic, Aly tried to think logically about her options. Obviously, if she didn't try to retrieve it, she wouldn't risk death so that there was a pretty good reason to just go to Braxin and confess she'd lost it. On the other hand, if she *did* take the risk and *did* find it down below without anyone catching her, she wouldn't have to face the awful possibility of never seeing her team again, of possibly being locked away. Or worse, like Sarah, who may very well be getting experimented on this very minute.

So, there could be an option worse than death. So, what did she have to lose if she went down below and tried to get her techband back?

Unlatching her fingers from the railing, Aly slowly turned her head over to stare at the elevator car only a few yards away.

If no one caught her. *If.*

She thought of the nillium again and of his threat, and her heart began to pound wildly. Her throat tightened and turned dry. Lightning and thunder crashed several more times before she decided to move. She made her way toward the car and hesitated before waving a hand over the scanner. The door opened and Aly stepped inside. She stood thinking for a moment longer before finally pressing the button for the last level. She took a deep breath and held it as the elevator started to move downward.

The natural and artificial light slipped away, as did the storm above, the rain lessening somewhat, turning into nothing more than a light drizzle as the water was stopped by rock and platforms above only to trickle and cascade the rest of the way down to the bottom. The darkness grew more vast and was only barely fought back by the bulbs along the cave face and the few floaters hovering along each level. As Aly made her way down, she looked for the bright-red floater but feared it had already beaten her to the bottom. The system of rock around her began to warp and change, becoming more smooth and symmetrical, showing the slightest hint of some man-made design.

When the elevator car finally hit the bottom with a not so graceful *thunk*, the doors opened, but Aly didn't step out right away. Instead, she peered out, staring into the darkness beyond where few lights could be found, most circling the elevator and a few feet ahead, focusing on the ground like a spotlight.

Never having set foot at the bottom before, Aly felt like she had just been transported to a whole other world. A world that knew nothing of daylight or the sun. Just endless night.

She imagined if the underworld were a real place, it would be something like what she was seeing now (or not seeing) and so feeling the uneasiness of being in such thick darkness was no great surprise.

Because she was a being of the light above, trespassing in this kingdom of night where its god ruled and he didn't much like her at all and she was very much unwelcome.

But damn if she was going to turn back now. So, she straightened herself up and walked out of the elevator and—

And rushed right back in, her palm ready to slap a button for any level above. Only the barest amount of courage stayed her hand because something roared in the distance and it sounded *huge*.

"It's okay, Aly. You're good, you're cool," she said softly to herself. The roaring grew more distant, until it was nothing more than a dull rumble. Whatever it was seemed to move on. Aly brightened the lights attached to her slipsuit, specifically around her wrists, and pointed her arm out in front of her. The light only pierced a few feet in front but it was enough to at least see where she was walking. Aly took one step then another until she dragged herself away from the elevator car and away from the comforting set of lights around it, setting off into the dark unknown.

* * *

Aly got lost a few times and had to backtrack until she could see the pinpoint lights of the elevator car. There was no way the floater could have gotten so far in, and yet, she found no trace of it. As she searched, she also got sidetracked a few times by the curious elements she found as she went along. The ground, for instance, was rocky in many parts, but in a few parts, it was actually soft and full of moss. Another curious thing was the set of pillars she happened across. Pillars that supported nothing in particular and were not natural by what she could tell. It seemed to her they were long-lost ruins of some ancient people. But who in their right mind would actually live down here?

And once she got her mind to wander just like her feet, she found herself lost again and had to once more backtrack the way she had come.

When she finally set on a path that focused on her true goal, she walked for an impressive amount of time before she finally caught the dullest red light blinking in the distance.

When she got to the source, she stopped and looked down into a small ditch to see the floater there, ripped down its middle with its wiry tentacles laying everywhere around it.

That explained why she hadn't found it right when she came out of the elevator. Because it had been dragged away.

With a shuddered breath, Aly circled her light around the area but found no movement. Quickly, she climbed down to the floater to search in vain hope for her techband among the debris.

She turned the bulb of the floater's head aside and saw no band caught in its remaining tentacles. She cursed under her breath then searched around.

There was nothing. Not even parts of the techband to be found. Aly dropped her shaking hand and felt she needed to sit for a moment and think. As soon as her butt plopped on the ground, she heard the sound of something behind her, and she quickly stood back up.

For a minute, it sounded like a hyena, with a high-pitched laugh-like call. But there were definitely no hyenas around here, though she wished there were because she would take a hyena over whatever just made that noise. The sound came again, to her left, and she whirled around to face whatever it was. She pointed her hand up and saw something shoot past her light, making her shriek and stumble back.

The cries of many responded to her own, and, as Aly beamed her light in every direction to catch a source, her light fell onto a creature so vile she gasped.

It smiled back at her, showing its razor teeth, and Aly screamed.

CHAPTER ELEVEN

"That's odd," Ryziel heard Nar say behind him as Ryziel dropped the last bit of minerals from his canister bag into the converter tank. Not nearly enough. And he had been at it all day.

Tired and annoyed, Ryziel dropped his bag and rubbed at his brow. "What is?"

"An alert just popped up of an intruder nearby." Nar, at the console, brought up a separate map of the surrounding area. "Looks like someone came down and is just aimlessly running around and"—Nar looked closer—"they are going pretty fast. Weird."

Ryziel didn't bother to look over at the map that Nar was studying. Every so often, a miner somehow found their way down below and were stupid enough to go exploring around, only to meet their death. Many, if not most, of those on Lethe thought it was him, but it was never the case, though he allowed rumors to fly in hopes it would be a warning to others. Some, it seemed, still didn't bother to listen, but the sluths would get to them before they even had a chance to find his lair, so it didn't matter much anyway.

"Let me just see if I can get a reading on their tag," Nar said.

"Don't bother. They are as good as dead anyway," Ryziel replied indifferently as he went to unzip his slipsuit and strip it off, ready for a hot bath.

"Yeah, probably, but I'm curious if it's another tylian. They said one got found close to the bottom the other day in the forum, but it didn't look like a usual sluth attack from what I read. Plus, they are going pretty fast," Nar stated.

"Do what you like. It won't matter." Ryziel got the slipsuit halfway off before Nar made a curious little noise.

"Oh, it's not a tylian."

Ryziel untied the side satchel from his waist and placed it by the canister bag. He checked his techband for any messages from Xilya and found none. She would be down again soon enough anyway. He would get some tools ready for her when the time came as she had reluctantly agreed to help with harvesting. The work would still be slow as hell, but at least he would have someone else to help him.

"Uh, Ryz..."

"I'm going to take a bath. Xilya will be down at some point, so look out for her when you—"

"It's a human."

Ryziel stopped, confused. "What is?"

"The signal just outside. The one running around. It's a human," Nar said. The urk looked back as Ryziel turned toward him and stared blankly. "You know, that race you were looking up the other day?"

It took Ryziel a moment to understand, and, when he did, a strange sort of feeling overtook him. Something closely resembling a sense of dread. He didn't move at first but his eyes immediately shot to the screen behind Nar.

"Which one?" Ryziel asked in a low whisper.

Nar stared at him oddly, as if noticing the stillness taking him so suddenly. Then he turned back to the screen. He entered into the techband's data and brought up the record linked to it. The screen popped up and showed them who it belonged to:

· · ·

Aly Smith

   Human

   Age: 24

   Physical: gold-red hair along head, blue-green eyes, pale, soft-skinned, small

   Home planet: Earth

   Job Skill: Mechanic

   Background: Found by Xolis enforcers, led by Captain Marzin, on tradeship, being transported to [undisclosed]. Brought to Yilsand for rehabilitation and integration into Xolis system. Currently stationed on Lethe Maws.

   Threat: low

   All Vaccines given. No known illnesses.

   Testing still underway

Before his brain even registered what the hell he was doing, Ryziel was out the door and blindly racing down the dark tunnel, with Nar's shouts echoing behind him.

He knew he could find her easily, but he didn't know if he would make it in time. His receptors began to vibrate, and he caught her scent in the air, but the sluths must have already found her, and she could be getting ripped apart even now. A low, violent rumble tore from his throat, and he forced his legs faster, his muscles tensing and burning with each step.

His vision—perfect in the dark—could see in the distance outside the tunnel from which he came, a dance of lights and the sluths circling them. As he bolted toward them, he noticed one sluth with a techband in it jaws, but thankfully, no hand to accompany it.

As soon as they sensed him, the sluths immediately started their terrible shrieking, their eyeless faces turning every direction, their white flesh turning gray. Ryziel didn't hesitate. He caught one by the neck, crushed its vocal cords, and flung it against a nearby boulder. The rest backed away, their wide mouths twisting away from their usual grins, going slack as they hissed and bent their backs at him, ready to flee or strike.

Ryziel made sure they fled.

Blood wet the rocks as claws and teeth collided in a fit of violent fury. Ryziel roared out as he chased them from the wide cavern, catching one after the other, crushing bone and slicing skin. The ones who got away shrieked with terror as they disappeared into the wide darkness. Ryziel watched them go with breathless, seething anger, his Drega wanting to rise up and finish them. He forced it back.

When he was finally able to calm himself, he went looking for Aly's body.

He could only think the worst, after all. He could smell the blood in the air before he had made his first strike and knew it must be hers. He ignored the numb dread that kept welling up in him and started searching. When he finally did find her, it was a shock at first to see that she actually wasn't dead.

But she was close.

He crouched down beside her and assessed the damage. She had been bitten in several places and sliced in a couple others. Her slip-suit was ripped open, her chest bare to him, and he had to shove his Drega back down in disgust at its lustful wanting even now before continuing on. Blood seeped down her shoulder from a deep bite and trickled down her arms. A large, nasty bruise was already beginning to form along her neck, with a few marks scattered across her face.

None of her limbs looked broken, which was good, but there was a lot of blood. And judging by how frail she was, he could lose her any moment.

As Ryziel stretched his arm out to touch her, bracing to fight back his Drega in the process, Aly opened her eyes and saw him.

Her face went ashen. She began to shake badly, her teeth chattering, a whimper falling from her mouth, which quickly turned into a shrill cry. She tried to back away, but it was a futile effort as she could barely move from where she sat against a rock. Ryziel feared that if he touched her, she might go into shock (if she hadn't already by seeing him), but if he didn't take her now, she would certainly die.

He went for her again, and the words that escaped her (and the sound she made with them), hit him like a punch to the gut.

"Please, don't hurt me."

Ryziel flinched. This time, he didn't hesitate. Despite her little cries and pleading moans for him not to hurt her, he picked her up as gently as he could, cradling her against him. She placed her little hand against his bare chest, feebly pushing against it, and Ryziel let her because he was more concerned about getting her back to the lair than about his Drega, even if it did rear up just like before. He shoved it back again, taking deep breaths and forcing his legs to move. He began to run fast, maybe a little too fast, but he feared if he stopped, he wouldn't be able to fight back his beast, and he didn't have time to keep her from touching him in that moment, so all he could do was run.

And pray he wasn't too late.

CHAPTER TWELVE

THERE WAS DARKNESS AT FIRST. A WHOLE LOT OF IT. THEN THE smattering of dreams or perhaps memories, though Aly couldn't tell the difference. She could only remember parts of these "visions." She remembered Blue; remembered seeing his face contorted with some hard emotion. Maybe anger. Or Fear.

She remembered hearing his voice a lot. Hearing him yelling to someone, then feeling herself being let down on a cold, hard surface. She felt arms on her, keeping her in place, Blue's face once again above her.

Then came the pain. Awful, awful pain.

There was nothing memorable after that. Just one last dream of her standing on the edge of some cliff with Blue there beside her, the sun setting before them. The sun disappeared, bringing the night, and Blue was no longer there. A horrifying monster with sinister eyes and a wide, wicked grin had taken his place.

Aly had started to scream, only to wake up instead. Her eyes fluttered open, her head feeling fuzzy, her vision blurry. She blinked several times and licked her lips, finding her mouth and throat dry.

She turned her head to one side, and the room moved, disorienting her. She squeezed her eyes shut then opened them again and saw a wall full of...well, stuff. Robot parts, sheets of metal, silver coil wires, and broken tools, to name a few. Those were what she could identify, at least. Some of the objects she had never seen before, like a dark green sphere with black etchings across its surface or a strange transparent tray with shiny, grid-like designs. Aly carefully tried to sit up, pausing to let the dizziness pass, until she could sit bent over enough without feeling like she might vomit.

She was in a small bed, lying only a few feet off the ground. Ahead of her was an open doorway covered by a black curtain. Aly straightened and could see a blue light glowing through a crack in the doorway. Carefully, she maneuvered herself into a different position and was shocked to feel little to no pain. She peered down at her torso and pushed the blanket off.

She no longer wore her slipsuit but a dark gray robe instead. Underneath, there were bandages wrapped around her torso, but when she peeled some of them off, she found the skin underneath to be nearly healed. There was no scabbing or crusted blood, just a slick, clear oil that smelled similar to peppermint. Aly took off the robe and unraveled the rest of the bandages to touch at her skin. Someone had used expensive, medical-grade salve on her. And possibly some other advanced surgical tools. She had seen such things used before, when Jamie had been injured after being taken off the tradeship by the enforcers. Her cut had been deep, but they had used strange tools to seal the wound. Aly remembered Jamie's contorted, screaming face at the pain; then after, her look of shock as her arm started to heal before her very eyes. Within only a couple hours, she had been healed completely, not even leaving a scar.

Aly stared down at her own body now and wondered who had done this to her. Then she remembered seeing the face of the nillium above her.

Had he done this? But why? Why, after he had threatened her to never go below?

Her memory started to come back ,and she remembered how she

had been attacked by a group of pale, eyeless monsters, thinking for certain she was going to die alone in the dark, when the nillium had appeared. She might have felt relieved then, but after their last meeting, she only felt more afraid, believing him to be some deadly executioner who had come to finish the job.

Maybe if she hadn't been so terrified, hadn't been going into shock from the pain, she might have thought over why he was running so fast to get away instead of ending her where he had found her.

Thinking on this now, Aly's heart did a little flip. She drew the robe back tightly against her then scooted off the bed. She rose and went to stand before the black curtain then slowly pushed it away.

The blue light blinded her for a moment, making her squint. Aly blinked and put up her hand until she was adjusted enough to see. Her eyes widened, mouth gaped open, and she stood there, staring.

Beyond, in the center of the large chamber, was a ship.

It wasn't a huge ship, by any means, but certainly big enough for a decent-sized crew carrying several loads of cargo. Its dark steel shone in the blue light cast on it from above, with four wings stretching out on either side, one missing most of its shell. The front was narrow and the back bulkier, with lights built around the sides like teeth. The design of it seemed familiar to her and, after a moment of staring, Aly realized why. It reminded her of the tradeship that had found her and the team.

Her stomach dropped and Aly's eyes instinctively began searching for an exit out of the chamber. At one cave wall, she saw a large metal door shut tight and wondered where the latch was to open it. Searching around for any movement, she took a cautious step out of the room then slowly made her way down a short set of metal-grate stairs. Clutching her robe close, she winced at the cold ground on her bare feet and went on tiptoe, searching around for any slipsuit or pair of clothing that might give her some warmth from the chilly cave air. Her mind began to race with even more questions as her eyes danced around the cavern. Where was she? Where had the ship come from? Who was keeping it here? Was it the nillium? Or Traders?

She noticed the dull hum of something nearby and a soft knocking coming from a set of large tanks against the opposite wall. As she moved closer to the door, she spotted a large console back by one wall, displaying a map of a cave route she had never seen.

Curious, she went over to it and looked down. She gazed at the pinpoints of colors before her and reached out her hand toward the holographic image.

"Hey, human, what do you think you're doing there?" someone called out behind her. Aly jumped and whirled around but saw no one.

"Hello?" she called in response. She moved back toward the ship and gazed around its sides. She heard the rattle of something above and looked up to see someone moving across the ship's roof.

"Hello?" Aly called again, craning her neck to see. There was a quick shifting sound then a sharp clang.

"Down here, human."

Aly turned her gaze downward and nearly jumped as she found herself standing next to what looked like a—

Well, she couldn't really describe in a realistic sense, only that the creature reminded her of a goblin. It was small, with sharp, flat ears and beady black eyes and a flat nose. It wasn't green like the ones she'd seen in books, however, but a pale yellow instead, with dark swirls across its face.

And it had metal legs.

"When you are done gawking," the creature said, "why don't you go on and sit over there?" It pointed to a thick metal table on the other side of the ship with a set of metal chairs.

"Oh, um, I'm sorry. I didn't mean—"

"Yeah, yeah, sure." The creature waved. "Over there. Go on."

Aly pursed her lips then turned toward the table, eyeing the creature once more before cautiously making her way over. There was a circular grate in the middle of the table with a blue fire glowing underneath. A metal pot filled with boiling water sat on one side of the grate.

Without asking, the little creature came over and took up a small handleless cup on a shelf nearby, dropped a pill-like bag inside, then filled the cup with the hot water using a large spoon. He then plunked the cup in front of Aly.

"Drink that and wait here," it said.

Aly stared down at the steamy cup before her. "Um, what is this? And where am..."

She looked up and found the little creature already loping away, back to the ship. "Wait!" she called, scooping the cup up in her hands. She rushed after it and got in its way before it could disappear back into the ship. "Where am I?" she asked.

The goblin snorted, "Somewhere you shouldn't be, honestly." It moved around her to continue walking until Aly blocked it again.

"Am I still at the bottom?" she asked.

The goblin sighed. "Yes. Now, if you don't mind, I have a lot—"

"Why am I here?"

"Trust me, I wish I knew," the goblin mumbled, attempting to walk around her once more. "But that stubborn ass couldn't even give a straight answer."

Aly thought she knew who it spoke of. "So, this is where Blue lives?"

The goblin actually froze and looked back at her with a confused, albeit curious expression, and Aly's face heated as she realized her error. That nickname was supposed to be a private one.

"Who the hell is...wait, you are talking about Ryziel, right?"

Aly drew a lock of hair back behind her ear and shrugged. "I don't know his name. I only know him as the nillium who hides in the underground."

The goblin grunted and turned away. "Yeah, that's him. Funny name to give him, though, lady. A little too on the nose don't you think?"

So, that was his name. Ryziel. Aly felt like some great secret had been revealed to her. She clutched the cup in her hands tighter and brought it closer to her chest. "This is his home? Ryziel's?"

"Yeah." The goblin turned fully toward her and gave her a stern sort of look. "And if you so much as speak about what you saw here, you can bet I will force a memory pill straight down your throat. I would have done it as soon as you woke up, but I was ordered not to touch you, and right now, I don't really care to lose another limb, so..." It turned away and walked back into the ship. "So, just go sit down and wait for *Blue* to show up."

Aly's face heated even more. She didn't try to stop it again. Instead, she turned back to the table and sat down. She would've asked more about the ship, but she could see the goblin wasn't in the mood to be bombarded by questions. Nor did it seem inclined to help her find clothes or anything else of the sort. She could go looking, but something told her it was better to wait. Wait for the nillium to return from wherever he was.

* * *

The enforcers lurked at the bottom for at least an hour before they gave up their search for the human woman. Ryziel watched them in the dark as their tracers scanned the area where a dead sluth lay, where the human's techband *should* have been but was nowhere to be seen, at least not by them.

"I see no trace of her," one said. A krull female. "We should just go back up. Judging by this sluth and the blood everywhere, I'd say she's a goner."

"We will have to make a full report," said another. A lygin with a scar across one eye. "The captain will want to know."

Ryziel's eyes narrowed, a sneer partially twisting his face.

It had driven him to near rage at first to learn that there were enforcers lurking not far from the lair. Even those on Lethe knew not to come down to the bottom. Whether by threat or payment, they had done well to stay far away. Until now.

And it didn't take Ryziel long to figure out what drove them downward, despite his efforts. Orders by Marzin could not go ignored, no matter the threat or bribe. And when Ryziel learned of their whereabouts not even an hour after bringing Aly into his home, he could guess what they were searching for.

But what greatly bothered him wasn't so much the reason they had come down but the why. Why were they searching for the human woman? Why was her techband linked to their tracers in the first place? Why did Marzin want her looked after?

These questions disturbed him, and he was almost curious enough to go searching for answers. Especially as he watched the band of enforcers walking around in his territory, looking for the girl.

"Let's get going. Before the Dark One shows up," the krull added, looking around nervously.

"Perhaps he knows where she went," said another lygin male, smaller than the first. "Maybe he could aid us..."

The other lygin moved the sluth body with his foot and looked under it with his light. "No. If anything, he would have killed her himself if he found her down here, and he won't take kindly to us lurking around. Yva is right, we should go. Likely, the sluths got to her first, anyway."

The band was in agreement. They swiftly left for the nearest elevator. Ryziel waited until they were fully out of sight before he moved. He slid off the rock where he had been sitting and took out Aly's techband from his bag.

It hadn't taken him long to find it, and when he had, he'd quickly unlinked the tracer system before the enforcers got to the mark where their tracer said it was supposed to be, leaving them to think it ended there. Let them think she was dead for now until he could figure out what the hell he was going to do.

Because he certainly couldn't keep her in the lair. By now, she might even be healed, and if she had rested enough, she would have to go back up toward the surface. Because she shouldn't be near him. He saved her life, and she certainly would be too afraid to come back down a second time, so he would need to take her back up without being seen. He would have to reactivate her techband and decide whether or not to give her a memory pill, which could potentially alter her memories completely, or risk trusting her not to go telling everyone that he had a ship. Especially Marzin, who would definitely want to know what happened to her.

Ryziel bared his teeth as he trudged back to the lair. He'd put the whole mission at great risk just to save this human woman. But he had no time to decide what he should have done once he saw the techband had belonged to her. His mind had already been made up, whether he cared to admit it or not.

He could imagine what his brother would think if he had seen him racing to save a non-nillium female. He would have been amused, somewhat, but also greatly concerned.

What, now you are the savior of the lessers, Ryziel? Don't forget who you really are. Because they won't.

But then Aly didn't know who he was or of his past. So, maybe it didn't matter. And it wasn't like he had saved her out of some sudden need to be heroic, he had done it because...

Because he still didn't have her figured out. That was all.

Ryziel slipped through the tunnelway that led to the hidden metal door several paces inside. When he got to the door, he paused, standing before it for a moment as if to prepare himself. His receptors began to vibrate, making his brow tingle. He closed his eyes and caught the scent of something sweet, reminding him of the velblum flowers that grew in the gardens of the First House. His brow furrowed at a single memory in those gardens, and he brushed the vision aside. Now was not the time to think about the past.

Opening his eyes, Ryziel went for the lock on the side of the door and plugged in the code to unlock it. The door began to rise before him, spilling blue light out into the tunnelway. He ducked inside then closed the door before it reached the top, hearing the sounds of Nar shouting nearby.

"No, for the last time, human, I don't need your help! Your impatience is astounding. Just sit down, will you!"

Ryziel looked around and stopped as his eyes scanned over to the ship and saw the human, Aly, standing before it, the light from the ceiling casting down on her like the moon had the night he first encountered her. She turned her head, a smile playing on her lips, until it fell as soon as she saw him, her eyes going wide, fear paling her features. She clutched at a mender in her hand, her body tensing as she stared at him, her lips parting ever so slightly. Ryziel caught himself staring back and took a step to move, only to still as he noticed her flinch. Her eyes skimmed down to his hand and her face seemed to pale more as she saw her techband dangling in his fingers. She opened her mouth to say something when she was sharply interrupted.

"Ryziel, you're finally back," Nar said from the top of the ship. "This human of yours," he pointed down to Aly with the end of his wrench, "can't just sit down for even five minutes. And she won't stop asking questions. I can't even get one part done without her interference. I knew it was a bad idea to bring her here, but would you have listened? No! I was this close to tying her up and gagging her, you know? This close!" The urk disappeared back into the ship with a huff, the sounds of banging and shuffling continuing as usual. Ryziel looked back at Aly, who smiled sheepishly, her face now red.

"I, um, I wasn't sure how long you would be," she said softly. A lock of hair brushed at her cheek, and she quickly curled it back behind her ear. Her body was still tense, the mender's end pointed at him, perhaps unconsciously, as if ready to use it as a weapon. Ryziel didn't respond. Instead, he took a few quick steps toward her, ignoring her nervous response. He held out her techband, and she looked at it for a long moment then gazed back at him as she carefully took it from his grasp.

"Thank you," she said.

Ryziel watched as she placed the band back on her wrist, checking for any lasting damage.

"I thought it was lost for good," she said casually. "I figured I was royally screwed."

Ryziel got most of her meaning. "You're lucky the sluth didn't get far with it."

She looked back at him then. "Sluth?"

"The things that attacked you."

She made a silent 'oh.' "The things...you saved me from."

It sounded almost like a question, like she wasn't entirely sure if he had meant to save her or if he had just taken her with a plan to do something worse than the sluths, and she hoped that he could confirm or deny her fears.

Ryziel felt compelled to answer honestly. "Yes."

Her body seemed to instantly relax, the mender in her hand even going a little slack, causing the robe to slip ever so slightly off her shoulder. "Thank you."

Ryziel clenched and unclenched his hands and nodded, trying desperately to look anywhere but at her. Because if he did, he knew his eyes would fall right to the curve of her neck then downward to stare at her small frame. He already had an image of what lay behind the robe. A body not so unlike nillium women save for the color and texture. He had gotten a good glimpse of everything when he had been forced to undress her then mend her wounds. His mind had been a blank slate then—only a few times did he have to leave the room to keep his Drega relaxed but otherwise, he kept his mind somewhere else completely, focusing only on the need to fix what was before him.

Still, that had taken tremendous willpower on its own. Now that she was before him, alive and well, he dared not even cast his eyes down to her nor meet her gaze, in fear his mind would go wandering somewhere he didn't care for it to.

"Your wounds should be almost healed. If you need to bathe, I can show you the washroom," he said, turning away.

"I would like that," she said.

Ryziel nodded and started toward the ship, moving around its right wing over to a wide, open alcove in the back, walled off with various sheets of metal and a curtain. He drew the curtain aside, revealing a large mineral barrel abandoned at some point by miners and now used as their makeshift tub. Ryziel went over to the empty barrel and brought up a hose from the tank beside it, filling the tub up with hot water. He knew she was behind him watching, but he made no move to look back at her as he waited for the base to fill. When it was through, he turned off the water and drew out the hose then stuck his hand in to make sure it wasn't too hot. When he was satisfied, he took up a bar of soap sitting on top of the tank and handed it to her without looking.

"I will bring your clothes and set them just outside. When you're done, we will discuss getting you back up to the surface." When she said nothing, he braved a glance at her. Their eyes met, and he thought she looked a little awestruck.

"That's it, then?"

Ryziel blinked. "What?"

"You...you aren't going to punish me?"

As juvenile as that sounded, Ryziel could see she was serious. She really thought he meant to harm her.

And how could she not, you idiot? You threatened her at Shadowpoint.

Ryziel turned his head to hide the grimace on his face. "No. I'm not going to punish you," he said quietly. He rubbed his jaw then looked back at her. "But you were a fool to come down, almost getting yourself killed."

She frowned, her eyes dropping. "I didn't do it to challenge you or upset you, trust me." She glared back up at him, her eyes more fierce and bright than before. "My techband dropped all the way to the bottom, if you can believe it." She laughed a little. "And wouldn't have been an issue if it hadn't been for that stupid ruling Marzin decided to place on us. On the humans, I mean."

Ryziel straightened, raising his head as he looked down at her. "What ruling?"

Aly lifted the techband up. "He gave us new techbands and said if we lost them or broke them, we would be punished under Xolis law." She dropped her arm and shrugged. "I don't know what the punishment would have entailed, but I was afraid that I would be taken away from the others. So, when my techband fell...I decided to take the risk and go searching for it."

Ryziel's eyes narrowed. Of course, the enforcers didn't want the human techbands destroyed. Otherwise, they couldn't trace them. Still, he was curious as to why.

"So, yeah, I can't tell you how relieved I am you found it because —" Aly's eyes widened. "Oh, no." She looked at him as if she had yet again done something wrong. "They are tracing it. They said they were going to watch us. The enforcers might..."

Ryziel shook his head. "It's taken care of."

Aly's brows furrowed. "Taken...care of?"

"I unlinked the tracker system. They won't find you here."

"Oh." Aly brought up her techband, brushing her fingers over the screen as she looked over it curiously. "Damn, if I had known it could be turned off, I would have just done it myself!"

"It's not as easy as just switching it on and off," Ryziel said. "It takes at least some knowledge of a techband's programming system. I learned to keep mine untraceable for some time."

Aly glanced up at him, her mouth curving slightly at one side. "Ah. Don't suppose you could teach me that little trick, huh?"

Ryziel turned his head to the side to look over at the ship. "No. Once I get you back to the surface, it will have to be turned back on."

Because the more he thought about it, maybe it was a good thing the enforcers were watching the humans closely. As long as she didn't return to the bottom, it meant someone would be looking out for her when he couldn't, meaning he (hopefully) wouldn't have to worry about her getting hurt again. And distracting him from his work with the ship. Why should he care or worry about the reason she was being watched? At least someone was, meaning it didn't have to be him. And that was a *good* thing because he couldn't waste any more time.

Still, something at the back of his mind was troubled by the enforcers' sudden attention on the humans, namely of the one before him. But he had to put the feeling aside. He had other things to worry about.

When Ryziel peered back down at Aly, he couldn't help catching the look of disappointment on her face, which she quickly hid when she saw him looking at her.

"Of course," she said, smiling. "I understand." She went to turn for the tub then paused. "Thank you again, Ryziel, for saving my life."

He met her eyes again. He didn't bother to ask how she knew his name. Nar was never good at keeping information to himself.

"The water is getting cold," he said, unlatching from her gaze and turning fully away from her. "When you're done, I will take you back." He stepped out of the washroom and pulled the curtain closed, leaving her.

CHAPTER THIRTEEN

ALY SAT IN THE NOW LUKEWARM WATER, CONTEMPLATING WHAT she was going to do. When she first stepped into the tub, she had accepted Ryziel's need to take her back to the surface, understood fully that it was absolutely necessary, so the others would know she was okay. That she wasn't dead or lost in the caves and that she could continue on working as if nothing had happened.

She accepted this fully and understood it needed to happen.

But then she started thinking about the ship, which she could see the top of just over the edge of a metal sheet of wall. As she soaped herself up and rinsed her hair, she continued to glance over at it, and her mind kept on turning and turning.

Because while she had been waiting for Ryziel to return to the lair, Aly had turned to studying everything around her, from the ship to the map on the console. She observed the large tanks sitting by the one wall, with a large machine attached to a laser head next to them, and the tools on a table nearby, and it didn't take long to put two and two together.

They were fixing the ship. They were harvesting minerals and using the tanks and the laser machine to create the materials needed to rebuild the ship. They were trying to escape Lethe Maws.

And as much as Aly knew it would be hard to convince them, she also knew she couldn't leave without trying to persuade Ryziel to let her and her crew on the ship.

Unless the goblin was telling the truth and did have a memory pill, Aly wasn't going to forget what she saw, and if she left without saying a word, she knew she would regret it.

This was their chance.

So, once she made up her mind that she was going to say something, she then thought about how, exactly, she was going to convince them.

The first thought that popped into her head was blackmail. She knew they had a ship and were trying to fix it, and if they didn't let her and her team on, she could go to the enforcers and tell them about it.

But she quickly threw that idea out the window. One, because Ryziel could probably find a way to warp her memory if he liked. Two, if he couldn't, he could just tie her up and leave her in the underground until they were done. And three, he could have thought of these very same ideas (and he probably did), yet he still was adamant about taking her back to the surface. He either somehow trusted her (which was unlikely) or he had some other reason. Regardless, how could she blackmail the very person who had just saved her life? She wasn't heartless. Desperate maybe, but not heartless.

So, here she was trying to think of other ideas. The water was turning cold, and she knew she was running out of time. As she rinsed one last time, Aly stepped out of the tub and padded over to the curtain where her slipsuit lay just outside, mended somewhat with sealing tape. She pulled it in through a slip in the curtain then quickly began to dress, putting her techband on last. Once secure to her wrist, she glanced down at it and frowned.

If she couldn't convince Ryziel to let her on the ship, perhaps she could persuade him to at least teach her how to turn the tracking off.

He seemed very adamant about not teaching her, but Aly thought maybe she could move him without begging.

Once she had her belt in place, Aly stepped from the washroom and silently made her way around the ship. As she heard voices, she slowed, until she saw Ryziel and his companion beside the console with their backs turned, looking at the map.

"I'm telling you, Ryz, it isn't a good idea," said the goblin, looking over the map from a high chair. "Unless you want every nasty beast in a ten-mile radius to hear."

"We could set traps, here and here." Ryziel pointed to places on the screen Aly couldn't see. "And if I can acquire a few drillbots, we could set up a distraction point some distance away."

"That will only work for so long. And some creatures are smart enough to go looking elsewhere and avoid traps."

"Me and Xilya should be able to get at least a container full before anything too bad shows up."

"And if something 'too bad' does show up?" the goblin said, looking up at his companion.

"Me and Xilya can handle it."

The goblin didn't reply to that. Instead, he said, "Where is Xilya, anyway? I thought she was supposed to be down here by now."

"I had her wait when I noticed the enforcers lurking around."

"Ah."

"She will be down again soon enough, once..."

"Once your little human is back where she belongs. Got it."

Ryziel crossed his arms. "Xilya and I can start on this end of the cave system and work around. There is a blockade here and only two entrances. One we can watch while the other can be trapped. There's no other way in unless something can fit into the smaller openings. But anything that size won't be looking for a fight."

The goblin snorted. "Says you. You've never gotten into it with a pack of nighthorns." The goblin crossed his arms as well. "And speaking of fitting into small spaces, we still don't have any way into those tighter areas because, I'm sorry Ryz, placing explosives is just asking for trouble, We had a load of it when we blew our way into this very cavern, remember?"

"We might not have a choice," said Ryziel. "Unless you can get one of your own to—"

"And, again, I'm telling you it isn't going to happen!" The goblin threw up his arms. "I really don't see why you don't just go up above and recruit some lone miner. Any of them would probably do what you say, and you could threaten to keep their mouth shut through the whole process."

"Because most of the miners are also too big to fit," Ryziel responded. "Even the smallest lygin would have to squeeze their way in. And likely, they will get stuck in the process..."

It was then Aly realized she had slowly snuck her way behind them, listening to every word they said like it was some kind of beacon in the dark.

It was so obvious what they needed. If she believed in any higher power, she would almost take it for a sign.

"I could do it," she blurted aloud.

The goblin jumped and turned toward her, scowling, while Ryziel dropped his hands to the console and slowly turned his head to fix her with a sharp gaze.

"I could do it," Aly repeated.

The goblin made a strange grunt. "Firstly, it's rude to eavesdrop, human. Secondly, hell no."

Aly glanced at Ryziel then back at the goblin. "Why not? I've had to fit through small spaces before when working above. I might be able to help—"

"Because you're a walking liability and probably the least durable species on Xolis by far," the goblin stated. "Your skin looks more breakable than the pillows my mother made for den children before they were old enough to walk. One bad fall or cut on a rock and you will probably be bleeding all over the place. Trust me, I saw enough when Ryziel brought you. And I am not helping to patch you up again."

Aly felt heat rush to her face at that. She knew they had to have seen pretty much all of her to help fix her wounds. Knowing Ryziel had didn't leave her too embarrassed but both of them together...

Aly cleared her throat, wrapping her arms around her waist. "I'm more durable than you think. And the slipsuit protects me...well, maybe not from the things that attacked me but certainly from rocks, at least."

The goblin snorted and turned away. Aly looked to Ryziel instead, who had remained silent, watching her.

"I can help..." she said softly.

Ryziel didn't move, but she could tell from his expression he was thinking. He turned back to the console, looking down at the map, rubbing his fingers underneath his jaw.

"Nar is right, it would likely be too dangerous. Unless humans have some natural inner defense, I see no qualities that tell me you are able to protect yourself."

Aly opened her mouth then closed it when he side-eyed her.

"Grex have venom, krull have talons, urk," he pointed to the goblin, "are quick climbers and runners and can see in the dark. There are things in the deep underground where one needs to be able to fight or flee if they have to."

"I can use a weapon," Aly said as she unclasped her waist bag and took out a pocket-knife.

Nar laughed. Ryziel didn't. He rubbed at his face some more, his eyes looking over her like he was struggling with some deep inner issue that was more than her feeble attempt to convince him she could help.

Aly dropped the hand holding the knife. "All right, maybe I'm not fit for the wilds or anything, but I *can* get into tighter places. And you need someone to do that. And you said yourself a lot of things can't fit into those spaces, so I can at least hide."

"Great," Nar said. "And I suppose we will just have to keep you from getting killed at every turn."

Aly shrugged. "There is risk to everything, is there not? And," she turned her eyes again to Ryziel, "if you are with me, you could protect me."

Ryziel's expression turned dark, and Aly feared she might have said the wrong thing. He looked away from her, his head bowed over the map.

"No," he finally said, after a long silence. "No. You have to go back toward the surface. I can't use you."

Aly wasn't sure if he meant that as an insult or a polite way of saying he didn't want to abuse her as a worker. Either way, disappointment jabbed her in the chest.

Before she could get in another word, Ryziel moved away from the console and headed to the other side of the cavern, disappearing into a different cave opening closed off with a black curtain.

Aly watched him go then looked back at Nar, who was eyeing her.

"Honestly, human, you either have a lot of guts or no brains. You almost died out there. And you probably think sluths are the worst there is."

"I'm gonna take a guess and say they aren't," Aly said.

"Far from it. Some things get to the surface every so often, sure, but most of those things are harmless compared to what you might encounter past the mine's defenses, down in the deeper parts." Nar shook his head. "And if the enforcers are watching your kind, the last thing we need is for them to come sniffing around again."

Aly looked down at her techband and frowned. "Ryziel can unlink the tracer..." She glanced back at him. "Please, I want to help."

"Why?"

Aly's eyes shifted toward the ship, and Nar's eyes widened.

"No. No way, no how. Forget it, human." Nar's ears bent back slightly as he bared his tiny teeth. "You're just gonna forget you even saw that ship. Forget you saw any of this, and just go back to what you were doing. Stick to the mines and don't think about ever coming back down."

CHAPTER FOURTEEN

ALY STOOD SILENTLY BY THE LARGE METAL DOOR AS SHE waited for Ryziel to take her back above. She checked her pockets and bags one last time and was surprised to find everything still where it should be despite a few hours ago, when she had been running for her life with the sluths cutting into her with their teeth and claws. The suit would have to be replaced despite the sealing tape fixed along the rips, but thankfully, she had a spare in her unit.

She checked her tools and found only one to be in need of a repair. Her other belongings, though few, were dirtied but not broken. She brought her sketchbook out briefly to check the inside and was relieved to find the pages undamaged, including that of her unfinished sketch of Ryziel.

"Time to go."

Aly quickly snapped her sketchbook closed and shoved it in her bag, glancing up to see Ryziel standing beside her. She smiled at him and nodded. "Okay, let's go."

Ryziel loosened a part of his belt and gestured for her to take the end. "Hold onto this and stay close."

Aly frowned at the belt end but took it without protest. Ryziel turned for the door and unlocked it, waiting as it rose slowly.

"I will relink your techband once we get to the elevator. If anyone asks, you tell them you got lost and that your techband went offline. They will think it odd, but they will likely believe you."

Aly didn't respond as she stared at the back of Ryziel's head. She took him in as if it were the last time, wanting to keep an image of him in her mind when she finished her sketch of him. Maybe she could even find coloring utensils. But then, she would never be able to get the blue of his skin right or the silver markings along his neck. But maybe she could at least get the shape of his eyes right this time, even if she could never find the color of those silver and gold orbs.

Ryziel peered back at her, and Aly turned her gaze away. Her throat felt a little tight as she gripped his belt in her hand. She nodded to him, and he started for the tunnel beyond the door.

"Keep your lights off and trust my steps," he said as they entered the tunnelway. Aly did as told and turned the lights off on her suit.

They went quickly, Aly keeping up as best she could with Ryziel's long strides. She only stumbled a few times, but after a while was able to stay beside him without an issue.

It was a surprise to see the glow of the elevator shaft not far ahead after they had only walked in silence for maybe less than a half hour's time.

When they got to the point where the lights overhead beamed above them, Ryziel stopped at the elevator shaft and waved his hand over the pad. A light blinked on to indicate a car was making its way down, and all they had to do now was wait.

Aly let go of his belt as Ryziel turned toward her and their eyes locked.

"Guess this is it." Aly gave him a smile, though it didn't feel genuine. "I...promise not to say anything about what I saw."

"I believe you." Ryziel gestured for her to lift her arm, and Aly did so. Careful not to touch her, he went through her techband's programming system and relinked the tracer. "You're good to go."

"Great."

They stood silent for a moment longer before Aly couldn't stand it any longer. "I could still help you," she said.

"It's out of the question."

Aly brows raised, surprised by his sudden response. "Why?"

Ryziel looked away, refusing to meet her gaze.

"I'm really that much of a pain to you, aren't I?" Aly couldn't help laughing. "I know the others say I'm a pain in the ass, but you really don't like me—"

"It's not that."

"What did I do? Is it my very existence? Do I smell bad?"

"No, it's—"

"I mean, you could have left me here." Aly threw out her arms. "But you didn't. And *you* came up to *me* when we first met. But then you act like sharing the same plane of existence with me is excruciatingly...awful." Aly dropped her arms and shrugged. "But I have to be honest with you. I don't care what you think. I don't. I know who you are. I know enough about the nillium, the 'oh so great nobles of Xolis,' to see that you think me beneath you. But I don't care. I want to help you rebuild the ship, and I want me and my team to have a seat on it. I know this is probably super disrespectful, but I'm too desperate to care." Aly refused to look away from him, even if it made her heart pound to see him glaring at her with such silent regard. She waited for him to speak, but he didn't say a word. Not one. The elevator car reached the bottom, and the doors opened.

"Ryziel, please—"

"Get inside."

Aly felt heat rise in her face and neck. She would have shouted at him, but she knew that would only make things worse. So, instead, she did as he commanded. She stepped inside and glared back at him. When she didn't move to press a button, Ryziel reached his hand inside and hit on level fifteen without looking. The doors closed, and Aly almost reached for him through the metal bars. Almost.

Before the elevator began its ascension, Ryziel finally met her eyes once more. Aly didn't dare say another word, but she let her eyes do the talking. Ryziel's only response was a cold stare of his own. As the elevator rose, he backed away slowly, and Aly watched him disappear in the darkness below.

* * *

Ryziel stalked back to the lair, feeling a little put out, to say the least. If he were any other nillium, he might have taken offense to Aly's outburst, but really, he could care less at the moment. What he cared more about was the thought of allowing Aly to aid him in any way with fixing the ship.

Because the very idea was absolutely lunatic.

It wasn't just the fact that she seemed too delicate or fragile, that the image of her limp body in his arms even now still burned in his brain, and that the mere thought of taking her deeper into the mines was appalling at best. To put her in that kind of danger was insane.

And yet...

And yet. She was most definitely small enough to fit into the spaces they needed to get into. And it wasn't an impossible idea that he could easily watch over her. As long as she was close and he stayed right by, he could undoubtedly protect her. He was thoroughly confident he could, in fact, keep anything from getting to her. And if they were quiet enough, maybe, just maybe, it was possible they wouldn't have to worry about anything at all.

So, what really got to him was the fact that it was a perfect idea.

And he refused to indulge it. Because as much as he was in desperate need to get to the minerals he sought, he couldn't have Aly there with him. Because...

Because there was the unfortunate fact that he, too, was considered a danger to her. His sole purpose was to fix the ship, yes, but he still didn't understand Aly and why she made his Drega slip from its hard-kept cage. And that still scared him. If something like what had happened with the sluths were to happen again, he didn't know if he could handle it a second time.

And what if she touched him again and he lost it?

Yes, that should have been the last good reason not to risk her return. But still his conscience tried to fight him at every turn.

You are desperate to get back. With her help, you could get the ship restored faster. You've trained to suppress your Drega before. This is no different. Just an unexpected challenge. Fight it off, keep her at a distance, but allow her to help, and maybe nothing will go wrong.

Maybe.

Ryziel unlocked the door to the lair, trying to calm himself, when he came face to face with a purple and red demon.

"Xilya," Ryziel greeted the vrisha female with a nod. "I didn't see you come down."

"I took the stairs."

Ryziel walked past to stand by the ship, ignoring her curious eyes watching him.

"I heard we had an unexpected visitor," Xilya said after a pause.

Ryziel's lip curled back slightly, and his eyes shot up to look at Nar on top of the ship, who didn't meet his gaze as he worked. "Yes," he said, in a low voice. "It was nothing. Just a small...mishap."

"Oh?"

Ryziel turned to her with a blank expression. "She was sent back up. She won't say a word. It's done with."

Xilya bowed her head and sauntered over to the map. "Is it, then?"

Ryziel followed her over. "Yes, it is."

"Nar says she wanted to help...in exchange for a place on the ship." Xilya lifted her eyes to his. "That true?"

Ryziel kept his gaze on her, his receptors vibrating, heat simmering in his chest. "Yes. And before you say a word, I absolutely forbid it."

Xilya's tail scraped lazily along the ground. She scratched at her throat indifferently. "Well, that was stupid."

Ryziel stared at her with a fiery glare, and she stared back in challenge.

"Was it?" Ryziel said softly, keeping his anger barely in check. "And what in Nihl's sight makes you say that?"

Xilya was unaffected by his seething expression, one of the very few who didn't turn or cower from his venomous gaze.

"Because she has seen everything already. She knows what we are up to. And instead of threatening to go to the enforcers and the Xolis Council, she is willing to actually aid us in the one thing we need most." Xilya's eyes narrowed. "Honestly, Nihl Ryziel, why *wouldn't* we take such an opportunity?"

"I have my reasons," he said.

"And they are?" she asked.

"I can think of one," Nar called out. "We don't have room to stow away a bunch of humans."

"I find that highly unlikely," Xilya responded. "We can make room easily. What else?"

Ryziel rubbed at his throat. "I have...personal reasons."

"And they are?"

"I don't need to tell you."

Xilya let out an impressive growl, and Ryziel met her with his own.

"Damn your stubbornness, Nihl Ryziel. Who cares if you have some strange issues with the girl?" Xilya hit her fist against the edge of the map. "You should know something. I was messaged again by the urk who gave us the map. With the storm season fast upon us, the water rises below and moves, shaping the earth. In a few cycles' time, he says there will be a great flooding below. This is why the cave systems constantly change and the urks are always looking for new systems. Is this not true, Nar?"

"It's true," responded the urk. "There are places that had been sealed off for ages because of the waters but then would become reopened after great floods moved the current. Yurza's Keep had been one of these at a point if I'm not mistaken."

"So, you see," Xilya continued, "we are running out of time if we want to grab as many minerals within the Keep as possible and have the chance to use the tracer to look for the ionx we still desperately need. So, if I were you, Nihl Ryziel, I would rethink forbidding the girl to help. I would think hard. Unless you can come up with a different plan very soon."

Ryziel closed his eyes and rubbed them, baring his teeth. This changed things. But could he put aside his fears and allow Aly to return? He barely knew her and yet he could no longer say he didn't care about what happened to her. Not completely.

Because all it took was one bad day. And even if she was still mostly a stranger, she was an innocent woman who his subconscious felt compelled to protect, even if he didn't yet understand why.

"I will...think on it," was all Ryziel could say.

Xilya bowed her head, giving him a stern glare. "Very well. But I would think quickly if I were you."

CHAPTER FIFTEEN

Aly stood by Braxin's door, waiting to be let into his work unit, preparing herself for the inevitable shouting match that was likely to occur. She hadn't gone to him right away. Instead, she had slipped back to her own unit to replace the ripped-up and poorly patched slipsuit for a new one, throwing the bad one in the trash. She messaged her team after that. Then, knowing she couldn't avoid him, messaged Braxin, who immediately responded, ordering her to come to him.

When the door to his work unit finally opened, Aly came face to face with two enforcers, a krull male, and a lygin female. Braxin stood between them.

"Get in here, Smith."

Aly did as Braxin commanded, the door closing behind her. She glanced at both of the enforcers who she'd seen around before but only at a distance.

"Sit down," Braxin said.

Aly did.

The krull came over and gestured to her techband. "Give it up so I can assess it," he said, almost like a parrot with his throat moving and beak opening and closing. Aly took off the band and handed it to him. His talons carefully tapped along the screen as he maneuvered through the programming. Aly watched him with only a simmering of anxiety bubbling in her stomach, fairly confident they wouldn't find anything unusual.

"Care to tell us where you were?" the lygin asked.

"I was at the bottom," Aly responded.

"And what were you doing there?"

"My techband slipped off my wrist and fell to the bottom. I went to go retrieve it but couldn't find it right away, so I went looking. When I did finally find it, I was lost." Aly had her answer rehearsed ever since Ryziel had left her at the elevator. It wasn't a total lie, at least.

"And why, then, did you not call for aid once you found it? Or use a map to find your way back?"

Aly was prepared for this question too. "The techband stopped working. When it fell, something must have gone wrong."

And, as Ryziel had predicted, they looked at her oddly. They didn't respond, though they did glance at each other with a sliver of suspicion.

Aly shrugged. "Sorry, I don't know the tech very well, but I did mess around with it while I was down there, and I must have fixed it somehow because it seems all right now, and I was able to find my way back up."

Still, they said nothing, but Aly made sure to keep herself looking as innocent and naive as possible. Something she was fairly good at, based on experience with her family.

"So you're telling us," the lygin said, with yellow eyes now narrowed, "that your techband just went offline somehow and you went so far from the elevator that you could no longer see it?"

Aly shrugged again. "Guess so."

"And your suit lights stopped working too, huh?"

"I tried to use them, but it was so dark that they didn't really give me a good sense of direction."

"And you just walked around in the dark for several hours..."

"Sometimes I stopped to rest."

The lygin's eyes narrowed some more. "And you encountered nothing down there?"

This time, Aly had to look away. "There were these things that chased me. But I was able to hide from them."

The krull and the lygin looked at each other again. The krull handed her back her techband. "It isn't broken. I can't find anything that says it might have been meddled with..."

The lygin exhaled through her cat nose, her whiskers twitching. "We will make a report. For now, see to it that you stay on the upper levels," she told Aly. "And if your techband falls off again, do *not* go looking for it." The lygin nodded to Braxin and started for the door, the krull following behind her. "We may have to return to ask follow-up questions. For now, you will have a strike to your name. See to it that you don't receive another."

The enforcers left, leaving Aly alone with her not-so-cheerful looking boss.

"Got lost, did you?" Braxin said, eyeing her intently.

Aly met his gaze. " I did. Is that so hard to believe?"

Braxin tapped his clawed finger against his console, watching her. "Perhaps not...though you look rather well-kept for someone who has been down at the bottom of the mine for several hours."

Aly clasped her hands. "I took a shower before I came here. I didn't want to dirty your workplace."

This time, Braxin's eyes narrowed. "And the things that chased you?"

"Like I said, I hid. They didn't see me."

"And was that all you encountered down there?"

Aly could see from his expression that he thought she might be hiding something, but Aly didn't give anything away. "No. Should I have?"

Braxin rolled his shoulders. "It is just very surprising. Since few return from the bottom alive."

"I guess I am very lucky, then," Aly said, unwavering.

Braxin's mouth turned up slightly, revealing one sharp tooth. "And you saw nothing of the nillium, then?"

Aly shook her head. "Not a trace."

Braxin frowned, rubbing at his chin. "Really?"

"Really," Aly said. "I got lost in the dark. I hid from the eyeless creatures, then I continued on until I found the elevator. That's it."

Braxin still didn't seem totally convinced, but he let it go. "Return to your unit for the day. Consider yourself very lucky this time, Smith." He pointed a finger at her. "You won't be reprimanded or tried unless they find evidence that your story doesn't add up, so I would be very careful if I were you. Because if they do find that you are lying, you will be punished severely."

Aly rose from her seat. "Well, then it's a good thing I have nothing to worry about." She turned from him and made for the door, her heart pounding wildly as she could feel his eyes burning into her back. She left his work unit without saying goodbye and slowly let out the breath she had been holding as she walked past the open room full of crates and out into the passageway.

"There you are, Aly!"

Aly turned just in time to see Mark rushing down the opposite end. Behind him were Kate and Julian, followed by Cilia and Jamie. Mark hugged her unexpectedly. Surprised, Aly returned it. As he released her, Julian gripped her shoulder firmly with his large hand.

"You all right?" he asked, forcing her to look straight at him.

Aly smiled and nodded. "Yeah, I'm okay."

"What happened?" Kate asked from beside Julian. Before Aly could answer, Kate also hugged her unexpectedly. "My god, all we heard was that you went missing. And then they told us not even a couple hours ago that you were dead. It was horrible."

"We were just planning a memorial for you and everything," Mark commented.

Ethan and Davis caught up just then and gave Aly a casual wave, which she returned.

"My techband fell off and I got lost," Aly replied to Kate. She gave them a quick rundown of everything she had just told the enforcers, leaving out minor details.

"Little miss sunshine got lost in the dark." Ethan shook his head. "And still came out unscathed. Maybe I need to stick near you more often, with all that luck you're hoarding."

Aly smiled. If only they knew.

"You are one brave, girl," Cilia said, patting her not so softly on the back. "Even I don't think I could have kept it together down there."

"It was pretty terrifying at first," Aly said honestly.

"What was it like?" Davis asked.

"Let's not force her to relive it," Julian replied.

"It was just...really dark," Aly said.

"So, you didn't, like, find anything interesting down there or anything?" Davis asked.

For once, Aly had to steady herself before answering. "No...nothing, really." She shifted her eyes away from theirs. "Just some strange rocks."

"So, no sign of Hades or his three-headed dog?" Ethan joked.

Aly smirked. "No."

"What about that nillium? The one they keep warning us about? That was his turf, right?"

Aly shook her head. Taking a deep breath, she let out a little laugh in hopes it would hide her wavering voice. "No. No sign of him. Just a bunch of rocks."

A few looked a little disappointed.

"Jeeze, they all hype up that place for nothing. What a joke," Ethan said. "They probably just don't want anyone wandering around for no good reason. Maybe the nillium isn't even real, just some made up boogey-man."

'Oh, he's real all right,' Aly thought to herself. 'And he is one stubborn jerk.'

Julian wrapped an arm across Aly's shoulders and brought her close. "Let's get out of here, eh? How about come back to mine and Kate's unit, and we will make some dinner to celebrate? It'll be a tight fit, but we will manage."

The others agreed and so did Aly, feeling suddenly happy to be back with her team. Even though she was still disappointed by Ryziel's rejection (and starting to feel the creep of guilt at having to keep the ship a secret from them), she was thankful to have her team no longer worried for her. To see them actually glad to have her back.

"Come on, Aly." Julian said, pulling her gently away. And Aly went.

* * *

Days passed, bringing more storms with them. It seemed to rain nearly every day now. Aly tried to go back to her usual work, to forget everything that happened below. The first day wasn't so hard and the second day was manageable, but the more days that went by, the more her mind began to wander, her concentration blown away into the netherspace of her mind, replaced by fantasies that were unlikely to ever come true.

One, specifically, entailed her getting on the ship. Of her and her team making their way out of Lethe Maws and through space in hopes of returning home. Or if not home, perhaps somewhere— anywhere, really—better than the mines.

She also thought a lot about Ryziel. About his refusal to let her help him and how distant he had seemed, even though he had just rushed to save her life for no reason at all. How he confused her and kind of infuriated her, really, and maybe she would just go down below again after all and give him another piece of her mind while maybe trying to convince him a second time...

Yeah, no, that was a stupid idea.

Aly stuck to the upper levels and refused to go farther than the twentieth floor. She tried her best to stay around others and messaged Julian every so often to let him know she was okay. She got up early for work and went straight to her unit after her shift end. She didn't mope around or try to speak to anyone.

She was on level eighteen, trying to fix a large caster—a sort of flood light—when her concentration (or lack of) was broken by the sudden rush or people at the corner of her eye. Medical staff were coming out from the medical hub nearby. The hub wasn't large in any sense, which said a lot about the Xolis Council's need to provide treatment to those on Lethe. The staff rushed over to the elevator only a few yards away as the car came up and the doors opened.

From the car stepped out two miners carrying a third, a grex from what Aly could make out. The grex was limp in their arms, his head swaying back from his shoulders, tongue slipping from his mouth, his skin a sickly pale green. Aly dropped down from her position by the light to get a better look. Something was on the grex's stomach—something like a pile of brown and green vines or leaves, clumped together in a sort of mass. A few miners watching flinched away. Confused at first, Aly watched the medical staff press the pile of mush against the grex's stomach, and she realized it was his guts.

Her stomach rolled, and Aly had to turn away, hand against her mouth.

"Ripped up just like that tylian," Aly heard someone mutter close by.

The miners holding the grex gave him over to the medical staff, who took him inside.

"No way he's surviving that," said another miner.

"What could have got him?"

"Don't know. Something really awful, though."

Aly turned back to the light and quickly went to fix it. When she eventually did get it working again, she made for the elevator where the two miners who had been carrying the grex still stood, talking in low voices with the others, including a few other grex who wanted to know what had happened to their kin.

"We found him on the lower levels, by one of the stairways," said one, a tylian, his feelers flattened against the shell of his head.

"Did he have saliva foaming at his mouth?" asked one grex. "A purplish liquid?"

The tylian shook his head, and that seemed to alarm the grex.

"No venom was used, which means he didn't even try to defend himself," one grex commented.

"Unless he was caught by surprise before he could," mentioned another.

"I don't know. There were several wound marks in various places. It certainly looked like he was in a fight," said the tylian.

The grex seemed deeply disturbed as Aly passed by, making her way over to a separate elevator so as to not be in their way. As she took the elevator up to nine, she thought heavily about what she had seen and heard and what it meant.

She thought of Ryziel again but shook her head.

No, he couldn't have done it. Otherwise, she would surely have been one of those being carried off the other night. It was more likely that it was a sluth. Though it seemed odd that the grex's body, like that of the dead tylian, was so intact save for the torn stomach. The sluths would have at least eaten him, like they had likely planned to do to her before Ryziel had come. And they wouldn't have left his body on one of the other levels. She was pretty sure they didn't know how to work an elevator or find the stairs let alone navigate them.

So, something else was down below coming up to hunt.

There were things far worse than sluths. That's what Nar had said. And she believed it. Maybe she should just be thankful she even got out of the bottom alive at all. Maybe she really needed to put the ship and everything behind her and just worry about her life and the others. Maybe she should even consider asking Braxin to have them work in the warehouses after all.

Because, as awful as that might be, clearly, nowhere was safe in the mines. And, even though the enforcers were tracking them to keep them "safe," she would be a fool to believe that they could actually stop anything from harming them. They certainly hadn't done a great job the night she went below and almost got catcn.

The elevator stopped at nine, and Aly slipped out, making her way back to her unit. She stepped into her apartment and began to take off her suit when another thought came to her.

Ryziel could protect them if he cared. She learned enough about the nillium at the refugee facility to know they were a powerful race; strong, agile and fierce. Some of them were even said to have strange but useful abilities. They were acknowledged as the First for a reason. Their strength and power were what made them the elite of Xolis, which was why the other races respected and revered them.

But the problem was, the nillium also didn't have a reason to care about anyone else. Unless it benefited them. Aly thought she had that chance to make Ryziel care but, as much as she could have helped, Ryziel didn't want it. Not from her.

Feeling suddenly anxious and a little down. Aly went straight for the shower, turning on the hot water and making it steam. She took her time cleaning up as she thought about everything that had happened. Trying desperately to think of a way to help her team.

By the time she was done, she thought again about the ship. Maybe she could sneak onboard. Get out of Lethe herself and return home to tell the others so that they could come rescue the team. Or just sneak the team onboard with her somehow.

Unfortunately, she had no way of remembering how to get to the lair, and she was definitely not going to risk the lives of her crew members to go searching around the bottom for it.

Sighing, Aly stepped out of the shower and wrapped a towel around her. As she dried her hair and started the kettle for tea, a knock sounded at her door.

Frowning, Aly thought it must be Mark, coming to check on her for the night as he had been doing the last few nights since her return.

"Just a minute," she called to him. She searched around for a suit then elected instead to put on her robe. Quickly tying it around her, she went to the door and opened it.

"Sorry, I just got out of the shower and—" she froze as the door slid open and she saw it wasn't Mark checking on her.

Ryziel stood before her, a dark blue shadow surrounded by the dim white lights of the hall behind him.

"Oh," Aly said, standing in the doorway, too shocked to move.

Ryziel's eyes met hers then flicked down her body then quickly looked away, looking anywhere but at her. "I need to talk."

Aly blinked, not sure what to say at first, still stunned that he was actually in front of her. "Okay," she said.

They stood there for a moment as she watched Ryziel's eyes shift down one side of the hall then the other. He glanced back at her. "Can I come in?"

He wanted to talk to her, inside her unit. It took Aly a moment to process that and then another to respond to his request.

"Um, sure, okay." She shifted out of the doorway so that he could pass by her. His bulky, tall frame barely slipped through the door as he stepped inside.

As the door closed behind him, Aly moved over to her kitchen. "I was just going to make some tea," she said as she fumbled around for a second cup. "Would you like some?"

"I'm fine."

Aly looked around and saw Ryziel standing in the middle of her unit, his head almost scraping the ceiling. He glanced around at her things, showing a smidge of interest, especially when his eyes fell on her bed, to the sketchbook lying open in the center.

Aly swept over and picked it up, closing it and setting it down on a shelf nearby. "Would you like to sit?"

Ryziel flicked his eyes once more over the bed, as if contemplating it, then shook his head. "I won't stay long."

"Okay." Instead of having to brush past him to sit on the bed herself, she leaned against her kitchen counter. "So...shoot."

Ryziel looked at her confused. "Shoot?"

"What do you want to talk about?"

He straightened, putting his arms behind his back, and didn't say a word at first. His head turned to gaze out the window, the bright lights from the casters making his pupils shrink to pinpoints. Aly watched him curiously, waiting.

"I...may need your help," he said and winced as if the confession hurt.

Aly crossed her arms. "Is that so?" She tried her best to keep her excitement restrained as much as possible, though she couldn't help the tiny smile forming on her lips.

Ryziel glanced back at her and seemed to notice. He rubbed at his neck, and she could see he was still a bit irritated at the prospect.

"Yes," he said plainly. "I...may be willing to rethink my decision. If your offer still stands."

When he said no more, Aly waited a moment longer before saying, "It does. I can't tell you how—"

"And if I do decide to let you return below and help with rebuilding the ship, you will swear to follow my orders without question," he said. He looked away from her and paced the room. "As long as you are down below, you will not go anywhere without me. You will do your part for however long you are needed then you will return above after. There is no arguing or negotiating, understand?"

Aly pursed her lips. A lock of hair fell against her cheek, and she brushed it aside. "I suppose that's fair," she said quietly.

Ryziel nodded his head. "Good."

"And our place on the ship?" Aly asked before he decided to leave without another word.

Ryziel looked back out the window, to the darkness beyond. "There are eight of you, correct?"

"Nine, technically." Aly's stomach dropped as she remembered Sarah. She hadn't thought about how they were going to get her back. She would have to worry about that later. "But eight of us are here now."

Ryziel scratched at his jaw and sighed. "All right. They will be given a place. But you will not inform them of it until the ship is fully built. And once you do, they will have to remain silent. If one speaks of it, you all will lose your chance. Understood?"

Aly moved off the counter to stand closer to him, ignoring his sudden stillness as she did so. "It's a deal, then," she said and put out her hand.

Ryziel stared down at her open palm like it was completely unfamiliar to him and he wasn't sure what to do with it. Which wasn't completely wrong. It wasn't like human customs were universal.

Aly understood this, and she quickly dropped her hand.

"A deal," Ryziel agreed. He turned for the door and before he could slip out, he looked back at her. "What is the lowest level you are allowed to enter?"

"Level twenty," Aly said.

"Then meet me tomorrow on level twenty when your regular shift begins," he replied. The door opened and he peered out, making sure the coast was clear.

"All right, great." Aly stepped behind him with a grin. "I will see you then—"

He walked off without glancing back at her. Aly poked her head out of the unit to watch him go, a strange feeling warming her. She returned back into her unit and let the door close soundly. Her smile stayed on until she slept.

CHAPTER SIXTEEN

It was only drizzling down on twenty from a light mist that had made its way into the lower levels, the storms quieting momentarily, keeping back the rain. Aly pretended to inspect a generator, checking for faults though knowing it was in perfect working order. No one seemed to care nor notice her, so it probably wouldn't have mattered anyway, but she would have felt silly if she had just stood around, searching every stairway and elevator car for Ryziel like an expectant puppy.

She hadn't said a word to her team like she promised, letting them believe she was working, though she began to wonder and soon worry about how exactly Ryziel planned to bring her down without being traced by her techband. If they were to unlink it again, the enforcers would grow very suspicious indeed.

She tried not to think too much about it, though her heart thumped harder the longer she wandered on twenty, in fear someone would eventually catch on that she wasn't really working.

As she finished inspecting the generator and began to make her way over to a charging station, she caught a sudden movement at the corner of her eye and turned to see Ryziel hiding just within the entrance to a small tunnelway. He gestured for her to come. Glancing around to make sure no one watched, she approached him carefully. As she neared the tunnel, he slipped farther in. Once she stepped inside, she walked a little way then halted before bumping into him.

Ryziel seemed to look her over carefully before pointing to her wrist. "Take off your techband and give it to me."

Aly did as he asked, slipping the band off and placing it in his big hand. She watched as he took it up and began navigating her screen, going through the band's system. Aly tried to peer over to see what he was doing exactly, but it was too hard to tell in the dark.

"Um, just my two cents, but won't just unlinking it again make the enforcers really suspicious and start looking for me?" she said.

"I'm not unlinking it," Ryziel replied without looking at her. "I am using a unique set of codes within a premade program to make the tracer think you are somewhere you are not."

"Oh." Aly thought about it. "So, like a VPN?"

Ryziel actually stopped what he was doing to look at her. "A what?"

"Sorry, a virtual private network. It's something we humans would use so that others couldn't trace us online...er, through a shared database system or whatever."

"Something like that," he said and went back to reworking her techband. "Nar and I made it up last night. It will allow you to go below without your techband setting off where you are. Instead, they will think you are somewhere on one of the higher levels. You will still be able to send and receive messages and make calls, though I will ask that you don't while you are down in the lair. If it is an emergency, we will return to another level." He made a few more adjustments then handed the band back to her. "Every hour, the location will change so anyone who can see where you are will think you are moving around. When you return toward the surface after your shift, you will turn off the program I just set, and it will relink to your exact location. I will show you how to turn it on and off later."

Aly slipped the band back on. "Got it."

Ryziel shifted his eyes back down the tunnel and seemed to pause, as if waiting for something to appear. When nothing did, he started for the stairs.

"The way is clear. No one will see us," he said. "When we come to an empty level, we will take the elevator the rest of the way down."

Aly nodded, though he didn't see. She followed quickly behind, keeping her suit lights dim enough to not cause attention but bright enough to see her steps.

They made their way down to the last level of the mine. Once they left the elevator and started again across the great open space that was the bottom, it seemed no time at all before they entered the tunnel hiding the metal door and were back at the lair.

As they entered and the door closed behind them, Aly saw Xilya talking with Nar by the console. They turned their heads to her, one looking annoyed, the other slightly amused.

"So, you have finally chosen," Xilya said to Ryziel. "Good. I take it we go down today?"

Ryziel made for several bags near the metal table with the central grate. "Yes. As soon as everything is packed."

Aly stood between the console and the table with the ship ahead of her. She stared at it now with hopeful anticipation. Several days ago, she never would have thought she would be back to see it, back in this chamber, back with...him. She looked over as Ryziel picked up the bags and a set of metal containers with straps attached off the ground and set them on the table, opening them to fill them with the things they would need for their journey. His back was turned to her, allowing her to admire his broad shoulders and slim waist without him noticing.

"So, human," Xilya said, stepping away from the console to stand beside her. Aly stiffened considerably, taking in the rather aggressive and sharp physique of the female vrisha before her. They really were terrifying, especially up close. "I take it you have no training whatsoever in combat or heavy terrain?"

Aly glanced behind her at Nar, who gave her a fiery sort of glare, then slowly shook her head. "Afraid not."

"I see," said Xilya. "Would you say, then, that you are at least agile? Could run at great distances if need be?"

"Run?" Aly said.

"From possible dangers," Xilya explained. "I'm sure you have already been warned of the many things that lurk in the deeper below."

"Oh. Right." Aly shifted, looking at her feet. " I think I can run all right."

Nar snorted. "Oh, she certainly proved she can run when the sluths were chasing her. Not that she was quick enough or strong enough to not get caught."

"It won't matter," Ryziel said as he continued to fill the bags. "She won't need to run for any reason."

Because he—or rather they, as it seemed Xilya was joining them— would be there to protect her. It wasn't said but implied enough that Aly understood. She could see by Ryziel's hardened expression and Xilya's bowed gaze that bringing her was a considerable risk they were now willing to bear.

"If you have a spare weapon, a shooter even, I could probably defend myself if need be," Aly said, glancing between them, not wishing to seem suddenly such a burden.

They were each silent until Nar burst out laughing.

"Ah, she can't be this thick-brained, can she?" he said, leaning back in his high seat by the map. "Oh, lady, you are naive. This is why I really think this is a bad idea."

"Quiet, Nar," Xilya hissed. The vrisha female looked back at her. "There are no weapons here, softling, save those you see before you."

Aly looked between Xilya and Ryziel. "You mean you'll—what? Pummel the monsters with your fists?"

Xilya made a sort of shrug. "More or less. And if that doesn't work, I have my second choice right beside me." She brought up her tail and swung it close to Aly, who flinched at the small dagger-like spike at the end.

"And...Ryziel?" Aly shifted her gaze slowly over to him.

Xilya smiled. "He has his own advantages too. Though he has yet to offer to challenge me in a fight, I believe he is capable of holding his own."

Ryziel's mouth thinned as he tied the bags closed. "It's time to go. Nar, link us up and be ready. We leave as soon as the canisters are pressurized." Ryziel went over to a large metal chest by the wall and opened it. He sifted through a few unseen items until he took out one in particular and turned back to Aly. "As for you," he said, approaching her with a dark oval-shaped object now in his hand, "you will wear this."

Aly took the object, turned it, over and saw that it was...

"A...helmet?" she said.

He made no comment as he went past her to gather the bags. She looked back at the other two then back down at the helmet with its black exterior and blue shield.

Funny how she had always believed helmets just never existed on Lethe Maws, considering the section leaders never gave them out or spoke of them as a necessity in the mines. Yet, here one was, likely stolen from a storehouse above. Aly shook her head, thinking it probably still wouldn't do her much good. Even so, she didn't protest.

"Safety first," she said and put it on.

The way into Yurza's Keep was not an easy one when compared to navigating one's way through the upper levels above. Though they called Ryziel's territory the bottom, it was not the end of the caves altogether. Just the bottom where the mines used by Xolis ended. Beyond that was uncharted, unmapped territory, at least within the mine's mapping system. There were no elevators to take, no stairs to climb down save for those made by ancients long ago, but even they were not like the stairs within the mine, which consisted of grated metal steps and bolted-in railings; instead, they were carved from the very rock and spiraled downward within narrow passages.

Once they made their way to a separate tunnel system on the eastern side of the large rocky field that was considered the bottom of the mine, they found one of these ancient stairways. Ryziel led the way down, keeping Aly between him and Xilya, careful to watch the steps to make sure none had crumbled away since the last time he had taken them. He turned on the light to his suit so that the others could see and understand what was ahead of them, but Ryziel himself did not need the lights to see. He had always been capable of seeing in the deepest black, his eyes adjusting so that everything several dozen paces ahead could be seen almost as clear as day. Xilya herself also had a sense of night vision, though hers was not comparable to his.

Aly, on the other hand, judging from those few moments he had walked with her in the dark, was completely and utterly blind. Even with the night vision activated on her helmet screen and the light of his suit shining the way, she stumbled several times and almost fell against him once (and he thanked Nihl that she didn't, her hands catching on a low boulder instead). His receptors tingled from her nearness, but after several days of meditation and working to stifle his Drega, Ryziel was confident he could at least control it with her near, though whether that was true if she were to touch him or he were to touch her was another story, and at that moment, he didn't care to test it.

He kept his eyes ahead and his focus knife sharp, listening and observing around him for any potential threats that might be close by.

The sluths had kept their distance, likely sensing him, clearly not wanting a repeat of their violent encounter from before. Nothing met them along the stairs, either, and that was good.

After several winding passageways and a few more stairs, Ryziel had them stop for a short rest, more for Aly's sake then for him or Xilya, but he was pleased to find she was in no way tired and, after a quick drink of water, was ready to continue. So they did and, after a slow climb down into another level and then across a narrow passage with a high ceiling full of spiked rocks Aly said her people called stalactites, they came to the first doorway leading into Yurza's Keep.

Ryziel stopped and went ahead first, checking to make sure the way was clear. There were some new holes he noticed along the walls and a few piles of crumpled rock indicating something had passed by some time ago, but he sensed nothing around and felt it was safe to continue. They went on through the doorway, clearly man-made with odd markings carved into its frame. Ryziel noticed Aly observing them carefully.

"Who were they?" she asked as they walked on past the door. "The ones who made all this?" She gestured around to the markings along the cave walls.

"A civilization long dead," Xilya replied.

They reached the end of the first passage to a second doorway, one that led on to a stone bridge stretching across a murky river. It was then Ryziel forced Aly to hang onto his belt, as patches of the bridge had crumpled away, some in the very middle, needing to be carefully walked around.

They crossed swiftly, Aly continuing to hang onto his belt even after they made it across and over to the third and last door, when he told her it was okay to let go. She did so but did not move to follow. She, instead, looked up at the impossibly tall doorway, with one frame still half clinging to one side and the other crumbled on the ground beside it.

She seemed ready to ask a torrent of questions, so Ryziel said, "We need to keep moving. We are almost there."

Aly looked back at him and, after a pause, nodded. They started again, with her now following closely behind.

Once past the door, however, she stopped again to gaze around in wide-eyed wonder.

"My god...this place is huge," she said aloud.

Ryziel stopped, as did Xilya. He watched her looking around, her human astonishment somehow amusing to him. Though he supposed he couldn't blame her. Even he couldn't help being impressed the first time he had come down into the Keep, a place with a ceiling so high one couldn't see the top, with hundreds of pillars as large as the watchtowers on Nihl, standing in rows that seemed to stretch several hundred paces. The ground underneath consisted of a black stone with ivory etchings carved deep to form an intricate, unique design. Some of the pillars and sections of the ground, however, had been broken apart by something equally as large. Something Ryziel didn't care to ever meet.

"This way," he said in a low voice. The two followed as Ryziel made a sharp left, crossing behind a pillar, over to the side of the vast chamber where a slip of a cave entrance could be seen, no more than a sliver against the giant, smooth cave wall. Turning sideways, Ryziel slipped through with Aly and Xilya doing the same. After a short distance, they broke through to the other side into a large tunnelway —not nearly as big as the ones leading into the Keep but still equally impressive. The cave walls here were not carved as nicely as the others of the Keep and there were no ancient markings adorning the walls. It was clearly a more natural passage made from a dried-up waterway.

They went on a little farther down one end till they came to a central chamber. One filled with dozens of separate holes and crevices, some wide enough for him and Xilya to pass through and others so small and low one would need to crawl. A large cavity took up a portion of one wall to the left while to the right, a short distance down, another large entranceway was blocked by a pile of rubble.

Ryziel stopped and dropped his bag. He brought up his arm and tapped on the screen of his techband. "Nar, we're inside."

There was a short click then the urk's voice responded. "I can see you on the map now," he said. "The tracer is synced and tied to your signal, so you can let it go."

Ryziel took the tracer from his bag—a small silver and black orb—

and twisted it then flung it into the air. The orb lit up with blue light and hovered.

"What's that?" Aly asked.

"Tracer," he said, watching as it floated around some more then, as it scanned around, flew by and headed down one of the small holes that led through to another set of passages on the other side of the chamber.

"What's it tracing?" Aly asked.

Ryziel flicked his eyes down to her. He didn't see any reason to keep the information from her, since she was bound to keep everything else a secret. "Ionx," he said.

Her expression was one of silent surprise, and Ryziel could not have expected anything different. Everyone who came to Lethe Maws knew of ionx and knew how astoundingly rare it was to find, as well as the nice payout one would receive if they found any. He didn't mention to her, however, that he wasn't looking for it for the money.

"Are we...looking for that here as well?" she asked after a pause.

"No. There is none here." Ryziel went back into his bag and took out a slim can of dustlite and shook it while Xilya dropped her own bags and brought out a few tiny lanterns, setting them alight around the chamber. "Here, we are looking for tython and byril, one is shiny gray the other a bluish-green. If you find aulion, toss it. We won't need it." Ryziel went over to one of the smaller openings in the chamber and began spraying the dustlite beside it with an X. He heard a sharp gasp behind him and stopped to glance back and see Aly looking astonished once again.

"It glows!" she said pointing to the blue X before him. "Is that paint?"

Before Ryziel could respond Aly came up beside him and placed her hand on the X. "Amazing. I could use something like this," she said more to herself than to him.

Uncertain what she meant, Ryziel took a step back. "It's to help mark your progress. You'll start here and work around. Xilya will be working the other end, and I will be right nearby, at this wall." Ryziel tossed the can over by his things and gestured for her to take off her bag. She did so, and he opened it up to take out the dissolver, a shiny metal gun with a small cylinder-shaped canister affixed to the bottom and top.

"This is what you will be using to find the minerals," Ryziel said, handing the dissolver to her. "Once you get deep enough inside, use the trigger and spray along the wall. The chemical won't hurt you but will start to dissolve the rock. Most of the minerals should just drop out, but if not, you can use a small chisel to weasel it out." Ryziel took out a chisel from his own side bag and handed it to her. Then he took up a metal canister and untwisted the lid. "Once you have the minerals, you will place them in here and close it tight." He gave it to her then stepped closer to the small opening, crouching down. "I will be close by watching you as I work. If you hear anything or see anything beyond where you are working, tell me immediately."

Aly nodded her head and crouched down beside him. She turned on her suit lights then peered inside. She seemed to hesitate before beginning to crawl her way in. Ryziel watched her go, making sure she was able to move inside without issue. For a brief moment, he felt a strong urge to follow her but knew that he couldn't. Instead, he watched her take up a crouched sitting position then turn on the gun and begin to spray the wall beside her.

He watched her for a long moment. When he was satisfied she would be fine, he forced himself away.

* * *

It was an hour or so into their work when they heard the noises. Ryziel's receptors vibrated, and he knew whatever it was was just beyond the outer wall. He looked to Xilya first, who gave him an icy glance, then he immediately rushed over to where Aly worked.

As he crouched down to look at her, he saw that she had turned deathly still, her eyes wide in the darkness.

"What is that?" she whispered.

Ryziel could make numerous guesses but judging by the shrill screeching, he made his bet on nyghi, large vicious beasts that roamed in small packs. He mentioned this to her, and she seemed to shiver.

"It sounds like...like banshees," Aly said. "Or cats fighting to the death."

Ryziel wasn't sure what any of those were, but he trusted they were things from her world that sounded similar. "They should pass soon. As long as they don't pick up our scent, we should be fine."

This didn't seem to calm her much so Ryziel continued with, "I will be right here. Nothing will get to you."

This worked better. She calmed considerably, even gave him a nervous smile.

"You could probably take one on yourself with no issue I'll bet," she said.

Ryziel met her eyes and was surprised to feel a smile playing on his lips. "One of them? Yes, if I was trapped and had no choice but to fight. But I would prefer to hide if I could."

"Oh? Why is that?"

"Besides talons that could shred a man in half? Venom. Painful enough that you would wish you were dead."

A loud shriek rattled the walls nearby, and Aly tensed once again.

"They wouldn't happen to be related to the grex by any chance, would they?" She laughed nervously as she edged her back against the rock behind her. Ryziel studied her closely and could see she was joking for the most part. He could also see she was talking to keep the edge off.

"No, not at all," he replied, wanting to help distract her. "The nyghi are different in every way. I've only seen one once from a distance, but I have heard their shrieks many times. I'd say you'd have to see one for your own eyes to understand, but I would prefer we didn't."

Aly nodded. "They don't happen to just kill someone and leave them lying around, do they?"

Ryziel frowned. "No. They will eat whatever they kill."

Aly closed her eyes and slunk closer to the rock. After several moments, the shrieking died down until it was nothing more than a distant echo far away. Aly took a slow breath and looked back at him.

"Looks like they passed." Ryziel looked back at Xilya and saw she had hunkered down by the cave wall and was now returning to her work. Ryziel turned back to Aly. "It's okay now. Let's just keep going."

* * *

They finished without another incident. An uncommon occurrence, Aly was told, after so many hours in the Keep.

Once they had filled up their containers with minerals and sealed them tight, Ryziel went on ahead through to the narrow passage beyond to make sure the way back was clear. Once he returned, they packed up and headed out, this time with Xilya taking the lead and Ryziel guarding at the back.

As Aly pushed through the narrow passage and came out to the massive chamber on the other end, she was once again awestruck by the unimaginable size. It was like walking through a giant's hallway or perhaps a god's. As they walked onward toward the door, she swept her gaze across the vast hall and along the pillars and realized she could see farther than her light entailed because there was a grayish blue glow illuminating the very chamber. When she tried to pinpoint the light's source, however, she was unable to grasp its exact location.

She slowed then turned her head back to Ryziel, who was trailing closely behind, and pointed across the way.

"That light, where does it come from?" she whispered.

Ryziel shifted his eyes around, focusing on the pillars in the distance. "It is muirlemp," he said softly.

"What is that?"

"A type of fungus plant. It glows in the dark."

"I've never seen it before," Aly said. "On Lethe Maws, I mean."

"It can only be found outside the mines," he replied. "It used to grow in abundance closer to the surface until the mining destroyed most of the environment and all the various flora."

"You mean there is a whole ecosystem down here?" Aly said, astonished. Oh, how Kate, their ship bio-expert, would freak at the idea. Such a promising chance to study and extract, if only Aly could tell her anything about it.

"Yes, a whole other world, if you know where to look," Ryziel said.

Aly gazed back across at the glow from the muirlemp. "It's been pretty terrifying so far but...this is rather beautiful. Maybe I'll try to recreate it."

"Recreate it?" Ryziel asked after a short pause.

Aly glanced back at him with a sheepish smile. "Er, draw it, I mean. Though it won't be the same in just my mind's eye. Better to actually have a sample to look at...not that I'm asking you to find me some plants or anything."

Ryziel didn't respond to this, and Aly turned back to following Xilya, who had already made it to the door and was waiting for them.

As they continued their trek out of the Keep, Aly couldn't help studying once more all the strange markings along the door and the bridge. As they passed by a large obelisk-like marker standing within the center of the bridge at its edge, Aly saw carved within it the shape of a woman, faceless, with a sharp crown hovering just above her head.

"Was she their Queen?" she asked as they crossed the river and started through the door.

"Pardon?" Xilya said, turning her head slightly.

"You said this was called Yurza's Keep. And that it was home to a civilization. Was she their ruler?"

"Perhaps so? I don't know much of the lore of this place as the others do."

Aly looked back at Ryziel again, who shrugged. "Nar claims she was an ancient who was guardian to the underground Keep and its city. His people may still have old texts within their libraries about her, but most of what is known is lost. Though some say she still lives, lurking in the passages below, others say it is only a ghost or something else that haunts the Keep, that fools one into thinking it is her."

Aly shivered at that. And here she thought she had gotten away from such things as ghosts and haunts, as if they were mostly an earthly invention. But no, even in the vast reaches of space, there are still the unknown terrors of the dark.

They slipped quickly through the last door and through to the passage beyond without issue. It wasn't until Aly came to their first set of stairs that she realized how far down they had come and how much she would now have to climb.

As she hesitated on the steps, she felt Ryziel close behind her, giving her the strength to press forward.

She kept up with Xilya up to the sixth stair, but by then, she was breathing much more heavily, trying her best to keep up with Xilya's long gait. She stuck to watching her feet as they climbed, trying not to notice Ryziel having to slow at her back.

As they came to a small chamber, Xilya called a halt, and they stopped.

"Let's take a quick rest," she said and plopped her bag down before Aly could protest. Neither the vrisha nor the nillium looked in any way like they needed to stop for a break, but she sure as hell did, and she wished that didn't bother her but it did.

'Damn but if I had used the stairs in the mines more,' she thought bitterly, sipping her water. Her eyes shifted around the cave room, trying to distract herself from her sudden embarrassment at feeling so inferior, when she caught sight of a bright glow along the ground and along the side of a wide crevice. She wondered how she hadn't seen it before, but perhaps her eyes hadn't adjusted yet and her lights had been much brighter when coming down. As the two talked quietly behind her, Aly stole herself over to the dazzling blue light trailing the cave wall until she reached its end. There before her was a budding plant, illuminating a beautiful blue-green hue along its petals like some fairy had sneezed magical glitter all over it.

Deeply mesmerized, Aly crouched down before it and thought to touch its leaves but then decided against it, not knowing whether it might be poisonous. She was about to call to Ryziel to ask him to tell her what kind of plant it was, when something fluttered above her, making her turn her head upward, casting her light along the ceiling above.

And, in doing so, revealing the large, white-eyed, bat-like creature crouching above her.

Aly gasped, stumbling to her feet, falling back against something hard behind her as the thing hissed and went to pounce. Aly shrieked and turned, covering her face against the hard surface that she had run into only to feel said hard surface wrap itself around her and quickly drag her away. Aly heard the sounds of a guttural growl and the shriek of something in pain followed by a sharp crunching sound and a loud shifting and howling before the noise died away.

Aly felt the hard surface that gripped her vibrate, then she heard the sound of another growl. When she dared peek upward, she found Ryziel's face, stone-still, with eyes as cold as ice, glaring down at her.

Aly let out another little gasp and jerked back, but he didn't release her. Not right away.

"Nihl Ryziel..." It was Xilya who spoke. Her voice was low and cautious, as if she were speaking to a man holding someone hostage and about to pull the trigger. Or, in Aly's case, rip her throat out from the look Ryziel was giving her.

He bared his teeth, his mouth quivering, his eyes narrow silver slits. He snarled down at her, and again, fear gripped her. Something told her to not look at him, to keep her hands off him, so she dared not touch him to move back, just kept her arms tightly at her sides. As if she were caught in the grip of a wild animal, she dared not move.

She closed her eyes and took a deep breath, waiting for...she wasn't sure what, but she knew something wasn't right. Something triggered him. Something, perhaps, of her doing, though she couldn't say what. All she could do was wait.

After several blessedly short moments of his ragged breathing, Ryziel finally let her go.

He didn't so much as look at her as he stepped away.

"Take the back, Xilya," he said in a dark voice. "Stay with her. I need to...go on ahead."

Without another word, he took up his bags (and Aly's) and continued on without them.

Aly stood there for a long moment, too stunned to move. Xilya took up her pack and approached her.

"Let's keep going," was all she said, as if pretending nothing had just happened.

"W-what was that?" Aly asked.

Xilya looked down at her with quiet regard. "A baelev. Creatures that use the glowing plants to lure their prey."

Aly didn't remark that she hadn't exactly meant the bat and Xilya didn't give away whether she thought that Aly meant otherwise.

The vrisha also didn't look ready to tell her anything more, so Aly let it go. For now.

"We're almost to the mines." Xilya waved Aly on to the next passage. "At least we shouldn't fear anything else meeting us from above."

CHAPTER SEVENTEEN

THE NEXT TIME ALY WAITED FOR RYZIEL TO TAKE HER BACK down with him, she was almost convinced and equally afraid that he would not come for her. The day before, when he'd brought her back to the surface levels, he hadn't looked at her, hadn't spoken save for the few grunts of a reply when she asked a simple question. If she had thought he seemed uncomfortable in her presence before, he was definitely irritated now.

She could probably understand him being upset if it had something to with her drifting away from him in those moments when they were so close to reaching the mines. But when she tried to apologize, it seemed to do nothing for him. He'd blocked her off, and there was no way to break those walls.

So, she forced herself to let it go and wait, even if she didn't yet understand his anger or his unhidden dislike for her.

Because that must be what it was. Something about her irritated him. She had theorized this before. But it seemed there was little she could do to remedy it. If it were her character, she would not force herself to change who she was, and if it were her general existence, well, he would just have to deal with that as well.

She told herself she would keep her distance, that in a way, he was like her new boss so that's how she should treat him. He was not her friend because he clearly didn't want to be and no matter how much that stung, she needed to respect his decision.

So, when he finally did show up (to her great surprise) to take her back down, she gave him a curt nod and nothing more.

Stepping past him to take the stairs down, she did not look up but knew he followed her silently from behind. Once they made it to an empty level, they took the elevator the rest of the way. Aly watched the lights pass by, wondering what fresh hell they might encounter today in the deep below, when she heard Ryziel shift beside her.

"I'm sorry about the other day," he said quietly.

Aly felt her body relax, actually feeling her muscles untighten and her jaw unclenching, not realizing how tense she had been. Her arms, which had been tightly crossed, loosened then fell to her sides. She glanced over at him and saw he looked calmer and less uptight than the day before. His eyes drifted over her face, watching her expression carefully.

She quietly watched him in return until she cleared her throat and said, "It's okay. I'm sorry, too."

He looked away and nodded his head. " We will be more careful today."

Aly arched a brow at him, though he didn't see it. "Yes, I will be more careful not to get on your bad side...or any of your sides." She smiled as she gazed at him. His mouth curved slightly, and for one crazy moment, she thought he was actually blushing.

"I should have warned you about the baelevs," he said. "And everything else we might encounter. I just didn't want to..."

Aly tilted her head. "Didn't want to?"

Ryziel side-eyed her then instantly looked away. "I didn't want to scare you."

Aly blinked. Then, as if like a sneeze she couldn't hold in, she let out a soft hiss of laughter.

He didn't want to scare her.

"Well, I hate to say that almost failed miserably," she said, with another fit of laughter.

Ryziel's silver gaze shifted back over to her as he frowned. "Almost?"

Aly sniffed and shrugged. "I'm still here, aren't I?"

Ryziel watched her for a moment then let out a hiss of breath. "You are."

"Though...I was scared a few times. I'm not running just yet...I guess the pressure now is more terrifying than anything I've encountered so far."

"Pressure?" Ryziel asked, confused.

Aly nodded. "The pressure to help my team. Failing them scares me more now."

Ryziel was silent for a long moment, Aly almost believing he was finished speaking altogether, when he said, "You want to return home..."

Aly bowed her head, crossing her arms once more. "They do. And I guess I want to as well. Or at least not to be here."

"I can attest to that," Ryziel said.

Aly looked back at him with a curious glance. "You are...trying to go home too?" she asked cautiously.

Ryziel met her stare. "Yes."

"Back to your family?"

"To my brother," he said.

Aly tucked a strand of hair back behind her ear. "On Nihl right? That is where they say all nillium are from."

Ryziel seemed to study her carefully before nodding. "Yes."

"They say it's like a paradise there. Is that true?"

Ryziel glanced away just in time for light to spill past the car, catching the silver fire in his eyes. "Yes," he said in a low voice, his expression darkening. "It is beautiful."

Aly hoped she hadn't touched on a sensitive subject but also didn't want to stop their conversation. "Earth is pretty, too," she said without hesitating. "At least in the places not destroyed by people."

Ryziel's expression lightened as curiosity took its place. "Your people...destroyed part of their own planet?"

Aly frowned, her eyes dropping. "For many reasons, and not all on purpose. It's...a long and complicated history. Once we started expanding into space, a lot of people left it behind. Some refused to leave, wanting to restore what was lost. Others...just wanted to expand their empires, no matter the cost." Aly closed her eyes and, for a brief second, thought of her own family then swiftly shoved those thoughts aside.

"And you chose to leave?" Ryziel asked.

Aly shifted her eyes back to him and nodded. "I...let's just say I didn't agree with my family's values. And if I couldn't agree then I didn't deserve to be a part of it."

Ryziel looked at her, surprised. "You were cast out?"

Aly clenched her jaw, an old bitterness festering in her stomach. "For the most part. Yes."

Ryziel did not speak again for a long while. The elevator came to a stop at the bottom floor, and they stepped out into the darkness beyond. They walked for some time before Ryziel chose to speak again. "You and I have that in common, then," he said at last.

Aly turned her eyes up to him, though he could not see her as she followed him from the back, her hand grasping his belt.

"Your family...disowned you?" she asked when he had said no more. It was strange. Though they were so completely different and from separate worlds, some things didn't change when it came to family. It made her oddly sad.

"My mother, no. She passed on when I was a babe," Ryziel replied. "And my brother, never. He had wanted to hide me away, though I refused, not wanting him to lose his position. It was my father and uncle who cast me out."

Aly thought for a moment on whether she should ask further, understanding it seemed deeply personal to him. But by his calm reply, she felt it was safe to continue. "Why did they?"

Ryziel turned his head slightly toward her. He did not reply right away, and Aly waited patiently, understanding if he didn't want to answer and say any more about it.

"I was...I am different from my kind. When I was born, instead of hiding me from sight, my father chose to use me for his own insidious purposes. I became his weapon in exacting justice and fear in those who opposed him. I was trained to fight, to use my differences to his advantage. When I grew, I accepted my place and my position as it was the only way I was allowed to be considered his son and be a part of his house. But...one day, I refused his order. My uncle, who had hated me from the beginning, convinced my father I would someday overthrow him if not kill him. My father, afraid of this possibility, chose to cast me from his house and send me here as punishment for defying him."

Aly listened to all this with silent awe. "Well...you certainly got me beat."

"Eh?"

"I only got thrown out 'cause I didn't care to work in the family business. And be forced to comply with my family's outrageous rules. Work for them, get married to some friend of the family, make babies who would eventually be subjected to the same rules, and never leave Earth...I forced myself to endure until I was out of school. Then no more."

Ryziel glanced back at her with a curious gaze then grunted. "It is...hard when you cannot be what they want."

"It is," Aly agreed. She watched his back for a long moment and frowned. "And I think I'm fine with never going back, honestly. To them, anyway. There are other places I could go." Aly went quiet as they walked then continued with, "Do you think they will take you back when you return?"

Ryziel took a moment again to answer then said, "My father is dead. Only my uncle remains. It is my brother I wish to return to. He will accept me back...once my uncle is dealt with."

Aly didn't dare ask what he meant by 'dealt with.' It was his business alone, and honestly, his uncle did sound like an ass. If she thought to judge Ryziel on his actions, she kept her opinion to herself. "My siblings wouldn't take me back. It's good you have a brother who will. He sounds like a good guy."

Ryziel turned his head and grunted again. "I haven't spoken to him in a long time. They've made sure of that. But I know I can trust him still. I know when the ship is ready and we leave Lethe Maws, that I will speak to him again. He will not stop me from returning and challenging my uncle. And then I will be by his side."

Aly smiled behind him, though a strange pang of some deeper emotion stabbed at her, and she realized it came from the thought that once they left the mines and he dropped her and her crew off somewhere, she wouldn't see him again. She didn't understand why, yet this bothered her. She didn't know him that well still, but she felt a connection through this shared confession.

"I hope it all works out for you," she said softly.

Ryziel looked back at her, and his eyes lingered longer than usual before turning away. "You as well."

* * *

They returned back to the Keep without issue. Ryziel, however, still forced Aly to hang onto his belt, even with Xilya at their back just as a precaution. Nothing crossed their path, though they heard the sounds of beasts moving about in the darkness. None drew near, and Ryziel hoped it was because they could sense him and knew enough not to come close. Once they made it to the chamber with the abundant source of minerals, they got to work right away.

Through the course of his work, Ryziel found his eyes drifting back over to Aly, watching her intently. When he realized he was staring, he brushed it off and went back to work. He thought about their talk on the way to the lair and how he had confessed so much to her. Things only Xilya and Nar knew of. Things he didn't expect to tell anyone else. But he didn't regret it or feel upset. In fact, he felt better after telling her, maybe because he had felt guilty about what had happened the day before. About how his Drega had slipped again in front of her, and in response, he had shunned her. He'd felt confused at first as to why he felt so guilty. It wasn't like him to be ashamed about avoiding someone when his emotions ran high. But with Aly, it just seemed different. Maybe because she didn't understand. She was so innocent. This led to him feeling the need to apologize (something he wasn't used to), and when she asked him about his past, he felt strangely obligated to answer her. As if her knowing would make her understand.

Though he still hadn't mentioned anything about his Drega, about why he was different from his kin other than in just a physical sense alone. That was something, perhaps, for another time, but he had a feeling he couldn't avoid the subject for long, not if another incident like the day before happened again.

He caught himself staring at her again from across the chamber as his thoughts wandered. He watched her delicate little hands brushing at the rock as pieces crumbled and slid from the wall. How it would feel to have those hands sliding across his chest and stomach. He thought of her hand pressing against him the night he had carried her back to the lair, and a low growl slipped his throat. Embarrassed, he turned away quickly and focused more sharply on the cave wall before him, forcing his mind back to his work and nothing else.

"Nihl Ryziel, I think it's time we left."

Frowning, Ryziel looked back and saw Xilya and Aly sitting nearby, their mineral canisters already full and tightly shut, ready to return to the lair. Ryziel looked down at his own and saw his canister, too, was full to the brim with another pile of minerals scattered around it. Cursing silently, Ryziel moved from the wall. Hours must have gone by, but he somehow hadn't noticed.

CHAPTER EIGHTEEN

They had gone one whole week down in the Keep without one major incident. Major being a cave tunnel falling in on them or a nyghi (or anything just as foul) finding them. And, though it was still taking more time than he liked to acquire the necessary minerals, Ryziel was pleased with the progress they had made so far now that Aly was aiding them. As she was able to squeeze into some of the more narrow holes that he and Xilya couldn't get to, she had helped greatly in extracting those minerals they desperately needed. She worked efficiently enough and, though Ryziel a few times had to remind her to not wander away and to be more quiet while they worked or made their trek, she complied and did not argue, cooperating with him and Xilya as best she could.

He still had to prepare himself for the worst every time they made a trip down to the Keep, to meditate and calm himself beforehand as fear still gripped him every time he forced her to travel down, afraid of the dangers that lurked close by. And to calm his Drega, which he had to do after he sent her back up as well.

He sat on his bed now, breathing slowly in and out, trying to force his mind into a state of black nothingness. Trying not to think about how Aly looked at him in the dark when she thought he didn't see. Or her instant reaction to rush close beside him whenever something slithered past a cave nearby, looking to him for protection, then smiling with relief when he told her everything was fine. Trying not to think about how she had brought herself against him the time the baelev attacked her. Trying not to think about her at all.

Ryziel closed his eyes. The ship's front exterior was nearly done. Nar had done a good job at fixing it. The shell of the ship would be completed in only another week's time. There was only the interior left and the fuel. The ionx they still had yet to discover, but the tracer was looking, and something had to turn up eventually.

Black nothingness. His mind went blank, and he breathed in slowly.

A trace of a flowery scent caught in his nostrils, a phantom scent that lingered even after she was gone. Ryziel drew his lids open and found himself on the terrace of his father's house, the First House, the ruling house above all others. He sat on a bench, the sun at the edge of the horizon. The first night of the month was upon him. The flowery scent from the plants surrounding the terrace caught again in his nose, and he inhaled slowly then rose to stand.

"Nihl Ryziel..."

He turned toward the feminine voice and saw the nillium female before him, tall, slender, golden, and beautiful in her black slip of a dress.

"This is the first night you have been here," she said, with a smile playing on her lips. Her long receptors caught in the last glint of light from the sun.

Ryziel frowned deeply at the female. She wasn't supposed to be here.

He couldn't remember her name, and it clearly showed on his face and with his silence because she let out a soft laugh and said, "You don't remember me, but we met at a gathering at the Third House, my home. I am Tazeen."

Tazeen, yes, he remembered now. He remembered how she

looked at him from across the room, her eyes always meeting his, her smile always there to greet him.

"What are you doing here?" he asked.

She stepped closer, and Ryziel's first reaction was to step away. He backed away one step then stilled.

"I wanted to see you."

He didn't believe it, not at first. He turned from her then, ready to leave her. "Did he send you?" he growled.

"Who?"

"My brother."

Another little laugh. "No, I come of my own will."

Still, he found that hard to believe. "What do you want?"

He felt her approach behind him, felt her come close, too close. Still, he didn't dare move. "If my father sees you, he will punish us both."

Her hand touched his lower back, and he nearly hissed. The gesture was too intimate for strangers. But it told him enough.

She slid her hand upward. "Are you not allowed to be with another? Are you forced to be alone?" she said.

"Yes."

That stilled her hand. "No one needs to know. I want you, Ryziel."

Ryziel refused to move. In the back of his mind, he remembered this conversation well. This memory stirred him even now. He could stop it if he wished, but he didn't.

"No," he said. "You don't know what you want. You don't know anything about me."

"I know enough."

He almost laughed at that. It was as he suspected. She was lured by his darkness, likely by the rumors about him. He heard enough of what they said from his brother. Most nillium women feared being in his presence. But there were those few, just a few, who wanted the danger and nothing more.

He remembered clearly what he had said. "You're not afraid?"

"I'm still here, aren't I?"

Ryziel's frown deepened. That, however, he did not remember her saying.

He turned back, and Tazeen was gone, and Aly stood in her place. She smiled at him. "I'm still here," she repeated.

"Why?" he asked.

She put her hand in his and he was surprisingly calm, his Drega remained sleeping.

"Because I am home." She turned her arms out, showing her wrists to him, showing him the smatterings of bruises along her hands and arms. "I'm home."

Ryziel stared down at them then back up to her and saw bruises along her neck. She smiled at him again, and all he could do was stare, confused and disturbed till the vision went black before him.

Ryziel opened his eyes and saw the cave ceiling above him, realizing he was lying on his bed now and must have somehow fallen asleep. He sat up and looked around the room that held nothing more than a bed and a chest with his things. He got up and pulled back the curtain, closing off his room to the great chamber beyond, seeing the ship before him and Nar nowhere to be seen. He wouldn't sleep again, not after that dream, so he left the room and headed for the ship to work on it alone.

* * *

Aly's team suspected nothing, even though she was way more quiet than usual at their meeting, this time in a storeroom that Julian had somehow convinced Braxin to let them use. She listened to their conversations, mostly about trying to talk once again with the Xolis Council about letting them off Lethe Maws and their arguments about whether it was really worth it (which it wasn't), about Sarah who they still hadn't heard from, about the enforcers watching them, and what it all meant. Old news, but there was nothing more for them to talk about, or at least nothing they wanted to talk about.

Briefly, Ethan mentioned about the bodies that were showing up at an alarming rate now, all pale and shredded, all seemingly drained of blood or so he heard a medical staff saying. No one wanted to talk about that, though, not even Aly. She had asked Ryziel and Nar about it when they were back in the lair after a shift, but, besides the talks about it on the forums and posts, they were uncertain either, only that they were watching carefully, both knowing that there were unknown dangers even they might not know about in the caves below.

So, they stuck to talking about something that didn't utterly terrify them, to something that would keep hope alive, no matter how small. Aly wished more than ever that she could tell them about the ship and what she was doing. At one point she was even close to considering the idea of asking Ryziel to allow the others to help, knowing that the work could be done even faster with eight humans instead of one. But she thought quickly against it because she had made a promise not to tell and couldn't be sure one of them wouldn't let something slip. Also, she couldn't ask Ryziel to try to protect eight humans when one was enough.

No, as much as it pained her, she had to wait, knowing that when the time did come to tell them, they would be more than relieved and wouldn't hesitate to take their place on the ship.

When she wasn't thinking of the ship, Aly's thoughts immediately went to Ryziel. Lately, she had been trying to decipher every expression or word or movement he made, as if he was a puzzle she needed to solve. She wished she could ask him more about his life, about his ways, but harvesting minerals in tight caves didn't make it easy to talk, especially when one needed to make sure nothing heard them while doing so. When it was just them alone as he brought her back to the mines, she did engage him in casual conversation but nothing more, suddenly feeling too shy to ask him to bring up his personal life or past.

Every night, it seemed, after she returned from the Keep, she would just sit in her unit, staring out the window or drawing in her sketchbook. Besides one new drawing of Xilya, it was filled now with nothing but him, and she shuddered to think of the utter embarrassment she would feel if the others ever found it and looked through it. They'd think she lost her mind.

And maybe she had.

She feared to grow distant with the others, but her mind just couldn't seem to focus unless she was down below. Before she knew it, the meeting had ended and she caught a few looking at her, probably wondering why she had nothing to say. She said nothing still, except for a short goodnight before turning away for her unit.

"Hey, Aly, wait up!"

Aly turned her head as she walked, to see Mark waving for her to wait for him. He caught up to keep step beside her. "Hey, I was wondering if you wanted to meet me after our shift sometime, just you and me?"

"Um, sure." She didn't look at him, her arms crossed, her mind still somewhere else.

"You okay? You seem pretty out of it lately."

She glanced at him and gave him a forced smile. "Just tired."

"Same," he said. They walked in silence until they came to their shared hub. Aly went to her door and Mark hesitated at his. "Whatever you're going through," he said. "I'm here to talk, anytime."

Aly looked back and, this time, gave him an honest smile. He was a good guy, she knew it. And in that moment, she wished she could go to him and tell him everything, but she knew she couldn't. Instead, she said goodnight and slipped into her unit. She pressed herself against the door as it closed and sighed, suddenly feeling lonely. But it wasn't Mark's company she wanted.

Tomorrow. All she could think about was tomorrow.

* * *

When Aly returned to the lair, she was surprised to find that Xilya was not there per usual.

"Xilya has been asked to work in another part of the mines," Ryziel replied when Aly asked when she would be coming down. "Today, it is only you and me."

Aly couldn't help notice her heart beating a little faster. She put on her helmet and drew up her bags in silence. She caught Nar's gaze from over by the console, and he shook his head as if he were displeased but said nothing and turned away.

They made their way down, Aly holding onto Ryziel's belt as always, watching the darkness around her for any signs of trouble. Ryziel moved forward without hesitation, even though he seemed more quiet and on edge than usual.

"Something smells odd," Aly said softly, as they made their way past the fifth stair. It was a bitter smell, like vinegar.

Ryziel did slow then. He seemed to be sensing around for something then continued on. "A creature marked the area, but they aren't around now. Something might be hunting nearby."

Aly shivered but followed close, never slowing, even when Ryziel's pace quickened.

The closer they got to the mineral chamber, however, the more the scent seemed to die off. There was nothing she could see that was odd or out of place. As they slipped into the narrow passage, Ryziel did stop just before entering the other side but didn't wait long to pull her through.

Aly looked around at the few glowing Xs now illuminating the chamber from the holes she had gone through. One portion of a side was nearly finished, and she felt like she'd made good progress.

"Do you think we will have enough minerals soon to make all the materials for the ship?" she asked as she released his belt.

Ryziel dropped his bags by a nearby wall and began to unpack. "With the tython, almost. Byril, we still need more of."

Aly dropped her own bag and made for one end of the cave when her foot stepped into something cold. She jumped back with a yelp and cast her light down to see a pool of water forming on the ground.

Ryziel came up beside her and cast his light on it as well. Blops of water hit Aly's helmet and she looked up to see water trickling down.

"I hope it doesn't flood," she said.

Ryziel turned away. "We will be done and gone before it does."

Aly looked back at him. "So, it will?"

"There is a possibility, but I'm not worried."

Aly thought about the Keep being underwater and wondered if it had been a great flood that had destroyed the civilization that once lived in it. "I couldn't fathom living underground like this," she confessed.

"Because of the dark?"

Aly looked back at him. "Not necessarily." She thought about it. "Though maybe that too. But just the idea of being, I don't know, trapped."

Ryziel took out his dissolver. "To some, maybe it's more a feeling of being secure. They never had to worry about the dangers on the surface."

Aly snorted. "Yeah, just whatever came around from underneath. And that is way too many things for my liking. On Earth, there are, like, maybe a handful of things I can think of that live in caves, and they are pretty harmless."

"Your world sounds fairly safe, then," Ryziel said, the hint of sarcasm not going unnoticed by her.

Aly smiled. "No, not at all, really. But I would never choose Lethe Maws over it, that's for sure."

"Few would. Only urks remain now that those of the Keep are gone."

"Speaking of, I think Nar would agree I wouldn't fare well down here," Aly said, taking up her own dissolver. "In fact, I think he would prefer I was anywhere but down here with you."

Ryziel made a low grunt as if to agree. "Nar is slow to trust. And quick to think the worst about everything. Most urks are."

"I can't blame him." Aly crouched down to the most recent hole she was working on then looked back at him. "Whatever happened to him?"

Ryziel went over to the wall he had been working on and started to spray the liquid fire onto the wall. "He got caught by something, possibly a nyghi. His legs were gone, and he was dying when I found him. I was able to restore him and return him to an urk den. A few weeks later, he came back with metal legs, saying he wasn't returning home and that he was going to help me escape Lethe Maws in return for saving his life."

"He chose to leave his family to help you?" she asked as she, too, began to work at the rock face before her. One thankfully closer to him, so they could talk in low voices.

"He was no longer of use in the den. The urk pride on working together to survive. Their worth is judged by what they can do for others. When he could no longer work to help provide, he was seen as a burden."

"That's awful!" Aly said a little too loudly. She winced. "Sorry. So, he had to leave?"

"He didn't have to, but he would have been looked down upon. So, he chose to leave instead."

Aly thought it over as she worked. A bunch of outcasts, that's what they were. "What will he do then when the ship is finished? Where will he go?"

Ryziel shrugged. "Maybe come back to my home and serve me there if he so chooses. Though it is debatable whether he'd care to, since the sun rarely sets on Nihl. And urks cannot see in the sunlight."

Aly paused in her work to look back at him, wide-eyed. Both these realizations were equally fascinating, but she chose one to ask more about. "Nihl doesn't have a nighttime?"

"It does in the southern regions of the planet, though they are few and short. In the city of light to the North where I am from, however, night only comes once a month and only for an hour."

Aly had heard of places on Earth having seasons where the sun rarely set. They called it the "midnight sun." But that only lasted for maybe six months if she wasn't mistaken. She had also heard of civilian worlds within the governing system having odd hours or irregular days and nights but nothing to the extreme to which Ryziel mentioned.

"What do you do on that night?" Aly asked.

"There is a ritual held. 'Nihl's reawakening,' as they call it. Some Houses settle down into fasting and prayer, others just have gatherings. I didn't encounter much of them myself, admittedly. I was usually on an...assignment for my father."

Aly understood that feeling. She missed a lot of parties with friends, all because her parents told her she couldn't go, usually because they wanted her studying to fulfill her role in the business. A business selling shipping bots to the military, of all things.

They continued on with their work, Aly spraying the cave walls, waiting a turn till the chemical foamed over, then pulling and scraping away the rock till a mineral was found.

When they were halfway through, Ryziel called for a break, a usual routine when they came down so that Aly could rest a moment and eat something to regain her energy. Usually, it involved Xilya teasing her most of the time about human needs and their ability to survive, and Aly took it pretty well, thinking she was doing pretty good, all things considered.

With Xilya gone, however, it was just her and Ryziel, and she was feeling glad for it. They hunkered down by their packs, and Aly took off her helmet. She brought out a few meal bars from her bag. Nothing extravagant in the least but it was exceptionally filling. She offered one to him, and he hesitated before taking it.

"Thank you," he said.

She unwrapped hers and took a bite, chewing it slowly, trying not to grimace. Trying and failing.

"What's wrong?" he asked.

"Does everything here have to taste like a lump of stale bread dipped in salt? Half the time, I don't even know what I'm eating."

Ryziel's eyes flickered at her in amusement as he unwrapped his own. "When it comes to these...I'd say you don't want to know."

"Please, don't enlighten me." She took another cautious bite, chewed, and sighed. "If there is one thing I miss about home, it's the food. Southern cooking was probably the only thing good about my home life. And when I didn't have that, I had everything else. Burgers, pizza." Aly sighed again. "I'd kill, seriously kill, for a stack of fries with a shake." Aly looked over at Ryziel and her face heated as she realized he probably had no idea what she was talking about.

Ryziel took a bite of his own, his expression never changing. "I miss Nihl food too. Valsh and nebaa bread will be the first meal I have when I am back."

"I bet it's good. Too bad Shadowpoint doesn't expand into a diner."

Ryziel snorted. "Miners are so used to their drink, food is rarely appreciated here, I think."

Aly smirked. "And that's really just another reason why this place stinks."

Ryziel's mouth curled, and he let out a soft laugh. "It does. Though, I'm willing to bet the ancients of the Keep had something better to offer."

"I hope so. Maybe sluth was a delicacy."

Ryziel grimaced at that. "Now you are just trying to make me feel sick."

Aly laughed. She took one last bite of her bar, offered the rest to Ryziel, who soundly refused, then threw it back in her pack. She downed some water then stood up. "Well, I guess we should get back to it."

Ryziel nodded, agreeing.

Aly looked around the cave system, shifting on her feet. "Um, I might need one more second though, if you don't mind. Over there somewhere." She gestured into the dark tunnel beyond.

Ryziel looked at her, confused. "Why?"

She shifted again on her feet. "For privacy..."

Ryziel frowned then realization seemed to hit him. "Ah." He looked to the dark. "All right, but stay where you can see me."

"Will do."

Ryziel watched her as she started for the dark tunnel. When she looked back, he was still watching her. She cleared her throat, and he seemed to get the message. He looked away, pretending to turn back to his work. Smiling to herself, Aly turned the lights off on her suit and moved on a little farther into the dark around the bend of the tunnel, where she could hide but still see Ryziel from afar. She did her business quickly and started back to join Ryziel when something caught her eye.

From within a crevice not far above, a green gem glowed. Aly had never seen such a rock before and was curious what it might be. Thinking she could easily dislodge it from where it was and show it to Ryziel, she started to climb up the rock and stretched out her arm.

As her hand nearly clasped the shining gem, however, it seemed to pull away from her. Aly frowned in confusion then stretched for it again, but it once again evaded her.

Annoyed this time, she clicked on her suit lights and aimed those on her wrists toward the glowy green object.

A giant worm stared back at her, the gem, its eye. Aly gasped then yelped. She lost her footing on the rock and fell to the ground with a loud thunk, chunks of rock falling with her.

"Aly?" Ryziel called.

Aly coughed and waved away the dust that drifted up around her. The worm slithered back into its hole out the other side.

"What happened?" Ryziel was now beside her.

Aly picked herself up and brushed the dust off her suit. "I'm an idiot, that's what," she muttered with embarrassment. " I'm sorry, I guess I didn't learn my lesson the first time..."

There was a sudden shriek from close by. Aly froze, as did Ryziel.

It started as one, one very close by. Then another sounded farther in the distance. Then another, until there were several.

Ryziel eyes flashed through the dark. "*Keva*," he hissed. A word she didn't understand but was certain was a curse. "Get into one of the smaller holes and hide. Now."

Aly jumped and did as he ordered. She snuggled herself into one and crouched low. "What is it?" she cried as the shrieking grew louder.

"The nyghi," he growled, backing himself against the hole where she hid. "One must have been close enough to hear us. It's called to its pack."

Aly's body went cold. "Ryziel, come hide with me."

Ryziel didn't move.

"Please, you said yourself you could only take on one or two, but this sounds like a whole lot more than that."

Ryziel crouched beside the entrance where she hid and looked back at her. "Just stay here. Whatever you do, don't move." Ryziel went for his bag and rifled through it until he found what he was looking for.

It was a metal insect with a drill for a mouth. Aly had seen it many times before in the mines and fixed a few.

"What are you going to do with a drillbot?"

Ryziel clutched it tightly in his hand. "Distract."

Before she could say another word, he was gone, leaving her alone in the dark. Her heart pattered wildly in her chest, leaving her panting. Sweat dampened her neck, falling down her back. The screams continued on until they slowly faded, and the noise of a drill could be heard in the distance. Soon, the shrieks died off enough that Aly could hear the soft dripping of water nearby. She waited a little longer until she heard the scraping of something close by and the sound of footsteps.

Ryziel crouched down before her. "We need to go now," he said. Aly could hear the urgency in his voice and knew they weren't out of trouble. She scooted out of the hole then flinched when Ryziel grabbed hold of her wrist and pulled her up beside him. Before she could even process that he was touching her, he was taking her through the narrow passage out of the cave system, back into the larger part of the Keep.

"Our bags!" Aly hissed, almost tugging away.

"Leave them." Ryziel tugged her back, heading through the passage until they came out the other end. Holding her still, he pulled her quickly behind one of the giant pillars. His eyes flitted from one side of the chamber to another, as if he could see something she couldn't. "Keep your lights off, stay beside me no matter what."

Aly nodded, her body shaking. She couldn't see anything past the first row of pillars save for the area where dim blue light showed from the muirlemp. Everything else was just black shapes. She clamped her mouth shut, afraid that if one of the shapes were to move, she might scream.

Ryziel waited a moment longer then slowly led her out from behind the pillar. They went straight for the exit, until Ryziel halted suddenly and let out a sharp growl.

Out of the shadow of a great pillar, a creature appeared, barely visible in the natural light, but Aly saw enough to feel the blood drain out of her face. It stalked forward, its yellow eyes glowing at them, its lips pulled back to show long, curved teeth. Its head looked like a lizard with no scales or muscle, just bone with a thin layer of skin pulled tight over it. Around its neck and across its back were quills so dense they looked like black fur. The rest of it looked like the body of some kind of beast, like a lion or a wolf with razor-sharp talons and a long, whip-like tail. It hissed at them and a set of quills along its neck quivered.

Aly didn't need Ryziel to tell her what it was. She knew it must be the nyghi he had spoken of.

Ryziel brought her behind him and hissed back. The nyghi actually drew back, as if put-off by him at first, as if it could see Ryziel was not mere prey but a predator like itself. Still, it did not flee but instead elected to pace before them, blocking their way out.

"Get back, Aly," Ryziel said, releasing her. Aly obeyed right away, stepping back toward the pillar to give Ryziel space. Ryziel crouched down low, ready to strike as the nyghi started to circle him.

'He's going to be okay,' Aly thought as her back hit the pillar. 'He said one wouldn't be an issue. He will be okay.'

The nyghi went to strike, and Ryziel dodged, moving so quickly Aly barely saw it. The nyghi, however was quick also and moved to strike again. Ryziel dodged once more then struck out his fist, slamming it into the creature's face. The nyghi yelped and backed off, shaking its head. Ryziel went for it, ready to take it head-on, but he stopped suddenly and dashed to the side as another nyghi appeared from the dark.

Aly felt her muscles tighten as if ready to bolt. Ryziel slowly shifted back, his eyes never leaving the nyghi's.

"Ryziel," Aly whispered. One of the nyghi turned its head toward her, and she pressed herself closer to the pillar.

Ryziel slowly straightened, his head bowed, his shoulders rising and falling. He tilted his head toward her, his expression dark, his silver eyes flashing, alight with a violent fire.

"Go," he said in a guttural voice. "Run. Run and hide."

Aly shook her head, her eyes wide, panic rising deep in her. "I can't...I won't leave you."

"Do as I say." He looked away from her. "Wherever you go, don't come out. No matter what you hear. Stay where you are. I will come for you."

Aly didn't move.

"Did you not hear me, woman? Go. Now!"

The snap of his voice made Aly jump. Whimpering, she looked behind her, back into the darkness across the Keep. She wouldn't be able to get around them, so she would be forced to go farther into the Keep, into a place she had yet to see. She took one last look at Ryziel then took a deep breath and pushed herself away from the pillar. She flew down the great passage, a passage that seemed a mile long, and heard the first piercing cries of the nyghi behind her. She dared not look back, even when she heard the sounds of them fighting, heard the sounds of their shrieks and of Ryziel's roars.

CHAPTER NINETEEN

Ryziel's control of his Drega was slipping. Though he tried to contain it, with every bite and slash from the nyghi and every bone shattering hit he brought down on them in turn, he could feel the rage building. A primal, wild fury of power chipping away at his sense of self, bringing the beast to the surface. A mindless, violent creature that only ever saw three choices: Hunt, fight, and—since discovering Aly—breed.

Now it was looking for a fight, and if Ryziel let it go, he knew he would win. But at the risk that he would be caught in the hold of his Drega for some time, perhaps hours, before he would be able to come down. And, with Aly close by, that wasn't an option.

Unfortunately, the more the nyghi attacked, the more his Drega awakened. He knew if he didn't let it go, he very well might die.

That would have been all well and fine if it meant protecting Aly. But knowing that the chances of her making it back to the lair alone, with more nyghi close by and the threat of other monsters in the dark, was slim at best. No, he couldn't leave her. He could only pray that, if he did lose himself, he wouldn't find her. Because if he did, he didn't want to think about what he might do.

The nyghi struck, one from the back, another from the front. Ryziel dodged them both and swerved around to swipe at the one behind him, catching it in the eye. It barked and staggered back as blood gushed from its now open eye socket, shaking its head away. Ryziel went to strike again but he was pulled back by the second, its jaws crunching over his arm. He growled and twisted around to bash the creature in the middle of its skull. The creature dropped down, releasing him, and he took that moment to jump against its back, wrapping an arm around its throat. The nyghi bucked, but Ryziel held tight, not paying attention to the quills that were now piercing his chest and stomach. The searing pain swept up his torso like licks of fire. As his vision went in and out, Ryziel tightened his hold around the nyghi and gripped its upper jaw. The creature struggled, but as soon as Ryziel had a good hold on it, with a quick thrust, he snapped its neck. The nyghi dropped to the ground with a dull thud, and Ryziel backed away, breathing out in a guttural, bestial noise. His awareness was waning as the pain from the quills heightened. Ryziel shook his head, desperately trying to pull back his Drega. He pulled at the quills, dislodging some, allowing blood to trickle out from the wound. The upper half of his slipsuit was in shreds, but that didn't worry him. He squeezed his eyes shut and tried to take deep long breaths. Tried to bring himself back.

But as the remaining nyghi crept up behind him and swiped his talons along Ryziel's backside, tearing the skin, the last of Ryziel's control disappeared.

* * *

Aly ran until she came to the other side of the long passageway that was the Keep. Her legs burned, as did her lungs, but she dared not slow down. Only when she reached the back wall did she pause, searching every which way for a door or opening. She ran parallel to the wall until she found such a one, a door made of some strange dark metal. She pushed at it, but it was so heavy it barely moved. Only with all the strength she could muster was she able to squeeze herself past and enter the room beyond.

What she found, however, was no mere room. In fact, for one brief moment, she thought she had stepped outside somehow. Out into an open meadow under the night sky. As she gazed around in confused fascination, she realized it was not a meadow but a garden filled with bioluminescent plants, and the night sky was, in fact, a ceiling filled with glowing muirlemp.

She would have thought it breathtakingly beautiful if she had a moment to stroll around and study it, but, with every fiber telling her to hide, Aly rushed onward down a lighted path and followed it until she came to the very center of the garden.

From there, another obelisk-like rock sat with markings around its sides and a set of crystals at its top. Aly chose to hunker down behind it, crushing herself against its cold face. She turned off her lights and tried to calm her shaking limbs, to quiet her loud breathing. The shrieks and roars died away, leaving only the still silence around her.

She remained there for what felt like hours, watching and waiting, until she couldn't stand it any longer. Fear still gripped her, no longer for herself but for Ryziel. She turned restless and peeked out from the side of the stone monument, searching the dark for any signs of movement.

For one panic-driven second, she feared something bad had happened to Ryziel and that he wasn't coming for her. This terrifying thought almost pulled her away from the stone obelisk until she heard the door to the garden entrance open then slam shut.

Flinching, Aly drew back against the stone, trying to remain as still as the cold rock she hid behind. She pressed against it, her head turned to the side, hearing...nothing, nothing at all, but knowing something was in the garden with her.

She could run, but she knew the chances of outrunning anything were extremely low. Hiding seemed her only option, but she hadn't expected to find the large open chamber with few places to hide, the obelisk being the largest by far. Still, her eyes searched for anything,

anything that could aid her. A distraction of some sort. Or a weapon...

Her eyes fell over the ground and she saw broken pieces of crystal that had fallen off the top of the obelisk. Most were too big, some nearly as thick as her neck, but one shard in particular looked small enough for her to grip, and its blue end was sharp like a dagger.

As she heard a low growl behind her, Aly leapt for the crystal shard then twisted around, ready to stab it into whatever beast was coming to attack her. She raised her arms and started to swing but then she froze, her eyes widening, lips parting.

"Ryziel...?" she whispered. She lowered her hand, taking in his dark shape. He stood there before her, and another low growl vibrated in his throat.

"Ryziel," Aly repeated, but he did not respond. She could only see the dim outline of him, nothing else. Slowly, she pressed against her wrist, turned on her light, and cautiously aimed it at him.

The light hit his face and body, and Aly stumbled back a step, gasping.

The shape before her was indeed Ryziel. But he was different in every way. His body was bent, his face a snarling demon, his eyes, narrow slits, were bright with silver fire. Fangs bared, he hissed as the light passed over him.

Aly's heart leapt to her throat at the sight of him. She backed away, crystal now raised once more toward him.

"Ryziel, what's wrong?" Her voice quivered.

Ryziel didn't say a word. He followed her as she stumbled back. His eyes, though glaring down at her, didn't seem to see her. He looked feral, like one of the monsters that roamed the deep underground, ready to take her and turn her into a nice meal.

Her eyes, which hadn't left his own, fell down to his now bare chest, where the suit had been ripped open, leaving him naked from the waist up. There, she saw the quills stuck in his chest and the blood dripping down his stomach, staining his blue skin red.

"Oh, god," Aly said. "They got you." She cast her light down and saw the puddles of blood forming on the ground

Ryziel tilted his head, apparently completely unaware that he was bleeding out. He wasn't himself at all, and Aly was still frightened of him. But she was also frightened of what would happen if he didn't get help fast.

Trying to stifle her fear, she inhaled a deep breath and took a careful step forward. "It's okay," she said as calmly as she could. "It's okay, Ryziel."

She got two steps closer and started to slowly reach out her free hand toward him, but he let out a sharp hiss. Aly jumped but refused to back away. "Let me help you."

Before she could even touch him, Ryziel swiped at her, almost catching her hand. He fell to his knees and remained there, but he would not let Aly come near.

Desperate and uncertain what to do, Aly remained still, not daring to move any closer. He wouldn't let her touch him, but if she didn't stop the bleeding, he would pass out soon and likely die. And judging by his ragged breathing, she was running out of time.

Aly wiped away the sweat from her brow and looked at her techband. She had Nar and Xilya registered now into her techband's list of contacts. If she called one of them, they might be able to help.

Thinking Nar would be more readily available, she called him first.

"What is it?" Nar said, picking up.

"Nar," Aly's voice cracked. "Something bad has happened. I need your help."

"What happened?"

Aly told him everything. About the nyghi attacking and her having to run and hide and Ryziel finding her.

"Nihl's hide," Nar cursed under his breath. "How bad is he?"

"Really bad. And he won't let me near him. He won't speak, and he tried to attack me when I got close. He's not himself, Nar. It's like...he isn't even there. I don't understand. He's bleeding out fast too."

Nar was quiet for a moment then said, "He hasn't touched you, has he?"

Aly shook her head, though he couldn't see it. "No. But he's collapsed on the ground."

"All right. Are you near his pack at all?"

Aly frowned. "No, why?"

"Can you get to it?"

Aly looked over to the garden entrance. The pack was way back in the cave system where they worked. It wouldn't be impossible to get to, but there could still be more nyghi out there. She would be completely exposed.

"I...I think so, yes."

"Get to the pack. Inside should be a medical kit. When you have it and are back at Ryziel's side, I will direct you further."

"Got it." Aly dropped her arm. She looked back at Ryziel, reluctant to leave him but knowing she didn't have a choice. "It's going to be all right. I will be back."

Ryziel watched her as she cautiously went around him, making sure not to pass close enough where he might be able to grab her. When she was far enough away, she met his eyes one last time before shutting off her light and turning for the door.

* * *

Aly stuck to the wall, her hand gliding against it to guide her down the long passageway, pausing behind each pillar to check for any signs of movement. She saw nothing and heard nothing. But that didn't mean something wasn't there.

Trying to remain as quiet as possible, she crept down the way. The scent of something bitter and strong stung her nose—something like that of alcohol or citrus. The farther she got, the stronger the smell became, until she had to keep a hand over her mouth.

By the dim blue light of the muirlemp, she could see a set of large mounds scattered across the great hall. She dared not put her light on to see what they were, but they didn't move, so she figured them harmless.

When she got to the narrow passage, Aly carefully slipped back inside, trying her best not to make noise as she scraped along the rock. At the end of the passage, she paused and put on her light, directing it into the cave system beyond. Nothing waited inside, and she let out a breath of air, her body relaxing. She moved toward the end of the system till she found the packs, then lifted her techband.

"Nar, I found the packs."

"Good," he replied. "the medkit should be inside. It's a shiny metal case. Everything you will need should be inside. Don't be afraid to give him the bluym too."

Aly wasn't sure what that was but decided to ask later. She rifled through Ryziel's pack until she found the case Nar described. "Got it."

"Good. Now get back quickly."

"There's a bad smell outside the cave," Aly confessed. "Like...the smell of nuri."

"That would be nyghi blood. Stay clear of that."

Aly nodded and swallowed, her mouth suddenly feeling very dry. She grasped the handle of the kit in a tight grip then turned back to the narrow passage.

As she once again slipped back down the hall, using the wall as her guide, she looked to the mounds again across the way and realized they must be the bodies of the nyghi. Or at least parts of them. Her stomach dipped, and she covered her nose once again, afraid she might vomit. There was an echo of a cry in the distance, but Aly ignored it, refusing to stop even to check around.

When she got back to the garden door, she squeezed herself inside then waited for the door to close fully before turning her light back on. She made for the obelisk at break-neck speed then slowed considerably as she drew closer, directing her light around it until she saw Ryziel crouching behind it like she had been before he found her.

He still did not speak save to growl at her, exposing his fangs. The yard around the obelisk was covered in blood, but Aly kept still, easing to the ground to set the kit down. She raised her techband once more.

"I'm here," Aly whispered.

"All right, open the case," replied Nar.

Aly did so carefully. Inside, she found a number of tools, a thick, black bottle, a clear bottle filled with what looked like nothing but water, a small red bottle, several gauze-like tapes, and a cleaning rag.

"Do you see a tool that looks similar to a mender but with a flat laser at its head?" Nar asked.

Aly dropped her light down to get a better look and saw such a tool, one which reminded her of a scanner. "Yes," she said, picking it up.

"Take that, the clear bottle, and the salve in the black bottle. You will need to clean out the wounds first," Nar explained. "Pour the liquid from the clear bottle onto his wounds and wash the blood out. After that, you will use the tool then the salve."

Aly took the three items, along with the rag, and inched closer to Ryziel. His response was to hiss at her again, his body growing tight.

"It's okay, Ryziel, I'm going to help you." Aly slowly moved closer but was beginning to hesitate, afraid he might strike at her. Her fears were confirmed when he lunged toward her, almost catching her foot, causing Aly to jump and drop the black bottle.

The bottle hit the ground, cracking open like an egg, causing salve to spill out in thick globs onto the ground.

"Damn," Aly cursed and stepped back. "Nar, I can't get to him. He won't let me."

There was a short clicking sound from her techband. "Try the red bottle, then. If you can get him to swallow some of the bluym, he should calm down."

"Should?" Aly responded, unconvinced. She set down the other items then picked up the red bottle. "What is it?"

"Its liquid bluym. A drug. Helps with pain and calming the mind."

Aly squeezed the bottle then looked back at Ryziel, who was starting to remind her of a trapped tiger. His eyes glowed back at her with feral heat, and his mouth split wide. The image reminded her of something she thought she had seen before, perhaps in a dream, and it made her shiver.

She watched him for a moment, unsure how to proceed. If she got close, he would strike at her. But he didn't try to attack her otherwise. It might be because he was weakening.

She took a step toward him then stopped as she became aware of something. He was still able to move. He could come at her if he wanted but he didn't.

Aly thought about it a second longer then, before she lost her nerve, she uncapped the bottle and moved swiftly toward him.

She flinched as he struck out but forced herself not to draw back again. His hand caught her wrist in a near painful grip, but she didn't hesitate. She shot out toward his face with the bottle in her other hand and practically struck him with it, the rim of the bottle hitting his fang. Liquid splashed his face, dripping down his mouth. Ryziel whipped his head back and snarled. He didn't loosen his grip on her, but he did swing her around not so gently. He dipped his head forward and licked his lips. Though she knew it was only from tasting the bluym, it looked to her like he was licking his chops, ready to take a bite out of her. Aly whimpered but didn't move, watching him, wide-eyed. She dropped the now empty bottle and waited for the bluym to take affect or for Ryziel to strike.

Ryziel's grip didn't loosen. He was still for a moment, as if confused. He looked toward her and blinked. Aly brought up her free hand to do...she wasn't sure what, and he gripped that one too.

"It's me, Ryziel. I'm right here," Aly said as softly as she could without breaking. "I'm right here."

He licked his fangs, tasting the last remaining bluym. He

watched her carefully, his eyes locked to hers, then he pulled her closer.

Aly stiffened but dared not pull away. His savage face drew close to hers, but she dared not look anywhere but him. His head tilted slightly, his mouth turned downward. She felt his breath on her throat, and she shivered again.

He growled low then his mouth suddenly pressed against her neck. There was a slick heat as his tongue grazed her skin. Aly was too shocked to move.

"Hey, human, are you still there?" Nar's voice rang out. "What happened?"

Aly didn't speak. She lifted her head up and swallowed hard, but she dared not speak. Ryziel lapped her again then opened his mouth and let his fangs slide along the soft skin not covered by her suit.

'He's going to bite me,' she thought. But as horrifying as that might seem, she wasn't completely afraid. The way he moved on her wasn't like an animal who was ready to devour a meal. This hunger was different.

He pressed his teeth against her skin, but he did not break it. Aly winced as he let up then pulled away.

His grip loosened on her wrists and his body bent forward, his head coming to rest on her shoulder. Aly remained motionless for another minute before attempting to pull away, gently pulling out of his grip.

"I'm here," Aly said aloud. "I think he's starting to relax."

There was a hiss from her techband. "Thank Nihl," Nar said. Cautiously, Aly drew away, allowing Ryziel to remain bent forward. Quickly, she went for the medical tool, clear bottle, and rag and came back to kneel before him. She looked over the wounds, noticing the ones also on his back. She moved around to his backside and uncapped the clear bottle then, with careful precision, began to pour the contents onto his back.

She braced herself, thinking he could rear up and roar, but to her shock and relief, he did not. What she presumed was disinfectant did not sting or burn. Feeling more confident, she let the liquid trickle down his back until the blood was washed away and his wound clean.

"Now what do I do?" Aly asked Nar.

"Turn on the surgical tool and place it as close to the wounded skin as you can without touching."

Aly moved closer, her legs almost touching his. She went to place her hand on Ryziel's back but froze. Something told her it was best not to touch him if she could. She shifted around behind him instead, to get a better position, then turned on the scanner-like tool. Its yellow light sparked in the darkness, and it made a soft whirring sound as she brought it down onto Ryziel's back.

As best she could, Aly tried to keep it from touching him and was thankful when he didn't move. She watched in silent awe as the slashes along his back closed up, mending into new skin before her very eyes. She was sure he would react then, but he didn't, and she wondered if it was the bluym now taking full effect.

When she finished, Aly stepped back to assess any more damage and was satisfied the back of him was fixed. She eyed the salve on the ground, knowing she was probably supposed to smear it over the mended skin to keep it from scarring, but, again, she was reluctant to touch him. Instead, she rose and moved to Ryziel's front where, now seeing her kneeling before him, Ryziel straightened so he could gaze at her.

They locked eyes, and Aly could see he was still not all there, but at least he was calm, and that was enough for now. Once more, she took up the clear bottle and poured the liquid along his chest and stomach. There were still a set of quills stuck in his skin, but Aly hesitated to touch them. She worked on the open wounds first, cleaning then sealing the skin. When she was through, her eyes settled back on the quills poking out of his chest.

She looked up at him. "I have to get these." She gestured to the quills. She had no idea if he heard her or even understood what she was saying for he didn't move, his expression never changing. Aly lifted her hand and reached out.

When her fingers grasped the first quill, Ryziel's hand shot out and once again wrapped around her wrist. Aly froze, watching him carefully, then began to pull.

It was then he reacted but only with a soft hiss. Blood gushed out from the opened wound where the quill once stuck, but Aly ignored it and went for the next. Ryziel didn't let go of her wrist nor did he look away from her as she pulled each one out. When the last one unlatched from his skin, Aly did the same cleaning routine with her free hand and sealed the skin. When she was through, her body went limp, forcing her to sit. Ryziel didn't let go of her wrist right away but that was okay, she just needed to breathe.

"It's finished, Nar," Aly eventually said.

Another soft click from her techband. "Great. Now just wait a few hours, and he should come around."

Aly's round eyes shot down at her techband. "A few hours?" she breathed. "You can't be serious."

"I am. Also, you should probably get away from him now. It might be a while before he is stable."

Aly pursed her lips as her eyes flitted over to Ryziel's hand, still gripping hers, and how close his body was. "And if he never is?" Aly asked, almost in a shrill voice.

"He will be. The bluym should help a little. Also, I've messaged Xilya. She won't be able to get to you until after her shift. So better to just wait."

Aly wiped another bead of sweat from her forehead. This was absolutely insane. Who knew how safe they were even now, let alone in a few hours? But she wouldn't leave Ryziel, not for any reason.

"If anything else happens, let me know," Nar continued. "I will check in and make sure everything is all right. Just let him do his thing. Leave him alone, but don't go far from his sight."

Aly wasn't exactly sure what 'let him do his thing' meant, but she guessed it involved his recovery, seeing as he had lost a lot of blood.

"The salve jar broke," Aly said before Nar clicked off.

"That's unfortunate. He probably won't be too happy to find a bunch of scars marring his skin, but I guess it can't be helped."

Aly glanced at the marks forming on Ryziel's chest where the wounds had been. She frowned. "Why does he care?" She knew she sounded a little indifferent but she only meant it out of curiosity.

"Nillium with marks are seen as...well, to not put it so lightly—ugly or flawed. Ryziel gets enough shit from just being a darkborn nillium—an outcast amongst his kind and an omen to some. Scars would probably only hurt his ego even more. And since he's looking to return to Nihl and be accepted amongst his kind again...I'd say scars will only hurt that goal."

Aly's frowned deepened. With a guilty glance, her eyes fell on Ryziel's body. She didn't respond right away to Nar, and he took that as a sign to click off. Ryziel still gripped her wrist but when she pulled away, he reluctantly let her go. She stepped back over to the salve on the ground, still solid and usable to a degree. Aly scooped a small bit into her fingers then returned to kneel before Ryziel. He watched her with half-lidded eyes. When they finally did close and he began to breathe slow and steadily, Aly took her chance to reach out and touch the mended skin, spreading the salve gently below his shoulder.

She watched him with a sharp, nervous intensity, pausing in her effort to see how he would react. When he didn't move, she continued, her hand slipping to his chest then down to his stomach where she could feel the tightness of his muscles, his body hard as rock but his skin smooth and warm under her careful fingers. She traced along the mended skin then along the silver markings that weaved along the sides of his stomach. Heat rose in her face as she stared down at his torso, and guilt ripped at her again, this time for touching him like she did, even if it was to help. She drew her hand back and rose her eyes to his face, only to see him staring at her.

Aly licked her lips to say something—likely an apology, afraid that she might have offended him or angered him again. But before she could speak, Ryziel moved on her.

It was both slow and fast, all in one graceful movement. He had her lying on her back, his body flush against hers. Aly let out a little gasp as he brought her arms up over her head and pinned her wrists together with one large hand. He was like a giant on top of her, his body nearly crushing hers. She didn't move, however, or struggle under him. She was surprised but not alarmed; nervous but not entirely afraid. Her body turned hot quickly from his own warmth on top of her, from adrenaline still coursing through her veins, and from her own growing desire that she had kept reined in for so long.

"Ryziel," she breathed. Whether she meant to or not, she lifted her hips to move against him.

He was still for a long moment, though his chest vibrated with a low rumble. It was like he was on the edge of a knife waiting to tip over, but he remained unmoving, and Aly wished she could read his mind, if he were thinking anything at all.

When his free hand did move, it settled between her breasts then moved up to her throat, his thumb stroking her jaw.

Aly shivered unexpectedly. She had touched him, and he hadn't turned angry. He didn't snarl down at her or try to scare her. Instead, he was touching her like a lover.

A spark popped in her brain, a realization hitting her like a strike to the head.

He didn't hate her or her touch, he wanted it. But he had been fighting this desire—until now, and perhaps only because he was lost in himself.

Aly's heart, which had already been pounding heavily for some time, now felt like it might burst in her chest. She wanted to touch him again, but he held her wrists tight.

His eyes, which had been staring at her face, flicked down to her lips and then her throat. His hand moved back down till it touched at the collar of her slipsuit. He lingered there for a mere second before he gripped the edge of her suit and ripped it down with one violent tug. The suit—which was supposed to be durable against any element —tore in two down the middle, exposing her left shoulder and breast. She inhaled sharply as it ripped then again when Ryziel's mouth came down once more on her neck; his teeth nipped and his tongue trailed along her skin as he moved across her shoulder then downward until his fangs grazed her breast and nipple.

Aly moaned, her back arching, hips pressed against him. He moved in response, and she felt the hard length of him pressing against her belly. She felt all the heat in her body slip down between her thighs, and she writhed under him, trying to open her legs more in invitation.

All he needed was to peel the rest of her suit off along with his and take her, hard and fast and with wild desperation, and she would be undone. His hand began to take hold of the rest of her suit as if to do just that when he suddenly froze.

His mouth unlatched from her and his head snapped upward to release a sharp, furious hiss. Aly went still beneath him as his eyes went wild, searching the dark, his teeth bared at something unseen.

Breathless, Aly tried to shake her head clear. A loud rumble sounded nearby, low like thunder. She tensed, her head turning to the side as if she might have imagined it. There was silence until Ryziel growled low, and a few seconds later, the sound of thunder rang out again, closer.

"What is that?" Aly said, more to herself than to him.

Then, with no warning at all, she was being picked up and thrown over Ryziel's shoulder. Before she could even blink, they were racing away, farther into the garden.

"Ryziel? What's happening?" she tried to say but the breath was knocked out of her as he leaped through glowing bushes and budding plants. She was astounded that he could move so fast and carry her at the same time when only a moment before he had been mortally wounded.

She felt him slow as he approached the left wall of the garden then she both heard and felt the hard kick as his foot connected with another door, slamming it open. He slipped them through then made a sharp right, and Aly saw what looked like a courtyard beyond the shadows of dozens of pillars. Ryziel ran alongside this courtyard, never breaking speed. Aly lifted her head up as best she could and saw a soft blue light casting down from the roof above, illuminating the chamber and the balcony above. Ryziel turned again, taking them up a flight of stairs, and Aly wondered if he even knew where he was going or if he was just running as far away as he could get from whatever threat was close by. He continued on down the side of the courtyard, now along the second level, until he halted and climbed up the side of the wall. Aly could see a large broken statue crumbled to pieces below them. Ryziel climbed into the deep alcove where the statue once stood then brought her down from his shoulder, wrapping his arm around her tight. He swerved around, placing his back against the inner wall. Aly twisted her head and body around to see down into the courtyard. There was a bridge not far past where they hid, broken in half as if something had crashed through it. They waited, Ryziel as still as the statues around them, while Aly trembled, breathing hard, crushing herself against him.

The rumble of thunder came again, along with the sound of something slithering against the ground. Something massive. Aly dared not look but she knew whatever it was was making its way along the courtyard down below. As the sound quieted, she dared peek around and saw the tail end of a scaly back slide out a doorway into a chamber beyond.

When all was silent, Aly let out a slow, painful breath. As she looked up at Ryziel, he watched the courtyard below. Without letting her go, he brought them both down, seating himself back against the alcove as best he could. Aly didn't try to release herself from him. Instead, with a weary sigh, she let her head fall to his chest, uncaring that she got salve in her hair and on her face.

Several long moments passed, and the adrenaline that had been pumping through her body began to disappear, bringing on a deep, unavoidable exhaustion. With Ryziel's chest rising and falling below her and his arm safely around her, Aly began to drift away. As her eyes closed, she thought she heard a hiss of breath and a whisper of words with it saying, "I'm sorry."

CHAPTER TWENTY

ALY AWOKE IN THE DARK, HER EYES FLUTTERING OPEN AS A SOFT white light flickered and passed over her face. Confused, she blinked several times and lifted her head. Ryziel remained unmoving against her, his arm still around her waist even as he slept. He did not stir when the light passed by again, and Aly slowly turned her head to see the source of it.

It was hard to make out at first, but as Aly shifted around a little more to get a better view, she saw in the distance a blur of light moving across the other side, just across the second balcony opposite them. Aly's face twisted, her eyes squinting against the light, trying to make out what exactly it was.

With a short repetition of flashes, the light seemed to morph, no longer just an unidentifiable blob but into that of a woman. A tall, slender woman with a halo crown above her head and a flowing white gown.

Aly stared at the woman with a silent sort of fascination, too stunned to speak. The woman was more than beautiful, she was otherworldly, like a fairy queen or an angel. She walked with long fluid steps across the balcony, as if she merely glided with no real effort at all. Her slender face, which had been pointed forward, turned slightly in their direction, and Aly had to stifle a gasp.

Her eyes were pupil-less, white, shining. They stared at everything and nothing. And though they looked around, they didn't seem to see her.

Aly was thankful for it. As beautiful as this maiden was, there was something incredibly off about her. Something Aly couldn't explain but which gave her a sick feeling of dread. It was like the woman's light sucked in all else, making the darkness around her somehow even blacker, deeper. A giant shadow moved above the woman, following her; but for the life of her, Aly couldn't make out what it was, only that she had a sudden and terrible intuition that she should remain completely still and silent, not even daring to try and wake Ryziel.

The woman eventually passed and morphed once again into a blob of light before fading away into the darkness beyond. Aly remained staring into the dark, deeply astonished and disturbed by what she had seen. It occurred to her that there was no end to this strange, terrifying underground world, and, as enchanting as it could be, Aly longed more than ever to get on the ship and get as far away as she could and never look back.

* * *

He was in the First House. His father's house and his brother's house. But never his. It was night, and the lanterns were lit—hundreds of them, like little suns. His brother was there with him. They sat in his private chamber, one that stood beside his own. Korzien had demanded it and had somehow convinced his father to let Ryziel have the adjacent rooms, ones that were connected by two doors with a short antichamber and nothing more. He had always wanted Ryziel close to him, even as children. Perhaps Ryziel had thought in the beginning to be suspicious of it, some untrusting thought he had with anyone who tried to get too close; that they were looking to gain something from him and nothing more. But his brother seemed to prove time and again that wasn't the case. He alone had taken Ryziel under his careful guidance when no one else would. Not in fighting and killing—Ryziel's father had seen only to that—but in all other things, from diplomacy to social hierarchy to understanding the ways of court to pleasing a woman. Korzien alone made him understand, and Ryziel was never ungrateful. When Ryziel was under any sort of scrutiny, it was Korzien who defended him. When the young men of the First House—cousins—found him in the outer courtyard, looking to pick a fight, Korzien was by his side.

Many times, he stood by him, even took blame for him when he did wrong, and Ryziel—though not much for prayer—silently thanked Nihl for his brother.

He loved his brother. That was a fact. And for a long time, he firmly believed he could love no other. He pledged himself long ago to always be by his side and that he would one day return to give back all that Korzien had done for him. Because his brother was all that he had. He was everything.

But Korzien was not without his faults, though no nillium would admit to having them. He did what he liked and spoke what he thought, and few could argue with him. He believed firmly in a nillium's right to rule. To have firm dominance over all others. And Ryziel never argued this. For Korzien was the voice of what the nillium had always believed since the beginning. He preached it. And Ryziel never spoke against him nor ever voiced his doubts. Because, despite his differences and the rumors about his lineage, he was nillium, so to doubt one's own was unacceptable. Therefore, Ryziel simply let Korzien do and say what he wished and rarely did he ever refuse him. Except perhaps this night. One he wished he didn't have to relive, even in a dream.

They sat at Korzien's table in his private room, and his brother smiled over at Ryziel as he brought a cup to his lips then set it down gently. "Take your pick, Ryziel," he said smoothly.

Ryziel did not let his eyes drift over to the ground where the women knelt. He looked only at his brother. "It is...unseemly, if not forbidden, to bed servants," Ryziel said softly, his hands clenched in tight fists.

Korzien laughed low. "Ah, brother, let's not waste time arguing about such things. You and I both know many nillium of the upper houses take pleasure in those who serve them."

He did. His brother included. But it wasn't so much that as it was the thought of taking a random servant—one he was certain Korzien had forced to comply—to his bed and knowing they only laid with him because his brother had willed it. There would be no joy for either of them.

"You have nothing to fear," Korzien said. "You understand the workings enough."

"It's not that," Ryziel said.

Korzien leaned back, observing him carefully. "You want a nillium woman. And you could have one, but you've refused. Out of guilt or fear, you won't say, but I know you enough to know it is one of those. I only wish to give you this one gift. You deserve to know the pleasure of a woman. It is your right to know, Ryziel."

Ryziel almost laughed. "There are many things you claim I have the right to, Korzien, yet still, I remain closed from such things."

Korzien waved a hand, dismissing him. "Father is a jealous coward."

Ryziel did not respond to this. Only Korzien could say such a thing, in front of servants no less, and know he would never have to fear punishment. Ryziel, on the other hand, knew if he did choose a woman to take back to his rooms and such an occurrence was found out by his father, he would likely be whipped. He was made to be his father's assassin and silent servant and nothing more. Otherwise, he was supposed to remain a ghost—or shadow in his case—in his father's home.

"The night hour will end soon," Ryziel finally said. "Father will wonder where I am. He wants me to make a visit to Nihl Wronin at the Fifth House and his kin. I will likely have to take out their head servant for spying." He rose but did not leave right away.

Korzien tapped his fingers along the table and sighed. "One day, you will come around, Ryziel. And stop being so afraid." He picked up his cup and drank it down then stretched out his hand until a servant took the cup from him. "If anything, to be afraid to love is unseemly."

"Since when have you loved any woman?" Ryziel said.

Korzien hit him with a sly grin. "Oh, I have loved many. In fact, I am about to love these ones here since you will not."

It was then Ryziel finally looked at them. The women kneeling. Servants with their faces covered by hoods, all quiet with heads bowed.

As he walked away from his brother, the room began to dim.

"It is time you learned, Ryziel," his brother said behind him.

A light flashed out at him from a distance, beaming back and forth. The dream broke as the light hit his face, dissolving like smoke. His eyes opened, and he saw the light beaming across the opposite wall from where he hid. He closed his eyes again then opened them, watching the light dance across a balcony passage on the opposite end then cast down to a courtyard below. Coming around, he started to lift himself up when he felt something heavy on him. He looked down and became very still as he discovered Aly snug against him, her suit ripped down one side, her soft hair brushing over his shoulder. His arm was around her tight, and when his brain finally caught up to his senses, he realized they touched skin to skin and his Drega did not stir.

In shocked disbelief, he did not move at first, fearing he might still be dreaming. But then the light came back around, beaming in his face, and he saw it was attached to the shape of something. Something very real and stalking about below them.

A growl ripped from his throat before he even had a chance to assess what it was. His arm tightened around Aly, and he thought he heard her make a small noise, but he didn't cast his eyes down to look at her, only to watch the light aim up at them. There was then the sound of something clambering up the wall and that something poked its head up at them. Ryziel pulled Aly closer to him, baring his fangs at the unseen intruder, when the light turned off and he saw the something was actually a someone.

"Nihl Ryziel, you growl at me one more time, and I will take it as a challenge." Xilya's sharp face came into view as she pulled herself up the rest of the way to brace herself firmly before them.

Ryziel let out a hiss of breath, his muscles relaxing. Aly stirred against him, her face turning to Xilya.

"You came," she said as if not quite believing it.

"I said I would, didn't I?" Xilya began to lower herself, and Ryziel took that moment to unwrap his arm from Aly, letting her sit up from on top of him to slide to the edge of the alcove and let her feet dangle.

"Come on, come on," Xilya said, and Aly hesitantly dropped down with Xilya catching her and placing her on her feet. Ryziel waited then dropped beside them.

"Took you long enough," Ryziel said, rolling the ache out of his shoulders.

Xilya snorted. "I wouldn't even joke. If it weren't for Aly, I wouldn't have come at all."

"How did you know where to find us?"

"Nar locked onto your location and sent the map my way. Took me a little longer to find you once I got into the Keep, but I was able to trace your scent." Xilya brought up her techband and clicked it on. "Nar, I have them. We are returning now."

"Thank Nihl," came the urk's voice.

"You didn't see anything as you were coming in, did you?" Aly asked, fear still showing in her gaze.

Xilya shook her head. "Everything was still...perhaps a little too still. Which means we should move quickly."

Ryziel could agree to that. He reached out for Aly on instinct but then quickly drew back.

No. Just because he had somehow managed to restrain himself—or rather his Drega had kept from reacting—when he found her against him, didn't mean he had free reign to touch her. Memories of what happened after the nyghi attacked were a blurry, chaotic mess at best and, though he was more than relieved to see her unharmed—to see her looking at him without fear—something in the back of his mind told him a lot had happened and eventually those memories might resurface. His eyes fell down to the rip in her suit and a fire burned in him. Something told him he had done that. But as their eyes met, she did not look at him horrified or disgusted. Instead, her face turned red as she kept the suit up with one hand in order to not expose herself. He could ask her what he had done. But not here. Not now.

"Nihl Ryziel, when you're done staring, can we go?"

Ryziel forced his eyes away from Aly to look at Xilya, nodding his head. "Lead the way."

They made good time exiting the Keep, and, to their great relief, nothing appeared out of some place unseen to stop them. Ryziel agreed that the area seemed unnaturally quiet. No howls or cries in the distance, and even the muirlemp seemed dimmer than usual. When they came upon the corpses of the felled nyghi, the scent of blood still permeated the air, but surprisingly, there was little blood left to be seen. Even the bodies seemed thinner somehow...smaller, as if drained. Aly tried to study them but Ryziel refused to stop. She clung to his belt tight and kept up with him as best she could, though he drove her hard, keeping at a light run. He knew she was tired still from everything that happened, but he wouldn't dare slow or rest. Not yet.

"What about our packs?" Aly mentioned as they came to the first door of the Keep.

"We leave them for now," Ryziel said. "Best case, they will be there once I return. If not, they can be replaced from above."

Aly said nothing. She stuck close by him. He could hear her ragged breathing and felt her steps faltering, but still, he refused to stop.

They passed the bridge then the long passage after. When they got to the first set of stairs, Ryziel gave a quick pause. He looked at Aly again and saw sweat glistening on her brow. He knew forcing her upward without rest was unfair, but he didn't want to stop, only to return to the lair. They had been gone for a long time, and he had a feeling her shift in the mines had ended at least a couple hours ago. If he didn't get her back soon, enforcers might grow suspicious as to why a human was working overtime.

He thought for a moment, then made Aly release his belt.

He turned toward her and tied her gaze with his. "It's a long climb up. I should carry you."

She said nothing at first, her eyes averting from his. "I wouldn't want to make you uncomfortable."

She might, it was true, but damn if he cared at that moment. If he had somehow been able to keep himself from harming her while in the hold of his Drega, then, by Nihl, he could carry her and be just fine.

"Let me carry you, Aly."

She looked back at him with her round eyes. Then, slowly, a smile grew on her face. "Okay, thank you."

He stepped closer to her, their bodies almost touching, even then. He took a deep breath then scooped her up and brought her to him. He waited for a reaction and was both astounded and relieved when there was very little. His receptors did hum slightly, and there was a stirring in his lower belly, but his Drega merely lifted its head and nothing more. It did not rise up as quickly or as violently as before, and Ryziel was able to push it back down with ease. He tensed slightly when she put an arm around his neck, but he felt in control enough to continue on with her cradled to him.

He turned, ready to start up the stairs, when he noticed Xilya watching him. She gave him a curious stare, one that said, "Are you sure that's safe?" and his return glare was to answer, "It's fine." She nodded, turned from him, and continued on. Ryziel followed behind her.

With Aly in his arms, they climbed fast, able to make the travel in half the time. When they finally broke from the tunnel leading into the bottom of the mine, Ryziel told Xilya to go on ahead back to the lair and he would meet her there shortly. She went as asked, and Ryziel began moving in the opposite direction.

"Where are we going?" Aly asked.

Ryziel glanced down at her then straight ahead. "To the elevator."

"Oh." She sounded disappointed somehow, but Ryziel didn't ponder or ask why. She had to get back to the safety of the upper levels.

"If anyone asks," Ryziel said, "you fell and got caught on a rock and lost track of time."

"That...seems a little fantastical, don't you think?"

"If you play innocent and naïve, they will think it possible."

"Ah," Aly said. "Well, it's a good thing I'm a pro at that."

A smile curved his mouth. He quickened his pace until the lights of the elevator came into view. As he approached, he set Aly on her feet then waved his hand over the pad to call an elevator down.

"Well, that was one hell of an adventure." Aly laughed. "But I think I'm good for a little while."

"That won't happen again," Ryziel swore. He looked over to her, ready to ask her what exactly had happened, what he had done, when he froze, the heat draining from him.

Aly had lifted her hair back to expose her neck and there, across her bare shoulder where her suit was ripped, were the markings of bruises in the shape of teeth marks.

"And there goes another suit," Aly continued on, not noticing his sudden icy silence. "Damn if Braxin will give me another. Good thing I have one last spare. Otherwise—"

He grabbed her arm and pulled her to him. Before she could say a word or yank away, he gripped the cuff of her suit at the wrist and ripped it upward.

"Ryziel! What the hell are you...Oh."

He didn't hear her. Everything around him was black, and the only thing he saw was the bruises encircling her wrist.

She tried to pull away from him, but he refused to let her go.

"It's nothing," he thought he heard her say. "Ryziel, it's really nothing. My skin bruises like a peach, always has, it couldn't be helped."

Couldn't be helped...

Something new rose in him, a different sort of fury he had never felt before.

"You let me do this to you," he whispered. "You said nothing. You were just going to go back up and say nothing."

"I didn't even know, honestly. I mean, it's a little sore, sure, but it's nothing."

"It is!" he yelled. She drew back, looking suddenly afraid, and he chose then to release her. She staggered, wrapping her arms around herself. He turned from her, unable to look at her.

"Tell me," he said in a low voice. "Tell me what happened."

"Ryziel—"

"I want to know!"

Aly went quiet. She stayed that way for so long he almost turned around to face her and demand again, when she said, "You weren't yourself. You were badly wounded. I went back for the medical kit in your pack then used the tool inside to mend your wounds. You...you swiped at me, but you never struck me. When I got close enough, you grabbed my wrists as if you thought to keep me back, but you didn't. You let me help you. You just didn't know your own strength."

Ryziel closed his eyes, desperate to keep his anger under control, trying to ignore that she just told him she went back for the kit, back into the very hall where the nyghi had been roaming, just to save him.

"And your neck?" he asked.

Again, she was quiet for some time until she said, "I fixed your wounds, placed the salve on you, then..."

"Then?"

"You were on top of me," she confessed with a wavering breath. "You tore my suit then bit me."

Ryziel opened his eyes but couldn't find words.

"But it's all right. I know you weren't yourself. You didn't hurt me. You didn't even break the skin."

A memory was coming to him now, still slightly blurry but more discernible. Of Aly's face below him, flushed and breathless, not filled with fear but with an undeniable urgency.

"What happened after?" he growled, ignoring the sudden fire in his lower belly.

"Nothing. Something frightened you. There was a sound like thunder then you had me over your shoulder and running. We hid until Xilya found us."

"You swear that is all?"

"Yes!"

He closed his eyes again, rubbing them. To think he actually believed he could keep from harming her while under his Drega. To think what would have happened if something hadn't come and frightened him, hadn't stopped him.

And he could imagine. An ache grew in him as did his anger.

"Ryziel, I..."

"I want you to stay above," he said. "For now. I need you to stay away from me."

"No."

Shocked by her sudden refusal to obey, he finally looked back at her. "Yes."

"I don't want to."

"I don't care what you want."

She frowned. "I wasn't afraid, do you hear me? Sure, you could have attacked me or something, but you didn't. Ryziel..." She gazed into the darkness then looked back at him, her eyes bright. "Please, don't turn me away again."

They stared at each other until Ryziel heard the elevator door open behind him. "I don't have a choice," he said.

"Yes, you do. You just don't want to face what you're feeling."

"Oh? And what is that?"

Aly's face reddened but she didn't hesitate. "You ached to touch me back down there," she said softly. "When I touched you, I could see you wanted me too."

Ryziel clenched and unclenched his fists. "I wasn't myself. You said so yourself."

Aly crossed her arms. "Maybe you were more yourself than you know."

"You don't know what you're talking about."

"Then explain."

Ryziel turned his head away, his jaw clenched tight. "All nillium have a darkness in them. A beast they call their Drega." He looked back at her. "It is our primal half. Most control it with ease. Especially those with a meek nature. Only when greatly angered to violence or some other powerful emotion might one's Drega appear. When it does, for some, it is only a stirring, for others an all-consuming flame. Everyone is different."

"And you?" Aly asked.

"It is always there. It just slumbers."

Aly nodded. "I see. And you think it is separate from you?"

He had thought so. "Yes," he said uncertainly.

"Even though you saved me and protected me while supposedly under its sway?"

Ryziel didn't know what to say. She couldn't understand.

He turned from her again, keeping the door to the elevator open. "I need you to go."

"So that's it, then?"

"Yes."

He both heard and felt her step closer to him, felt her close to his back. "Fine. But I'm coming back down."

"No, you aren't," he hissed.

"I will have Xilya take me down, then. I want to finish my work."

His hand tightened on the door. "You will not go down there without me."

"Well, according to you, I'm not safe with you, so how else am I supposed to finish my work?"

"By not coming down at all!" he snapped.

"So, I'm to be punished because you got mad that *you* supposedly hurt me? Even though I said I was fine?"

He tilted his head over his shoulder. "No, it's more than that."

"How so?"

Ryziel growled. "It doesn't matter."

"I don't believe you."

Ryziel looked away. "You don't know what I'm capable of."

"Well, I have some clue based on what I just saw down below."

They were quiet for a long moment. He didn't move to force her into the car, but she didn't go willingly either.

"Ryziel, please." Her voice grew soft again. "I'm not afraid. I'm still here. I...I want to be with you."

His chest tightened. How those words should have brought him utter bliss. And on one half, they did. But on another, all he could think about was her marked skin and all the what-ifs.

No, she should stay away. And if she wouldn't do as he asked then...

Without warning, he felt her hand touch the middle of his lower back. His Drega lifted its head once more as fire licked his insides. With a sharp hiss, he swerved around, took hold of her, and backed her against the side of the elevator shaft.

"You think I want to be with you?" he said, his voice almost shaking. "You aren't even my own kind." He placed his hands to the side of her head and leaned in close. "You are beneath me." He watched her carefully, tilting his head slightly, his eyes drifting over her upturned, pale face. "I don't want you near me, human, do you get it? Whatever happened down there was a mistake. It meant nothing." His eyes met hers as his head tipped downward. "You mean nothing."

Before she could even respond, Ryziel straightened and turned away. He forced himself not to look back as he stalked away into the dark, leaving her.

CHAPTER TWENTY-ONE

ALY CURSED AS THE GENERATOR THREW SPARKS AT HER, blinding her for one headache-inducing second. She blinked and wiped at her eyes then shot up and placed her back against the cave wall. The generator smoked and sputtered, but she didn't return to fixing it. She watched it instead then slowly slid to the ground, bringing her knees to her chest.

Eight days, a little more than a week, since she'd heard anything from down below. She had hoped Ryziel would come up on the second or third day to take her back, maybe even to apologize, but by the fifth day, as she waited for him on the twentieth floor and he did not show, that hope started to die. By the sixth day, she stopped going to the twentieth floor all together.

She told herself that she wasn't upset by his words. That he didn't mean them, not really. But no matter how much she tried to make herself believe it, her heart told her otherwise. The ache never disappeared, and the tightness and nausea never lessened. Her mind wandered through dark thoughts, lost.

She didn't hate him—she didn't think she ever could. But when she was at her lowest, she wished she had never met him on that bridge. Wished she had just stayed away and kept with her team; with her own kind, who were the only ones she had left. She should have listened when they told her to stay away from the others.

But then she told herself if she hadn't met Ryziel, she never would have seen the ship, and that was their one chance home. And that's what mattered.

He might not come for her or let her help now, but she didn't think Ryziel would be so heartless as to go back on his word. They would still have their spot because he wouldn't leave them here after everything. She had to believe that.

And if that was the last time she saw him then so be it. She would say goodbye and they would never see each other again. Forever separated, galaxies apart.

Her lip quivered, and her hands tightened around her legs, but Aly refused to cry. Her crying days were over, left back on Earth with her estranged family.

She swallowed down her feelings and picked herself up. It began to rain again as she went back to the generator, the droplets hitting the metal with a hiss.

A few minutes later, after several more attempts to reconnect the generator's system, her techband went off. Heart jumping a little, she checked it and saw it was from Mark. He wanted to know if she was free after her shift.

Disappointment swelled in her as she went back to work, ignoring the message. Then her thoughts began to wander again, and her eyes drew back down to her techband.

She should see him and talk. She hadn't been engaging with the others enough lately and they noticed. And maybe what she really needed most was to talk to someone.

She lifted her band and responded back with a short reply then returned to the generator.

* * *

Mark was waiting for her by the end of a bridge that went across a small pool and waterfall on the fifth level. The water cascaded down into a deep, narrow chasm on one end, down into darkness. Mark leaned against the rail, looking down this chasm, when she approached.

"Hey." She gave him a smile, though it didn't meet her eyes, and he returned his own.

"Hey, Aly." He hugged her with one arm, and she, in turn, wrapped one around his backside. They sat down by the edge of the rail, and Mark took a small metal bottle out of his pack. "Care for a drink?"

Aly arched a brow at him. "Drink?"

He handed the bottle to her, and she took a careful sip. The bitter tang of the svas stung her throat, and she grimaced.

"Where did you get that?" she choked.

Mark laughed and took the bottle back. "Ethan and Davis have been going to Shadowpoint more. And started sneaking nuri and svas out with their canisters, hoarding it in their units." Mark rolled his eyes and took a swig.

"I thought you didn't drink?" she said, eyeing him curiously.

Mark shrugged. "A place like this will change a man."

Aly laughed for the first time in a while. "Yeah, I can attest to that."

They smiled at each other then sat quietly, drinking from the bottle and watching the water falling.

"Julian is going to talk to you soon, just so you know."

Aly looked over at him. "Oh? And why is that?"

He took another drag from the bottle then set it down between them. "He's noticed how distant you've seemed lately. You know the man can sense a troubled mind a mile away."

"Do I really look that troubled?"

Mark shrugged again. "Honestly, I'm sure we all do. But you've been the most positive one here until recently. And I guess seeing you looking so down has made us nervous. I mean, if the sunshine queen isn't smiling, something is definitely wrong."

Aly did smile then, but it was a sad one. "I just...this place is taking a toll on me."

His hand gripped hers, and Aly almost flinched. She stared down at his hand in hers, but she didn't pull away.

"You're not alone, Aly. Remember that."

'Then why do I feel like it?' she thought. Even though she knew she shouldn't, somehow, she felt more alone than ever.

"I...I just," Aly began. She looked straight at him and frowned. "What do you do when someone you've come to really care about turns from you? Or doesn't want you around them? How do you cope with that?"

Mark looked back at her with a confused frown. "This someone we know?"

Aly shook her head. "No. No, just hypothetical." He looked at her a little suspiciously but didn't pry. He looked down at the water, thinking.

"That's a good question," he said. "Obviously, it's not good to force yourself on them. If they need their space then that's what you should give them." He was quiet for a moment, staring at the water. "It's hard but...if you truly care about someone, you learn to let them be. Coping is all you can do. It means working on yourself, to be a better person so they can see that you can be separate from them and still care. That you could be there for them and it means nothing more than that. To be selfless for their sake." Mark let out a short laugh. "Or maybe I'm just talking out my ass."

Aly shook her head. "No. No, that's good, actually." She looked down at the water too. "I think you are right."

His hand tightened in hers then released it. "Maybe that's why I should tell you that I care about you. But I get that what happened on the ship between us was enough. I understand if you don't feel the same way."

Aly closed her eyes then opened them slowly. "I care about you, too. But as a friend."

She saw him nod. "I had a feeling," he said. "And you know what...it's okay. I'm glad to be just your friend."

Aly's throat suddenly tightened. She looked back at him, and for a brief second, wished she felt for him like he did for her. Truly wished it. Because that would make everything so much easier.

But no, she was in love with a man from another world. Who wouldn't even touch her.

She leaned in and hugged Mark, and he did the same.

They talked for a little while longer, until the rain started to fall harder.

"Let's get back before the rain gets worse," Mark said, starting to stand. He offered his hand, and she took it, standing up with him.

They walked together back to their hub. Before they reached the door that led into the hall attached to their units, Mark stopped her. "It's going to be okay, Aly," he said. "Whatever happens, it's going to all right." He leaned in and kissed her on the cheek. Aly didn't mind. She smiled back at him, thankful.

* * *

Ryziel watched the pair from the edge of a stairway. He'd waited several days to come above, only to check on Aly, just to make sure she was safe. Or so he told himself. He'd been working harder than ever within the Keep, the last few days spent working through the night and rarely even returning to the lair. If anything crossed his path between the Keep and home, he made sure they regretted it. With the scent of nyghi blood still permeating the air and with him stalking the Keep in a dark mood, most living things stayed far away. Xilya came down many times with him but never stayed for more than her shift.

After he returned, he barely spoke. Not even to Nar. He went to his room and tried to meditate, and when he couldn't do that, he worked on the ship. Neither Xilya nor Nar said a word, though they knew something had happened and that it had affected him in some way. Even Xilya knew it was best to let him be.

When the fifth day had come since Aly left, he began to grow restless. But it only made him work more. It wasn't until Nar found him sleeping on top of the ship that he told Ryziel he should take a break. Ryziel did but only to go stalking through the caves at the bottom of the mine. Climbing down stairways and passing through tunnels, not thinking where he was going, just moving. Eventually, his travels brought him to discover a sluth nest. He destroyed it and a few of the stragglers, tearing his way through it until there was nothing left.

On the seventh day, a report went out on the forum that another body had been found. Nar had a mind to ask an urk cousin if there was any similar trouble in the dens, to which he replied back that there wasn't but that there were rumors going around as to what it might be. This was the final tipping point for Ryziel, and so, on the eighth day, he went looking for Aly.

And he found her with another human. The one that he had first thought to be her mate but had quickly discarded the notion when he saw how little time they spent together and how her attention had been focused elsewhere. Still, seeing the man touch his mouth to her again didn't make him feel any better. Because, though they might not be mates, the intimate gesture could mean they were courting. And that *definitely* didn't make him feel better.

But she wasn't his. Though his brother might tell him otherwise, he couldn't make her his. Because he was a cold-hearted bastard, and if he tried to stop her from being with another, after everything he had said to her, then he was a selfish one too. It wasn't fair to her, and he knew it.

So, though his Drega trembled, wanting him to rush forward and clock the man out of the way for touching her, the part of him he could still control said to just back away and be thankful she was safe. Even if leaving hurt.

He made his way silently back down, his mind like the storm clouds high above, when his techband went off. He stilled on the stair and saw it was Nar.

"What is it?" he answered, not too nicely.

"Nihl's hide, Ryziel, get back down here quick." The urk sounded breathless, excited. "Xilya is coming too. You both need to see this."

"What is it?" he repeated.

"Ionx," Nar said. "We've found it."

CHAPTER TWENTY-TWO

Ryziel entered the lair and saw Xilya already there, talking with Nar beside the console.

"Where?" he said, his heart still racing after flying down the stairs. Xilya moved to the side so Ryziel could see the map.

"Below Yurza's Keep. Literally right below it, in fact," Nar said. He pointed at the map below the area of the Keep, where tight clusters of yellow dots showed bright. And not just yellow clusters but blue and green ones also. All the minerals they would need, ready for the taking.

Ryziel stared at them with a tight frown. "That's...impossible. We've looked all through and around that area. How could we have missed this?"

"The tracer somehow missed a hidden passage here." Nar pointed at a section just past a tunnel, where a narrow opening could be seen. "It was well-hidden too. If the tracer didn't pick it up the first or second time, something must have been blocking it."

"And whatever was blocking it," Xilya continued, "wasn't doing so when the tracer was searching for a third time."

Ryziel glanced at them both and then back at the map. "Are you saying you think someone or something is intentionally keeping it hidden?"

"That's exactly what I think," Nar said. "In fact, if you notice how the minerals are clustered in a pattern, not scattered like the others were, that shows us that they aren't just sitting in the rock like that naturally. They are being stocked."

"Stocked." Ryziel's eyes narrowed. "As in..."

"Someone or something is hoarding them," Xilya said.

They each studied the map, not speaking as their minds turned over this alarming piece of information.

"Whatever it is, it's smart," Nar stated, breaking the silence. "Real smart."

"It can't be any of the miners, could it?" Xilya asked.

Ryziel crossed his arms. "No, they likely wouldn't have survived long enough to hoard that much, and we certainly would have seen someone or at least traces of someone by now."

"How about one of your kind, Nar?"

Nar shook his head. "No way. I might be out of the dens, but even I would have heard about it. And that would have taken a lot of urks. No way that would have been kept secret, and they wouldn't go hoarding it away from the dens, especially so far from them."

Ryziel stared at the map, thinking. "Then it is something from the Keep or far below. Something that has been down there for a long time."

"Great," Nar said.

"Your people have tales of older things in the deep, correct?" Xilya asked Nar. "Since the time of the ancients?"

Nar rubbed at the bridge of his nose. "There are always tales or rumors of things. But that's all they have been."

"Doesn't mean one of them couldn't be true."

"I'd prefer if they stayed untrue," Nar said.

"Xilya, didn't you say that the rainwater would eventually flood the whole area?" Ryziel asked.

"Yes," she answered. "And that part should be no different."

"So, that means when it floods, this hoarder shouldn't be able to get to the minerals."

"Not unless they can breathe underwater," she said.

Ryziel and Xilya looked over at Nar, who stared back at them. "I mean, there are, like, dozens of species that could breathe in both air and water and just as many that can hold their breath for days," Nar said, throwing up his hands. "But I'm fairly certain none of them are smart enough to do this." He waved a hand at the mineral clusters.

"The tales of things below," Xilya said to Nar, "do your kind have written claims about them? Or are they only through word of mouth?"

"If there are written stories," Nar said. "They would probably be in the urken archives."

"Do you have access to them?"

"No, but I can," he said confidently. He swiped the holographic image of the map aside and brought up a set of data written in the urken language. "They've been serializing everything digitally since one of the libraries got destroyed by a cave-in. Shouldn't take more than a few minutes to crack into it."

"Good," Ryziel said. "Once you have access, start looking for all mentions of myths involving water-based creatures."

"Got it," Nar said, continuing to sift through an urken database.

Ryziel brought his gaze over to Xilya. "You and I are going to go investigate."

Xilya bowed her head to him. "Do you think it wise to go near there before we know what we are dealing with?"

Ryziel left the console and started for the opposite side of the chamber, where a metal shelf sat. "We won't be going in yet, obviously," he called back to her. He took up a green orb from the shelf and returned to where the vrisha female stood. "We will use a nighteye." He held it out to her, and she took it carefully. "We will get close then send it in and have a look around."

Xilya turned the orb in her hand. "Not a bad plan." She offered it back to him, and he took it. "When do we leave?"

"Right now," Ryziel said, turning away again to place the nighteye in his pack.

* * *

They stayed down below for several hours, half the time traveling then sneaking their way over to the passage leading to the hidden chamber, the other time waiting as the nighteye took a full image of the room. When it was finished, they didn't stick around long to wait for anything to return. They quickly made their way back to the lair before half the night was through.

As soon as they returned, they uploaded the image feed to the console. As it played, they watched carefully, their faces twisting more and more into hard-set frowns.

"That's a lot of holes," Nar said flatly. "Tight ones."

Xilya slapped him lightly across the head. "Don't be crude."

Nar rubbed the back of his head, giving her a venomous look. "I wasn't," he snapped.

They watched as the nighteye circled around the chamber, showing an elevated view of a room punctured with small holes similar to those in the cave system where they had originally been harvesting. Only, these holes were even smaller and set in what were clearly rows, confirming that something had made them.

"Every single one is filled with minerals, all the way to the back," Ryziel said. He rubbed at his face. "Made to be hard to get into."

"What could this thing need with all these minerals anyway?" Xilya asked, glaring at the image. "It can't possibly use or need them for anything."

"Your guess is as good as mine," Nar said as he tapped at the console and brought up the urken archives on a separate screen. "But I've found a few possible culprits." He tapped the console again and brought up about five or so entries. "I've ruled out a couple, since they are more of the 'swimmer only' variety, as this thing clearly walks as well as swims. That leaves these few, and I'll tell you right now—none of them are nice and fluffy. I'll read deeper into each and see if one fits with what we are dealing with. "

"Good. I will start organizing supplies for each of us." Ryziel backed away from the console and started to head for the supply cabinets.

"Hold, Nihl Ryziel. I think we should discuss a plan of attack first." Xilya spoke as she gestured toward the screen. "After all, it could very well be trapped."

Ryziel paused to think on this. "Very well," he said. "Tell me what you have in mind."

Xilya left Nar to read over the entries, moving to Ryziel's side. "Firstly, I think if we are dealing with something extremely advanced and just as equally nasty it would probably be good to at least have a backup plan, rather than just sneaking inside and hoping for the best."

"Sound theory," Ryziel said.

"So, we should prepare both for a distraction for the best case scenario and to arm ourselves for the worst."

"Arm ourselves?" Ryziel tilted his head. "I didn't think you were one for the use of weapons. If we had any..."

Xilya shook her head. "It is not so much weapons but more something that could really do a great deal of damage to a creature without us having to necessarily fight it. Because I think both you and I can agree that we don't need another incident like what happened with the nyghi—"

Ryziel looked away as his face twisted, trying not to think about it.

"And I cannot say I could necessarily fight it on my own." Xilya bowed her head, moving a little closer to him. "So, we use something that not only could keep it away but could also get us out in case it trapped us."

Ryziel's eyes flicked back to her, his mind working as he stared at her. "You want to use bombs?"

He guessed correctly as she nodded her head once. "Like the very ones used to break into this chamber."

Ryziel cast his eyes back to the area of supplies, where he knew a few bombs still sat, left over from when they had been breaking through chunks of cave wall to find the ship. "It would be loud...it could draw others."

"It could, but I don't think it will," Xilya stated. "Did you see any hint of life or sense movement as we neared that hidden den?"

Ryziel shook his head. "None."

"Because the things below know not to go near. They know something lurks there that would keep them far away. They will not come." Her eyes narrowed at him. "The bombs could be our protection and distraction."

"We would have to be careful how we use them, though," Ryziel said, rubbing his jaw. "We don't want to spur a cave-in."

"True, we would need to be careful. Keep the charges low. Don't use them unless absolutely dire."

"I will gather flashers as well. Though they draw some creatures to them, they might help depending on what we are dealing with," Ryziel said, still eyeing the supplies, thinking.

"Good." Xilya shifted her tail around and that seemed to be the end of their planning as she started for the door. "Ready the supplies, then. I will go above and get Aly."

Ryziel jerked his head around at her. "What?"

"I will bring her down so that she can be ready to go with us."

Ryziel choked down a snarl. "You will not. She is not going to be a part of this."

Xilya gave him an unhidden look of exasperation as she turned on him. "Must we argue this again? How many times do I have to tell it to you for it to sink in? We can't fit in those small spaces. We need someone who can."

"Nar will—"

"Nar will come this time, yes, as we won't be making a second trip if we can help it and need all the help we can get. *All* the help we can get." Xilya pointed at him, but Ryziel continued to shake his head.

"She can't come. It's too dangerous," he growled, turning from her, not wanting her to see his panicked expression. But she was right, of course; in all logical sense, they needed Aly again, no matter how much he didn't want to see it.

Xilya snorted. "So was taking her down to the Keep. But she went and she survived. We need to gather as much of what we can get in this hidden room and, hopefully, do it without disturbing anything. If we can do that, it will be no different than what she has dealt with before." Ryziel didn't speak, his mouth drawn thin. "And if it bothers you to have her close to you, then you needn't worry, I will guard her while you protect Nar."

Ryziel scowled, beginning to pace. "We have no idea what we are dealing with. I won't put her life in jeopardy again. I won't."

"Guys..." came Nar's voice, like a soft noise in the background, barely discernible.

"She has every right to be here, as much as us. We all risk something. And if I'm not mistaken by Nar's story, she had to do a great deal by herself when you were in your beast's hold."

"Guys," came Nar's voice, a little louder.

Ryziel growled low. "That won't happen again. And you sound so sure we will get in and out fine, but if you are wrong and something happens..."

"If it makes you feel better, I will protect her with my life. How about that?"

"And what if we're wrong? What if it isn't just one thing?" Ryziel swung his arm toward the console. "What if it is many things? How will we be able to—"

"It isn't!" Nar said, almost yelling.

The two went silent but didn't look away from each other.

"What do you mean?" Xilya spoke first.

"It isn't many things. It's definitely one thing," Nar said, swinging around in his high chair. "It's her."

Ryziel looked over, as did Xilya, and they saw that Nar's face was ashen.

"It's her," he repeated softly.

CHAPTER TWENTY-THREE

Aly was working on the repair of another drillbot when Julian suddenly appeared out of the elevator and stepped over to her platform. The rain was just a light mist, a dazzling gleam of particles against the harsh light of the castors. It reminded Aly of the first night she had met Ryziel, and it had put her into a sour mood. When she saw Julian, her mood lifted slightly but only enough to greet him with a weak smile.

"Mind if we talk?" he said as he approached, gesturing for her to stand. Aly did, wiping her damp hands on her suit. She followed him over to the opposite side of the platform, near the rock wall and out of the way of others, knowing that this 'talk' must be the one Mark had warned her about.

"I thought you'd be working," Aly said as they stopped at the edge of the platform.

He leaned forward against the rail, looking down into the abyss. "They decided to let us off early." He shrugged. "So, I thought to find you."

Aly raised her brows at him. "They...let you get off early?"

He glanced back at her, and the side of his mouth curved up in a slanted smile. "No. A joke. I slipped away. I have no warnings this month, so I can afford to be a little rebellious. Just like someone I know." He bumped her arm with his, and Aly chuckled.

They looked over the edge and were silent for a long moment before Julian elected to speak again. "Did I ever tell you that me and Kate had been stationed on Freya for a few months before joining the Grayhart mission?"

Aly looked over at him curiously. "The civilian world? Why?"

He stared around until his eyes met hers. "We were thinking of settling down there, to try to start a family. It's a lovely place, really, the terraforming done a lot smoother than others." His eyes fell from hers. "But then we were called to join the mission, so we put our plans off. After all, who would say no to the chance to go looking for alien worlds? To study them? It's like every sci-fi nerd's dream. Too bad they don't tell you it's not like the movies, eh?"

Aly smiled but said nothing. 'Some of it can be,' she thought. 'And that makes it even stranger.'

"So, me and Kate talked it over, and we think that this whole exploring thing might not be for us. And that's okay. Just because it is a chance of a lifetime doesn't mean you have to take it."

Aly's brows furrowed as she watched him, watched his mouth turn up into a smile though his eyes were dark with some deep emotion.

"So, if we do ever make it out, we are going to go back and start that family. 'Cause that can be an adventure in itself. Maybe not to all but it can be. And it is enough for us." He looked back at her again, his smile fading a little. "I know your home life is bad, Aly, but you don't have to be alone. If you wanted to join us, you could."

Aly's eyes widened at this sudden offer. "You would...let me stay with you?"

Julian placed a hand on her shoulder, and the touch was welcome as she was desperate to have it. Even just from a friend.

"Family can be made anywhere. That's at least one sure thing in this universe. And my crew is my family. You are welcome to join us. And, you know we are always here to talk. When we come out of this, as I'd like to believe we will, we will go home together." He squeezed her shoulder. "Whatever is on your mind, whatever is bothering you, you will come and talk. Me and Kate will always listen."

Aly felt her throat tighten. She nodded her head but couldn't seem to form words except for a quiet, "Thank you".

He smiled and patted her back. "I better get back to work, but we will see you at the next meeting." He started back for the elevator then turned. "Don't be late." He winked and left.

Aly watched him go, her hand splayed across her neck. She had a place to go now if she ever went home, something she'd always wanted. She should be happy, but...

Her eyes fell across the entrance to a stairway just across the other end of the platform, and she froze. A figure stood watching her. A very big red and purple devil.

Xilya waved her over, and Aly didn't hesitate. Once she got to the entrance, she opened her mouth, but Xilya spoke first. "You're needed below again."

Aly licked her lips. "He...needs me?"

Xilya's eyes sparked with amusement. "We all do. Come."

* * *

Xilya fiddled with Aly's techband, messing with the code of the tracer program, before they made their way downward, telling Aly she would explain when they were below. They took the stairs for two levels until they found an empty elevator and took it the rest of the way down. As they stood silently while each level passed, Aly glanced over at the vrisha female, wringing her hands as if to keep them warm. Her eyes lingered, tracing the pattern of Xilya's hard-edged scales along her neck.

She'd never really been alone with the alien before, and she began to realize she'd never really talked to her about anything, either. At least nothing important. Nothing about home and all that had happened. And she wondered how much Xilya knew. Perhaps nothing. Or maybe she'd left after. But then Aly thought that couldn't be. She was sure the alien would have acknowledged Aly's race when they first met if she had.

"Am I making you nervous?" Xilya said, shifting toward her.

Aly smiled. "Only a little."

Xilya grunted. "It is expected. Most are put off by my kind." She flicked her dagger-tipped tail, hitting the back of the elevator, leaving a thin black mark. "I can't imagine why."

Aly chuckled nervously. "You are intimidating up close."

"As opposed to far away?" Xilya huffed. There was a glint of amusement in her eyes as her mouth widened. Her eyes traveled down Aly's body, studying her carefully. "It is funny, though... most who I encounter usually have the same reaction—an instinctual drive to run or cower and maybe piss their pants."

Aly shifted on her feet, her eyes falling to the floor. "I'm sorry they judge you like that."

Xilya shrugged. "I am used to it. And really, it's hard to blame them." Her eyes shifted over Aly again, now curious. "You didn't react that way, though, did you? When we first met."

Aly bit her bottom lip and forced herself to meet the woman's eyes. "I guess I didn't."

Xilya's deep red eyes narrowed at her. "I thought it rather ironic. As soft and small as you are, to not be so completely afraid."

Aly didn't know what to say. She swallowed hard as her throat turned dry. She should come out with it but was suddenly afraid the vrisha might not believe her and be upset. She didn't know why she thought that, but it made her hesitate all the same.

Still, though, Xilya's eyes did not move from hers. "Maybe I should do an experiment sometime and see how the other humans react," she said thoughtfully. " See if it is a species trait, to not feel fear of something that looks like it would prey on them...or maybe it is just you?"

Aly had to look away then, knowing she couldn't keep it a secret, especially if Xilya was being serious. She stayed quiet a moment longer before saying, "I...we know about you."

"You...know about me?"

Aly looked back at her and nodded grimly. Xilya tilted her head. "And what, exactly, do you know?"

"My kind and yours have met before."

From what little expression Aly could gather, this confession did surprise her. Xilya blinked once then turned her body completely toward her, making Aly do the same.

"How?" she said.

Aly let out a deep breath and brushed her fingers through her hair, wondering where to even begin. She thought maybe first she should start with a question of her own, to gauge how much to tell Xilya. "How long have you been on Lethe Maws?"

Xilya was taken aback by the question but thought it over and said, "If I can remember...about five years by Lethe's cycle, give or take. I arrived a year after Nihl Ryziel."

This time, it was Aly's turn to be taken aback. She had never thought to ask how long Ryziel had been on Lethe, and she wondered for a brief second how long it had taken them to find the ship and how long they had been trying to rebuild it. She was curious to know now that they were so close to finishing but instead asked, "And how long have you been away from home since coming here?"

Xilya thought it over again then said, "Three years."

So, she'd arrived on Lethe a little after everything had occurred. Or ended, as it were. Aly thought over her words then told Xilya what she knew. "One of your own got captured by my kind."

Xilya's eyes widened at her in what Aly could only assume was a dumbstruck expression, then she burst out laughing. A chittering, hissing laughter.

"It's true!" Aly said. "But he did it on purpose."

Xilya fell silent and frowned, scratching at the scales underneath the collar of her suit. "What was his name?"

"Xerus."

She went still. When she said nothing, Aly took the moment to explain. She told Xilya everything she could remember, everything that she heard from the news sources that had kept up with what had happened on the Lazris base, and the eyewitnesses who had survived to tell their tale. By the time she was finished, they were at the bottom, heading toward the lair.

She waited for Xilya to say something as they walked, Aly holding onto the woman's belt like she would with Ryziel. Xilya was very quiet for most of the walk until she finally said, "So it is over, then. The war."

"Yes," Aly said, though it hadn't been a question.

"And this woman, this Dr. Hart, she was taken to Tryth?"

"That is what they claim," Aly said. She didn't tell her that Dr. Hart had left all her records saved in a cloud file for them to find, information about the vrisha and their planet. But not its location.

Xilya was quiet a moment longer until she whispered, "Thank *Veradis* and *Rikasha*...it was not all lost, though I had failed my mission." She let out a deep sigh. "Now more than ever, I must return."

Aly nodded. "After all that had happened, there were a lot of changes with military control. A new program was started, the Grayhart project, a mission to find other civilizations for non-violent and scientific purposes." She looked up at Xilya, at the outline of her in the vast dark. "We had hoped to find Tryth and re-establish contact."

Xilya slowed and twisted her head down to look at her. "I wager you hadn't expected to 're-establish contact' here of all places. My, what a small universe."

Aly smiled up at her. "Yeah, I guess it is." They kept walking, and Aly felt a sense of accomplishment. She let out a little laugh. "If you see Dr. Hart when you go home, tell her we said hey."

* * *

The doors to the lair opened, and Xilya stepped inside with Aly right behind her. Nar was at the console, looking up at the screen, but he swiveled around to greet them. Aly smiled and waved hello, and Nar grunted in response. He seemed paler to her, wearier. It was only him she saw at first in the chamber. She looked around, over the ship and along the cave sides to the packs sitting by the grated table, searching, her heart thumping a little faster in her chest.

"Everything is ready to go," Nar said flatly. "The packs, anyway. I can't say the same for myself."

Xilya made a clicking noise. "I'm sure it won't be as bad as you think."

"Yes, it will."

"Where are we going?" Aly asked as she stopped in her search, with growing disappointment, and looked back at them and the console.

The two didn't speak at first, and Nar turned back in his chair. "You fill her in."

"Very well," Xilya said. She gestured for Aly to follow her and stand beside the console opposite where Nar sat. She brought up a map, which Aly looked down on. It had clusters of colors, yellow being the most prominent. The area was not unlike the one they had been working in before, only more enclosed, with one noticeable entrance. "We have discovered a new room filled with every mineral we could possibly need including,"—she pointed at one of the yellow clusters—"ionx."

Aly's eyes widened, her mouth gaping open slightly as she stared at the map. "That's all ionx?" she breathed with astonishment.

"Yes, as well as a few clusters of tython and byril, enough to finish the ship I imagine."

Aly could scarcely believe it. All her time on Lethe Maws, she had been told (mainly by Braxin) how precious ionx was and how incredibly rare. A miner was lucky to find maybe one every other season. And here, before her, was a map that showed a whole chamber filled with it. Enough for billions of credits. Enough for a miner to be wealthier than some of the richest silions in Xolis. Probably even some—if not most—of the nillium too.

"How?" was all Aly could seem to say.

Xilya was quiet for so long, Aly eventually had to look up at her. She caught the vrisha looking over at the urk, who wouldn't meet her gaze.

"What is it?" Aly asked, intrigued but uncertain.

Xilya scratched at the side of her neck. "It is...not a natural occurrence that these minerals are here." Nar made a sound, and Xilya fixed him with a fiery glare before looking back at Aly. "Something has placed them there on purpose."

Aly frowned, her mind taking that information in to slowly work through it. "Something...?"

"A slight inconvenience."

Nar shot his head around at them with an alarmed expression. "Slight inconvenience?" He nearly choked. "A *slight* inconvenience." He let out a laugh. One that was clearly meant for how absurd he thought her comment was and not because it was funny. "I don't know what your kind considers a slight inconvenience, but *Coria* is no such thing."

"Fine." Xilya waved her hand indifferently. "Perhaps, then, she is a respectable foe, at best."

Nar rubbed a hand over his face. "You vrisha would think that. But I'm telling you we should just forget this whole thing."

"That isn't going to happen because this is our one chance."

Aly listened and watched them bicker before raising her hand. "Um, sorry, but who is Coria?"

Nar stopped his arguing with Xilya to look straight at her. "A wicked she-beast, that's what. An ancient, nasty, monstrous, fiendish—"

"We get it, Nar," Xilya interrupted. "She's an old creature from the deep," she explained to Aly. "Possibly around when the Keep still held its people."

Aly's brows furrowed as she looked back at the map. "And she is just...hoarding these minerals?"

"As it would seem."

"Why?"

"Possibly for her own selfish purposes," Nar said, bringing up a page of texts on the screen. "But also, to lure."

Aly didn't like the sound of that. "To lure what?" she asked nervously.

His look told her all she needed to know. "The urken texts say she would use several methods to trick victims into following her somewhere far and unseen. They say she would usually disguise herself in some way as something one would trust, but if that didn't work, she would use objects of temptation depending on what might work best, such as jewels, crystals—"

"Minerals," Aly blurted.

"Exactly," said Nar. "She lures her victims then feeds from them, draining them of all blood then discarding the husk of a body."

Aly felt her own blood draining from her face. "Those miners...you think?"

Nar nodded grimly. "The texts mention that, after the fall of Yurza and her Keep, the she-beast went into slumber. Even when the rains came and flooded the chambers, she would not waken, which meant she could keep breath underwater." The urk closed out the text and turned his chair around. "But all signs say she's awake now, and she is feeding."

Aly felt a chill run through her then jumped a little when Xilya placed a hand on her shoulder. "It won't be so bad, you'll see," she said confidently.

Aly looked up at her, wondering if Nar was right, that she might be a bit delusional. "And how, exactly, do we plan to get inside and grab all these minerals without her noticing?"

"Simple, we—ah, Nihl Ryziel, there you are."

Aly twisted her head around and her eyes immediately locked with Ryziel's. Her heart fluttered and her stomach flipped as Ryziel slowly approached. He did not smile at her. In fact, he looked irritated or maybe even sad, though she couldn't imagine why. She stared back but only for a brief moment before she forced her eyes away and turned her head. She had to remind herself what he had told her the last time they spoke. And to keep her distance. She felt a pang in her chest, but she dared not look at him again as he came up beside her.

"I was just telling Aly about the mission," Xilya said, oblivious to the sudden tension in the air. "So—here, girl, are you listening? We will go down together. Me and Ryziel will make sure all is clear and guard the entrance while you and Nar will go in and fill as many of the canisters as you can. The minerals are set deep inside a series of tight holes. They may be hard to get into, and you may have to shuffle your way inside. If anything happens, you will immediately stop and come back to our side. Me and Ryziel will each have bombs that we will use if the situation absolutely calls for it. It should not take us long, a few hours at most. Enough time before our shifts would ever end. However, if in case we don't return in time, your techband has been updated, so at the end of the shift, it will show your location inside your unit until the next day. We don't want another close incident like last time."

"Hopefully, no one goes knocking on my door," Aly commented.

"A risk we will have to take," the vrisha said, then looked over Aly's shoulder. "Are you ready, Nihl Ryziel?"

Aly didn't glance up at him but could feel his heat at her back.

"If I feel even the slightest disturbance, we are turning back," he said, with an edge of finality that no one would dare argue against. He sounded as irritated as he looked, but there was also a hint of defeat in his voice.

"I'll take that as a yes," Xilya responded in a much lighter tone. "And you, Aly?"

Aly went to speak but was promptly cut off.

"You don't have to do this."

Aly turned around, her eyes landing on Ryziel's face. He glared down at her. His expression changed, his eyes, at first sharp and icy, now turned pleading. She clenched her jaw and did not give. "I am ready," she said softly.

"Good," Xilya said. "Let's go."

CHAPTER TWENTY-FOUR

ALY picked up her bag and put on her helmet then immediately returned to Xilya's side, ready to take her belt, trying her best to ignore the nillium's silvery gaze, which still lingered heavily on her. Nar, with great reluctance and a lot of muttered curses, joined Ryziel at his side. He did not reach up for Ryziel's belt but instead threw his pack and set of canisters over his shoulder and waited. Xilya opened the door, and as soon as they stepped into the dark, Aly grabbed hold of her belt, wishing it were Ryziel's but not daring to ask to switch.

They went quickly, at a pace Aly could just barely keep up with without stumbling. Ryziel had made sure to be at her back with Nar bounding beside him, easily staying with him despite his stubby metal legs. They took the familiar route down into the Keep, only, when they got to one passage close by, they took a separate stair, one Aly had not noticed before.

Down they went until they came to a very large passage, not as gigantic as the great hall of the Keep but still impressive. The air was chilly, Aly's breath fogging the glass of her helmet. The area was different somehow, and Aly couldn't place what it was at first, only that she had a growing sense of anxiety that began to turn into an unexplainable fear. The farther they went, the more she started to understand why and realize what it was.

There was nothing. No sense of life. Even in the Keep, she heard the calls or the hollers of something in the distance, and if not that, then at least the dripping or rushing of water. There, she saw the light of muirlemp patches all around or other strange plants and the tracks or scents of something that had passed by. Even the flutter of what she thought might be the alien-equivalent to bats along some of the ceilings if she happened to have her light on and was looking above. There was always life, though she might not have seen it as clearly before. But here, there was nothing, and somehow, that seemed terrifying.

The silence was heavy, just like the darkness, as if it were a living being cloaking them with its translucent skin. The others remained quiet, though their steps did not, and the noise now seemed so much louder, making Aly more alert, more anxious.

After what felt like a long stretch of time walking, Xilya finally halted and pointed to the cave wall to her right. Ryziel and Nar stopped as well and carefully dropped their packs. Aly looked around where Xilya had pointed but saw no door. Confused, she looked at Xilya then Ryziel, who drew close to the wall. After a short pause, they together pushed against a smooth part of the rock and, to Aly's astonishment, made it move. The rock slid back first then, as they pushed it aside, it revealed an opening, and Aly realized it was a door. A very craftily hidden door.

Aly took a step forward, and Nar caught her arm. When she looked down at him, he shook his head and mouthed for her to wait. Ryziel and Xilya slipped inside first to see if the chamber was empty. Aly struggled to keep calm as she waited for their return, ready to bolt if need be. When they did return, she was relieved but not much calmer.

"Coast is clear," Xilya whispered. "Go as quickly and as silently as you can. Once a canister is filled, come back and switch it for a new one. Go for ionx first, as much as you can get. Me and Ryziel will be just outside, guarding the door." Xilya took out a small gray orb from her pack and shook it. It began to brighten steadily, and she turned back to the opening and threw it inside. Nar stepped forward and immediately went into the chamber. Aly hesitated, tightening her grip on her canister, and started for the door. A hand suddenly caught her before she entered, and she was shocked to look around and see it was Ryziel.

"Aly." He seemed to struggle with his words, his expression hard to read. "I'll...be close by. Be careful."

Aly felt her throat tighten as he said her name. She smiled at him and nodded her head. He did not release her right away but when he did, she went straight for the entrance and didn't look back.

The room was well-lit now by the strange flashy little orb that brightened it with harsh white light. Aly could see all the various nooks and holes, most along the wall, and she realized she would have to climb to get to the ones way at the top. Thankfully, there were those at standing height that she could easily reach. She decided to go for these first. She came to one snug hole and could see she would have to shuffle her way in. Hands shaking slightly, she set her canister down then pushed her way inside and began to crawl with her elbows and legs.

What was really strange as she made her way through was that the hole was smooth rock on the inside and square-shaped. It didn't seem naturally formed at all. As she wiggled to the end and saw a soft yellow glow, she forgot about the strangeness of it at first and started reaching for the glowing metallic rock that she knew to be ionx. Using one hand and arm as a shovel, she dragged the pile of rocks with her as she shuffled and pushed her way back out. Thankfully, the hole wasn't that long, and she was able to feel her legs dangling out in no time. She brought the ionx to the front as she moved her body out of the hole then quickly opened her canister and began sifting the ionx, which looked like fiery diamonds, inside it. She didn't dare look around her to see how Nar was doing or glance at the door. Her heart raced as she went straight for the next hole.

Just like the first, she pulled herself inside, dragged out the ionx, and placed it in the canister. She did this several times without issue and was beginning to feel a lot more confident and maybe a little less terrified. On the fourth hole, she chanced to look around just for a moment as she filled the canister up and realized the chamber didn't look naturally made either. In fact, by the way of the harsh light, it looked like a chamber she might find in the Keep, with many box-like holes and even alcoves, a couple of which she noticed had statues sitting within them, one split with a deep gash down the middle and another without a head. There was even a slab in the middle of the room, for what purpose she didn't want to even imagine. Because something about the chamber really unsettled her. It felt almost familiar, and she gathered that it was because she had actually seen something like it before back on Earth. Something like...

A tomb.

Aly couldn't stop staring around, her body frozen in place. What little heat she had left in her body seemed to slip away into ice. Her heart hammered in her chest, and her mind went black. No, she couldn't panic now, not now.

"Hey, human...hello? Why are you just crouching there? We need to keep going." Nar came into her periphery and waved a hand over her face. Aly blinked.

"It's a tomb," she whispered.

"Eh?"

"A tomb," she said louder. "This is a tomb." She couldn't seem to stop saying it.

Nar looked around then back at her and shrugged. "Yeah, so? Come on, we need to keep going."

Aly's lip trembled as he left her to return to his work. She closed her eyes and took a few breaths, telling herself she would *not* run out like a little girl and go crashing into Ryziel's arms where it was safe...no matter how badly she wanted to. Her eyes drifted to the door, and she could see the two figures standing in front of it. They both watched the passage and the room intently. Ryziel noticed her looking over and frowned with concern. "What's wrong?" he asked, tensing as if ready to run to her.

Aly shook her head. "Nothing," she stammered. "Nothing. I'm fine." Not wanting him to see her fear, she ducked back to the next hole and pushed through. She made quick with the fifth hole, knowing now that it was really meant for a corpse. She almost laughed, thinking how oddly Earth-like it was to see such a place made for the dead to rest. Just like the ancients from her world. Strange how things weren't always so different.

With one canister filled, she rushed to switch it out with an empty one. Nar, she noted, was already on his third. Feeling ashamed for being so slow and wanting the deed to be done as quickly as possible, Aly began to pick up speed, forcing her mind away from bad thoughts and focusing solely on her task. She shuffled her way through each square-shaped opening and grabbed the ionx inside, taking no notice of Nar or the others that were quietly talking, of Ryziel saying he thought he heard something and stepping out into the passage, or of the light from the orb beginning to dim. She was so focused, in fact, she hadn't heard the faint sound of rock sliding away from the roof above (no one had really heard it) or of a dark shadow slipping along the wall.

As she moved out of yet another hole and started to place the ionx in her canister, a shout rang out from the passage beyond, and the door slid shut with a loud bang. Aly felt her body shake. She heard Nar let out a sharp bark close by and saw the bright light from the orb fall to nothing but a dim glow. Aly stumbled back, hitting the wall, her eyes wildly searching the dark. She was about to call out to Nar when another bright light shined out of nowhere, nearly blinding her. Aly put up her hands against the light until she could truly see what it was. When she did see, she felt her heart drop to her stomach.

The glowing lady, dressed in a flowing gown, a halo crown above her head, smiled at her.

"How clever of you to find my little treasure trove," she said in a silky voice. There was a sudden pounding on the thickly-laid door, but the lady paid it no mind. She held out her hand to Aly. "Come. I will give you whatever you desire, for I have the power to do so."

Aly was awestruck. Though something in the back of her mind screamed for her to get away, she could not move. The lady was so lovely and her voice so sweet it put her in a near daze. She shook her head but, as if unable to refuse her, Aly began to reach out her hand.

"Don't!" someone yelled. "It's a trap!"

As if those words struck a chord in her, Aly forced her hand down and pushed the lady from her mind. "No," she said and backed away.

The lady dropped her hand with a frown. "Too bad," she said sweetly. And her face began to twist, her mouth growing wider, showing off long sharp teeth. "I'll just have to catch you the boring way."

From the corner of her vision, Aly saw Nar throw another small orb up into the air. Light burst from it, bathing the chamber. The lady disappeared, and, in her place, the shadow loomed overhead, but it was no longer just a shadow.

Aly scrambled away and let out an ear-shattering scream. The thing above her hissed back. It retreated a long tentacle from its head, one with a glowing tip, to have it sit alongside a set of other tentacles that grew like a mane of hair along its back. It smiled down at her with a mouth not unlike a snake or an angler fish, with several rows of long curved teeth. It crawled across the side of the chamber wall. It had a body similar to a long-limbed panther with its talons fully extended. Its sightless eyes didn't even glow in the dark nor did its oily black skin shine with the light. It seemed to absorb the light like it was made from a black hole. It hissed at Aly again and started to scrape its way down the side of the wall toward her when the door blew open, rock and debris spraying into the chamber.

Aly dodged some of the bigger rocks, but a few smaller ones struck her back and arms as she covered her head. There was a gut-twisting shriek, and Aly tried to open her eyes, but the dust blinded her. She could hear the sounds of roars and shouts around her as another scream began to slip from her throat. She slipped to the ground and crawled blindly away as the shadowy beast loomed still above her. As the debris and dust began to settle, Aly caught Nar nearby with a dark egg-shaped object in his hand. He went to throw the object when one of the beast's tentacles slammed right into him, throwing him back, forcing him to drop the object. It rolled toward Aly, red lights blinking across its side and at its ends. It took Aly a second to understand, and, once she did, she grabbed it and chucked it toward the creature.

She had hoped the bomb would land across the creature's back but, not giving herself time to throw it properly, it instead bounced and landed behind the beast's left leg, where it unconsciously kicked the bomb back to hit the slab in the center of the room. The bomb went off, destroying the slab and the ground beneath it, flinging rock up in every direction. Aly could see nothing once again as the dust clouded everything around her. She ducked her head, trying to keep low to the ground and crawl away somewhere, anywhere that wasn't near the horrifying nightmare-born monster shrieking and hissing close by. Her hands cut against rock, and her shoulders ached, and she thought she could hear her name being called. She wanted to crawl toward the voice but feared she would be stomped and slashed to death any moment by the tentacles and talons that she could still hear sliding and scraping across the room. She reached out her hand, moving back farther, until she felt the back wall and could just make out one of the holes.

Just as she thought to hide herself inside it, there was another massive explosion, this time from above, with a flash of blinding orange light that fell across the monster's back. The creature screamed, as did Aly, while more debris rained down from above, some bits hard, others soft and fleshy. The she-beast went sprawling backward, falling back to hit the ground with a loud crack. As it did, the floor beneath it crumbled then split on one side, and Aly suddenly felt herself sliding away down into darkness.

CHAPTER TWENTY-FIVE

The massive creature dropped, its body rolling to the side then sliding peripherally, sinking partially down into the ground where a crater-like hole had been made in the center—its body wedged itself into it, covering it. It did not stir, its mouth hanging open with jaws split wide, blood-trailing down its head and neck.

Ryziel knew it was dead before it hit the ground. If he felt some relief in that, it was short-lived because all he could think after was that Aly was somewhere still inside, possibly crushed by a rock or by the creature's body that lay limp in the center. Dust began to settle, and Nar hobbled out from the side. Ryziel shot over to him, made sure he wasn't too badly hurt, then began desperately searching for Aly, calling out her name.

"Check the holes," Xilya said to him as she checked on Nar, who now sat by the edge of the broken door panting, one metal leg dented and roughed up by rocks.

Ryziel did as she advised and searched wildly through each hole. "Aly!" he called, reaching his arm through a few but coming out empty. Desperation grew to panic as his head turned each way, but he saw no sign of her, no movement. He began to check under rocks but found nothing.

'This is my fault,' he thought. 'I let her be put in danger again and now...'

Now she may very well be dead.

That thought spurred him on, and he began to fling rocks away, digging through rubble, reaching his arm through square-shaped holes.

"Ryziel...Ryziel...Hey!"

Breathless, Ryziel swerved around and saw Nar stretch out his shaking hand to point at the center of the room. Confused, Ryziel followed his pointing finger to the monstrous corpse, and his heart leapt to his throat. He stalked over to the giant body and tried to search underneath it, terrified of what he might see. He lifted several limbs but found nothing below save for a narrow portion of a hole that the beast was now covering.

"It was...quick," Nar said, still trying to catch his breath. "But I saw her go under as the floor...collapsed."

Ryziel checked around the corpse then attempted to lift it. He knew he had strength to do so, but the beast had wedged itself so fully into the floor that it was stuck and, as heavy as it was, Ryziel couldn't move it off the opening. Cursing, he was very close to hacking it apart with his bare hands to get underneath when Nar made another sound.

"She slid down. A piece of the floor is...is slanted but still intact, which means it...most likely hit another tunnelway below."

Ryziel thought he understood. She may well have fallen underneath and could just be lying below, possibly injured. He brought up his techband and called her, praying he might hear something. The call went through, but there was no answer. He cursed again and withdrew his band.

"Xilya, take Nar back to the lair. I'm going to search for her." He started for the door, his mind tracing a mental map in his head of possible stairways or passages. The duo did not argue, but Xilya did fix him with a concerned stare.

"Find her if you can...but be prepared for what you might discover," she said carefully. Ryziel didn't need to be told. He turned for the door and left without another word.

His mind raced as he flew down passageways and through inner chambers, looking for stairs or cave openings leading downward, struck by images of Aly's mangled body covered in rocks or her head split open from the fall. Even when he did eventually find his way below, he couldn't tear those images from him, and the more he searched, the worse they got. Then, as he continued to find empty rooms and caves, another awful thought hit him: he may never actually find her.

Suddenly, the idea of returning to the hidden chamber and cutting the dead thing open in order to get through to the broken floor below was very tempting. He had no more bombs, but he could find a sharpened rock or crystal. But if he did that, he risked moving the creature where it might fall through the floor and drop on Aly, crushing her. If not that, then the rest of the ground might give and fall as the beast may be the only thing keeping it intact. So, he continued to fly through caves in desperate hope. He checked the map on his band several times but the Keep and the tunnels around it were a maze, and it only showed him where the tracer had gone, not any of the undiscovered places beyond. He could only use his senses, and he did so to the best of his ability, following the vibrations of his receptors, seeking a familiar scent.

Those damning thoughts of Aly being dead or injured or lost drew out dark and intense emotions that burned him from the inside. As he raced through the endless passageways and began to call out her name, uncaring of anything that might hear, he could feel the guilt gnawing at him like a flesh-eating parasite.

He had pushed her away. He had hurt her. And he hadn't even apologized. He never forgot the look on her face when he had said those harsh words to her, words he wished he had never given voice. Words that could never be true in his heart, no matter what he was supposed to think or feel as a nillium.

And perhaps worse than that was that he hadn't thanked her. Hadn't even shown his gratitude for what she'd done for him while in his Drega's hold. She had helped him despite her fear. She had been so brave. And what had he given her? Nothing. Except a constant reminder to keep her distance.

Ryziel's face twisted, a low growl ripping from his throat. He pushed on and knew he wouldn't stop searching, even if he collapsed from exhaustion—wouldn't stop until she was found, even if all he found was her lifeless body.

As he went on through the endless dark—a place Aly was lost in, alone—he felt the fire in him grow cold.

He hadn't apologized, and he hadn't thanked her.

* * *

The first thing Aly felt was something sharp grating against her face or rather several sharp things. She turned her head away and felt herself blink, though the black nothingness across her vision didn't change whether her eyes were open or closed. This brought her mind to focus immediately, and she came around enough to realize she was lying on the ground. A few seconds after processing how she got there, she remembered she had been in the hidden room with Nar when that monster, Coria, had found them, and she had felt the floor drop under her, and she had been falling, falling for what felt like forever.

No, maybe not falling, exactly, but sliding. First from the collapsed floor then down some more from a sediment of smooth rock onto what she could only feel now as a pile of loose rubble underneath her. Thinking this now, she steadily sat up and felt around her.

She moved her arms then her legs then turned her head from side to side and bent her back. She took off her helmet and found the front was broken, one side split across the top. She touched at her face and skull but found them dry then she patted at her torso and found her suit intact. She let out a deep sigh and, besides the soreness across her back, she felt no serious pain. She touched at her arms and felt their tenderness and knew it was likely from the rocks that had pelted her. But she was okay. She wasn't greatly injured and that's what mattered most.

Carefully, she tried to stand, but the rocks under her were not stable. Instead, she crawled her way off the pile until she touched solid ground. With shaking limbs, she stood and, besides being a little shocked, she felt fine, good even, as her adrenaline began to wear off.

She looked around, realizing she still couldn't see a thing. She turned on the lights at her collar, which were dimmer than usual but gave her enough to see at least a few feet in front of her.

The passage wasn't large by any means. In fact, it was rather small compared to most, though it was still big enough that several humans could walk side by side. It went down straight, with no obvious curves or bends, and, since the opposite way was blocked by rock, Aly would have no choice but to follow the path forward.

She took a step then realized she didn't know where she was, and neither did the others. They didn't know what happened, didn't even know if she was alive. Heart pounding, she brought up her techband and went to make a call, but then she heard something slither by the wall. It could have just been her imagination, but it was enough to make Aly drop her arm and bolt away, in fear that Coria somehow wasn't dead (she had only seen the fall, after all) and that the creature might be trying to slink its way into the tunnel Aly was now in.

So, she ran blindly down the passage, passed an open door, and went up a flight of stairs. She only slowed when she started to see the soft glow of what she thought had been muirlemp, only it was moving and that spurred her onward even more.

She fell onto the landing of the stairs, breathing hard, and quickly looked back behind her. But she saw nothing coming up to attack her from below. She fell back for a moment on the cold, smooth rock, trying to catch her breath, then she slowly rolled over and stood back up. There was a soft beam of light ahead of her, sneaking out from under a door not too far ahead. Aly chose to head toward it, hoping it might be one of the others looking for her.

She crept to the door and pushed it open just enough to see inside and saw it wasn't Ryziel or Xilya or Nar. She opened the door all the way and stepped inside and just stood there, staring.

It was a vast chamber, which was nothing new in the Keep, where she clearly was now. It was what was in the room that brought Aly to stop dead and stand there in complete awe.

It had to be the throne room, that's all she could think. Giant statues stood straight and proud along each wall between thick pillars that connected an arched, vaulted ceiling. A large throne-like chair sat at one end, with a high back and twisted metal legs welded to the shiny black floor. And behind it, an even larger statue of a crowned woman, the very same one Coria had been trying to imitate with her false light. Yurza, the queen of this dead kingdom.

All these things, which had been made by long-gone ancients, were now covered in muirlemp. From ceiling to floor; from head to toe. Aly slipped farther into the room, and she could see something else giving off light, some kind of insect fluttering about the glowing fungi. Something like a firefly.

Seeing them suddenly made Aly want to cry and laugh all at the same time. Her throat tightened, and her eyes began to sting, but she refused to let tears fall. She smiled and laughed softly instead, wishing she had her sketchbook with her but then knowing she would easily be able to recreate it from memory if she had to because she would never forget this place. This world that was so different from home.

She walked toward the throne and saw another door below Yurza's feet. Without a thought, she passed through and entered into a garden not unlike the first one she had found a little more than a week ago. Only here, there was nothing but crystals of every color and size growing from lush beds of moss along the ground. She walked over and stared at one massive crystal close to the middle of the room and then finally came to her senses, remembering the others were still probably looking for her, so she brought up her techband once more to make a call.

"Aly."

The low, pained voice brought her around, and there, she saw Ryziel standing only a few feet away, an open doorway to his back. He looked...different, and it took a moment for Aly to figure out what it was.

There was no more tension in him, no obvious look of annoyance or quiet discomfort. Just relief, unmistakably drawn across his face.

"Aly," he said again, as if he couldn't believe she was before him. He started toward her, and it was her turn to tense. She took a step back, and he halted.

"It's beautiful, isn't it?" She didn't know what she was saying, really, but she felt like she had to say something to keep herself from bursting into tears at the sudden sight of him. Or from rushing into his arms only to feel him grow rigid then crying and making a fool of herself. He straightened but didn't look around, didn't take his eyes from her.

"It is," he said after a moment, relief turning to concern.

Aly's mouth quivered as she forced a smile. "It really is."

They were silent for a long moment, and Aly thought she could be calm enough now to just walk away, calm enough to pretend she was okay and wouldn't make a foolish attempt to touch him like the last time. She took one long, deep breath then focused on the door. "We should get back. I'm fine to walk." She took a few steps, thankful that her knees didn't give out or that her voice didn't crack.

Ryziel blocked her way. "Look at me," he commanded. Without hesitation, she did, though she wished she hadn't because, as soon as their eyes locked once more, she felt her control slip. Unmoving, she nearly gasped as Ryziel's hand reached out without warning and brushed his fingers through her hair.

"What are you—"

"Thank you," he said, his hand lowering slightly. "For everything."

Aly stared up at him, shocked to silence. His fingers slipped past her hair and carefully touched against her neck. Then her jaw. Then her face. He didn't flinch or hiss. Instead, he moved closer, his face nearing to hers.

"I'm sorry," he whispered. "For everything."

Aly watched him a second longer then closed her eyes, wanting to only feel the touch of his fingers against her skin, to feel the heat of his body close to hers. She tilted her head up, and he brushed her hair back behind her ear then cupped her face with his other hand. She opened her eyes and saw him glaring down at her with his silvery gaze before his mouth came down on hers.

She knew it was meant to be a kiss, though it started off more as a nuzzling of his mouth on hers. She didn't mind. When he lifted his head and watched her again, she felt the breath leave her in a heavy sigh. His hands moved from her face to fall down her shoulders and then grab at her waist, bringing her closer, drawing her into him. She raised her arms then dropped them again to her sides.

"Touch me," he said. "I want you to, Aly."

Heart fluttering, she watched him carefully then hesitantly lifted one hand and placed it firmly at the center of his chest. Ryziel closed his eyes, and she felt him breathe deep. A soft growl vibrated against her palm, but she took it as more of a purr than anything. He gripped her wrist, gently this time, but didn't push her away. Slowly, she let her hand fall down to his stomach. She felt him shiver.

He peered down at her with an intense, half-lidded gaze as she stopped her hand by his hip. Uncertain by his expression if she should continue, she went to pull away, but he held her fast.

"It's all right. I can handle it," he said softly.

With eyes locked, Aly freed her hand from his then raised it once more, this time touching the side of his face, fingers trailing along his cheek and jaw. He closed his eyes again, tensing briefly then relaxing, pressing himself against her hand.

Aly watched, transfixed, his skin smooth under her fingertips, curiously hot, though he didn't seem to sweat. She traced down his neck then curled her fingers under the collar of his suit. She tugged lightly, hoping with every move she made she didn't overstep and make him uncomfortable. Fearing he might pull away from her at any second.

Ryziel opened his eyes slowly but didn't tell her to stop. Daring to ask with her hand, Aly tugged again at the end of his suit, and he seemed to understand. Without a word, he brought his hand up and unzipped his suit, letting it loosen from his hard body. Carefully, Aly peeled it from him till the top half hung off his waist, leaving him bare before her. She placed a hand against his chest once more, feeling the heat of his skin and the hard pounding of his heart in the middle of his chest. She held there for a long moment, just feeling it against her palm until she slowly let her hand fall downward, feeling every tense muscle along his stomach. She felt him tremble and heard him hiss softly and she paused. She brought her other hand up and placed it on his waist, and still, he didn't move.

"How bad is it now?" Aly whispered.

"Not bad..." His hands clenched and unclenched at his sides.

"Should I stop?"

Ryziel shook his head. "I want to feel you."

At that, Aly drew closer, grazing her fingers along his ribs. She didn't know how much he could take before he might lose it, but she was willing to test and see. She brought her face close to his chest and exhaled before pressing her lips to his skin. She heard him inhale sharply then felt him grip her shoulders, but she didn't stop, trailing her mouth lower.

As she was pulled back by his grip, her first thought was that she had gone too far and that he was going to shove her away, but instead, she found herself being pressed against a mossy rock, Ryziel holding her in place with his hips. She could feel the hard part of him between her thighs as he placed his hands on each side of her, his face close to hers.

She could see he was still there, still in control, but he clearly didn't want to stop. And, really, neither did she. Feeling confident this time that he wasn't going to force her away, she took hold of the edge of her suit and unzipped, letting herself be exposed.

Ryziel's eyes flickered down her body. With one hand, he took hold of her suit and slowly peeled it from her. His eyes darkened as he looked at her. Though the room was cold, Aly felt far from it.

"You were right," Ryziel said in a low voice. He bent his head down and nuzzled her chest, the slick heat of his tongue grazing against one breast then he nipped her. "Some deeper part of me did reveal itself while in my Drega's hold. And it's been killing me." He nipped her again, his tongue swirling, and Aly threw back her head and moaned. "I don't think I can stand it any longer. I don't want to fight anymore either. I thought I lost you." He raised his head slightly then, as if readying himself, he tugged down the rest of her suit, dropping it beside her, and let out a shaky breath. He took hold of her wrists in one hand, placing them over her head. "I think I can control it now because I know what it wants. Because...it is what I want."

Aly gazed up at him, knowing he was waiting for her to tell him no, to tell him to get off her, but she wasn't going to say it. Instead, she licked her lips and said, "Then take what you want."

Ryziel shuddered, his free hand stroking her ribs and down the side of her thigh. "You aren't afraid?"

Aly shivered at his touch. "I'm still here."

He shut his eyes and growled low. He lifted her leg up, placing it around his waist, lifting her body slightly so that it fit perfectly against his. Carefully, he dropped his hand between her legs and stroked his fingers along her, exploring. Fire rose in her lower belly and a terrible ache with it. Aly moaned, lifting her head once more as his fingers slipped inside once than drew out.

"I don't want to hurt you," he said suddenly.

Aly dropped her head and looked back at him, pressing her hips into him, watching him bare his fangs in a groan. "You won't."

With that, he tugged down his suit just enough so that she saw a glimpse of his male sex, not so unlike a human's except for the pointed tip and curved shaft. He bent his legs slightly, and Aly felt him pierce her. They each gasped as he slowly slipped inside and was buried deep.

He didn't move at first, and it took all her will not to arch against him. He steadied himself then thrust into her, letting out a sharp hiss as Aly felt him throb inside her. Heat rose up her neck, and Aly flushed, feeling the thick heat of him fill her so suddenly. But he didn't falter or stop. He gripped her leg and stroked deep again.

He moved on her slow, trying to master his self-control, and Aly squirmed against him, wanting him to go faster. She could feel herself tightening, like a spring ready to be let go.

He breathed hard as he watched her rise and fall before him, his eyes sharp, never leaving her. Then, he let go of her, slipping out of her and releasing her from the rock to bring her down beneath him on the ground.

He pinned her below him, and Aly bent her legs up as he pierced her again, this time with one hard thrust of his hips. He began to move faster, more urgently, and Aly clung to him so as not to slide against the floor. He was heavy and huge on top of her, his hard, bestial movement bringing her to the peak of orgasm until she finally cried out, making him almost pause as if afraid he had suddenly harmed her. When he saw he hadn't, he continued on, faster, until his release came, this time with a loud groan.

Breathless, Aly dropped her shaking legs and turned her head to the side, feeling sweat drip down her back. Ryziel lay on top of her, with his head buried in her neck, and there they stayed for a long moment, with just their breathing and the drip of water nearby the only sounds in the room.

"Ryziel..." she breathed. He rose slightly to face her. He looked so calm, too calm, but inside, he was as revved up as she was. His hands, warm and gentle, moved across her body, kneading at her. She licked her lips, ready to speak again, but he bent down and gave her another one of his nuzzle-kisses. She smiled and wrapped her arms around him, returning his kiss. "I think," she said as he lifted his head, "there was no stopping this, was there?"

Ryziel looked down at her, his eyes still bright. "No," he said, his fingers once more brushing the side of her face. "No, there wasn't."

And she could see he meant it. His expression was that of a man no longer willing to fight nor wanting to. She'd never seen him look so calm.

"And you're feeling...all right?" she asked timidly.

Ryziel peered down at her, and she thought she saw his mouth widen. "More than all right." He actually grinned at her, and she gazed up at him, almost alarmed. His smile, along with his relaxed features, almost made him look like a stranger.

Aly stared as if seeing him for the first time. Then, slowly, she smiled back. She laughed and pulled herself to him, feeling him grunt as she smacked her body against his. He drew his arms around her, and they stayed that way for a long while, until his techband went off.

"I should get it. It's Nar, likely, wondering here I am." He released her gently and pulled up his suit then answered the call. Aly took the moment to stand and pick up her own suit. Heat rose in her face as she glanced down at herself, realizing she needed a shower and her suit a good wash. She put it on anyway, with a tight grimace, just as Ryziel ended his call.

"They know you're safe now. Let's get back to the lair." He rose and pulled the rest of his suit on, turning back to her, eyeing her, still with that eerie calmness and smug grin. He stretched out his arm, offering his hand to her. Aly glanced down at it, a warm feeling swelling in her chest. She took it gladly, his large hand wrapping fully around hers.

He didn't move right away, as if wanting to just feel her hand in his, and Aly didn't say a word, letting him enjoy her touch. He pulled her once more to him and nuzzled her head then turned for the door and led her away.

CHAPTER TWENTY-SIX

Ryziel woke to the smell of flowers and thought for one odd second that he was back in the First House. Yet, as he opened his eyes, he found instead that he was lying in his bed within the lair on Lethe Maws, with golden red locks of hair brushing against his face and chest. He gazed at the top of Aly's head, wondering if he was awake or dreaming. By the solid warmth of her body against his, he knew it to be real. With a deep sigh, he pulled her closer, his arm wrapped protectively across her.

The room was dark and chilly, the only sound that of Aly's soft breath as she slept soundly beside him. It was likely still early enough that he didn't need to wake her yet, but soon, he would be forced to. He took a great risk to have her stay.

He hadn't cared last night, and he didn't care now, though he should. If someone realized she wasn't in her unit and found out her techband had been compromised, it could create serious trouble. But they had made it this far, and damn if he would let her go now.

Aly stirred but did not wake as a low grumble sounded in his chest. Ryziel closed his eyes and lay silent until she was still once more. He thought again about last night, his mind wandering through the events, still shocked by how everything had come to be. And the blissful relief afterwards. It was like a weight had come off him, but in reality, it was something even greater:

His Drega had been quelled.

And, by Nihl, that was some kind of miracle. He had been afraid at first, though he had been prepared for when it lifted its head at Aly's touch. It hadn't risen much more than that, and, though his desire drove him, he had kept his control, and at the end, the beast had calmed as if satisfied. He had let go and given in, and she hadn't been hurt. She, who was so brave. She, who was worthy. He could almost hear his brother laughing, saying "I told you so," and he grimaced at the thought.

Yes, he certainly couldn't pretend he didn't care for her now. And by his right as a nillium of the First House, she was his now, alone. And that was just fine. That was more than fine. Let his brother laugh.

Ryziel brought his mind back to last night and the image of Aly. Even the ship now barely preoccupied his thoughts as much as it had in the last few months. And he knew they were at the last leg now of its completion. With Coria dead and the hidden chamber still stocked full of ionx and the other needed minerals, they could easily return and take it all. Then, in only a few weeks' time, the ship would be fixed, and they would be off Lethe Maws for good. Yes, this should be the focus of his thoughts, but instead, he thought only of Aly. Of her soft body beneath his, not just in the crystal garden but in the bath they used once returning to the lair, then in his bed after. Now that he had let go of his fears, he was starved for her. And there was still plenty of time to make up for all those lost moments.

Aly stirred again, and this time, her eyes fluttered open. She groaned softly and turned to face him. When she saw him looking down at her, she smiled, her small hands coming to rest against his chest. He took one of them and brought it to his mouth with a kiss— that touch that he knew was intimate to humans, though he knew it wasn't exactly like how they did it but he would work on that.

"What time is it?" she asked.

Ryziel rubbed a hand across her back. "Early. But I will have to take you back up soon."

She groaned and seemed to mumble something along the lines of "do I have to?" while rubbing her face against his chest.

"Afraid so, yes. But only for a day. It would be best for you to work and be seen so that no one suspects anything."

She sighed and rolled onto her back. "And I have to see my team. I can't miss a meeting, or they will start looking for me."

He tightened his hold on her. "Such as that man?" He didn't mean to sound annoyed, but it couldn't be helped. She looked at him with confusion.

"What ma—do you mean Julian? Or Mark?"

Ryziel didn't say anything. Mainly because he didn't know the man's name.

"You...saw us together?"

He looked away from her and shrugged, realizing his mistake. She stared back at him. "You were watching me?"

"I...just wanted to make sure you were all right." He looked back at her and could see her brows were raised at him, but she didn't seem agitated. If anything, she gave him a sly little smile.

"Well, Julian has Kate, and Mark is just my friend. We aren't together. But I'm glad to know you were at least thinking of me, even after you told me I couldn't come back."

Ryziel's mouth tightened into a frown. He still felt the guilt of that moment, even now.

A sudden idea occurred to him then, and the frown flipped back to a smile. "By the time you return, we will have gathered a lot of the minerals and started reworking them into materials for the ship."

"Can't I come down and help—"

He shook his head. "One day above and I don't need you going anywhere near that place again. With Xilya and Nar, it can be done quick enough." He brushed his fingers along her jaw. "But I will have a different task for you when you return. For you and me alone."

There was a wicked spark in her eyes and next thing he knew, she was on top of him. She straddled his hips, and he felt himself grow hard beneath her. Her delicate hands trailed along his chest and stomach, and he thought he could never get enough of her touch.

"You don't have to call it that, you know," she said, laughing. "It is not a chore to be with you like this." Her hand slipped down till he felt her hand grazing the hard length of him.

He groaned and gripped her hips. "I don't mean this. Something that involves you and I traveling to another part of the Keep. One last time."

"Oh." Aly's hand gripped him and moved him to her center, where she eased him inside her. She sat firmly back against him and he could feel every bit of her heat tightening around him, making him bare his teeth with a hiss. "Then I am more than happy to help."

He laughed. "I'm sure you are." He moved his hips up to meet her and watched her tilt her head up, arching her back.

"Will it be dangerous?" she said.

"Possibly."

She said no more, only moved against him, and he was content to let her.

* * *

Moving the minerals out of Coria's hidden den was as easy as he had hoped it would be, though it did still take the whole day to do it. Once they were collected in full and taken back to the lair, Nar had the tanks ready to harvest them completely. It would take several days for such a large batch to be ready to process into actual usable materials, but after that, it wouldn't take long to use them to patch the ship and have it running. What was estimated to take several more months now would only take weeks, and Ryziel was more than ready to be gone and sailing toward home.

"All works out in time," Xilya said as they set down the last container and began to help Nar fill the tanks. "You are still certain about giving the ship over to me once you return home?"

"I'm certain," Ryziel said. He would have no more use of it. Once he and his brother were reunited, he would have plenty of other ships at his disposal.

"And the humans—I assume they will come with me until I can set them on a path toward their own home?"

"All except Aly, yes."

Xilya paused in dumping her container to look at him. "She will return to Nihl with you?"

Ryziel didn't slow as he emptied his own. "Yes."

Xilya didn't say anything at first, but Ryziel could practically hear her thoughts. "What is it?" he said.

"As happy as I am to see you two finally getting along, I can't help wondering if that is such a good idea."

Ryziel forced himself not to rub at his temples or his receptors. "Why?"

"Because of your people's laws about non-nillium subjects."

"What about it?"

Xilya shrugged, as if it were some casual remark. "She wouldn't have the same privileges as the others, would she? And she isn't a silion either, which means..."

Ryziel glanced at her, with a frown. "She would be under my care and protection. I would have my brother pardon her."

"The same brother who practically lives by nillium law?"

Ryziel said nothing. It didn't matter at the moment. What mattered was that they got off Lethe Maws. That he got to Nihl and challenged his uncle. What happened after was of little consequence, he was certain. His brother loved him as he loved his brother, and he would give him this one thing because Korzien would see how much Aly meant to Ryziel and allow her to be his chosen mate as he so wished it.

"And what about Aly?" Xilya said, as if hearing his thoughts.

"What if she does not wish to return to Nihl with you? What if she wants to go home?"

Ryziel hadn't even considered that. He realized this was a fault on his part, but it had seemed so obvious to him, that there was no possibility of her not returning with him.

"I will ask her, then, if it will make you feel better," Ryziel said. "When she and I are back in the Keep."

Xilya's eyes narrowed at him. "Why in hell are you returning there this time?"

Ryziel actually smiled at her. "A surprise."

CHAPTER TWENTY-SEVEN

"So, where, exactly, are we going?" Aly's hand tightened around Ryziel's, not out of fear (she was used to the dark now) but with excitement. Though the water splashing at her feet did worry her a tad. The waters were beginning to rise, just as Ryziel had mentioned before and per Xilya's warnings. The rush of water could be heard dully through the rock walls, droplets falling in splats on her head. But Ryziel didn't seem concerned at all as he led her down a flight of stairs toward the Keep.

"You'll see soon enough," was his only answer, but she could see by the glint in his eyes that whatever it was he had them doing wasn't just the usual mineral run.

They came down to the landing of the stairs then through a tunnelway till they passed a shorter, narrower bridge with fast running water beneath them, and Aly had the suspicion that they were entering some secret side entrance to the Keep, one yet seen. They slipped through a narrow open doorway and took several turns through obvious corridors till they hit a set of wide stairs leading down. This time, Ryziel slowed but didn't hesitate to go down them.

"We won't have a lot of time," he said. "Till the waters consume this place. But I think we can make it."

Aly didn't respond, only followed, trusting his guidance. Even when they came to the end of the stair and the water hit her ankles, she didn't pause, thankful she couldn't feel the icy cold through her suit.

At the end of the stair was a wide double door with a long gash slashed across one side and down the other. Aly's heart fluttered at the sight of it as Ryziel approached. With his weight, he pushed on one side and, with a loud crack and a groan, the door opened. They waded inside, into a long, wide-open chamber with nothing but water on the ground reflecting the muirlemp above and what looked like a tree at the center. A metal tree with glowing buds sprouting from its ends. Ryziel ignored the tree and pulled Aly around it, the tree brightening considerably as they passed, until they splashed their way over to the other end of the room and the tree returned to a dim glow. He stopped at the next door and placed his hand on its surface.

"This door is locked pretty tight. I need you to keep watch for me as I break it." He released her hand and started to examine the door for weak points. Aly did as he asked and watched behind him, though she knew he could easily sense anything without her. She decided to indulge him anyway by keeping her eyes peeled for any movement.

Beside the occasional ripple in the water, which was probably only a worm, there was no sign of a threat. Behind her, she heard Ryziel work at the door with loud thuds and scrapes until there was another loud crack followed by an eerie creak as the door fell open. Aly twisted around, but Ryziel halted her from following.

"I'll go in first and make sure it's safe. Wait here."

"What if it is trapped?" she said softly, not sure why she was whispering.

Ryziel looked back at her with a sly grin. "That's what I'm going to find out."

Before Aly could say another word, he slipped inside. Cursing, she decided it was better to wait than to follow, in case something did happen and she had to call for help.

A few excruciatingly long minutes later, Ryziel returned, waving her inside.

"No traps that I can sense, or they are no longer working." He let the door close behind her, and she was only partially comforted by the thought that it couldn't lock them in, since Ryziel had broken the door. It was a small comfort as the room had no other doors or passages to leave it by. A dead end.

"So, what now?" Aly asked, looking around and finding nothing but an empty room except for a stone block against one wall sporting a mural of some kind and a few of what looked like chain-links dangling along each wall.

"Your guess is as good as mine," Ryziel said, studying the room for himself. "But something tells me there is a hidden door or opening in here somewhere. We just have to figure how to open it."

Aly's eyes went for the only possibility in the room: the stone block against the wall. Ryziel drew his eyes over to it as well. "Yes, that would be my guess too."

"How do we open it, though?" Aly approached it with him. The mural etched into the block was of a lady whom she was sure was Yurza again, only this time, she had two children beneath her, each holding what looked like a set of stars. Ryziel carefully placed his hands on the mural, looking over it. There didn't seem to be any hidden keyholes or levers, but Aly figured they might not hide a door the same as a human would. As Ryziel checked the mural, Aly went about studying the rest of the room. There were no markings on the walls. Unlike in the rest of the Keep, the smooth stone was curved, with no obvious cracks or crevices that could hint at the outline of some door. The floor was also covered by water, so she couldn't make anything out under her feet. She went across one side and checked one of the chain-links, cautiously pulling at it. Her eyes followed it up to the ceiling, where she saw a wide round shape like that of the moon cut into the stone. She stared up at it curiously then looked back at the chains.

"I think there's something up on the ceiling," she said as she returned to Ryziel's side by the mural. He nodded his head, deep in thought as his hands continued to slide along the block.

"See here?" He pointed to the three stars that the two children and Yurza held in their hands. "Look." He pressed his hand against one of the stars, and the stone piece sunk into the stone block.

Aly's eyes widened. She went over to one of the other stars and pushed on it, and it too sunk into the stone. They looked at each other then over to the third star—the biggest star—being held by Yurza. Together, while keeping their hands on the other stars, they pressed on it, watching it slip back into the stone.

There was a rumble, and the ground began to shake. Ryziel immediately shot over and brought Aly against him. As he pulled her away from the stone mural and into the center of the room, the chain-links around them began to tighten, and the floor below them began to rise.

Aly gasped and clung to Ryziel as the water sank then slid and fell in a roar across the edge of the floor, which was now no more than a circular slab that the chain-links lifted up toward the ceiling. Mist from the water blew into her face, and the smell of iron hit her nose. Ryziel's arm held tight around her waist as they peered upward and saw the ceiling open up above them.

They waited until the stone slab entered through the roof then came to a shuddering halt, bringing them into a completely different chamber. Ryziel lifted her off her feet to pull her off the stone slab, which was now in line with the floor. Aly looked down at it curiously.

"Too bad they couldn't have used that method for all the damn stairs in this place," Aly remarked with a twinge of bitterness. "Pretty sure the people living here would have liked an ancient elevator to take them between floors."

Ryziel chuckled. As he set her on her feet, he motioned for her to wait again as he checked the room. Aly circled around to get a good look herself and was startled to find it so...bright.

If by bright one meant coming out of a nearly pitch-dark cavern to a place that looked like dusk with the full moon.

High above, there was a narrow opening that seemed to go on forever. The ceiling and the room in general were nothing like those others places she had seen in the Keep. Instead of stone or marble, here it seemed to be made of some translucent blue rock or perhaps even crystal. Walls that shined as if by their own power.

"How...?" Aly breathed as she tilted her head back to look through the opening. She felt Ryziel come to stand beside her, looking up at it as well.

"An ancient trick. They used reflections to cast light down all that way from the surface. It seems whatever the interior is made of absorbs that light."

"It's beautiful." Aly dropped her head to look around the rest of the chamber. Rows of arched columnways made up a web-like maze around them. Along these columns were piles of objects, from chests to suits of armor. "What is this place?"

"I think," Ryziel said, picking up what looked like shiny red and blue gems, "It's a treasury."

Aly took one gem in her hand and held it to the light. It flashed a beat of red as she rolled it in her fingers. She dropped her hand and looked around the room, now stunned. "I think you're right."

Ryziel brushed his arm against her. "Come." He started down one columned path, and she followed.

"But how can this still be here after all this time?" Aly asked as they explored, her eyes drinking in all the shiny objects around her. "Wouldn't Coria or something have found this place and ransacked it?"

Ryziel shrugged. "Perhaps Coria or something never thought to look. And if they did, they didn't get far. The guardian likely saw to that."

Aly brows furrowed. "What guardian?"

"The one we passed outside the chamber below us," Ryziel said, searching around as if looking for something.

Aly looked up at him, alarmed. "You mean the tree?"

"Yes."

She stopped to seriously think about that for a moment then caught back up to him. "Why did it let us pass, then?"

Ryziel glanced back at her then across the chamber. "Honestly, I'm not completely sure, but my best guess is that it didn't recognize us as a threat."

Aly frowned, letting that sink in and deciding it wasn't worth trying to wrap her head around or contemplating for the time being. She didn't expect to understand ancient alien technology.

She caught Ryziel searching around again as she followed closely behind. "What are you looking for?"

"There should be a large chest around here somewhere with a— ha, there!" Ryziel skirted down another row of columns, and Aly nearly tripped over some sort of black mirror to catch up with him. Down the row at the very end was a statue of Yurza and the two children. Below them was a large chest made from the same material as the walls and columns of the room, carved with intricate markings across its lid. Ryziel crouched down beside it, but there was no lock to be seen or handle to open it. He checked all around it then sat back. Aly sat beside him to observe it carefully.

"What do you think is inside?" she asked, after a brief moment of silence.

Ryziel tilted his head. "Only one way to find out." He moved again to the box and began to slide his fingers across the surface. His hand pressed against one side and a piece of the chest popped out. He pulled at the piece and another slid outward.

"It's like a puzzle box," Aly said. "You have to put the pieces right to open it."

Ryziel thought it over then began to work it out in silence. Aly watched for the most part, giving her suggestions every so often. It took a solid hour or so by her guess before he slid in the last piece, and the lid opened with a click.

Ryziel lifted the lid, and they both looked inside and found a glowing sphere, like a large pearl with flecks of gold across its surface. Cautiously, Ryziel drew it out of the box and held it in his palm. They both stared at it in trance-like wonder. Suddenly, the sphere's glow went out, and the flecks of gold jumped from the orb to spread out before them in a burst of glittering light. Aly leapt back as Ryziel shot up, but the lights didn't pierce them or hurt them, they merely floated around them. They watched the colors move and then one specific speck of gold light became larger and brighter than the rest.

"What is it?" Aly breathed.

Ryziel watched for a long moment, his eyes darting from one set of lights to another. Then his eyes brightened in realization. "It's a map."

Aly gazed at the specks around them. "How do you know?"

"I was forced to memorize the Xolis map as a youth, and I recognize some of these systems." He looked back at the brighter dot of light before him. "This is the edge of Xolis." He pointed it out. "But there is no system here that I remember."

"But it's saying there is."

Ryziel's eyes narrowed. "It is."

Aly crossed her arms as she gazed at the bright spot. "What do you think it means?"

"It's a marker."

"To what?"

"I think...a planet."

"Do you think..." Aly dropped her arms. "Do you think some of Yurza's people didn't die? That maybe they...?" She shaped her hand like a ship, sweeping it toward the bright system.

"It's not completely impossible." Ryziel squeezed the orb in his hand, and the bright gold flecks returned to the now glowing sphere. He looked down at it with a frown and back at the box, which now lay empty. "It's a pity this is it, though."

"Why? Were you expecting something different?"

He glanced up at her with a sheepish smile. "I was hoping for a set of jewels."

Aly raised her brows at him. "Really? Jewels over something like this?"

Ryziel shrugged. "I wanted to give them to you. The most coveted treasure in the Keep."

Aly blinked at him. Then she smiled and laughed. "You don't need to win me over with jewels, you know. But I'm glad we found this."

Ryziel placed the sphere in one of his side packs. "Me too."

They started back for the ancient elevator, Aly refusing to take any of the other gems or treasures in the room, until a book on top of a chest caught her eye. She picked it up and opened it and let out a little gasp.

"What is it?" Ryziel said.

"Oh, it's..." Aly covered her mouth. She opened it up so he could see. It was a book of drawings; unbelievably intricate and beautiful sketches of the different parts of the Keep, of the flowers and plants, of beasts and of people.

"It's nice," Ryziel said. He looked at her and nodded. "You should have it, then."

"Oh, I don't know if I should take anything," she said, even though she clutched the book to her. She caught Ryziel giving her a sly grin.

"Take it. Better for it to be appreciated than sitting collecting dust."

Aly stared down at the cover, her hands tracing circles over its leatherbound surface. "I guess...all right." She placed it in her own side pack next to her sketchbook. Someday, she would show the others and tell them of this place.

With a satisfied nod, Ryziel led her back to the center of the room. With the tap of his foot on an inlaid star, the ground beneath them began to descend. As they slowly dropped down, Aly looked up one last time to see the light from above disappear as the ceiling closed back into itself, returning to the shape of the moon.

* * *

"How did you know to look for a place like that anyway?" Aly asked as they sloshed their way up a set of stairs, the water cascading down the steps in a foaming torrent. The water under the bridge they crossed earlier had already risen considerably since they left. The Keep would be under soon, nothing more than an unreachable ruin until the waters eventually fell away, deeper into the earth.

"I had the map leading to that secret part of the Keep for some time," Ryziel explained. "I acquired it by mistake when looking for the ship. The tracer somehow made its way into there, and Nar had an incomplete map given to him long ago by a deceased relative, claiming it was where Yurza hid her most coveted possessions. It wasn't hard to put the two maps together and see where it led. I told myself once the ship was close to being finished that I would go there and let Nar know what I found." He peered down at her with an amused expression as they made their way through a murky tunnel. "He'll probably be peeved to know I didn't bring anything back for him, but I will give him the map so he at least knows where it is if he wishes to go there himself someday."

"It's too bad," Aly said as Ryziel pulled her up over a fallen rock and set her on the other side. "If he tells his people, they will probably ransack the place when they get a chance and try to sell every little bit off to the miners."

"Perhaps. But maybe he won't tell them. And it may be a long time before the water recedes and it opens again. By then, who knows. We won't be here to learn of its fate either way."

He was right about that, she was sure. The ship would be long gone, and Lethe Maws would be a shadow in the blackness of space. They would be on their way home before they knew of anything that happened within the Keep.

Home.

Aly looked up at Ryziel, and a small sort of ache welled up in her chest. As they walked up another set of stairs, she knew if she didn't say something, the ache would swell till it burst. "Ryziel...when we get off Lethe Maws, um...I know you will return to Nihl."

He grunted but didn't turn to look at her as they walked.

"Will...do you think..." She had a hard time forming words until she finally just came out with it. "Will I go home with you?"

Ryziel slowed and looked back at her. "Yes."

Aly stared up at him. "Oh."

He looked away and continued, "It is what I wish...do you not want to?"

Aly took his hand in hers. "I want to."

He pulled her to him and quickly kissed the top of her head. The ache left her, and she had to force herself not to scream for joy.

Home. With him.

They came out to the bottom of the mine, and Aly had a sudden urge to run. To leap and bound like some crazy, high sprung deer.

"So, when we go to Nihl, I will stay with you, in your home?"

He gave her a funny look. "That's the general idea."

Aly laughed. "Right."

"I will request my brother allow you to be tied to our House and bound to me as my woman."

'That's a weird way of putting it,' she thought. Clearly, he must mean...

Aly halted after she began to jog down a familiar path. She looked back at him. "What do you mean bound? Do you mean...married?"

"In Nihl's way. Yes."

Aly went still as he came up beside her. She opened her mouth but wasn't sure how to answer. "What is Nihl's way?" she asked finally.

"It makes it official. A small ceremony, nothing more. If we were going by ancient nillium standards, I'd say I've already claimed you now as my mate. But my brother would want it done the modern way, I imagine."

"Ah." Aly felt a sudden odd mix of emotions, ranging from giddiness to anticipation to nervousness. To know he saw her as his mate was beyond surreal and made her heart pound with uncontrolled excitement. But some small voice at the back of her mind was a little unnerved.

He had never asked her. By human standards, you at least asked.

"What if I don't want to be your mate?" She blurted it right out and shouldn't've been surprised when he froze to stare back at her.

"You don't wish to be?" His voice was low and soft, and even from the dim light of their suits, she could see the hurt in his eyes.

It came as a sudden realization to her that nillium weren't used to asking for anything. Nor were they used to being told no. Even Ryziel, though different from his kind, was no exception.

"I do," Aly said and meant it. "But I guess I would have liked to have been a part of that decision, you know?"

Ryziel's mouth tightened. "I'm sorry. I shouldn't have assumed..."

Aly thought for a moment then said, "When did you decide I was your mate?"

Ryziel looked everywhere but at her. "When we first laid together."

Aly's brows rose. She had thought his answer might be when they slept together the second time in his bed but not literally their first time when in the crystal garden.

Aly smirked up at him and a sort of ridiculous idea snapped in her head. "How about this? We say we aren't, uh, mated yet because I didn't know. But I will give you this chance now to say we are if you ask properly." He opened his mouth, but Aly put her hand up to say quickly, "After you claim me again."

Ryziel frowned at her, totally confused, but the smile never left her face.

"I get a head start." Aly then turned from him and rushed into the dark. "If I make it to the lair, though, you're out of luck!" she called back. She laughed and shut off all her lights except for one on her wrist.

It was a silly game, she knew (and hoped she didn't just offend his alien pride) but she was feeling that swell of giddiness again, knowing she had him and he could have her. She slowed in her run, knowing she'd probably trip on a rock if she went too fast. He didn't call out to her, but she didn't stop, knowing he'd catch up to her easily. She dropped down to hide behind a rock and turned off her wrist light. She knew the tunnel to the lair was just ahead. Heart pounding, she turned her light on again and made a break for it, only to be completely swept off her feet before she even got to the tunnel's edge.

Aly let out a little shriek then laughed as Ryziel wrapped an arm around her and threw her over his shoulder.

"Woman, you are full of surprises," he growled. She saw the flash of his teeth and fire in his eyes. He walked a way back then brought her off his shoulder, only to pin her against a rock. "I will, however, assent to your request."

Aly inhaled sharply as he swiftly unzipped then pulled her suit down, exposing her breasts and stomach. His mouth was on her before she could even speak, his teeth nipping and grazing over her sensitive skin. Aly moaned, tilting her head back, allowing him to remove the rest of her suit along with her pack until each laid on the ground before them. She shivered, but his heat against her warmed her quickly. Aly could see little in the dark and through the haze of desire that he pulled from her, she wondered briefly if they should pause and continue in his bedroom. But he didn't seem concerned about sluths or anything at all, and she knew if there was any danger around, he would sense it, so she let it go and gave in with another breathless moan.

Without warning, he lifted her higher, until her legs were on his shoulders. His head dropped down between her legs, and Aly had to fight the urge to grip the horn-like antennas on his head as the slick heat of his tongue grazed her center. She rocked back, her body tightening instantly, the orgasm so intense she had to choke back a scream, a dull cramping stirring in her abdomen. She quivered, clamping her mouth shut, though her cries still vibrated in her throat. He lifted his head from her, their eyes locking as he pulled her back down then peeled his suit off just enough to release the hard length of himself and slide deep inside her. Aly bucked, but he pinned her fast, stretching her legs to set them on each side of his waist. His hulking body moved on her without hesitation, and all Aly could do was cling to him, her hands grasping at his chest and the curve of his neck. Above her own soft cries, she could hear Ryziel's hard breaths turn to low grunts then to deep growls. If she thought to be concerned by the sudden change, it hadn't crossed her mind. Only after another less intense orgasm hit her did she happen to notice his snarling face and unseeing silver eyes.

"Hey." Breathless, Aly placed her hands to the sides of his face. "Ryziel." She knew he had already finished in her once by the throbbing sensation against her stomach. She forced him to look at her, and he blinked as if coming out of a trance. He tried to say something to her, but the sounds came out wrong. Aly softly stroked his face as he slowed his pace against her but did not stop fully. His mouth came down on her throat, and Aly tensed as she felt his fangs graze her skin.

"Will...be my...Aly," he mumbled as his teeth nipped her ear. Aly gripped his shoulders and let him bury his face back into the curve of her neck. "Will you...be mine?"

Aly closed her eyes, and without another thought, said, "Yes."

CHAPTER TWENTY-EIGHT

It was night again at the First House. Ryziel once more stood on the terrace, looking out at the slip of light fading on the horizon. The lanterns were lit, and the scent of flowers filled the air.

"Take your pick, Ryziel."

Ryziel turned and saw his brother sitting at a table nearby, his mouth turned up slightly in a curious sort of grin. "Come on, just one," he said, taking a sip from his cup. "You can have any you like."

Ryziel looked around and saw a set of servant women kneeling before him, quietly obedient. Most he'd seen before, traveling the halls, cleaning, or cooking. But there were several he didn't recognize. Four, to be exact.

"What are they doing here?" he heard himself say, pointing to the human women seated with others, their heads bowed, eyes staring at the ground.

"They are ours," his brother said firmly. "Our women."

Ryziel frowned, not understanding. "That cannot be."

His brother sighed. "We need them, Ryziel."

He looked to his brother with alarm, who nodded at him. "Go on. Choose."

Ryziel didn't argue this time, even though he knew he was supposed to be taking care of his father's business. He looked back, and the only women now before him to choose were the human women, those he recognized seeing in the mines. His eyes fell over each until they stopped on one hooded figure bowing low, hiding her hands under her shawl.

"This one," Ryziel said, without even thinking. He had to have her. He didn't need to see her face to know it was his Aly. He came up beside her and gestured down to her. "I want this one."

His brother's eyes narrowed. "That one? Are you sure?"

"Yes."

"Very well. Take her, then."

Ryziel bent to pick her up, but she pulled from his grasp. A whimper escaped her, her body shaking. She hugged herself, hiding from him still. He tried to pull her to him again, but she merely turned away.

"Pity," his brother said, sighing again. "Some things just aren't enough."

Before Ryziel could ask what he meant, the night swallowed him and everything around him until all he could hear was the cries of a woman far away.

The cries turned into a hum next to him. Ryziel opened his eyes, and Aly's face came into view. He was about to ask her if she was hurt, but then the dream faded into nothing more than a shadow of a memory, and he could see plainly that she was fine. It was only a dream.

He watched her curiously as she wrote something in what looked like a small journal, her eyes drifting over the page in deep concentration. When they lifted to glance over at him, she gave him a look of surprise, then a timid little smile.

"Ah, I didn't realize you were awake," she said, seemingly embarrassed, and set down her writing tool.

"I only just woke." He lifted himself slowly on his elbows and peered down at the journal in her hands. "What were you writing there?"

She chewed on her lip and he thought it rather cute. "I wasn't writing."

"Oh?"

She hesitated for a moment, as if she was afraid to show him then lowered her hand so that he could see.

It was drawing, a rather good one, and it was of...

"You drew this?" he said with surprise. She merely nodded and let him take the journal from her hands. He studied his portrait more clearly, astonished by the accuracy of how she had depicted him, lying on his side across the bed. He flipped through the other pages and found many more drawings of him, all in different angles or poses, some just of his head or his eyes. He glanced back at her and saw she had gone red in the face.

"I might have gotten a little carried away," she said timidly, curling a lock of hair back behind her ear. He thought that cute also.

Ryziel shook his head dismissively. "You have a gift. These are very good."

"Thank you."

"You're almost out of pages, though," he said as he shut the journal and handed it to her. "I'll have to get you a new one when we get home."

Aly set the journal away in her pack. "Are there many artists there?"

"Some. Most talent comes from jewel-craft and clothing. Others are commissioned in architecture. But I could see many silions paying good credits for a drawn portrait, especially with an eye for realism like yourself."

"You think so?" She smiled.

"I do."

Her fingers made little circles on the bed. "I can't wait to see it. Nihl, I mean. I bet it's beautiful."

He took her circling hand and brought it to his mouth. "It is. And you will fit within it perfectly."

They laid together for a moment longer until Ryziel deemed it necessary for them to at least dress and start packing her things. It was still early, and she wouldn't have to return above just yet, but, while the minerals were still being converted within the tanks, he and Nar needed to start preparing the ship and all the possessions that would be stowed on board.

As they left his bedroom, Ryziel saw Xilya talking with Nar by one of the wings. On the grated table nearby was an iron-bowl filled with a sort of stew he had seen Nar make before, along with a pot of hot water and tea infusions. He followed Aly over and sat beside her. Not long after, Xilya and Nar joined them.

"Conversion is going smoothly," Nar said, settling himself on a high stool next to Xilya. "At this rate, we will be out of here in, I'd say, maybe two, three weeks tops."

"At least we never have to return to the Keep or the cave systems surrounding it. Now, it's just a waiting game," said Xilya, curling her tail around her chair.

"It was good timing too. You were right," Ryziel said to Xilya. "The waters have risen down below."

"What did you go back down there for anyway?" Xilya asked, her eyes shifting over to Aly then back to him.

Ryziel looked to Nar. "I used the map and found Yurza's treasury."

Nar's eyes widened. "Nihl's hide," he breathed.

"The way in is probably underwater now. But I will give you the map if you ever wish to return."

"Did you at least take anything?"

Ryziel looked at Aly then took the pearl-like orb out of one of his side-packs. "This." He handed it to Nar, who took it in both his little hands and turned it over.

"This is..."

"Some sort of star-map."

Nar grunted. "Strange thing to take..."

Ryziel shrugged. "Strange thing to have locked away in a treasury."

Nar nodded and handed it to Xilya so that she could also examine it. When she squeezed it, the gold flecks shot out, spreading across the room.

"See there." Ryziel pointed to the brightest and largest gold speck, flickering every so often with blue light. "There's no known system there, yet this map claims there is."

Xilya squeezed on it again, and the gold flecks returned to the orb. She handed it back to Nar.

"Interesting," Nar said. "Mind if I hold onto it to examine it some more?"

Ryziel shook his head. "Not at all."

Nar pocketed the orb then got up and began to set several cups on the table.

"What's this?" Aly asked, pointing to an iron bowl.

"It's called *Loshi*. It's an urken meal made for celebrations," Nar explained. "I figured, now that we know we will have the ship ready soon, this was a good enough time as any to, well, celebrate."

"And I couldn't agree more," said Xilya. She poured hot water into the little cups for each of them while Nar distributed the stew in steel bowls. Ryziel gave a tea infusion to Aly while dropping one into his own cup. As the pills soaked, Xilya took up her bowl carefully in her sharp hands and lifted it. "To the ship. May it safely fly us out of this hellscape and away to better worlds."

"Couldn't have said it better," Nar said, lifting his own. "To the ship."

Ryziel glanced at Aly, who met his eyes. She smiled at him and lifted her bowl. "And to home."

Ryziel smiled, lifting his. "To home."

They ate in silence for a short while until Ryziel noticed Xilya watching Aly with curious intensity. Her gaze eventually flicked over to his and their eyes locked. They stared at one another for a long moment before Xilya spoke.

"Speaking of home," she said, with a suspiciously casual air. "I am told you will return with Nihl Ryziel to his home world. Is that true, Aly?"

Aly swallowed her mouthful of stew and set her bowl down. "Ah, yes." She glanced at Ryziel then back at Xilya. "It's true."

"Hm." The vrisha female scratched at the side of her jaw indifferently. "And I take it, then, you aren't worried about being the only human left on Xolis?"

Ryziel's hand slowly clenched into a fist. Where was she going with this?

Aly cast her eyes downward, as if thinking, then slowly shook her head. "No. It doesn't bother me. I'll be with Ryziel." She looked up at each of them. "And I'm sure I can somehow keep in contact..."

"You think so?"

Aly shrugged but didn't seem to have an answer.

"The humans will come with me," Xilya said. "And, assuming your tale is true, that this Dr. Hart you mentioned is likely on my homeworld, she may know how to get them back to human territory. But the likelihood of them returning to find you is assuredly impossible." She took a sip of her tea then set her cup down. "I'm just saying if you choose to go to Nihl, there's no going back. You will never see a human again."

Aly frowned but didn't seem completely disturbed by this revelation. "I understand."

"Do you?"

"Yes."

Xilya sat back and bowed her head. "And you understand, then, that, no matter what happens, once you are on Nihl, you can never leave."

"Careful, Xilya," Ryziel warned softly.

She ignored him, her eyes staying on Aly.

Aly looked back at her, her brows furrowed tight. "If that is true,"

Aly began, "then so be it. As long as I am with Ryziel, it doesn't matter. It will be my home."

"A home you barely know anything about?"

"Enough, Xilya," Ryziel growled.

Xilya finally turned her eyes to him, her gaze almost accusing. "You are very sure you will be able to go and challenge your uncle without issue?"

The question was unexpected, but Ryziel knew his answer. "Yes."

"And you are very sure you will win?"

Ryziel took a hit from his own cup then set it down. "Yes, I am sure." He didn't think he needed to explain his plan, but he did so anyway. "I will challenge him on the First Night, when I am strongest. My uncle's ego will drive him to think he can still defeat me, even then. And, as heir to the house, my brother will allow us to fight."

"Just as you think he will allow Aly to be your bonded mate?"

Ryziel's eyes narrowed, and he waited a moment before saying, "He will if I ask it."

Xilya narrowed her eyes back at him. "And have you told her what it's like for non-nillium within the great Houses?"

"It doesn't matter."

"I think it does."

Ryziel bared his teeth. "We are done discussing this. It is not your decision."

"Not mine," Xilya agreed. "But hers." She gestured to Aly.

Aly looked to both of them. She was quiet for a moment, looking to Ryziel for reassurance. She turned back to Xilya. "I think it will be fine."

Xilya stared at her for a second longer. Then, as if it was no longer a concern, she tilted her head with a shrug. "So be it." She drank the rest of her tea and so said no more.

Aly's techband rang out like a little bell, letting them know it was time for her to head above. "I'll go get my things," she said hesitantly, looking to Ryziel as she rose from her seat.

"I'll be right there," Ryziel said to her as he went to stand.

"Let me take her up," Xilya offered. "I have to return to the top as well, and one tank is nearly complete. You could stay and help Nar."

Ryziel was ready to say no when Aly spoke first. "I don't see a problem with that," she said. She looked over at Ryziel. "If she has to return above then we might as well go together."

Ryziel couldn't argue with that.

Once Aly's pack was secure, Ryziel followed her over to the door. Uncaring if Xilya or Nar saw, he pulled her to him, wrapping his arms around her.

"Be safe," he said, nuzzling her ear. "I will come to get you later. Meet me at our usual place during mid-shift."

"You got it." She kissed the corner of his mouth then drew back. "I was thinking...maybe I can say something now about the ship to my team. Or at least just my team leader? So that they can be ready when the time comes."

He brushed a lock of hair back behind her ear. "We will discuss the possibility tomorrow. Until then," he grazed his mouth against hers, "see you, my love."

Aly kissed him once more and released herself gently from his hold to back away and stand beside Xilya. Ryziel's eyes flicked over to the vrisha with a tight glare, which she immediately returned. "See you soon."

* * *

Aly walked beside Xilya as they made their way across the bottom toward the elevator. She was so accustomed to the path now that she didn't need to follow behind. Xilya didn't seem to mind, though she stayed quiet for most of their journey.

"You really plan to take my team to Tryth with you?" Aly said as they walked up to the elevator.

Xilya waved her hand over the pad to bring down a car. "That's the idea, yes. From there, they may be able to track a way back to a human territory. Or perhaps one of them will know of better coordinates to go by, and I can drop them off at a human settlement. Either way, I'm certain they can be returned home without issue."

Aly nodded. "I'm glad. I will miss them...and you."

The alien didn't respond readily to this, and they waited in silence until the doors opened. Once they were inside and the car began to move, Xilya made a soft hissing noise.

"It might be very lonely on Nihl without your kin," she said.

Aly looked up at her, but the vrisha didn't meet her gaze.

"I think I'll manage fine. I'll make new friends."

Xilya scratched at the side of her face.

Aly shifted and cleared her throat. "Ryziel says it's beautiful there. It might even seem like Earth in some ways. He says there are some who might like me to draw—"

"You shouldn't go."

Aly stared at her, confused and, frankly, a little hurt. "Why?" The vrisha didn't say anything at first so Aly continued with, "Is it really because you think I'll be lonely? Because I told you I'm not upset—"

"You don't understand." The alien sighed, rubbing at one of her horns. "You won't make friends there. You won't have anyone. Except, I guess, Ryziel. You *will* be alone."

Aly frowned. "What are you saying, exactly?"

Xilya turned her head toward her. "What do you know of the nillium, truly? Tell me."

Aly thought about it then said, "I know they are a noble race...that most are members of the Xolis Council. I know they think a little too highly of themselves."

Xilya made another low hissing noise. "And what do you know of Nihl, their homeworld? That it is beautiful, that is all?"

Aly opened her mouth then closed it. "I...I know that the sun rarely sets there, at least in the northern hemisphere. And when it does, it is only like...once a month."

"The First Night, they call it," Xilya said. "The one night that lasts only an hour to which they endure once a month, yes. And Ryziel will challenge his uncle on this night, as you know."

"Right, because he's strongest somehow at night...like he said." Aly spoke the words but they sounded uncertain, even in her ears.

"Wrong. He isn't stronger at night," Xilya said bluntly. Aly opened her mouth to protest, but Xilya cut her off. "He isn't stronger. The sun, his planet's sun, weakens him."

Aly went still.

Xilya bowed her head. "It is so. He is stronger than probably most of the nillium within Xolis. But his very own sun betrays him. And his own people hate and fear him for it."

Aly shook her head. "I...that can't be. His father didn't trust him, and his uncle hates him, but his brother is there and cares about him."

"They are afraid of him because he is not of the light but of the dark," Xilya said, ignoring her words. "He is different. When he was born, they took him for an ill omen. It is only because of his father's choice to keep him alive and raise him to become his own personal assassin that he is still breathing at all. His brother likely has his own agenda."

Out of all her words, *assassin* drew Aly's focus the most. Ryziel never mentioned exactly what his father made him do, but she might have guessed. Still, the sudden truth didn't immediately disturb her. If it was true, he had been forced to do it. And, she was sure, he was no longer that now nor would he ever be again. "Things will be different. His father is gone. His uncle..." Aly crossed her arms. "He will be too."

"Yes, his brother will allow him to stay within his home. That is most certainly true. But Nihl Ryziel will still be an outcast to them."

Aly looked up at Xilya, wide-eyed as she said this.

"So." Xilya twisted her body around to face Aly. "What do you think they will see when you arrive? The non-nillium mate of an outcast?"

Aly clenched her jaw. "I guess so."

"No," Xilya said, her eyes a fiery blaze. "Not even that. Because, if you had bothered to ask, then you would know."

Aly felt a sudden awful cold, like an icy stone drop in her stomach. "Know what?"

"You would know that there are no non-nillium mates. That even silions of the highest cast are not offered such privilege. You would know that, because you yourself are not nillium nor even silion, that you will have no rights within that House nor on Nihl anywhere. Not even Nihl Ryziel's own brother would allow you to be called a lady of Nihl nor a nillium's mate." The fire in Xilya's eyes dimmed, replaced with a guilt-ridden sadness. "I have heard rumors of nillium women being hidden within their own homes, unable to leave, none seen off of Nihl in many years." She placed a hand on Aly's shoulder. "You would be kept out of sight from everyone, just like them, locked away for only Ryziel to keep you company when his brother doesn't call him away, which will be often. And it would be worse for you, much worse."

Aly swallowed hard, her throat suddenly tight, her mouth dry. "How...how much worse?"

Xilya's hand slipped from her shoulder. "You would be forced to serve under them. Nihl Ryziel would have little say, and something tells me he won't move against his brother—not even for you." She bowed her head low. "You would be nothing more than a slave."

CHAPTER TWENTY-NINE

Aly sat on her bed inside her unit, her sketchbook sitting on her lap, hands clenched tightly around it. Her shift would be starting soon, but she couldn't bring herself to move. She hadn't even taken her suit off once she returned to the unit after Xilya left her. She had just gone to her bed and sat there for a long time, thinking.

She thought about what Xilya said and refused to believe it. Her denial was so strong she considered putting the idea out of her mind altogether and continuing on as if the conversation had never happened.

But the more she tried to shut out Xilya's words, the more they came whispering back to her like the twist of a knife. And she couldn't ignore it any longer.

After all, why would Xilya have cause to lie to her? Why would she have any reason to make something up to keep Aly from Ryziel? She had no reason to do that, no secret motive. Aly had seen the honesty in her eyes, the pleading expression of someone who only wanted to save her from what could only be considered a terrible fate.

And that's exactly what it was. Even with all the love and trust she felt for Ryziel, she could not deny that the idea of being shut away and forced to comply with those around her did more than just terrify her. It broke her.

And suddenly, all she could think of was home. Not of Nihl but of Earth. How she had escaped a life of control and manipulation from her parents. And now, with all the denial stripped away, leaving doubt to grow and fester inside her, she knew her future might be doomed to bring her back into that same trap.

After hours of this dreadful thinking, Aly had come to the final numbing conclusion. That she would now have to make an important and life-altering decision: go with Ryziel and risk living a life in the shadows. Or return with her team and risk never seeing him again. The latter choice made the sharp pain in her chest hurt so bad it left her gasping. But the former choice left her shaking so bad she had to keep her hands clenched on her lap to still them.

Someone might say she had a third option, but she feared to even consider it because she knew what Ryziel would say, and his answer would only break her more.

She could ask him to not return home.

But where would they go? Back to her world? A place still new to the idea of life beyond human existence, still working to understand those aliens they had come to discover? The gyda might be on some of the bases, but even after so many years, they were still separated from the human communities. And then there was the vrisha and the whispers from those who still deemed them "hostile" even though they had yet to make contact with them again, ever since the Lazris incident. She knew they were discovering more civilizations, more races, but humans were still too afraid, still too uncertain, to allow others to integrate into their cities and homes. Ryziel would be just as unwelcome as she might be on Nihl. She couldn't put him through that.

And, besides, she already knew his answer. He had been trying for so long to return home, to return to his brother. She knew even she couldn't sway him not to go back, especially not now, when he was so close.

Slowly, Aly rose from her bed and, like a sleepwalker, went over to the kitchen, thinking for the moment she should just eat something before she had to work for the few hours until Ryziel came to get her. Then she would have to talk to him. At least try to make him understand her fears. They had time still before the ship was finished, and, maybe, just maybe, she could find a way to still make it all work.

As she finished with a small meal that she could barely keep down, she had started placing her sketchbook and tools in her pack when a knock started at her door. She went over to it without a thought and opened it.

A krull male stared down at her from the doorway, and it took Aly a moment to realize it was an enforcer. Her heart skipped a beat, but she merely smiled. "Can I help you?"

"Aly Smith, we are here to escort you to level three."

Aly frowned. Her eyes shifted past the krull to where two others waited by the wall. "Why are you taking me to level three?" she asked nervously. Level three was the beginning of the warehouses, along with the security hub, if she remembered correctly.

"Your team must go to level three immediately," was the krull's answer. "We are here to take you. Are you ready to comply?"

Aly didn't answer at first but didn't see how she had much of a choice. Cautiously, she stepped out of her unit and allowed the enforcers to circle her. She followed them over to Mark's unit, where the krull knocked on his door.

A moment later, Mark opened it, his eyes first meeting the krull's then slipping down to Aly. "What's going on?"

"You are ordered to follow us to level three. Gather your things and meet us in the hall," said the krull.

Mark hesitated. He looked back at Aly, who only shook her head. "Okay," he said. "One moment." He closed the door then, only a couple seconds later, stepped out into the hall with them.

The enforcers led them quickly down the hall and out of the hub to a waiting elevator, which they all entered.

"What's this about?" Mark whispered.

Aly glanced over and shook her head again. "No idea. They just said the team is going to level three." Her heart was racing now. She tried to prepare herself for what she feared might be another interrogation. Maybe they had caught on that something wasn't right. Maybe they had seen her leaving for the bottom or returning. Maybe they knew her techband was faulty. She was surprised at how calm she seemed on the outside, considering how afraid she was now. Her eyes shifted over each enforcer. She needed to get a message through to Ryziel but not with them watching so intently.

They got off the elevator onto the third floor and headed into a larger and taller building cut deep into the rock that rose up to the second and first floor, all the way to the top. Aly realized neither she nor Mark had ever been this close to the surface, at least not since they had arrived on Lethe. They made their way through the wide corridors and across one bridge, over a stock room, until they came to a pair of doors that opened as they approached. Beyond was a huge circular area with a wide-open ceiling that could be seen all the way to the top, surrounded by white and blue lights. Ahead stood what she estimated to be more than half of all the enforcers stationed on Lethe Maws (which wasn't many) and near to them was the rest of her crew.

"You two all right?" Julian asked as the enforcers brought her and Mark in with the group.

"I think so?" said Mark, uncertain.

"What's going on?" Aly asked.

Kate, who kept close to Julian, shook her head. "Not sure, they wouldn't say."

Braxin came out of the fold of men and women to stand before them. His yellow gaze studied them briefly, his mouth set in its usual hard frown. "The Xolis Council has decided," he said sharply. "Lethe Maws will no longer be your home."

They all stood in shocked silence, Aly worst of all.

"So, where are we going, then?" Ethan asked first.

Braxin did not speak. Instead, he bowed his head and left them without a word. As he stepped away, a wind shot down from above, like a sudden whirlwind. A ship covered over the open roof then dropped downward until it landed soundly in the center before them. The doors opened and three nillium stepped from the ship. Two they didn't recognize, while the third they knew almost immediately.

"Fuck," someone muttered. Aly stood rigid, her body gone cold.

Marzin walked across, with the two others at his sides, his black uniform billowing in the wind. As they stopped before the team, he looked them over without so much as a 'hello.'

"The bands," he said.

Right away, before anyone could argue or even struggle, the two nillium unsheathed a pair of red blades and cut the techbands from each of their wrists. They tossed them over to the other enforcers, who quickly dismantled them.

"Where are you taking us?" Julian asked.

Marzin nodded his head, and the nillium duo went around and began shoving them down to their knees. All the men anyway. Not the women. Marzin looked from Kate, to Cilia to Jamie and then to Aly. "You are to come with us back to Nihl," he said plainly. "Where it will then become your permanent home."

Aly thought she might be sick. "No," she said aloud before she could even stifle the words. Marzin stared at her, but Aly couldn't stop. "No, No!"

She thought she might scream. This couldn't be happening. The other women began to grow restless around her.

"What do you mean?" Kate said, stepping away from one of the enforcers, who tried to reach for her. "What do you mean our permanent home? We are supposed to return to Earth."

"No," Marzin said. "The Council has decided. You will remain in Xolis." After a nod of his head, the enforcers took hold of them. Julian and Davis started to stand but were promptly pushed back down.

Jamie cried out, and Cilia wrenched her arm but couldn't break free. They shouted and cursed, trying to pull away.

"What are you doing? Why are you taking them and not us?" Julian said, struggling in one enforcer's grip.

"Take them to the ship," Marzin commanded. The nillium did as ordered, dragging them away. Aly dropped to her knees, and Jamie, beside her, screamed. The other enforcers came around and helped carry them. Aly heard the men shouting. Julian rose again but was shoved back down.

"Answer me! Why are you taking them?" Julian shouted.

Marzin turned back but did not fully look at him. "They are ours now. We need them."

And that was all. Marzin left them, and Aly and the others were pulled away. Kate reached for Juilan, shouting his name. The others cried out, as did Aly, knowing more than any of them what was going to happen. Mark called out to her and Aly, without thought, screamed for Ryziel. Panic-driven, she clawed at the one who held her and beat at his arms, but there was no stopping them. The shouts and screams of her team rang heavily in her ears, but no matter how she fought, the ship drew closer and the men slipped farther away.

The enforcers who gathered around the men shoved them back. Then, as if time had suddenly stretched itself thin, turning seconds into hours, Aly watched as the enforcers drew out their shooters, aimed them at the men, and fired.

Aly saw Mark's face last before a flash of white light hit them and they each went limp on the ground. A piercing, awful scream ripped from Jamie's mouth, followed by a heart-wrenching moan from Kate. Aly went numb. She stopped fighting the man who held her and let him carry her the rest of the way to the ship. She felt nothing, thought nothing. All she could do was stare at the bodies of her crew spread across the floor and of the women fighting to reach them.

She couldn't even think of Ryziel in that moment or of the fact that she was leaving Lethe Maws without him. Leaving for Nihl.

She had no thoughts at all, as if she had left her body and was watching everything from afar. All until she was pulled onto the ship and the door closed behind her, shutting her away.

* * *

The first tank was finished, the second was more than halfway done, and the third (filled specifically with ionx) would follow soon after. From the converter, Nar began to create the ship's exterior parts while Ryziel began to sift through and reorganize all the necessary equipment they would need to bring onboard. A few things would have to be left behind, he realized, in order to make room for the humans, but it didn't worry him in the slightest. He would destroy any evidence that he had been there, returning the cave to nothing more than the empty shell it had been when they had first discovered it.

They had been working all morning when the wide outer door opened suddenly, and Xilya shot into the room before it had risen halfway.

"What the hell are you doing here?" Nar asked. "Aren't you supposed to be—"

"They're gone." It was the first time either Ryziel or Nar had seen her flustered. Her tail swayed from side to side her, her eyes searching around until they found Ryziel.

"Who?" Nar asked.

Xilya stared at Ryziel, and in some terrible way, he knew.

"The humans," she said. "I heard it for myself and saw the ship go. The men are dead. The women have been taken. Aly with them." She bowed her head at Ryziel, who hadn't moved, had barely drawn breath, his Drega woke in a violent fit as if someone had smacked it in the face.

"Where?" he managed to growl out. His body tensed to run, to fight, but there was no enemy to chase or to strike. Panic and despair and unfathomable rage welled in him instead. "Where?" he snapped.

Xilya did not snarl or snap back at him. Her expression only darkened as she said in a quiet but unfaltering voice, "To Nihl. They have gone to Nihl."

CHAPTER THIRTY

Nᴉʜʟ

The first thing Aly saw as she exited the ship was the light from the sun, an orange orb in the sky that dipped low to the horizon but never touched it. The light made her squint her eyes considerably, blinding her, forcing her to shield her face with her hands. She couldn't see much of anything around her except for the outlines of buildings nearby and the tan-colored ground beneath her feet.

She remembered very little of her trip to Nihl. All was mostly darkness and the soft, sometimes wailing, other times muffled, cries of the others around her. Even now, Kate's face had aged from the time between leaving the mines and landing on the hot, bright planet they tread across in that moment. Jamie, too, looked like a stranger, her face hollow and tear-stained. Cilia seemed the only one who had kept some of her composure, though she looked ready to kill. Aly had been silently numb the whole way. She did not cry or scream or fight. Instead, she had drawn away from the situation altogether, crawling deep into herself. A robot who only walked where Marzin and the others told her to.

Eventually, they stopped just before the gates leading into some courtyard and were ordered to declothe; to wear some kind of thin red dress similar to a sari with a hood and shawl.

Whether out of fear or hopelessness, they complied. Their suits were thrown away, though they were allowed to keep their packs. Then, hoods were tossed over their heads to hide their faces. They were marched through the gates, past the courtyard with a magnificent fountain and plants of a kind she had never seen. Things she might have appreciated and looked on fondly if the situation were different. If she were with Ryziel by her choosing and not ordered by Marzin.

Once they entered through a large set of doors and started down a large passage with open rooms to each side, Aly began to wake out of herself and memorize her surroundings. The house—as she was sure that was what it was—was more than just some mansion—it was a palace. The pink and tan walls were decorated neatly with glittering blue and green mosaics, the floor of the same color was carpeted with lush red and purple rugs; golden lamps sparkled with colors, some she couldn't even describe, and satin curtains swayed along the frames to each open doorway, beckoning them to enter. There was the smell of something sweet in the air, like roses or lilies, and she could hear the singing of birds somewhere unseen as they passed by a well-kept garden.

It was a paradise. A dazzling, beautiful heaven.

And she hated it.

They came to another set of doors at the end of the hall and stepped on through into what Aly could only describe as a lounge or sitting area. Couches and chairs made up most of the room, along with a smattering of tables, one of which seemed to hold enough food for a banquet. Statues stood within alcoves, reminding her of those found in Yurza's Keep, holding bowls of flickering flames.

Aly only took in these few details as they were ordered to a halt before a group seated in front of them, a regal pack of nillium in their finely cut suit coats and dress. Aly's eyes drifted over them and stopped dead on a man lounging in a chair, staring calmly back at them.

"Nihl Korzien." Marzin bowed his head slightly toward the man. Before the man could speak, a sort of whimpering cry escaped from Aly's dry lips. The man's gaze fell on her, and Aly stood there, shocked by her reaction as much as by the nillium male before her. A man who, by some unfair draw of the gene pool, resembled Ryziel in almost every way save for his golden skin and hair and his eyes.

The man tilted his head at her, amusement flashing in his gaze. "So, these are the human women we have come to hear so much about." His eyes flickered down her body, and Aly wanted to shrivel up and disappear right there. "Hm. Odd as they are, it is the same stirring as I felt before. You were right after all, Marzin."

Aly didn't know what he meant and didn't care to. She and the others stood as still and quiet as ghosts before his critical stare. He eyed each of them until he returned to Aly. With a gesture of his hand, Aly found herself dragged closer before him. He took her hand in his, turning her wrist upward as his fingers stroked gently at her skin. "What is your name, girl?"

Aly didn't say a word, though her lips trembled.

He smiled at her, and her stomach twisted. "Shy, are you? No matter." His fingers pressed lightly against her, and it took all her will not to draw her hand back.

Another nillium man, paler and smaller than the others, came over and pulled at a lock of her hair. "Ugly, if you ask me. I don't like their stubbed noses. Though this one has nice hair...and eyes."

"Zyr, you would bed one whether it had two noses and a scaly face," laughed another nillium beside Korzien.

Zyr snorted. "Hardly."

Korzien did not look away from her as his smile widened. "I think she's rather lovely." His fingers slipped from her wrist to press at her palm. "And she has delicate little hands, do you see? I'll bet they are delicate in their touch as well." His thumb stroked her hand, and this time, Aly couldn't take it. She pulled her hand away.

"Oh, she's feisty," said another man nearby. "Better watch yourself, Korzien, or she might bite."

Korzien's smile only slipped slightly, but his eyes never fell from hers. And Aly dared not look away.

"I agree with Zyr," said a female in a black hooded dress. "They are ugly. Don't bother yourself with them, Korzien, surely."

Korzien's eyes narrowed, but his smile never faltered. "No. I like this one." He took her hand again, gentle but firm. "And we can't blame them for being skittish, can we? Now," his hand tightened considerably around her, "what is your name, girl?"

She hissed in pain. "Aly," she whispered.

"Aly? Hm, not a very pretty name, but it's not your fault. Well, Aly, we are here to celebrate. Would you like something to eat? To drink?" He released her hand and made a gesture, and immediately, a pair of hooded servants (not oracles, Aly noted), with faces hidden under the thin cloth of their shawls, approached, though he promptly ignored them. "Sit down, the lot of you."

Aly and the others were pushed down into seats, with hers closest to Korzien. She could hear Jamie beginning to weep silently beside her, but none even looked at her. Cilia argued that she didn't want to sit and threw a few profanities their way, until she was slapped hard across the face and forced into silence. Though tears streamed down her cheeks, Kate kept her composure.

"Please, we just want to go home," Kate said, trying to use her most diplomatic voice. "We mean no trouble. It was a mistake that we found ourselves here."

"There is no mistake," Korzien said. "It is by Nihl's doing that you have been given to us. This is your home now. So." He gestured again to the servants. "Let us celebrate."

The servants came around and placed a glass in each of their hands, filled with some sort of yellow liquid. Korzien took one for himself, and the others around him followed suit.

"Let us drink to this historic occasion. An odd but needed gift from Nihl, who has answered our prayers." He began to raise his glass then lowered it. "Ah, but we are missing one, aren't we? Marzin, bring the other one down."

Marzin seemed to hesitate. "She may be resting..."

Korzien waved him off. "I think she will be happy to join us."

Marzin left, with another little bow of his head. As they waited, Korzien asked the others for their names. Kate spoke hers in a whisper that turned into a choked sob and neither Cilia nor Jamie felt compelled to answer.

"Maybe we should give them Nihl-appropraite names," said Zyr. "This one"—he pointed to Cilia—" can be called Sazia. Bull-faced. And this one"—he pointed to Jamie—" can be called Fila. For a simpering little—"

"Enough, Zyr," Korzien said, dismissing him. "Your words are irritating. Leave them be."

Aly had remained rigid beside him, silently battling with whether or not to confess in front of all of them that she knew his brother and that Ryziel would return home and show him what a mistake he was making. But in the end, she knew she couldn't risk it. Not when Ryziel was still stuck on Lethe Maws and could still get caught. She had to wait, knowing he would come.

Marzin returned, and behind him entered a small, hooded figure, another woman by her dress, holding a bundle in her arms. They stopped before the group and the hooded figure gasped, throwing back her hood.

Aly stared and so did the others, as Sarah, their lost crew member, stared back at them.

"You're really here," she said, her voice shaking, and the bundle in her arms began to cry.

* * *

They all sat quietly now, huddled close together, close to Sarah, who clutched tight to the child in her arms, returned to its slumbering state. There had been a sort of eruption, a break of emotions at the sight of her, each of them bursting into tears, reaching for her, pulling her to the ground with them, until they were quelled by the nillium guards, forced back into obedient silence. They listened to Korzien speak then drank the sickly-sweet wine offered to them, but their focus only lay on their lost crewmember and the child. A child who looked more nillium than human save for its faded color and softer skin.

"What did they do?" Kate whispered, clutching Sarah's arm. "What the hell did they do?"

"A little experiment," Korzien answered. "Thanks to Marzin." He nodded toward him. "What do you think? Would you make another?"

Marzin looked down on Sarah, who cast her eyes up to him then quickly looked away, her face turning red.

"If it is as strong as the oracles say. Perhaps." Marzin stood emotionless as he watched Sarah's back.

Aly felt a cold, sharp jab hit her stomach. The others looked down at the child, horrified. When they each in turn came to the realization of what that sleeping bundle meant and saw the sullen, shaking woman holding it, they knew why they had been brought to Nihl.

"Fuck this," Cilia said. "And fuck you!" she spat. She shot up. "I won't have one of those...those monsters! I won't!"

With a nod of Korzien's head, Cilia was slapped again into silence and shoved back down with a groan. Jamie began to wail again, reaching for her, but was promptly held back.

"In time, you will accept the inevitable," Korzien said calmly. He took a sip from his glass then set it down gently beside him. "For it must be as Nihl has wished it to be."

Aly shook her head, rage beginning to fill up her insides. She clenched her hands into fists and looked straight at the brother of her mate. "Why us?" she asked in a near whisper, trying to keep her voice from shaking. "Why would you want us? You have your own women."

The lone nillium woman in the room stared sharply back at her with a venomous, bitter gaze.

Korzien sighed. "Oh, we would wish that, trust me." He got up and went over to the lone female, taking her hand in his. She looked up at him, her bitterness turned sad. "Nihl, however, has punished them for some unknown reason." He brushed his fingers against the woman's cheek. "Our women, for many years now, have gone barren. Those who do conceive give us deformed monstrosities or weak, powerless babes who soon die not long after." He dropped his hand and turned to Aly. "And so, we were forced to seek other means. It is a sin to create and manipulate life through artificial means, so we had to get creative. We tried with many others: lygin, corax, krull, skra. None could conceive nor carry a nillium child in their womb. Yet, still, we tried, keeping our experiments secret." He came to sit again, leaning in close to her. "We began to lose hope. But then, what should be found on a lowly tradership but a new race." His hand reached out to her, and she grew still as his fingers stroked through her hair. "A strange little race that Marzin rescued and claimed they had made his receptors vibrate and his Drega stir for the first time in years." His hand reached out to her face, but she turned away. "Even now, I feel it too." He dropped his hand and sat back. "So, we kept one of your own by Marzin's choosing and gave her a nillium life. Then we waited." He turned up his hands and laughed. "And, by Nihl, it worked, didn't it? You see now for yourself. Though they will likely be weaker with their human blood, they are decidedly stronger than any yet made. A miracle." He picked up his glass and held it to the servant, who poured him more wine. "So. We brought you here now and we celebrate. Because you lot are blessed, truly blessed, to save us from our extinction. Perhaps you are upset now, but it's only because you have yet to understand how special you are. You, who might have been worthlessly growing and spreading somewhere in the universe for no real cause or reason now have a greater purpose." He held up his glass as he smiled prettily down at her. "And you will be thankful for it."

CHAPTER THIRTY-ONE

Xilya had not been entirely right. They were not made slaves—at least not yet—but they were locked away in the First House which, according to Korzien, was the highest house to Nihl, the ruling house, that all others bowed to. Maybe she would have thought it exciting or funny to think that, the whole time she had been with Ryziel, she had actually been with what was the equivalent in her world to a prince, but it didn't really make her feel much of anything in that moment of realization, only made her think of Ryziel, wondering if he had yet finished the ship, and if he was on his way.

No, they were not slaves. But like the slaves—or servants as they called them—they too were locked away, forced to hide themselves, like living shadows walking the grounds waiting for the inevitable which, to Korzien, would come on the day following the First Night. The night that came only once a month and lasted only an hour. And when the sun rose back into the sky, that was when they would have to face their inevitable fate. Submit and conceive and be locked away again until a child was born. And then the cycle would continue.

Nihl's months were longer than Earth's months, so, by Aly's

count, they were about twenty-five days into the current month, which ended on day forty-three. Very little time to wait.

In the days following their arrival, they were given their own rooms, their own clothes, were fed well and were allowed to stay together for most of the day. They were not disturbed by anyone, and the nillium mostly ignored them altogether. They could walk the grounds and the gardens and the many rooms, and if they were caught trying to walk out the front gates, they were taken back to their rooms with little more than a slap on the wrist, or in the guard's case, a hearty laugh and shake of the head. There were guards everywhere, just as there were servants and nillium and even silions visiting from other worlds or cities. Everywhere, there were people, so to escape unseen was impossible. And even if they did, they would have nowhere to go. The City of Light was a large, dense city, with the other houses spread across its territory. Someone would see them. The only hope was to escape to the shipyard, but that too was heavily guarded. They talked and talked every day, trying to form a plan but every sound idea was shot down by some logical and real problem.

And then there was Korzien. He left them well enough alone, but there were those few days when he cared to amuse himself with their company. Or at least Aly's company.

Yes, as awfully ironic as it was, he had taken a liking to her alone. In fact, one sundown, he gathered them together and made the grand decision that they should be chosen accordingly amongst those born of the First House so as not to cause any trouble at dawn after First Night.

"We have our pick, though it isn't much," he said.

"My father should have a choice, don't you think?" Zyr said from next to him.

"You're absolutely right." Korzien waved his hand, and a servant disappeared. A moment later, they returned, and Aly drew herself up straight as she stared into the eyes of the man who caused Ryziel so much pain.

"Uncle, you have been lurking in the house for days, and you have yet to meet those blessed to us by Nihl," Korzien said.

The man Korzien and Ryziel called uncle was older and rougher around the edges compared to the other nillium. Though he still had that same arrogant, rigid air about him, he also looked weary, almost sick even, his head bowed slightly, his mouth set in a hard frown, even his receptors curved in a sad sort of droop over his head.

For the first time on Nihl, Aly felt a spark of hope at the sight of him. Ryziel could beat him easily, she could even tell that. But still, the fear of what came after the challenge kept her worries the same.

It wasn't really the uncle she was concerned about.

Her eyes drew over to Korzien, jaw clenched tight as he sat back casually in his chair. "Go on, Uncle. If it matters not to you, then just pick one and be done with it."

The uncle snarled as he looked at the lot of them. "This is what you call me out of my study for?" He wheezed then coughed, his hand wiping at his mouth. "You might as well have brought me out to the farms and told me to pick out a drow from a herd of cattle."

Korzien smiled. "Very well, uncle, don't worry yourself of it then."

Their uncle left with a sneer and not another word. Korzien merely shrugged at Zyr, who frowned.

"I will choose one for him, then," he said. He looked over them each and his eyes fell to Kate and to Aly. "One of them, I guess." He pointed between her and Kate uncertainly.

"That one is mine." Korzien was firm as he said it, his golden eyes set hard on Aly, so she knew. "He can have the other."

"Cock-sucking bastards." It was Cilia who spoke, not in the Xolis tongue, but in clear English. With so many eyes and ears watching them, it had been Kate who suggested they talk in English, though only to each other. Cilia, on the other hand, couldn't help spilling a few profanities, thinking it safer to make sure the nillium couldn't understand her lest she get slapped again.

And it worked sometimes because Korzien only laughed. "I'll bet that wasn't very nice," he said. "Give her to Azil. He will have a good time keeping her quiet."

"Fine." Zyr looked to Jamie with a frown similar to his father's. "I guess I'll take this one. Maybe it will be out of tears by First Night and I won't have to look at its whimpering face."

After that, Aly was subjected much more to Korzien's presence. And, even then, she was mostly ignored, sitting beside him where he didn't so much as look at her as he talked with the others. But when he did look, he gave her a hard, thoughtful stare that lasted until someone got his attention.

Aly did not cower before him. Sometimes she even met his gaze with a hard stare of her own. She did not shout profanities or physically fight them, but she didn't cry or beg either. All she did was wait. For that was all she could do. Because the only chance they had was in Ryziel. And she knew he was coming for them. For her. He had to be.

On one particular sundown, Korzien once again commanded her to him. She was prepared for another dinner party where she would sit in obedient silence and be ignored. Maybe he would look at her again, and maybe she would look back at him and there would be nothing there but hate (except maybe a brief stab of pain as she gazed on a man who looked too much like her Ryziel). Then she would return to her room as if nothing happened, take out her sketchbook that she had secreted under her bed, and flip through the pages, maybe even draw a sketch or two if she wasn't feeling a lot worse than usual. Yes, she expected the same routine.

But Korzien always had a way of shattering her expectations.

"You know, girl," he said after a moment of staring. He never actually cared to call her by her name even, though he knew what it was. "There isn't much to be proud of in having you as my chosen one. You humans are so plain and small and, well, simple really." He said this in front of his nillium brethren, even in the middle of another's conversation, cutting off their story about a pair of grex they met in one of the cities to the south. "There's really not much there that one would say is especially fascinating or impressive, wouldn't you agree, Azil?"

The nillium sitting across the table from them looked over at her then nodded his head in agreement.

"And yet. There is something. Maybe it's just the Drega stirring. That instinctual need to mate, you know? It's such an odd feeling, though, to feel it for you."

Aly said nothing. She dared not even move as he settled himself closer to her.

"It's actually kind of...what's the word? Aggravating."

Aly remained still and didn't turn her head to look away from him. She licked her lips, knowing she shouldn't say a word but doing so anyway. "If I irritate you so much, perhaps you can dismiss me from your presence."

Korzien waved his hand and sighed. "I'm afraid that won't be any good. But it does make me wonder something. There are only five of you and a whole lot more nillium. Many sons that need to be made. I hate to think what kind of trouble that could entail. And I really don't want to have to kill you if it comes to it."

Aly kept herself from flinching, just barely, her eyes never leaving his. His hand stroked down her arm then took her hand. "It's like a need to keep you from others. Which is a problem because I will be expected to share you." His thumb grazed over her palm while he thought. "And the other girls can't take on all the burden. They will break so easily." He sighed again and dropped her hand. "Something will have to be done."

Aly didn't want to wonder what he might be thinking. She also didn't care for the idea of getting killed because he didn't want to share her. Not that she wanted to be shared either. He rubbed at his temples and his receptors before looking at her again. "Nihl works in mysterious ways. Why he would force his firstborn to mate with a low breed is worrying enough. But to have us feel for them is just as disturbing. Tell me, do you agree?"

The other nillium men nodded. Their eyes all drew toward her in a way that made Aly's stomach squirm.

He tapped a finger on her shoulder. "It is a fault which we nillium cannot have. Do you know why, girl?"

Aly swallowed hard. "No."

"Did they not teach you anything at that refugee facility? Tell me you know, then, what nillium means?"

"I don't know."

"It means perfect. As Nihl is perfect. But this union feels far from it. And, though I pray to Nihl for understanding, I cannot grasp the reason."

Aly said nothing, but in her mind, she saw an image of herself smiling wickedly at him. 'On my world,' her thought-self said, 'On my world, Nihl means nothing. Literally nothing at all, you son of a bitch. You are nothing. You mean nothing.'

She didn't voice it, but she hoped he saw the thought in her eyes.

He sat back and regarded her, a frown twisting his perfect features as if he had heard her after all. "Yes," he whispered. "Something will have to be done."

A couple more days passed. The women continued to talk, to try and form a plan, but that was all. And when they weren't talking, they were sitting around or walking and occasionally crying. Kate, now leader of the remaining crew, did her best to keep things together, to organize their gatherings, to be there to listen or be their shoulder to cry on, but Aly could see her self-control slipping day by day. Many times, Aly found her sitting alone, weeping quietly, calling out Julian's name.

The others were still trying to cope in the only ways they could. Jamie had resorted to mute silence, barely saying a word save for a few mumbles, and Cilia talked the loudest, the angriest, but had little to say that was worth saying.

Sarah surprisingly, was much more calm, much more cheerful. It was nice to see her optimism at first, until they realized it wasn't because she expected them to escape but that she had already given up entirely on the idea that they ever would, accepting that this was their new life. Many times, they watched with dread as she smiled and hummed to the child in her arms, watching their inevitable future before their very eyes.

Aly helped in any way she could, but she too found herself slipping away, sometimes for hours, just to stare out at nothing. An awful paranoia had begun to seep into her mind, one thought being that she could not even whisper Ryziel's name inside the house in fear that someone would hear and know he was coming. That they would find him, and he would be stopped before he could save them. It was why she hadn't brought herself to speak a word of what she knew to the others, even though it could bring them hope (regardless of whether they actually believed her). And when that thought didn't drive her mad, the second thought surely did: that Ryziel would come, but he wouldn't try to save them.

After all, she knew well enough from their talks how much he cared for and loved his brother. It took her several days to come to terms with the idea that, though she was certain he would return to Nihl to challenge his uncle, he would not, under any circumstances, go against his brother. And he might not fight to free them.

These dark thoughts turned to nightmares every time she slept. A few times, she hadn't bothered to sleep at all, though the thoughts never stopped, never went away.

And, unintentional or not, Korzien always made things worse.

"What is this?" Aly said one morning, staring down at her bed after coming out of the bath as a servant drew away the curtains. The servant turned to her, another faceless specter in a red robe, and bowed their head for no particular reason.

"It is a gift," they said.

Aly closed her eyes. She knew the answer, but she asked anyway. "From who?"

"Nihl Korzien."

Aly opened her eyes and stared at the jewels laid out on her bed. Blue sparkling gems with a touch of green, strung together on a necklace tied with pearls.

"Take it back," Aly said. "Tell him I refuse."

The servant bowed again. "I'm afraid I cannot do that. He says they are yours now."

Aly turned her head to argue, and she saw a pair of yellow eyes staring back at her, pleading. It was a lygin, a young one. Aly closed her mouth but did not move to touch the necklace. The servant left without a word, leaving Aly to dress.

She found herself wandering one of the many gardens. It was warm already and another clear, beautiful day, with a bright blue-green sky. The plants and trees swayed gently to a soft breeze, and she could smell the scent of something sweet in the air. The light, the warmth, the colors, all of it should have brought her at least some happiness. But, like its name, Nihl made her feel nothing.

"Ah, there you are."

Aly turned to see Korzien walking toward her, wearing his dark blue and gold-cut suit coat unbuttoned, a charming sort of grin on his face. The grin fell slightly when he stood beside her and looked down at her bare neck. "You do not wear my gift."

"No," Aly said flatly. "I don't."

"Pity. I would have liked to see it on you." His hand reached up to trail his fingers across her collarbone then slid up to gently encircle her neck. "They were the closest I could find to matching your eyes." He tilted her head up so that she was forced to look at him. His hand squeezed slightly before he released her. "Come, walk with me."

Aly didn't move. She glanced over at a wall nearby and saw the guards watching her. Not wishing to face the embarrassment of being dragged beside him at his command, Aly forced herself to walk.

"I have been doing a lot of meditating and some praying the last couple of days," he began as they walked. "And I have decided that I am no longer troubled by the idea of you being my chosen nor the feelings that come with it."

"Great," Aly said.

"If it is Nihl's wish, then it cannot be a fault. There is a good reason. You must have been made for us. But the conditions had to be right, so you were made somewhere else. This is why your kind have not been found in Xolis, yet you being here now is meant to be."

Aly listened but cared little to comment. She jumped as his hand came around her waist.

"And so, this union is right, but it is not perfect. But it could be."

She glared up at him, wondering what he thought could possibly make it right or perfect.

"I know you hate me, but it doesn't really matter in the end," he said suddenly, keeping his arm around her as they walked. "Things would be easier, of course, if you didn't. It doesn't take much to obey, really." He stopped walking to have her face him. "It doesn't take much at all. You have been a good girl so far and slip-ups will happen, I have no doubt. I am a patient man, but I also can't ignore defiance, even when mostly innocent." His hand came up behind her head to gently take hold of her hair. "Because obedience isn't hard. It's not." He tugged her hair so that she was forced to tilt her head. "So, when I say do something, there should be no need to hesitate. When I give you something, it should not be hard to use it. You can even say how much you hate it. I won't mind. I won't care." His hand tightened, making her wince. Her face turned hot, eyes stinging. "But you will do it. If I give you a gift, you will wear it. If I ask you to walk with me, you won't hesitate to think about whether or not you will. You just do. It will be better for both of us." He released her, and it took all her will not to reach up and rub at her head. A guard came through one of the garden entrances and whispered in Korzien's ear. He nodded and then smiled back at her. "Now, take my hand and follow me. We have visitors."

CHAPTER THIRTY-TWO

HE TOOK HER INTO A PRIVATE COURTYARD WHERE THERE WAITED five aliens of various races. Two were grex, huge for their kind, the third a scarred lygin and the fourth a slender, green-gilled, amphibian-like female of a race Aly had only seen a few times called skra.

The fifth she had never seen before except for maybe in a nightmare. She wasn't sure what to even compare him to. The only words that came to mind were *death* and *predator*. His dark purple skin seemed to absorb the light around him—his eyes, sunken into his face —were orange like the sun at sundown. He wore strange silvery-black armor, and what little she could see of his skin seemed to have bright patches or stripes of white paint brushed along it, which also covered his face, making it look skull-like. His ears were long and sharp, stretching past his head, where white hair grew thickly between them. There was so much to him that Aly caught herself staring.

The group huddled around the fountain at the center, heads turning as Korzien and Aly approached.

"I am glad you all could come," Korzien said, releasing her hand. "I am the heir to the First House, Nihl Korzien. I know you don't care to waste time on formalities or small talk, so I will get right to it. I have asked you all here for a simple job. One that won't be easy but will be rewarded well if completed."

They listened, expressionless. The fifth one's eyes drifted over to Aly, and she quickly looked away.

"Do you see this person here?" Korzien placed his hand on her shoulder. "This girl is called a human. They came to Xolis not long ago from traders. Through interrogating these traders and studying the few things they took, we know about their human ship and which planet it was found on. With the help of oracles and silion scientists we have charted a possible path that could potentially lead to human territory. Your job is to explore that territory and bring back what you find. Specifically," his hand squeezed her shoulder as he pushed her forward, "more human girls like this."

Aly looked up at him, wide-eyed, speechless. The purple alien drew out a blade from a sheath at his thigh and looked it over carefully. "That could take a long time, assuming your scientists are right," he said in a low but smooth voice.

"You'll be given all the necessary provisions," Korzien said, giving Aly a warning glare not to interrupt him as she shook her head continuously. "And we are confident that you will find something, at least a trace if not more. You will be rewarded depending on what you bring back, whether that be information or actual humans." He looked back over at them and nodded. "I am confident one of you will at least find something." His eyes drew over to the purple alien. "Especially from you, Nezka. From what I have heard."

Nezka's mouth curved ever so slightly as he flipped the blade in his hands. "And what have you heard?"

Korzien smiled back at him. "The rumors abound. The bounty hunter from nowhere who always finds his prey. Vesra's greatest killer, who likes his drink and his women even more. Who those call Voidstorm. Or so it goes."

Nezka stopped playing with his blade and slipped it back to his thigh. He looked over at Aly then back at Korzien. "I want half now and repairs done to my ship."

"We can discuss a deal after—"

"That is my deal. Take it or don't."

Aly waited nervously for Korzien to react, expecting a nod and one of the guards standing by the wall to cut the alien's head off for interrupting. Instead, he only grinned and laughed. "Fearless. I like you. Stay, then, for the day and we will talk. Same for the lot of you," he said to the others. "And because I am nice, I'll repair your ships while we do so, whether you agree to go or not."

'In other words,' Aly thought. 'Say no and we will blow your ship out of the sky as it leaves the atmosphere. Just because we can.'

The others seemed to know it. Only Nezka was unphased. He stood up, his legs slightly bent as he walked across the courtyard. The others followed suit.

"Oh, but one thing," Korzien said, stopping him. "You can treat yourself to the servants if you wish, but nillium women are off limits. And if I see you even touch one of our human girls, I will have your insides stripped out and hung off the outer gates. Do you understand?"

Nezka twisted around to face him. He glanced back at Aly, his eyes flickering down her body then back up. He smiled, and Aly caught a set of curved fangs poking out from his mouth. "Tempting," he said and disappeared.

* * *

Aly saw the hunters roaming the grounds throughout the day, a constant fear gripping her every time she encountered them. She wished she had done something, even if all she did was scream or shout or beat her fists, cursing them and Korzien in that courtyard. But if her silence seemed like cowardice on her part, she told herself it was the smarter thing to do. After all, what good would it have done her? No amount of screaming or shouting would stop them. All she might receive in return was a good solid cuff to the face from Korzien, silencing her for good.

But the more she watched the hunters walking around or talking to one another or even fighting in one of the courtyards, she wished she had at least put up some kind of fight.

Because the idea of them finding more humans and hunting down other girls for the nillium was sickening and horrifying.

In fact, she thought she might be sick now as she watched the pair of grex dueling in the wide courtyard close by.

Covering her mouth, she rushed down the passage, desperately looking for a bathroom. Unable to make it in time, she found a plant pot instead and vomited inside it. As her vomiting turned into a dry heave, Aly thought her nerves must finally be shot for good. She was at least impressed she had made it as long as she did.

When she was finished, she straightened and wiped her mouth with a shaky hand. Something had to be done. They had to be stopped. Someone had to stop them. She could mention to the others about the hunters but feared that sort of news might just be the tipping point to completely undo them. And even then, what could they do? There was no means to communicate with anyone, no one who would be able to help them. They couldn't get to the ships, they couldn't run, and they couldn't hide.

As the sun began to drop, servants lit lamps inside and opened curtains. One came to her now, ignoring the fact that she had just thrown up in one of the pots, to tell her that dinner would be served soon, and Nihl Korzien expected her by his side.

Aly took her time walking back through the house, clutching her stomach, which now throbbed with a sort of dull pain. The servant led her to a private room on the second floor, and, once admitted inside, she found Korzien, Zyr, and the hunter, Nezka, sitting by a table on the balcony, sharing some bluym in a pipe.

"Ah, there you are." Korzien gestured for her to take a seat beside him.

Aly hesitated before she stepped into the room and sat down, trying not to cough from the spicy smoke wafting in the air now tickling her throat. As soon as she took her seat, she was ignored, save for Nezka's eyes drifting over briefly, showing obvious curiosity.

"We can give you a pulse tracker. That should make it even easier to find them," Korzien said, continuing their conversation. "We've already taken samples of their DNA and synced them to those we have on-hand." He took a hit of his pipe, the burning glow of the tip catching in his eyes. "As we said, we don't want the males. You could dispose of them for all I care. Any defenses they have shouldn't be a problem, but it would probably be wise to be stealthy."

"I'm not worried about that. My ship has shadowcast siding and several detection blockers," Nezka replied, lounging back in his chair and blowing out a lazy trail of smoke. "But I'll need at least two ionx capsules. I can convert them easily enough into the engine bank."

Zyr grimaced. "Two capsules is a stretch, don't you think? By Nihl, you could be across the galaxy and back before using up even half of one."

Nezka shrugged. "A better precaution. Those traders probably had a decent store of their own, I imagine, if they made it to another system altogether to find these humans. And who knows how much these humans traveled before reaching the planet, if it is assumed that they were exploring. Which could mean they didn't get far or they had been sailing for a long time. Better to assume the latter." He tilted his head and glanced at Aly. "Just in case."

Zyr scoffed, but Korzien held up his hand.

"He has a point, Zyr. We can give him the capsules. We aren't hard up for them, and more will come in time."

Zyr tapped his fingers on the table then relit his pipe. "Fine," he snapped. "But only for him. The others will have to make do with a half capsule at most."

"Really, I only hired them just for the spread, but it is you, my friend," Korzien pointed, "who I am confident the most in. Find them and gain their location at the very least. If you bring back a few, even better. After that, we can start sending out our own ships."

Aly listened and felt her body turn cold then hot. She clenched her hands into fists on her lap, trying not to be sick again.

"And maybe, just maybe, if things turn out well enough," Korzien continued, "we'll give you one, a nice girl perhaps, like this one here, assuming there are plenty to go around."

Aly felt Nezka's eyes on her again, and this time, she glanced back, glaring, hoping he could see the hate there.

Korzien leaned forward and placed more bluym in his pipe. "I know you are intrigued by them. I can tell. I think it's their soft innocence that does it. They are so delicate. I am curious to see how they break in the bedroom." He laughed, his hand brushing the back of Aly's head. "And they are not always meek, mind you, though some have shown to be. But they can be fierce little things too, even in their silence. Isn't that right, girl?"

Aly didn't respond. She didn't turn her gaze away and neither did Nezka.

Nezka took another hit of his pipe. "Very...intrigued," he said in a low, husky sort of voice. A wicked spark lit in his eyes, and Aly felt herself blush.

Her stomach twisted and what she thought might be vomit coming up again was instead words. "You won't find them," she said softly. "You won't find any because we are all that is left."

A blatant lie right to their faces, but she could think of nothing else, and her desperation was too great to care.

They were silent, watching her carefully, Korzien's expression indifferent if not amused. "Is that so?" he said slowly, inhaling then exhaling smoke. He set his pipe down to look over at her more intensely. "That is a very grand statement if it is true." His mouth turned up ever so slightly as he stared at her. "Funny, though, the other girl, Marzin's chosen, said otherwise. She claimed there were quite a few worlds inhabited with your kin."

Aly clenched her jaw, her throat tightening. Damn Sarah and her betraying mouth.

Korzien leaned forward, his face close to hers. "Are you telling me she lied to us? Because if that is true, she will have to be punished rather severely. Perhaps, have her babe taken from her for a week or two or maybe have her tied out for a day with a few lashes across her back."

Aly's mouth trembled.

"Hm? What do you think?" Korzien said, unphased. "I can have it arranged today if it's true. I'll just have one of my guards slip into her room and—"

"It's not," Aly said, cracking under his gaze. "It's not. Please don't harm her."

"Ah. So, then, it was you who lied." Korzien sighed and gently cupped the back of her neck with his hand. "That really disappoints me." With casual effort, he picked up a short-curved blade sitting by a plate of cut meat and held it over a small flame at the center of the table used for lighting their pipes. Still holding her neck, he gripped her tight so she couldn't pull away. The now hot blade rose toward her face, and Aly choked down a tiny whimper. "I don't appreciate being lied to." The blade moved closer, and Aly tensed. "But because I like you, I will let you off with this one warning. Just one. If, however, you ever lie to me again, even if it is the smallest, most innocent lie imaginable, I will take this heated blade and make you suck on it till your tongue is ash in your mouth. Do I make myself clear?"

Aly nodded her head quickly, and the blade dropped.

"Good girl." He released her, and she let out a little hiss of breath.

They continued talking, pretending she wasn't even there, and Aly said no more, allowing herself to float away from the scene altogether, beginning to feel a dull buzz now from the bluym floating in the air. Only when her stomach rolled and she clutched at it, leaning forward, did Korzien look back at her.

"What's wrong now?" he said, more annoyed than concerned.

"I...I don't feel good. Can I please be excused?"

Korzien eyed her curiously for a moment then waved his hand. "Go, then."

Aly went, not bothering with so much as a "goodbye." She slipped out of the room and wandered aimlessly down one hall until she came to some other small garden and sat down at a stone-laid bench covered by a tree with purple leaves. She sat with her head nearly between her knees and just breathed in and out for what felt like hours. When the pain finally subsided, she lifted her head and saw that it was sundown. She was gazing around at the shadows forming along the outer edge of the garden, particularly around the several rows of pillars, when she noticed one shadow looking back at her with a pair of orange eyes.

Nezka watched her as he leaned against a pillar, his hand playing with a collar-like necklace set with violet gems across his neck; one she had yet to notice, just like the small gem-like beads that were set in the skin across his brow.

They stared at one another for a brief moment, until Nezka turned away and Aly shot up and ran after him.

"Please don't do this," Aly called out as he walked away from her down the passage. Nezka stopped and looked back at her. When she caught up to him and stopped several feet from him, she repeated, "Please don't do this."

"Don't what?" he said after a pause.

Aly gave him a grim expression. "Please don't hunt my people down. If you give them up to the nillium, they will be no more than slaves!"

Nezka closed his eyes then opened them slowly. "What can you give me?

Aly stared at him, rage seeping through her whole body, making her shake. "Give you?" she said, in quiet disbelief.

He stepped closer, and Aly flinched but did not move back. His face came close to hers, studying her. "There is nothing you can give. And I am not bound to save you."

Aly shook her head, feeling the sting of tears she refused to let fall. "No," she said. "But you could, knowing that it is right."

Nezka's hand came up, slow yet quick enough she barely had time to react. He touched the side of her bare arm, sharp fingers lightly pressing against her skin. It could have been a sensual touch if he had trailed his hand down like Korzien often did, but he did not, choosing to keep his fingers in place for a few seconds before lifting them away. "Right or no, it doesn't matter. I can't save you."

He turned from her then, and Aly watched him go before calling out to him once more. "If you loved someone, if you truly loved someone and knew they were to be taken away, never to be seen again, how would you cope? How would you survive?" She didn't know why she said it, just that she needed to argue, to make him understand.

Nezka turned back to her. "I don't love anyone. So, I think I'll survive just fine."

Aly's hands clenched into fists. "Then I hope someday you do. I hope someday you know how it feels to love someone and have them taken from you. And that you feel the pain. A pain like nothing ever felt before." She didn't raise her voice as she said it. She whispered it, hoping it sank in deep, moved him somehow.

But his expression didn't change. If anything, he seemed to give her a mocking sort of smile.

"And we will fight. We will fight you. Every step of the way." Before she lost her senses, before the rage consumed her, she turned from him and didn't look back.

CHAPTER THIRTY-THREE

The hunters left the next day. As the sun rose, Aly looked out her window, watching the ships leave the planet. A servant brought her morning meal, but she couldn't eat it, her stomach still set in knots.

She dressed and went out looking for her crew instead. She walked around, avoiding any nillium she could, until she found a small pavilion with Sarah inside, sitting alone with one of the few oracles kept in the house, her baby sleeping next to her in a pile of pillows.

"How is he?" Aly asked, looking down at the child that looked more nillium and less human each day.

"He had a better sleep than usual," Sarah replied, rubbing his belly. The oracle, in the usual white garment, bowed her head as Aly came to sit herself down beside them.

"What's the bot for?" she asked.

Sarah looked back at the oracle. "Just a precaution for the baby. She checks his status every day to make sure his vitals are good and there aren't any health problems."

Aly watched the child sleep for a long moment before turning her eyes back to Sarah. "Will you tell me what happened to you?"

Sarah didn't look up at her. She smiled down at her baby, brushing his hand with her finger. She didn't say anything for a long while, and Aly thought maybe she wouldn't, until she finally said, "They kept me at the facility. I didn't even know you guys had gone. They hadn't told me. I stayed there for some time. Then Marzin came and..."

"He..." Aly tried to ready herself. "He forced himself on you?"

Sarah's brows knitted together, and she shook her head. "No. He stayed with me. He kept me company and...I just felt drawn to him, somehow. I can't really explain it."

Aly knew. She closed her eyes and remembered the first time seeing Ryziel.

"So, well, one thing led to another and after," Sarah said, wiping her face, "after, he left, and when I was told I was pregnant, he came back but only briefly. He was cold after that."

Aly cast her eyes down. "I'm sorry."

Sarah laughed softly. "I begged him to stay, but he wouldn't. I begged him to take me with him, and he wouldn't. I carried the baby, the oracles constantly monitoring me, then," Sarah shrugged, "I gave birth, and only a day later, they came for me. That's when I was brought here. They waited a couple more weeks before they decided the baby was strong enough, then they brought you guys."

"I'm sorry this happened to you," Aly said, completely honest.

"I'm not. I'm upset about Marzin but...I have this baby now." She took Aly's hand and looked at her. "We can survive this. It doesn't have to be so bad. It was devastating at first, but you begin to accept it and, really, it's not so bad."

Aly shook her head, unwilling to believe Sarah meant that or that she understood exactly what was happening to them. All Sarah saw was her child, and somehow, that made her content, regardless of the circumstances.

Aly went to voice her thoughts when another wave of nausea hit her. She bent over with a moan, clutching her stomach.

Sarah's hand gripped her shoulder. "Are you all right?"

Aly licked her lips and tried to sit up. "My stomach...just been bothering me."

"May I take a look?" the oracle suggested, rising from her seat.

"Yes, let her look," Sarah replied. "She can evaluate you."

Aly started to protest. "I'm sure it's just nerves," she said, eyeing the bot nervously.

The oracle stepped over carefully and knelt down beside her. She placed her hand on Aly's stomach and her hand lit up blue.

"Analyzing," she said. Aly thought to pull away, but before she could make up her mind whether to do so, the oracle had already finished. "Done." Her hand dimmed. "Vitals are normal, no serious injury." The oracle stood up. "A healthy system undergoing its first growth cycle."

Aly looked up at the bot with a frown. "What does that mean?"

"I can give you liquid doxin for the pain," she merely said.

"Doxin?" Sarah's eyebrows rose. "Funny, that's what they gave me during my pregnancy." She looked over at Aly with a curious glance. "So, who—?"

"I'm not pregnant. That's not possible," Aly breathed. She shot up and backed away. "It's just nerves. The oracle is wrong."

"Aly, wait," Sarah called.

But Aly only shook her head, her body growing hot, sweat beginning to drip down her neck and back. She turned from them and hurried away. "That's not possible," she whispered, afraid she might pass out. "Not possible."

* * *

She sat alone in some corner of the house, trying to keep herself together, trying to not believe a word the oracle said, trying not to realize that, because of everything that was happening around her, she hadn't noticed she was more than a week late. No, she refused to believe. Because if it were somehow true, Korzien would find out, and he would likely kill her. She didn't believe for a minute he would care or even think about the fact that the baby would be his brother's. She didn't believe he cared for his brother at all; she believed that for a while now. Not once had he mentioned him, not once.

Taking deep breaths, Aly steadied herself, walking one step at a time back toward her room, trying not to have a panic attack.

Before she could reach for her bedroom door, a servant came out of nowhere and told her to follow them. Aly didn't need to ask where they were going. She could already guess.

When they got to the door leading to Korzien's private rooms, the servant knocked then entered, bowing before the nillium prince, who sat at his table by the window. Aly stopped just inside the room and froze, the heat dropping from her body, sweat turning to ice.

"You may go." Korzien waved the servant away without a glance as he flipped through Aly's sketchbook. "Come closer, girl. Come sit down."

Aly didn't move until Korzien's eyes shot up at her with a warning glance. Then she immediately made her way over and sat at a chair beside him. She stared in petrified silence as he shifted through the pages of her sketchbook, through the drawings of Ryziel, stopping to study each one with interest.

"These are very good," he said, without an air of sarcasm. "You have a unique eye, don't you? I confess, when the servant handed me the book and said it was full of drawings, I assumed they would be...well...a little different. More a look at your true feelings than any actual show of skill. And these," his fingers traced over one portrait of Ryziel, with his face turned as if gazing over something in the distance, "well...I think you've captured me rather well. Though having me half naked is a rather curious choice."

Aly sat, stunned speechless. Here she thought she was going to have to make up some well-placed lie as to why she had these portraits of his brother, praying he would believe her, when instead, he didn't see Ryziel at all but saw himself. The drawings weren't colored, though she did shade some parts, but she had to wonder how he couldn't be at least a little suspicious, especially when seeing the picture of Ryziel lying in bed. Surely, that would make him wonder.

But as she carefully observed him, she could see he wasn't toying with her nor was he just incredibly stupid or clueless. No, as she stared at him, she knew it was his narcissism, his bloated ego, that kept him from truly seeing and understanding. He honestly thought she had been sketching him all these days, and he was pleased to see it.

He tore a few of the drawings out of her book and held them up. "I like these the most. I'm going to keep them. I don't think you mind. After all, you made them for me, didn't you?" He smiled at her, and Aly, though pained, smiled back and nodded. He set the pictures down and looked her over. "This truly pleases me. I am glad that, despite your grievances, you are still so honestly drawn to me." He grinned at her, with an amused sort of look, hand splayed across the several pictures he had ripped out. "And I encourage you to make more. In fact, I think I know just the job for you." He handed her back her sketchbook, and Aly took it happily. "I think I will commission you to make a portrait of me. An actual finished one, in color. This will give you something to do other than mope about, and I will be proud to show it off." He glanced away from her to gaze about the room, as if thinking. "Yes, you can call it a gift for me. You can even present it to me on First Night before our joining. The others will be jealous, I am sure. The other girls have shown little talent in such things." He turned back to her and she made sure to keep her face expressionless, if not at least somewhat compliant. She would take this opportunity gratefully. Better this than the thought of what he might do if he had realized it was only his brother she thought of.

"Lovely. Now go on. First Night approaches, and I would have this portrait by then or be very... displeased." He waved her away and Aly rose. Clutching her sketchbook tight to her, she glanced back briefly at the drawings of Ryziel on the table then left without a word.

* * *

By the next morning, she had everything she needed to make Korzien's portrait, except Korzien himself. A large blank canvas stood in the center of a near empty room, with tables pushed back and a stool for her to sit at, with large windows all across the room to give her enough proper light to work by. Paints sat on a small table, along with brushes made from odd hairs and a slim ink-tipped tool that she assumed was meant for outlining. The room was located not far from Korzien's usual sitting area, likely so he could come in and check her progress when the need struck him.

Yes, she had everything she needed, but an artist could only be so accurate in her own mind, with nothing more to go by. She went to him, asking if he would sit in so she could use his image for the painting, but he only waved her off.

"Just use one of the sketches you made in your book," he said. "That should be enough. Nihl knows I don't care to waste time sitting there like a statue all day."

When she didn't move, he made it clear she was dismissed and to figure it out herself. "I am confident you can make it without me."

Hate stirring in her chest, she went back to the room and reluctantly used one of her portraits of Ryziel to sketch out Korzien's face.

It took her the better part of the day to do just that, mainly because she took several breaks, one to get sick again (this time in a decorative vase, sorry to whoever had to find it) and another to calm her nerves as best she could before she settled right into a screaming panic.

Days passed after that, each one melding into the other. She got up, sat with her crewmates for an hour or two, though not much was said, then went to her private room and worked on Korzien's portrait, anger slicing through her with each stroke of her brush. When sundown came, he would enter the room and look at her work, saying very little but looking satisfied enough that it would be to his liking. He might call her to join him for dinner or he might not. Either way, she ate very little and sometimes, when she was back in her room alone, she got sick but refused to think much about it.

First Night was quickly approaching, and the closer it got, the more anxious she became. She hadn't given up hope that Ryziel would come. But doubt had snuck up from nowhere and squirmed its way into her mind. Only when they were two days away from the dreaded night did she acknowledge the doubt at all. But she knew he had to be coming.

Unless, of course, something had stopped him from doing so.

She was sure if he had been captured that she would have heard of it. Korzien would have said something or Marzin would have come and announced it. The awful thought that he might have gotten off Lethe Maws but been immediately caught made her feel another kind of sick. The thought that he might not have made it out of the mines at all, that perhaps the ship couldn't be fixed, made her feel even worse.

Eventually, sundown on the last day came, and still, there was no sign or word from him. The dark emotions that had been filling up in her had nearly reached their peak, and she wondered in the end if she should just let them spill over or wait for them to burst out on their own. She sat at her stool, staring numbly at the nearly finished portrait before her, keeping her hands locked tight on her lap to save from taking her brush and lashing out at Korzien's face with violent strokes of red. Instead, she left it sitting nicely in the center of the empty room and made her away across to the place, where she knew Korzien must be waiting.

Within the sitting room, Aly found several nillium, including Korzien, Marzin, Zyr, and Azil, to name a few, along with her crew huddled together. The nillium talked and laughed as they ignored the women sitting with heads bowed nearby. As a mini celebration, Korzien had all the girls called to him to share in a meal with their chosen. The nillium ate, the women didn't. At one point, Korzien's uncle appeared, grimacing at them as he settled himself in a corner, covering his mouth as he coughed, and angrily waving a servant away from him. At the end of dinner, cups of sweet wine were distributed to each, and Korzien once again raised his glass in toast.

"To our human women, who have the honor of carrying our legacy onward. For tomorrow, once First Night ends and the new dawn begins, we will join together. May the children they produce rise above all others and rule for the many cycles to come. As Nihl so wills it."

They began to drink from their cups when a pair of guards entered the room and bowed.

"We regret to interrupt," one said. "But there is a ship that has come from Taquen. The crew wishes to meet with you and Nihl Zyr."

Aly had been drifting thoughtlessly away from the scene, but she suddenly came crashing back into reality at the guard's words.

A ship had come. Then it must be...

Korzien frowned, setting his cup down. "And why, in Nihl's Sight, should I even indulge in their request? Or not have them forced out of their ship and killed?"

The guard bowed again. "They say they are traders."

Korzien laughed. "An even better reason to kill them. How dare they land their ship here and not at one of the many other docks in the city?"

The guard glanced around the room, specifically at Aly and the other women. He came over and whispered in Korzien's ear. Korzien's expression, which had been slipping quickly into sheer annoyance, suddenly changed to one of shock.

"Really?" he said quietly. "That much?"

The guard whispered some more, and Korzien's eyes narrowed. He gestured to Zyr, who came over, and the guard spoke quietly to them both. The other nillium, feeling it was impolite to eavesdrop, went back to their own conversations. Aly leaned forward but couldn't hear a word, though she saw Zyr's face light up. He straightened and nodded to the guards.

"I'll go," Zyr said, loud enough for her to hear. "And see how true this is. If they lie, I will have them killed and their ship burned."

"If it is true, however," Korzien said, "have them return here so that I may speak with them."

Zry agreed and left with the two guards. Aly sat frozen, heart thumping in her chest. She heard Cilia mutter some kind of profanity beside her and Kate whisper to her to be quiet, but Aly barely noticed them or the others, her eyes never leaving the doorway, ready to see Ryziel come walking through at any minute.

It seemed like forever before anyone returned. When the guards finally entered again with a bow and Zyr walked past them, Aly felt her heart leap in her chest as another pair followed behind him, only to have her heart sink to her stomach when she saw it was not Ryziel or Xilya or Nar but two roughed-up men. One was a scarred lygin with a wrap over one eye and the other a very disfigured tylian, with long misshapen feelers, its bug-like skin a nasty shade of orange. They each wore drab flight suits with worn shields and faded patches, the tylian carrying a pack over its shoulder.

The lygin looked around the room, his one good eye falling on her and the other women briefly before turning to Korzien. The tylian didn't so much as flick his feelers at them.

"They tell the truth," Zyr said. "I saw the capsules myself."

Korzien brushed a finger over his mouth as he studied them. Then he smiled. "Come. Join us. We were just finishing dinner, but you are welcome to food and drink."

The tylian took the cup of wine a servant offered and drank it down in one sloppy gulp then grabbed another before one could be offered to the lygin, who refused it.

"I take it you have traveled a long way," Korzien said, eyeing the tylian with amusement.

"Very long," the tylian said, with a grated voice, as he wiped his mouth after finishing his second glass.

"And you bring with you quite the treasure."

"We are willing to make a good deal for it," the lygin said, his voice also rough. "If you let us stay for the day to refuel our ship, we can discuss a price."

"You come, unfortunately, at a rather bad time," Korzien said. "We are interested, have no doubt, but the next couple of days will be rather busy." Korzien looked to Zyr, who merely shrugged. He turned back to the two. "I don't usually allow traders to stay in the house or even land here at all, really, but because I am interested in what you have to sell and approve that you came to us first, I am willing to forgive." Korzien gestured to a servant, who came right away. "Have a room ready for them, somewhere on the east end," he told them. The servant bowed and left. "Since you are here, then, and we won't be discussing any trades for a day or two, come and stay with us."

The tylian looked like he was about to refuse, but the lygin bowed and said, "We welcome your hospitality." The tylian gave his friend a seething look, but the lygin ignored it.

They sat and talked for some time, and Aly, with her heart gone cold with disappointment, began to lose interest, her gaze slowly dropping, her mind beginning to drift away. It wasn't until her stomach began to turn over again and her legs became pins and needles that she decided to get up and walk. She did not leave the room entirely, as she knew Korzien would notice and probably have her whipped for leaving without his permission, so she elected instead to take a turn about the room and then out to the wide balcony that stuck out past the tall open windows. She looked out over the gardens and over the grounds of the house then stared up at the sky, hoping for a moment she would see another ship coming down, one that she recognized.

"What honor do you have to be here?"

Aly looked around and was surprised to find the lygin staring at her by the window. He came over and stood beside her to lean against the railing. She couldn't even bring herself to smile at him. They stood together, looking out at the orange and pink sky. "I heard about your kind. Humans," he said eventually. "But it is strange to see you here."

Aly looked over at him curiously. She thought about telling him the truth, that they were prisoners. Like the hunters, she knew no one was going to bother saving them. No one would go against Korzien or his nillium brethren.

But if she spoke the truth, it may only hurt her more.

"We are...guests. They believe we are meant to be here."

"Meant to be here?" the lygin said.

"Yes. We are...destined to serve them." She glanced at him then said, " As all those in Xolis are meant to."

"Are they?"

She frowned at him, her head turning, eyes drifting over to the nillium gathered in the room.

"You do not seem happy to be with them."

Aly closed her eyes, choosing her words carefully. "Can anyone be happy being something they are not?" Can anyone be happy...living a life someone else chose for them?"

The lygin was silent for a long moment, and when she looked up at him, she could see a sort of odd expression on his face, his eye regarding her with a deep, weary sort of look.

"Perhaps not, but they could be content if it is with someone they care about. And you care for the nillium, do you not?"

Aly said nothing, only let her eyes do the talking. The lygin seemed to understand. He looked down at her dress, at Korzien's necklace hanging around her neck, at her done up hair.

"They care for you, don't they?" His eye narrowed suspiciously. "They don't hurt you."

Aly's frowned tightened. She turned her head away, not wanting him to see her tremble. "What would you have me say?" she said.

"I am...curious to know what it is like for ones such as you to live in such a place like this."

Aly felt the anger rise quickly. All the sorrow, hate, and utter disappointment mixing inside her, turning into a toxic sludge. Her hands turned to fists and she twisted around to glare back at him.

"You want to know what it is like?" she said softly. "I was stationed on Lethe Maws. You know of the place?"

The lygin nodded.

"I was there for many months. I endured countless horrors, endless storms, and a darkness like none I had ever encountered. And yet," her voice shook, and she took a deep breath, "and yet, I would go back if I could. I would go back there before ever returning here."

The lygin went still, watching with intense interest, his expression darkening.

"If it meant being with the one I cared about, I would go back," she whispered. "Because this place is hell."

She left him on the balcony, left him to ponder her words, uncaring if he confessed them to Korzien, uncaring what happened after he did. She slipped away, too angry, too sad, too disappointed, to care.

CHAPTER THIRTY-FOUR

THE LYGIN AND THE TYLIAN DIDN'T HANG AROUND LONG. WHEN others began to disperse, they called on a servant to lead them to their room. They walked in silence the whole way, neither acknowledging the other except for when the tylian gave the lygin an aggravated sort of glance when the servant's back was turned.

As they passed through a courtyard and were taken into the east end of the house, the servant stopped at a double-sided door and opened it, stepping aside to let them enter. The pair lumbered inside, barely regarding the room to make sure it was to their liking before waving the servant off, who shut the door soundly. The lygin locked the door, and the tylian dropped his pack on the ground.

"You just couldn't help yourself, could you?" the tylian hissed. "For once, can't you put your feelings aside?"

The lygin bared his teeth as he walked about the room, shutting curtains, checking drawers. "I had to make sure she was all right."

"She looked fine to me, and I didn't have to move from my seat. I could see plainly enough from across the room. But, no, you had to talk to her."

The lygin rubbed at his face. "I needed to be sure."

The tylian huffed. "He noticed, too, you know. I saw him glance over as you two were talking. What were you thinking?"

"I wasn't," the lygin growled.

"Clearly."

Once all the windows were covered and the door was barred as well as locked, the pair faced each other then, each smacked their palms against the center of their chests. A flash, like a spark of electricity, rippled across their bodies until the image of the tylian and lygin disappeared, and Ryziel and Xilya stood in their place. Their suits shined with pulsing light, beaded black scales expanding and shrinking along the fabric, moving in waves as they readjusted to fit tight against their bodies. A large purple, diamond-shaped pad at the center of their chests shimmered with light before darkening.

"Well, I hope that little act didn't just put a whole lot of suspicion on us," Xilya said. "I wouldn't be surprised if we find a guard or two outside our door now."

"They would likely have them there regardless." Ryziel brought up his arm and began to tap on his techband. "Korzien would have outsiders watched as a precaution."

"I'm glad you're not too worried."

Ryziel glared at her as he lifted his band closer to his mouth. "We are inside, Nar."

"I'm standing by," came Nar's voice a second later.

"So," Xilya bent over and began sifting through her bag, "did you learn anything at least?"

"About what?"

"Is she safe or not?"

The grimace Ryziel had on his face since leaving the party deepened. "I...I don't know."

Xilya looked over at him, studying his expression curiously. "What did she say to you?"

Ryziel turned toward the window, but he didn't open the curtain to peek out. He bowed his head, shaking it slowly. He closed his eyes and saw Aly's face. Not the one he had come to know—the glowing, happy, loving face of his mate—but one with a pale, sickly look; with frightened, glazed-over eyes and a hard-set frown.

"She seemed...upset." He shook his head again and hissed low. "No, worse. She seemed..."

"Unhappy?"

Ryziel glanced at her and nodded, then cast his eyes to the ground. "She told me...she said this place was hell."

"Do you believe me now, then?"

Ryziel rubbed at his jaw. "I don't know," he whispered.

"Well, that's an improvement, at least," Xilya said. "Your denial is slipping. Maybe it was good you saw her after all."

"I didn't think..." He glared back at her and snarled, but it wasn't her he was angry with. "She didn't look hurt, but I could see that she was."

"You think he is harming her in some other way?"

Ryziel began to pace the room. "Korzien would have no reason...it makes no sense. It must be my uncle or one of the others."

"I told you he wouldn't treat them right. They aren't nillium—"

"I need to talk to my brother."

"You don't have much time."

He knew that well enough. It was a miracle they had gotten to Nihl when they did. It had been a torturous couple of weeks after Aly had been taken. He had slept very little, desperate to finish the ship. He thought he would lose his mind waiting for the tanks to finish, and once they did, he and Nar worked tirelessly to create the parts and fill the engines. Xilya turned to spying and hacking through various networks to give them any sort of information as to why the humans had been taken to Nihl. It was through Braxin that they learned of anything and only after Ryziel forced him to talk. When the lygin told him they had been taken to Nihl to serve at First House, Ryziel began to suspect why, though he didn't want to believe it.

But there was little else that could explain it, and when Xilya found the files on the human, Sarah, from the refugee facility's database, he knew then how they were meant to serve.

Knowing that was enough to drive him to complete the ship in a record amount of time. The thought of them touching Aly drove him into a violent rage that never left him.

When the ship was finally done, they left Lethe Maws for good, stopping only once to trade some of their ionx capsules in the shadow market for the shrouding suits they wore now. Disguising themselves as traders with more ionx than any found on Nihl made it easier to gain access instead of having to sneak inside. First Night was near, and, when it came, Ryziel would find his uncle and cut him down. It had taken all his will not to do so when seeing him in the room just now, but Xilya warned that he needed to wait for the sun to be gone, when he had all his strength.

Once his uncle was dead, he would go to his brother, and they would talk, and Korzien would give Aly back to him unharmed, once he understood what she meant to him. And he would make things right, and Aly wouldn't be afraid.

He would make things right.

"I could sneak out and find Korzien now. Try to get him alone..."

"I wouldn't risk it," Xilya said.

"I could explain everything."

"Things may have changed. Your brother may not be the same person now."

Ryziel stopped pacing to stare at her. "He's always been on my side."

Xilya stared back. "Perhaps, until now."

"He's never harmed anyone."

"That you saw."

Ryziel growled. "Once my brother has full rule over the House, things can change. He won't let the humans suffer."

"But he won't let them leave, won't let them out of the house, won't let them live their own lives."

Can anyone be happy living a life someone else chose for them?

Aly's words cut through him like a blade slicing across his heart.

"That is suffering," Xilya said when he said nothing. "And unless he is being told to keep the humans here by your uncle, I would prepare yourself for a hard truth. And while you come to terms with it, I will prepare myself to fight." She slumped down on the bed, tail flicking beside her. "For now, though, we must wait."

CHAPTER THIRTY-FIVE

As soon as Aly woke on the final morning, a knock came at her door, and several servants rushed into her room. Against her will, they bathed and dressed her then forced her into a red slip of a dress with a simple shawl and hood, which she was made to cover herself with. She ate little of the food they offered then was ordered to follow the guards that waited outside. They led her to Korzien's sitting room, where she saw her crewmates already waiting. All except one.

"Where is Jamie?" she asked as she hunkered down beside them.

Kate shook her head, and Cilia cursed under her breath.

"She should be coming," said Kate. "Maybe she is giving them a hard time."

They waited, but when the guards returned, they came back alone. Korzien stepped into the room not long after, wearing a white coat with intricate gold markings along its edges. He looked displeased.

"Your little friend has chosen to run off and hide," he said icily. "It is tragic for her, truly tragic. But once she is found, everything can be set right. For now, the rest of you can wait in here." Without warning, he gripped Aly's arm tight and dragged her up. "I will allow you to leave only so you can finish my portrait. I will expect it to be finished before night comes." He pulled her away and flung her out into the hall. Aly stumbled then righted herself, not daring to look back at him, though it wouldn't have mattered if she did because he had already gone. She didn't want to leave the others, but with Korzien already in a bad mood, she didn't care to make it worse in fear that he might lash out at her or the others. She marched into her private room close by and sat down at the canvas. She picked up her brush, dipped it in paint and worked to finish the portrait, hating it more and more.

She didn't know how long she sat there, too dazed, to numb to care. Her thoughts turned to Jamie, and a pang of fear settled in her chest. If they found her, Aly didn't want to think about what they were going to do. Jamie wouldn't get far. Wherever she hid now, Aly hoped she stayed there until night. Then, maybe, she might have a chance.

The sun slowly began to set as Aly placed the last stroke of color on Korzien's face. She went to set her brush down, her hand shaking, the blisters forming between her fingers starting to sting, when she heard the rush of feet and a screaming cry. Without thinking, she shot up from her seat and rushed out of the room, just in time to see a group of guards walk into the sitting room nearby. An eruption of howling cries went out, and Aly rushed down the hall and into the sitting room. She stopped dead at the entrance, frozen.

Kate and Cilia huddled around a body where guards had dropped it on the ground. Sarah sat far in a corner, clutching her baby tight as it wailed. The body she called it at first because she couldn't identify it. Until it turned its head, and she knew it had to be Jamie. Only her face was deformed, eyes shut tight, lips swollen and blue, blood gushing from her nose, staining her face and neck. She was limp on the ground, but she was alive, from the slow rise and fall of her chest.

Kate and Cilia clung to her, howling with rage and fear, and the guards stood silent around them.

Aly didn't move, didn't react, until she was pushed aside by Zyr, who gave her a dirty look before gazing down at the girls on the floor.

"Idiots," he spat. "You could have at least spared her face. How am I supposed to bed that?"

Behind him, Korzien's uncle appeared. He saw the body too and gagged. "Korzien has gone too far, damn him," he muttered. "And damn this whole thing. Guards, seize these two," he said, pointing to Cilia and Kate, "and bring them to my quarters. Azil can wait with me there."

They screamed as the guards pulled them away, kicking and hitting. Aly tried to move in front of them, to stop them, and was quickly shoved away. She fell to the ground next to Jamie, who moaned. Aly shook as she stared at her, her stomach rolling, but she refused to get sick.

"Where are you going, uncle?" came Korzien's voice behind her.

"We are taking ours to my rooms. I don't care to have mine beaten to a pulp. You move to stop me, boy, and you'll regret it."

"Go, then, uncle, and stay out of my sight."

Footsteps faded away, and Aly knew Korzien stood right beside her.

"It's too bad. She shouldn't have gone. This could have been easily avoided. Zyr, take her. Have an oracle come to fix her."

Zyr must have gestured to the rest of the guards because they began to pick Jamie up. "I want a better one next time, Korzien, do you hear me?" Zyr snapped. "I deserve a clean one, an obedient one."

"And you will have it, Zyr. I promise. Next time."

Zyr left, with the guards towing Jamie over one shoulder, blood dripping onto the shiny floors and pristine carpets.

"It's sad," was all Korzien had to say, in the most unemotional voice imaginable. He sighed, and she knew he looked down at her. "It's time we left. Come, let's move to the grand terrace and watch the sun set. I'll bring some wine."

Aly didn't move.

"Did you not hear me, girl?"

"I heard you fine, you asshole," she said in her own tongue, southern accent and all.

Korzien laughed. "What was that? Speaking in gibberish now? Funny, but I'm done playing games. Get up."

She did, and once she stood, she turned to face him. "We shouldn't forget your portrait, should we?" She walked past him, still holding her brush tight in one hand.

"I didn't say you could walk away from me."

"But it's so important, isn't it? Your precious, stupid portrait. We wouldn't want to forget it!" she shouted back at him as she rushed to her private work room. She stopped before the picture just as Korzien made it to the door.

"You'll have to be whipped for that, but I'll do it after the ceremony. If you come here now and be good, I won't punish you more."

"You are a bastard."

"What was that?"

"You heard me. A sniveling, cockless bastard. And I'm done doing what you say. I'd rather die than be controlled by you anymore. So, go on ahead because you'll never have anything from me. You can beat me, but I'll never do a thing to make you happy. Not ever!" Aly raised the sharp end of her brush and stabbed it into Korzien's portrait, tearing it down the middle. "I'll never praise you. I'll never draw your picture. Nothing. You are nothing to me." She stabbed and stabbed, till his painted face was in shreds.

She panted, limbs shaking as she dropped the brush, paint splattering on the carpet. He didn't say a word, and when she turned to look at him, she thought she might faint, but she took deep breaths, fighting to keep herself steady.

Korzien didn't look shocked. He didn't even look enraged. The closest she could come to identifying his expression was disappointment.

"That was the wrong choice," he said dully, shaking his head. "Stupid. And you will regret it." Calmly, he began to walk toward her, and it took all her strength not to go running. "You're right about one thing, though. You won't be making any more drawings of me. Or of anyone. You'll just have to learn how much I matter and how little you do."

* * *

Ryziel felt like a beast trapped in a cage. The sun was nearly down, and he paced the room, ready to burst right out of it as soon as the sun was gone. Xilya was much more calm as she sat on the bed. They had gotten little sleep, Xilya wanting to keep watch and Ryziel unable to shut off his brain. They ate a pack of bars and turned away any of the servants who came knocking on the door. Waiting, waiting

He had a clear memory of the house in his mind. He remembered well each and every room. His uncle's rooms were on the top floor, and that was where he would head first. Xilya would head around the outer walls to cause a distraction, or so she claimed. He didn't worry about what she had planned, not yet. Hopefully, whatever fight she cared to start wouldn't happen if he got to his brother first and made him see reason. He didn't ask her why she wanted to help or cause a scene, but he had a feeling it had something to do with Aly. She cared for her too, in her own way.

With blades ready at his sides (another small buy at the shadow market), he checked them each carefully one more time then turned to the door. His receptors vibrated lightly, telling him there were at least a few guards walking around nearby.

"Whatever happens," Xilya said, approaching the window to watch the sun disappear below the horizon. "Whatever happens, keep me and Nar in the know. And don't lose yourself, Nihl Ryziel."

"My Drega is under control," Ryziel said.

"I mean, don't lose yourself to your brother."

Ryziel looked over at her, confused, but she didn't bother to explain what she meant. The sun slipped away and brought the night. The lanterns were lit, and Ryziel and Xilya snuck out of the room and went their separate ways.

One hour. He had one hour till the sun rose again, but he knew he wouldn't need that much time to find his uncle and defeat him. Ryziel started for the east stair. As soon as he made it to the east terrace, he knocked out one guard and hid the body then slipped around a set of servants setting up a table. He weaved his way through passages, climbed around the side of one building, and slipped through another window then up a small stair.

At the end of one hall, he saw several guards stationed at his uncle's door. He crept into a spare room and climbed out another window and onto the roof till he hopped over onto a balcony. Another guard was there, but he knocked them out before they could even draw breath to shout. He placed them behind a bush then slunk over to the set of wide-open windows and peeked inside. There, he saw his uncle bent over coughing and Azil, his cousin, patting him on the back while two of the human women sat nearby crying.

"It'll be over soon enough," Azil said.

"Can't you shut those two up? I'm sick already of their wailing," Ryziel's uncle growled.

Ryziel watched as Azil tried to pull the women up but they wouldn't go, wouldn't separate from one another.

"I don't want this," Ryziel's uncle said. "Why would Nihl do this to us? Were we not his firstborn, his favorites? Why has he forced these creatures on us?"

Azil gave up trying to pull them away. "I don't know. But it must be for a reason."

"We know the reason. But it sickens me. I cannot be happy for it, I cannot."

Azil gently led the older man to a chair on the far side of the room. "I'll be back." He left him there alone, and if it were not for the women, Ryziel would think it a perfect moment, having his uncle to himself. Carefully, he entered the room through the window, and the two women spotted him right away. They gasped and cried out, and he gestured for them to be silent. His uncle looked over and, when he saw him, he scowled. "I knew you would come someday. I knew." He coughed and wiped his mouth, smearing blood on his hand. " I still believe you were the cause of all our suffering. The ill omen of a future that brought us deformed children and barren women. I truly still believe it. Your kind were supposed to be extinct. It was a sign from Nihl of our end. And you come now to finish it, don't you? To finish us." His teeth rattled in his mouth. "I knew I should have killed you when I had the chance."

Ryziel stepped over to him and unsheathed one of his blades. "Yes, you should have."

He struck fast, and his uncle didn't even flinch. The knife cut clean across his throat, blood spilling over his neat clothes. His eyes glazed over, and his body fell forward.

The women screamed behind him. A connecting door from one side opened, and Azil stood in the doorway, his golden skin turning ashen. Blade still in hand, Ryziel took a step toward him, and his cousin let out a strange sort of bark before bolting back into the adjacent room. Ryziel went to follow but the door leading into the passage beyond smashed open, and several guards rushed through.

"Nihl Kyzier, are you—" one of the guards stopped as he saw Ryziel. "Nihl—Nihl Ryziel?" His eyes dropped to the chair, where Ryziel's uncle now lay limp, then to the blade in Ryziel's hand.

"He is dead," Ryziel said. "Take me to Korzien now."

The guards were frozen, uncertain whether to obey his request or to seize him.

"Guards! Guards! Come quickly, there is someone on the roof!" Zyr's voice called down the passage. He stopped at the open doorway. "Some kind of demon is running along the—what the hell are you all doing in here?" He stomped into the room then staggered back when seeing Ryziel, a hiss escaping from his mouth. "You...you are supposed to be exiled to..." His eyes fell on his father and to Ryziel's blade, and when realization hit him, he let out a roar. "Take him!"

Hesitant, the guards drew their weapons, a few choosing curved blades and others, their shooters. Ryziel unsheathed another of his blades, preparing himself. It might have been a few years since he had fought, but he remembered everything well. The guards tried to circle him, but before they could get around him, Ryziel threw one blade into the neck of a guard holding his shooter. It went off in bursts, and Ryziel dodged to slice the thigh of one guard standing with a sword raised. As one guard fell limp to the ground, the other screamed and fell to his knees. Brilliant white light flashed across the room as a pair of guards tried to blindly shoot at him, only to be quickly cut down, one sliced in the belly, the other stabbed in the chest. They went down, and a sword-wielding guard charged him, blade raised. Ryziel kicked out, catching him in the stomach. His sword sliced part of Ryziel's leg, but he barely noticed. Ryziel rushed at the guard as he staggered back and caught him just under the jaw, ripping his blade away as the guard fell. A sudden sharp pain hit Ryziel's side, and he growled, pulling back to see Zyr with one of the shooters. Zyr's hand shook as he pulled the trigger, grazing Ryziel's shoulder as Ryziel leapt to one side then threw his blade, slicing Zyr's hand nearly in half. Zyr dropped the shooter and clutched his hand, screaming.

Ryziel picked up his blades then lunged over and grabbed Zyr by one of his receptors, pulling his head back.

"Where is Korzien?" he yelled.

Zyr bared his teeth at him, and Ryziel cuffed him hard across the face.

"Where?"

Blood trickled from Zyr's nose. "The main terrace," he spat. "But you won't defeat him, even in the night."

"I don't mean to defeat him." Ryziel let Zyr go. "He will listen to what I have to say, and he will lift all charges against me. Your father is dead and so Korzien will rule First House and unexile me."

Zyr let out a low, blood spraying laugh. "You've been away too long, Ryziel. Since your father's death, Korzien has already taken over. You killing my father changed nothing."

Ryziel stiffened. "That's a lie."

"No, truth. My father was too sickly to rule, everyone knew. He gave First House over to Korzien not long after Nihl Bizen's death. Korzien never meant to release you right away. Perhaps not at all."

"You're a liar," Ryziel hissed. "And once me and Korzien speak, I will make sure you feel the judgement of my blade first."

"Go on, then," Zyr said. "Find him and see. If he has not already taken his chosen to his bed." Zyr laughed again, and Ryziel thought to hit him once more. Instead, he left him there with the women and started for the main terrace.

* * *

The night was at its fullest when Ryziel came upon the main terrace, looking over the city. There were few guards patrolling, and those who were, he knocked out easily. Nillium walked by, thinking him no more than a shadow, until he finally found Korzien, staring out at the cityscape, with Aly crouching down beside him, head covered in her hood, hands hidden underneath her as she bent forward.

Ryziel walked calmly toward him, sheathing his blades. His eyes drew down toward Aly, wishing she would look up and see him, knowing he was here now, and she would be all right. Instead, Korzien twisted around and saw him first.

"Brother," he whispered in surprise.

Ryziel stopped before him. "Brother."

Korzien looked shocked at first but then his mouth curved slowly into a smile. "I am so glad you are here, as unexpected as that is."

"I freed myself from Lethe Maws to join you. Our uncle is dead." Ryziel's eyes drifted back to Aly, who still hadn't moved, her body shaking with each breath.

"I see," Korzien said, not moving to check on Aly nor even to embrace him.

When Korzien said nothing else, Ryziel frowned. "You rule First House now, and I would be by your side. My only request is that you give her to me. She is my mate."

Korzien tilted his head. "Is that so? And how is that?"

"We joined together when in the mines."

Korzien seemed extra surprised at that.

"Come, brother," Korzien said, his expression darkening. "The night is young, still. Tell me everything." He went over to a nearby table and poured them each some wine.

Ryziel glanced down at Aly then back at him. "I would see my mate first."

"She can wait."

Ryziel's mouth tightened. As Korzien's back was turned, he quickly crouched down and laid a hand on Aly's back. She flinched and cowered back from him.

"Aly, it's me. You're all right," he said softly.

She did not move nor even look at him.

"I said leave her, Ryziel."

Ryziel straightened and looked back at his brother. "I don't understand. What have you done?"

"She serves us now. She belongs to us." Korzien gave Ryziel the wine. "I'm sorry, I must seem off to you. I am just shocked that you are here, my brother." He put a hand on his shoulder. "But I am glad now of it. You should be here for this too. And after, we will speak and make things right."

Ryziel's eyes narrowed. "After what?"

"The joining." Korzien pointed down at Aly. "She is my chosen. To have my children."

Before Ryziel could even think of what he just said, Korzien gripped his shoulder tighter. "I did not know, though, that you had already claimed her. Forgive me. This happened before I knew of anything."

Ryziel stared, beyond words.

"It should have always been you and me anyway, right? This is fitting. You can stay by my side now, and we will share in this blessing together." He dropped his hand from Ryziel's shoulder. "And there will be plenty of others too. You don't have to chain yourself to only one."

A growl ripped from Ryziel's mouth, surprising them both.

No. No, she's mine.

The words struck him hard, and his Drega stirred. Ryziel turned from his brother and placed his glass carefully on the terrace wall. "I don't know that I can do that."

"You can because you are my brother and she is only a vessel, Ryziel." He laughed softly when Ryziel didn't respond. "You can't honestly tell me you've grown too fond of her?"

When he saw the look in Ryziel's eyes, his own brightened. "The great and terrifying Ryziel knows love, by Nihl, what a miracle. Too bad you've made the mistake of choosing one unlike your own. Don't worry, I felt fond of her too, at first. But I have learned to control such simple emotions. I will teach you, just like I have taught you everything else. A woman does not come between brothers, after all. That, you must see. You can feel for them, Ryziel, but they are still beneath us."

Ryziel took long, deep breaths, his eyes always turning back to Aly. Why did she say nothing? Why did she hide from him?

Korzien sighed. "Go on, then. Because you are my brother and to show it matters not to me, I will let you have her first. Go on and take her."

Fear stirring suddenly in his chest, Ryziel did go to her and did try to pick her up, to make her look at him, to take her away. What he got was Aly's cry of pain. She slipped from his grasp, clutching her hands tight against her. Stunned, he tried to go to her again, and she made a noise he had never heard her make before and wished he never had.

She wept below him, and it froze every bone in his body.

"What have you done?" Ryziel whispered.

"She had to be taught a lesson. But don't worry. She is still good to bed." Korzien nodded his head at her. "Though I would maybe keep her on her back."

Aly took gulps of air, then slowly, she looked up at him, tears staining her face, falling still as she shook before him. Her face twisted with anguish, and she raised her arms to expose her hands.

Or what was left of them.

Ryziel stared down at bloodied hands, fingers twisted and smashed, some even gone. Held barely together by thin pieces of cloth.

Seeing them, Ryziel found he could no longer speak. The only sounds filling his throat seemed to come from a wild animal, not from him. His vision began to blur until he saw nothing but Aly before him. He heard someone speaking but he couldn't even understand them. His Drega had risen to the surface, and he had let it go without a fight.

* * *

All there was, was pain. So much so, it was hard for Aly to think of anything else. She had been so consumed by it at first, she hadn't even recognized Ryziel's voice above her. But as the pain numbed, she had looked up, looking for mercy. When she saw Ryziel, she thought he might be a hallucination to make her feel safe. She had reached for him, only to see his face go dark, a snarl rip through his throat and his eyes to glaze over, no longer seeing her. Then he turned from her and faced Korzien.

Korzien tossed his glass, shattering it, then drew a blade from inside his coat. "Now, now, brother. You're upset, but you'll get over it in time, once I make you understand."

Ryziel lunged and Korzien met him. With every swing Ryziel made, Korzien seemed to dodge. Ryziel was quick, but Korzien matched him easily. They fought, equally skilled, though Ryziel's blows were more savage and wild and less coordinated. Blood splattered the ground as Korzien's knife sliced across Ryziel's hip. Ryziel slammed his fist into his brother's gut as the blade came across, and each staggered back. They struck and blocked, Korzien's knife making its mark along Ryziel's arm, leg, and chest. Ryziel caught at Korzien's coat, tearing it. He slammed into him, making them each fall back and forcing Korzien to drop his blade. Korzien growled, his face twisting, eyes growing wild. Fists flew, one knocking Korzien across the jaw. Korzien kicked his legs out wildly, trying to buck Ryziel off him.

Aly watched helplessly as they fought, until the sky began to lighten behind her. The sun was coming back up.

The sun weakens him.

And if Korzien was putting up a good fight now, Ryziel didn't have a chance when the sun rose. Pain and fear ripped through her as Aly cried out Ryziel's name.

Ryziel pinned his brother down and struck repeatedly, keeping Korzien beneath him. Korzien didn't strike back but instead, blocked the blows with his arms. His eyes shot over to the rising light, waiting. Ryziel began to breathe harder, his punches slowing. He grabbed Korzien by the throat, and in response, Korzien kneed Ryziel in the gut then tossed him off. He leapt up, grabbing Ryziel and pulling him down so that he now lay under him. Exposing his fangs, Korzien bit the side of Ryziel's face. Roaring and kicking, Ryziel shucked him off, and in turn, Korzien tore part of his ear clean off. Blood gushed from Ryziel's head and down his neck, but he didn't falter. He rose and came at his brother again.

"Give it up, Ryziel," his brother growled in a bestial sort of voice, dodging Ryziel's attack. "The sun rises, and I have the advantage."

Ryziel, panting hard, refused to stop. But for every blow he swung, Korzien blocked and struck him back. Ryziel began to waver on his feet. Korzien only smiled.

"Foolish, brother. I hate to have to kill you now. I thought I could make you one of us, but perhaps Uncle was right. You are a lost cause." He went to strike when a sudden flash of red and purple whipped past him, and one of his receptors was cut clean from his head, falling to the ground. He blinked, confused at first. Then he saw Xilya standing behind him, tail swinging. He roared with rage and prepared himself to fight when Ryziel picked up Korzien's cut-off receptor and swung, stabbing him in the throat.

Korzien went still, his eyes wide with shock. Hours seemed to pass as he looked on his brother with fury before he finally dropped to his knees.

As the sun appeared above the horizon, Korzien fell back, writhing on the ground, his white coat soaked with red. His head tilted to look over at Aly, his eyes gazing on her last before going dark.

CHAPTER THIRTY-SIX

THE SOUNDS OF GUARDS COULD BE HEARD SHOUTING ALL ACROSS the house. They were coming. Aly looked at Ryziel, afraid he was going to collapse as he looked down at his brother's body, his own body shuddering as he was still in the hold of his Drega.

Aly wiped the tears from her face. "Ryziel," she called to him softly. He looked at her, blinking slowly.

"Nihl Ryziel, you are injured, and the guards are coming," Xilya said. "We need to go now."

He didn't move until Xilya started for Aly, and he growled at her, baring his teeth.

"It's okay, Xilya," Aly said before the devilish female thought to strike at Ryziel in defense. "Ryziel, it's all right." She reached out her twisted hand. "Let's go."

Ryziel looked at her mangled hand for a long moment until the shouts of guards finally snapped some part of him back. He came to her and picked her up, cradling her. "Go," he growled.

Xilya started for the terrace stairs, and Ryziel followed. They hid in a spare room as guards rushed by. Xilya ripped off one of the curtains and tore it in half, wrapping one piece around Ryziel's head and the other around Aly's hands. When the area was cleared, they slipped out again and started back toward the ship.

"Wait, we can't leave my crew!" Aly cried.

"Don't worry," Xilya replied. "We aren't. I have three stowed away already. The fourth we will find."

Aly didn't ask which ones. She was only grateful to Xilya for finding them. They slipped through the passages of the house, servants screaming and running as they approached. Xilya took out a few unsuspecting guards as they entered one of the many courtyards.

"There!" Aly pointed to the pavilion, seeing Sarah sitting inside.

They rushed over, and Sarah screamed seeing them.

"It's okay, Sarah, we are here to take you home!" Aly said with a shaky voice, tears falling as her hands still burned. "But we have to go quickly, or they will find us."

Sarah glanced at each of them, her face pale, arms tight around her child, who began to cry.

"Trust me, Sarah, please!"

Before she could utter a word, Ryziel hissed and turned as Marzin walked into the courtyard with several guards.

"You are taking her nowhere," he said. "By the law of Xolis, you each are under arrest for the death of the prince and for stealing his property."

Ryziel looked to Xilya, and Xilya pressed a button on her tech-band then crept forward. "I don't think so. We are taking them with us. But you are welcome to try and stop us."

"So be it, then." Marzin gestured to his men, and they slowly began to approach.

Before they brought up their weapons, a blast as bright as the sun flashed across the sky, followed by another and another, until the ground shook beneath them from the explosions.

The guards faltered and cried out, some aiming their weapons, others falling to the ground.

"You can thank Nar for those later," Xilya said. "Now go. Take Aly back to the ship with this one as well. I will hold them off."

Aly shook her head, but Ryziel didn't hesitate. He motioned for Sarah to follow and she did so, cautiously. They backed out of the pavilion, shooters aimed at them but not firing as Marzin told them to hold lest they hit one of the girls.

Before Ryziel turned out of the courtyard, Aly got a glimpse of Xilya dodging and leaping, taking out men left and right till it was only her and Marzin. Fire blazed above them, keeping the men distracted as they rushed to help defend, leaving the house's docking area empty save for the ship. Aly looked on it, more tears filling her eyes. The door of the ship opened, and Ryziel rushed inside with Sarah behind him.

"Took you long enough!" came a familiar voice. Nar stepped away from the group of women, who each cried out with relief at seeing Aly and Sarah. Sarah sat down beside them, and Ryziel set Aly down carefully in a seat.

"Xilya is on her way. Start the engines."

Nar hobbled away to the pilot seat, and Ryziel knelt beside Aly. "I'm sorry. I'm so sorry." He kissed her knees instead of her hands, which hurt too much to do so. "I was wrong."

Aly smiled, even through the tears. "It's okay. Just get us out of here."

Ryziel nodded and went to sit beside Nar. She watched as they started the controls on the ship, which began to roar to life and hover over the ground. The door opened just as a set of guards came shooting into the dock, and Xilya slipped inside.

"And what the hell took you so long?" Nar called back at her.

Xilya raised up her hand, revealing another lone receptor, this time cut from Marzin. "Just wanted a souvenir."

Rolling his eyes, Nar put on a pair of goggles to see by then took hold of the steering of the ship and slowly began to lift off.

Flashes of light hit the ship, but, besides a little shaking, the ship didn't halt as it turned itself around and gained speed, rising faster into the sky than the sun in the distance.

AFTER

They traveled on for several days, only stopping once at a far-off port on the edge of Xolis. The port was mostly empty as it was situated on a barren, dry planet, but it was the safest place they could find. They knew Nihl spies would soon bring news of their landing, but they needed a second ship. In a private dockyard, they stood together as each ship was ready to fly.

"I will take them on the path to Tryth until a human signal can be found, as promised," Xilya said. "I will tell others of this place so that they can be ready for any threats."

"Thank you," Ryziel said.

"I still think you should come with us."

Ryziel shook his head, wrapping his arm around Aly. "It is ill-advised to travel so far while with child. I would not risk it. We will hide somewhere. Then maybe...someday."

Xilya nodded. "I will give you the coordinates." She looked over at Sarah, who bobbed her child against her hip. "Will you be going with them?"

"I think so. For now. I want my child to be around his own kind."

"So be it." Xilya bowed.

Kate and the others, who stood close by, smiled over at Aly. They closed the distance, and Aly embraced each of them.

"We will miss you," Kate said. "Don't worry, we will tell everyone to be ready for the nillium if they ever come."

Aly released her and frowned. "There are hunters who were paid to find us too. Look out for them."

Kate nodded. "We will."

"See you around." Cilia winked.

Jamie smiled, hugging her once more then looked to Ryziel and Xilya. "Thank you for helping us."

They each embraced Sarah after and said their goodbyes then made their way onto the second ship.

"So, where will you go?" Xilya asked.

Nar, who had been quietly standing by, came up and un-pocketed the pearly star-map found in Yurza's treasury. "We are gonna pay a visit to Yurza's descendants."

Xilya's eyes widened. "Do you think that wise? You don't know anything about the planet or the people there."

"From studying the texts of the Keep for years, I know a little of their language," Nar commented. "So, I can speak to them. And knowing what I know about the people, they were never a hostile bunch. Just had to live around a lot of hostile...well, things. Besides, the planet isn't far off, so we will only have to travel a short distance. And it's hidden. Xolis enforcers will never find us. We can check to see if it's safe. Worse case, we hide away from the locals. For a little while."

Xilya looked to Ryziel, who tilted his head in a shrug. "I would rather deal with them than anyone from Xolis. I am confident I can protect them."

"So be it." Xilya placed a hand on Ryziel's shoulder. "You are welcome to visit me. I would like to take you on in the fighting pits sometime."

Ryziel smiled. "You know it."

She bowed her head then looked at Nar. "And you keep out of

trouble." Nar rolled his eyes, muttering something under his breath. Xilya smiled then faced Aly. "You, also. And don't worry, I haven't forgotten to look into this so-called doctor you mentioned living on Tryth. It will be interesting to see how one of you survives on my world." She patted Aly on the head, and Aly grinned.

Aly watched her go, sad to see her friends depart but knowing it didn't always mean goodbye. Ryziel took hold of her, and they watched as the ship lifted off and flew out of the port to disappear into the clouds.

* * *

Ryziel watched the sun go down in the distance from a wide balcony looking over a sprawling cityscape on the edge of a bright green ocean. Two moons, one blue, one orange, hovered in the sky. Kyres and Eris, the Yurzans called them. Night and Day.

"A favored night to you," came a silky voice behind him. Ryziel turned and saw a tall female, gray of skin and black of hair, dressed in blue.

"And to you," Ryziel said.

"Many thanks." She came up beside him, looking out over the scene. "Our matriarch has told me to tell you that, as thanks for the treasures you have returned to us, she will give you the means to upgrade your ship. Or have a new one if you so desire."

By treasures, Ryziel knew she meant the star-map and the book of sketches Aly had picked up in Yurza's treasury, thankfully recovered from her unit before they left Lethe Maws. Treasures seemingly long lost to them. Though they had several other star-maps and drawings, the ones he and Aly found were of historical importance.

The Yurzans had left Lethe Maws after the death of their queen and the beginning of the drilling of the mines from Xolis. Feeling threatened, they knew they would have only three choices: Adapt, parish, or flee. They let their city fall and left for a world they had discovered through their telescopes and explored with ships. The planet, Elestyl as they called it, had a sun that was dimmer than others and could not harm them. And the nights were longer.

When Ryziel had landed their ship, the Yurzans had been worried at first, seeing the ship branded by Xolis. But as Nar spoke to the matriarch and heads of Elestyl, their defenses lowered, and they soon welcomed them, giving them everything they could need or want.

"Tell her we are forever grateful," Ryziel said.

The woman smiled and touched at her neck as a sign of respect. "Will you join us again tonight for dinner and talk?"

"Not tonight. My mate says she has a surprise for me. We will stay in our room."

The woman touched her neck again. "Very well. Good night to you."

"And to you."

She glided away, and as the sun touched the horizon, Ryziel too went inside.

"I'm telling you, Ryz," Nar said as Ryziel entered a large domed room with a computer console at its center. "These people surprise me every day. I was just doing some research on the history of their tech and, by god, they are way more efficient and knowledgeable than Xolis. It's too bad they are such a docile race, or they could probably make a formidable foe."

"I have no doubt of it," Ryziel said as he passed by Nar then stopped. "Anything from Xolis?"

"They still got people looking. A few ships even passed close by." Nar laughed. "The blocking system on this hunk of rock is insane. Might as well be a shadow in the darkness." The urk turned to face him. "It still might be some time, though, before they stop. We might be here for a while."

"I don't think any of us have a problem with that, do you?"

Nar shrugged. "Not really. At least here, I don't have to worry about the sun."

Ryziel smirked at him. "Me too."

"There's another thing. I was sifting through some of the Xolis networks to get a feel for any news that might be important. You should know Zyr has taken over First House, and there are rumors of rebellion from the other houses now that the princes are all gone and, well, no one likes Zyr. There is also talk of hunters, like Aly mentioned, going out of Xolis to look for humans. One of them is a nasty piece of work named Nezka."

Ryziel frowned, thinking he had heard that name before. "Sounds familiar."

"He's one of Vesra's."

Ryziel's eyes narrowed. He heard that name before too, a supposed crime lord who ruled over a city. Even Xolis enforcers stayed away, either too afraid to challenge him and his kin or paid well not to. "We should warn Xilya."

"I've sent word, but it will take time to get to her now that she's so far away. We can only hope this Nezka and others in his gang don't encounter any humans."

"We can only hope. But for now, we will have to stay hidden."

"You got it."

Ryziel left the urk to play at his computer. He strolled down one hallway, passing by a small room, where he saw Sarah playing with her son. She saw him and nodded with a smile and he did the same. He continued on till he came to a black steel door which opened to his touch. Inside his and Aly's bedroom, he found a half-eaten plate of food on the clear tabletop, their bed neatly made to one end and blankets and pillows flung around on the couches on the other end. On their private balcony, he saw Aly sitting alone, looking over what seemed to be a blank canvas. He stepped out to stand behind her, encircling his arms around her to nuzzle her neck and shoulder.

"Having a hard time with your painting?" Ryziel asked.

Aly turned her head to look up at him and smiled. "No." Her hand came up to touch his face, a hand partially fixed with metal, the joints bending and moving as seamlessly as if they were real. "It's finished, actually."

Ryziel looked at her then back at the canvas, with a confused frown. "Finished?"

Aly nodded then picked up a can of dustlite she must have found stashed somewhere on their ship.

"I don't follow."

Aly laughed then moaned, patting her now swollen belly. "Ah, every time I laugh, he kicks."

Ryziel placed a hand on her stomach, rubbing gently. "Is he making you hallucinate too?"

"Very funny. Just watch," Aly pointed out to the sea, where the sun was nearly set. As it dipped down into the horizon and its rays vanished, the sky darkened considerably and before his very eyes, the canvas began to change. What had been a blank canvas in the day turned slowly into a colored, glowing portrait of him made with the dustlite. A beautiful creation of blue and silver in the night.

"It's for you," Aly said. "My so-called surprise."

Ryziel moved around and knelt before her, kissing her hands. "It's beautiful, Aly."

Aly smiled and he held onto her, embracing her, laying his head on her lap, and closing his eyes, breathing deep.

He thought for a moment how, only a year ago, he would have never seen himself in this position. An image of his brother suddenly appeared then in his mind, shaking his head in disapproval.

"How can you be with her?" Ryziel heard the ghost of his brother say. "How can you love her as you do? How can you care for her and protect her like this and fight your own kind for her? How can you do this, Ryziel?"

Ryziel only smiled. 'Because,' he thought, 'she is everything.'

**Sign up for Olivia Riley's Newsletter for updates on
new releases, and promotions.**

Olivia's Newsletter

https://oliviarileyauthor.com

ALSO BY OLIVIA RILEY

Dark World Mates

Heart's Prisoner

Dark's Savior

Shadow's Chosen

Heart's Keeper

Vrisha Warriors

Xora

Axrel

Vrexus

Xeda

Sidonions

Shade's Embrace

Draka's Heat

ABOUT THE AUTHOR

Olivia Riley loves the frightening possibilities of deep space, where dark heroes and brave heroines reside. She is also a gamer and film nut.

Instagram: oliviarileyauthor

Facebook: OlivaRileySFR